PRAISE FOR TH

'The most assured crim
Lisa Jewell, *Sunday T*
The Family Upstairs

'The writing is so assured, the characterizations so rich and believable, the twisty storyline so gripping and unexpected. Christie Newport is definitely a star on the rise!'
Diane Chamberlain, *New York Times* bestselling author of
The Last House on the Street

'Just finished *The Raven's Mark* by Christie J. Newport. It's a crisp, tautly plotted police procedural with a phenomenal depth of detail and some truly shocking reveals. I was gripped! So impressed to read — many congratulations! A worthy winner of the Joffe Books Prize.'
Harriet Tyce, bestselling author of *Blood Orange*

'Twisty, tense and authentic — a compelling police procedural with real heart.'
Marion Todd, award-winning author of *See Them Run*

'Christie J. Newport has long been one to watch and now she's one who's truly arrived. *The Raven's Mark* is a superbly researched, compelling police procedural with a unique protagonist and some of the nastiest villains you'll have come across in ages. This is one Raven that will be making its mark on readers in droves.'
Trevor Wood, award-winning author of
The Man on the Street

'Taut, pacy and gritty story that kept me guessing the whole way through.'
Philippa East, author of *Little White Lies*

'A propulsive thriller with a flawed protagonist, a diabolical villain and enough procedural detail to make the setting life-like.' Douglas Skelton, author of *An Honourable Thief*

'Taut and compelling. Christie Newport has written a pacy police procedural with a compelling new heroine.' Andrea Carter, author of *Death at Whitewater Church*

'I tore through this dark, shocking and brilliantly executed police procedural peppered with eye-popping twists galore.' A.A. Chaudhuri, author of *The Abduction*

'The plot is gritty, deliciously dark and fast-paced with a host of colourful characters who keep the pages turning.' Kate Bendelow, author of *Definitely Dead*

'An utterly compelling and propulsive thriller that grabs you from the first page and refuses to let go!' Awais Khan, author of *In the Company of Strangers*

'Vivid, gripping and authentic, *The Raven's Mark* may be a debut but Christie J. Newport writes with all the assurance and skill of a long-experienced novelist.' Alison Belsham, author of *The Tattoo Thief*

'Just finished Christie J. Newport's upcoming debut novel and it is FANTASTIC! Very dark, very twisted, very clever, and utterly compelling. I literally read it in a day as I raced to uncover the truth. Highly recommended to all crime fans.' Sarah Bonner, author of *Her Perfect Twin*

THE ORDINARY MAN

An absolutely gripping crime thriller with a massive twist

CHRISTIE J. NEWPORT

The Preston Murders Book 2

Joffe Books, London
www.joffebooks.com

First published in Great Britain in 2024

Cover art by Dee Dee Book Covers

ISBN: 978-1-83526-327-3

*To those of you who saved my life in 2015. Special mention
to Amy Gilbert and Patricia Spooner.*

*And to my wife, Amy Newport who was
and is my number one supporter.*

*My family and close friends who were there to sell cupcakes,
hand out leaflets and more besides. My cousin Cherie
who jumped out of an airplane. My friend Ben who shaved his head.
Both terrifying feats for them, as Cherie's was death defying and Ben
had previously sported a ponytail.*

*You all restored my faith in humanity and gave
me back my life. Thank you.*

PROLOGUE

DCI Bethany Fellows

Nightmares have been plaguing me all night, jolting me awake repeatedly. It's as I'm drifting back off once again, and I'm halfway between sleep and wakefulness, that I hear it: the dull thud of a footfall. Sitting bolt upright, rubbing sleep from my eyes, I snatch my mobile from the nightstand and check the time — 2.30 a.m. I look around my bedroom feeling uneasy. Something is different. It's as though the very air has been altered. I must have been dreaming — there's no one but me in this house. I'm being paranoid. He wouldn't have the nerve to come here. I've spent weeks convincing myself that my home is safe from infiltration.

I pat my pillow until it is nicely bunched in the centre, then lay back down and pull the quilt up to my neck. I close my eyes. I won't let him win. I refuse to become scared in my own home. Besides, all windows and doors are locked and secure — that I am certain of. He would have no way in, not without me hearing something. A door being kicked, a window broken. I wouldn't have slept through that.

Rolling onto my side, my eyes start to feel the weight of sleepiness and flicker until they almost close. Almost, but

1

not quite, and it is in the not quite shuttered from the world moment that I see it, the shadow in the gap beneath my bedroom door. It hovers, then moves away. I know what I see — it's no mind trick.

There's someone here, now, in my home.

I swing my legs over the side of the bed, trying to be quiet. But as I make contact with the floor, the footsteps are loud and undeniable as they rush downstairs. I race to the door, swing it open — but whoever was there has already cleared the stairs. I chase after them and trip over the edge of my hallway rug. I swear at my mistake — I should have taped it down, at the very least. But I right myself, grab the banister, and launch myself down the stairs.

Taking them two at a time, my heart is thundering against my ribcage. My breath escapes in rapid bursts. Once downstairs, I round the corner into my hallway. The front door claps gently against the frame, not quite sitting in place. Sprinting forward, I shove the door wide and stare frantically up and down the dimly lit path.

There's no one there.

No car screeches past.

There's nothing.

But I know they were there — that they might still be there, watching, waiting for the perfect opportunity to catch me unaware, and then what? Maim? Kill?

I can't be certain of anything. I can't even be certain that I didn't sleepwalk again and leave the door open myself. That everything leading up to now wasn't yet another night terror. But something solid and immoveable in my gut tells me I am not safe.

I have a camera set up outside my home. It's pointing at the front of the house. I glance up and let out a frustrated shriek when I see it's swivelled out of place. I'd bet my last pound it's no coincidence, and that there is nothing useable on it.

I can't call this in. My position as detective chief inspec-tor is already precarious. There's no way I am risking them

2

saying I'm not emotionally or psychologically ready to be back at work. Or worse, them believing I really am in danger. If they decide the former, I'd be forced onto medical leave. If the latter, they won't let me near the office until whoever is doing this to me is caught. Either way, it would be months before they'd let me back.

I can't tell a soul what's going on, because there's no one I know and trust who would risk my safety by keeping quiet, not after what happened last time. If someone is really out to get me, and I know that they are, then I have to face them alone. I have to face *him* alone.

I step back inside, and am about to close the door behind me, when I hear a noise that sounds like it came from the darkness of the hallway. My heart is racing as I stare into the gloom. Then the sound is behind me, moving fast — I have no time to react as something hits me hard in the back. The force takes my legs from under me as I plunge forwards. The side of my head glances off the wall. I hit the floor with a crunch and the wind is knocked out of me. I see something moving in the shadows, and the intruder steps forward to stand directly in front of me.

I look up and our eyes meet. 'Oh my God,' I say, shocked at the sight of the knife in his hand. 'I trusted you.'

CHAPTER ONE

Nineteen days earlier...
DCI Bethany Fellows

I didn't call ahead, and now I'm beginning to regret it; the truth is, I was avoiding giving Danielle the opportunity to order me to stay away. I arrive in Longridge and drive to their home on autopilot, then park my car a little up from the Wilsons' modest semi-detached. My stomach is flipping around, making me feel like I've just stepped off the Waltzers. I get out of my car, then close the door with shaking hands and hit auto lock on my keys. My heartbeat speeds up during the short walk to their house. I can't even be sure they'll be home — hell, part of me is counting on them not being. I've been here so many times before that it's steeped in familiarity, and for some reason that wounds me. In their front garden, a small shrub sits in the centre of some circular stonework. There are potted plants around the perimeter of the garden, along with a selection of stone forest animals. From one of the ceramic pots, a colourful windmill hangs broken and limp. The last time I was here, it had been stood to attention. It feels strangely apt, like a portent — there for my benefit, if only I would heed its warning.

4

I look at the red front door — there's something different. At first, I can't put my finger on it, but then I see that the golden house number fourteen isn't as it was. The four had always been crooked, ever since I first came here — now the four is positioned the right way up, and I can't decide whether it's a good thing, a bad thing or completely immaterial. I hear evidence of life being lived streaming from the open lounge room window. There's a television blaring, kids squealing as they play and Diana's voice calling to ask if anyone wants a brew.

She sounds well, from what I can tell. I recall seeing her doped up to the eyeballs on antidepressants and looking much older than her forty-two years. She's improved so much that it makes me rethink. Perhaps I am being unbelievably selfish — maybe I should turn around and leave. There are too many reasons I have to do this. One, these kids are my kin; two, if it is Tom stalking me, then perhaps he is doing the same to Danielle and the girls. I can't do nothing. I don't want to scare her, but I have to know.

I falter, my hand poised to knock, and then I let my arm fall to my side, second- and third-guessing my decision. I see Danielle's face appear at the lounge window. My heart jumps into my throat — lodging there, a lump I can't swallow past. She vanishes from the window, and I wonder whether she is going to ignore my presence completely. Within a few seconds, the front door is opening, I look around at her — our eyes meet, and the time that's passed since I last saw her falls away.

I look past her and see she's closed the door leading from the hallway into the lounge. 'Danielle,' I say.

'Beth.'

Well, at least she's dropped the formality. It gives me hope. 'I . . .'

'What are you doing here?'

'I wanted to, to . . . erm, I've been thinking about you all, about Erin and Ava.' I sound weak, my voice low and insecure.

She shakes her head, her blonde bob swishing from side to side. 'You shouldn't be here. This isn't fair. We need to move on. All of us do.'

'But they're . . .'

'They're nothing to you, Beth. They are just two little girls you met during one of your cases.'

'You know that isn't true. They're my nieces.'

Her head shakes more determinedly now, her eyes narrow. 'No, they aren't. You need to get that out of your head. For your sake, but most important, for theirs. They have all the family they'll ever need. They do not need you in their lives. They don't need the chaos you'd bring. The memories you'd drag up. They do not need a connection to their so-called father. This has to be about what's best for them. You need to concentrate on sorting your own mess of a life out and leave us be.'

'My life isn't a mess. I'm just—'

She smirks, and it stabs directly into my chest — how can she be like this? We've all suffered at the hands of those poor excuses for human beings.

'Oh, come on. I made it clear you needed to stay away. We all did. And now look . . . here you are, making this about you. Well, it isn't, it's about them.' She stabs her finger towards the vestibule door. 'They need a fresh start, and that can't include you.'

'Why can't it?'

'Because of what you represent. You're the past, Beth, a past we need to move on from. I'm sorry if that seems hard, but it's the truth.'

'But they are my blood, whatever that means, and I would like to—'

'There you go again: *you'd* like, they're *your* blood. Like I said, Beth, this isn't about you.'

'I'm not saying it is. I know it isn't. But you have to at least let—'

'No, you're wrong. I don't *have to* let you do anything. I know this might seem harsh to you, but those girls—' she

6

looks back into the house, then faces me again — 'they are everything to me. I will protect them no matter what — nothing and no one else matters more when it comes to keeping them safe and happy. They've been through enough. They've lost their dad, their home . . . I am trying to rebuild their lives. They need stability and continuity. They do not need anyone else messing with their heads.'

I stare at her incredulously. 'What is it you think I would do?'

'Hurt them, even if you don't mean to. Maybe . . .' She looks hesitant. Her eyes avert momentarily, then land back on me with a determined sheen to them. 'Maybe it's in your blood.'

I feel sick. Of all the things for her to say. 'That's not right. It's downright cruel to insinuate—'

She appears guilt-stricken, her face softening, her voice, too. 'I know you wouldn't harm them physically . . . I've been thinking about this a lot, Beth, and I honestly believe Tom thought he could be better. That he could somehow wipe away his connection to his family and start again. I don't think he wanted to hurt us, but he did. In the end, he couldn't help it. I do believe that you want to be in their lives for the right reasons, but I can't take the chance of you hurting them, too. I just can't. I'm sorry. Now please, please just go.'

I step back. My chest tightens with the increasing distance as I move backwards. Danielle offers me the weakest of smiles. Is it gratitude that I'm leaving?

Anger and indignation rise in me like a tide. 'Those girls,' I say, pointing into the house, 'are as much my brother's blood as I am. If you honestly believe their evil, their darkness is inescapable, then you must think your girls' destinies are determined, too. Is that right? Do you think your own daughters were born evil?'

I watch her face fall.

'Well, do you? My mum was raped and murdered, for Christ's sake. Your sister was a victim? Well, so was my mum.

We are all bloody victims, Danielle. I am no more evil than your own kids. You know that. This is all just you looking to find someone to aim your venom at. Well, go on and take your best shot.'

Blood is rising into my face; I am flushed with rage. After everything that's happened lately, I am gearing up for a fight. I might be in prize position for Danielle to take everything out on, but I won't make it easy for her. I am sick of being a scapegoat.

'Just leave, Beth. Leave us alone to recover.'

My chest pulsates with anger, indignation. 'You aren't so innocent. You can't rewrite history to suit you.'

'What the hell is that supposed to mean?'

'You recognized Sigmund in the photograph I showed you. You could have stopped it all then. You could have spoken up, but you kept quiet. You bought him time. What happened after that is partly down to you. Accept responsibility for once in your bloody life.'

She falters, her face reddening. 'I didn't know . . .' Her expression hardens. 'They haven't charged me. They believed me when I said I didn't recognize him. It really doesn't matter what you think. So, like I said — just go.'

'Has Tom contacted you? Do you know anything? Where is he?'

'Are you accusing me of helping him? Are you serious?'

I open my mouth to continue my tirade, but she slams the door.

I get back into my car shaking with a whirlwind of emotions. She's just given me the incentive I need to do what must be done. I won't kowtow to anyone; no amount of misplaced guilt or self-recrimination will stop me. I can't bring my mum back, but I can avenge her death. The truth is, I haven't simply been at home moping since my suspension. Yes, for a week or so, that's exactly what I did. Then I pulled myself together and set about preparing for what I know is on its way. Because Tom will come for me. I don't know how I am so certain of that. I just know that I am.

Tomorrow I will go into work. I will sit in front of Dillon, and I will do everything in my power to convince her to clear me for duty. I need access to the resources they have — not to mention, it's where I belong. It's the place I always aimed to be. I won't allow what happened to derail my ambition. If anything, it has made me more determined to be the best detective I can be. Plus, Stanley Baker's face when he finds out his remaining son has been locked up, with me the person responsible for hunting him down, is a sight I'm hungry to see.

CHAPTER TWO

DCI Bethany Fellows

My disciplinary hearing had happened swiftly and with minimum fuss. What followed was a temporary exile. Now comes step two: convincing Dillon I am ready to return. I stand at the foot of the stairs leading up to the Major and Serious Crimes Northwest Division and my stomach begins to flutter. I'm not sure whether it's nerves, hunger, or the proximity of the place that, next to Aunt Margie's, feels more like home than anywhere else.

Once I reach reception, the fluttering turns to lead. I'm ashamed of having to book in like any other civilian. I have no pass anymore. I know the code, but that alone won't get me through the security door beside reception. Feeling disjointed, I stand in line behind a woman wearing a black suede mini skirt, knee-high boots and a red halter top. I suppose it is a Friday, but having said that, it's early afternoon.

Halter Top's voice rings out: 'Like I said, I need to speak to someone now. I'm sick of waiting. I've been waiting for over an hour already. I mean, what the fuck? Look around. There's barely anyone here.' The woman turns. Her lips are plumped with a ridiculous amount of Botox. Her false eyelashes almost reach her hairline as she stares me down. 'What the fuck are you lookin' at? Mind stepping back? You're practically on my fuckin' heels. Heard of privacy, have you?' She scowls.

The receptionist must be new. I've never seen her before; even so, she offers me a small smile of apology and understanding. I swallow the retort I sense bubbling up. I grimace at Halter Top and take a stride back, almost bumping into the row of black plastic chairs behind me. The overpowering smell of her sickly-sweet perfume is choking me, anyway. There's practically a cloud of the shit around her head. Despite its potency, it fails to mask the stench of stale cigarette smoke. It clings to every inch of the woman. Her hair, bunched up into a messy bun, moves as one mass when she shakes her head. She turns back to the receptionist to continue her tirade as the security door opens and Detective Superintendent Dillon West appears.

I don't know whether I expected her to be pleased to see me, but her stern expression sends my anxiety into overdrive. 'Beth.' She holds the door wide, and Halter Top shoots us both a dirty look. I step through, glad to be out of the overpowering mist of perfume and into the inner sanctum of the building I have missed like an amputated appendage. I could sense it the entire time, like a phantom limb.

'Are you fuckin' kiddin' me? I was first. I was fuckin' here first.' The rest of Halter Top's words are thankfully lost to the closing door. Once inside, I take in the large office space, the computer banks, tables, and the chairs all filled with my colleagues. Their eyes wander to me. There are some smiles, a number of waves, and a few look awkwardly away, as fast as is politely appropriate. Something in my chest tightens. It feels as though a hand is massaging my heart. It's not altogether a bad or a good feeling. A rumbling sensation begins in my stomach, and I realize what I am anticipating and fearing — seeing Millie for the first time in weeks. She'll know I have no choice, that I am not opting to make things right.

A flash of cropped dark hair and familiar chocolate eyes lifts my mood instantly. Amer rushes at me, then wraps his arms around my waist and pulls me into a bear hug. 'Aw, Beth, it's so bloody good to see you, mate. Jesus, feels like forever. How're you doing?'

'Congratulations on the promotion,' I say. 'You deserve it.' I regret not sending something, getting in touch. He's now the same rank as me, Detective Chief Inspector. I should have shown him I was happy for him, because I am.

'Thanks,' he says, sounding choked. With nervousness? Guilt, because he got on with things while I was gone?

Dillon clears her throat. 'Any danger of you having this little catch-up after our meeting, Amer? Beth's here for a reason today, and this isn't it.'

Stepping out of Amer's hold, I look at Dillon nervously. I'm akin to a stranger in my own home, at odds with the world around me.

'Come on, Beth, let's get this over with.' Dillon starts towards her office, me following behind.

I glance back at Amer. His eyes flicker away awkwardly, and he fiddles with his belt, a nervous habit of his. Something feels off about all this. My chest constricts as Dillon opens her door and gestures for me to go inside ahead of her. She steps through after me, then closes the door. I'm half expecting a firing squad as I sit down and gaze around at the familiar space. There are the same framed commendations adorning the walls, the same photographs on her desk. The same *Who's the Boss* giant mug, half-filled with coffee, beside a dangerously tall pile of paperwork. Everything's as it was, but it feels completely alien.

'So, Beth . . .' She sits down, takes a sip of her coffee, then screws up her face in disgust and fires the liquid back into the cup. 'Urgh, it's freezing. So, first things first — how are you feeling?'

'I'm good, yeah, I'm doing really good. Back to normal.' I hear myself talk and realize I sound as articulate as a two-year-old running on candyfloss.

She holds up a finger and lifts the handset on the left of her desk. 'One sec, I can't drink that.' Dillon nods towards her mug and presses the button that will link her to her newly acquired assistant. 'Chloe, yes, grab us a couple of coffees, would you?' There's a bit of mumbling from Chloe, her tone slightly too high-pitched for my liking. 'Yeah, thanks. Cheers for that.' Dillon puts the phone down, then leans forward in her seat. She places her wrists on the table and clasps her hands together. 'Now then, where were we? Ah, yes, you were telling me how you've utilized your time away from this place to reflect, to come to terms with everything that happened during the Brander case and the mistakes that were made.'

'I was?'

Dillon wiggles her brow.

'Yes, I was. I have been taking walks, reading, thinking. I've been re-evaluating my life.'

Dillon chortles. Then there's a gentle couple of taps on the door, and a blonde bombshell walks in carrying a silver tray adorned with two mugs and a China tea plate filled with a mouth-watering variety of biscuits. Dillon looks at Chloe, the tray and back to Chloe. 'Thanks,' she says, as the assistant places the tray on the desk between us.

'Can I get you anything else, ma'am?'

'No, thanks.'

As Chloe leaves the room, I note the flick of her eyes in my direction. She's inspecting me, sitting here in my two-piece trouser suit. Today I opted to put my hair up in a croc-odile clip, and to wear limited, sensible make-up and leave my leather jacket in the car. I'm attempting to rewrite Dillon's already ingrained impression of me. I needn't have bothered; she knows me too well. There's no fooling her into seeing something other than the version of me she has always known.

Sitting forward, I move my mug but don't lift it. I admire the biscuits with no intention of eating any. Looking up, I see that Dillon's eyes are fixed on me. She's giving me the death stare. The one that says she knows what I'm think-ing before I do.

'Okay, so I haven't been doing much of anything but brooding,' I confess, knowing there's little point trying to hide the truth, though the entirety of that truth is not up for disclosure. 'I've been a mess, to be honest. But—' I look her squarely in the eyes — 'I'm not now. I promise you, Dillon. I am not a mess anymore. In fact, I'm more together than I have ever been. I needed to fall apart, you see, so I could reassemble myself the right way. I know who I am now; I know what I need to do. I *need* to be here, working. With you, with the team. I need to come back, Dillon, please, please let me come back. It's a waste me sitting at home twiddling my thumbs when I could be here. It's where I belong. This isn't lip service, Dillon, I swear.'

I sit back and let out a long, slow breath. That's it, I've said it, I didn't know what I had to say until I was speaking the words but there they are.

Dillon's spiky blonde hair is a little longer than the last time I saw her, and she looks sharper — her face more drawn, cheekbones more defined. I realize that the Brander case didn't only punish me. It was traumatic for all of us.

Dillon lifts her mug and blows into it; a drifting wave of coffee reaches the far edge. She sits back, holding the mug between both hands before slowly raising it to her mouth to take a tentative, thoughtful sip. Her eyes peer over the top of it, watching me the entire time. I wait her out. A silence falls over her office. I'm not inclined to push her. She might know me, but I also know her. Pushing Detective Superintendent Dillon West is never advisable.

Eventually she replaces her coffee mug on the table, then drums her fingers against the side of it and takes a breath. 'I'm going to level with you, Beth.' Her mouth twitches and she scratches her nose. Aunt Margie's silly superstition rings out in my mind: *Itchy nose means you're going to have a fight*. I hope she's wrong. I don't buy into her many, many superstitions; still, the thought of her rarely fails to make me smile. Today I hold on to that smile; this isn't the time.

'You have been cleared to return to work on my say-so. We kept things in house, as you know. However, I want you to understand the magnitude of what you did.'

I nod along, while inside I'm jumping for joy that I can come back to work. Unless Dillon is about to kibosh it. 'Having said that, I understand why you did it.' She eyes the room as if the walls are about to sprout ears. 'Do not repeat that. Ever.'

I nod.

'The case was unique. I mean, none of us could have known the outcome.' For the first time since I arrived, her expression softens. 'It is what it is, Beth. You can't help who your family are, any more than I can help being related to my nose-picking, crotch-scratching uncle Ralph. But there you have it.'

'They're not my family.'

Dillon looks contrite. 'Yes, I'm sorry. You know what I mean, though, don't you?'

'Yes, of course. They're linked to me by DNA, but that's the extent of our link. They are not and never will be my family. They're a sick, twisted scourge on humanity, and we would all be better off if they didn't exist. But they have nothing to do with me coming back to work. I'm ready for this.'

I had considered telling Dillon about the postcards I've received sporadically since Tom vanished, which I'm certain are his idea of a joke. I'd worked alongside him for years, Detective Constable Tom Spencer. I hadn't known what linked us, that we'd both been sired by the same monster. I hadn't been able to see what Tom was, that he too was a monster, just like his father. None of us had seen it, but all along he'd been right under our noses. The postcards are always blank, every last one of them, but I know they're from him. I know he will continue to send them, until I find him. He can't leave me in peace. His hatred of me runs far too deep for that.

I'd made the decision before arriving here today not to mention the postcards. I can't tell Dillon about it, because if I do, she'll guard me like an Alsatian at a junk yard. I can't have her peering over my shoulder. I need to keep this part of my return to work in the shadows. Work cases as I always have; bring killers to justice while searching for my brother under the radar. I have to be the one to bring him in. It's not an ego thing. It isn't arrogance or even a vendetta. I honestly believe I stand the best chance of catching him, and he needs to be caught. The book he left behind, with the twenty-eight brands seared into pieces of torn flesh remind me of that every single day. On the last page, he'd written *'to be continued . . .'* and I know he means it. He is out there now, hunting. I'm going to stop him, and being here will make that more probable than simply possible. It gives me access.

Dillon lifts some paperwork from the pile and slides it across the desk to me. 'Read it, sign it. You will *not* keep anything pertinent to any investigation from me again. Am I understood?' She stares at me while tapping the sheets of paper with an outstretched finger. 'I mean it, Beth. Are we clear?'

Pulling the paper to the edge of the table, I grab a pen from the pot beside Dillon's computer. 'Crystal.' I can't help the small smile that teases my lips, until they give in completely, spreading wide. 'Thank you, Dillon.'

'Ma'am,' she says, curtly.

I feel colour rising in my cheeks. 'Sorry, ma'am.'

'Don't make me regret this. I'm putting my ass on the line here; I need you to understand that. I need you to grasp how serious this is, for both of us.'

My smile is long gone. 'I do understand, and I appreciate it. Thank you.' I scoot back in my seat.

She holds up a hand. 'I'm not finished.' I settle into my seat again, my heart hammering. 'Wait until you hear what I have to say before you go thanking me so profusely, although you should be damn grateful you're here at all.'

'I am.'

She drums her fingers on the desk. I want to reach out and still her hand.

'There's something you need to be aware of, and you might not like it.'

I grip my knees tightly. 'And that is?'

'After what happened, it will take time to earn my trust and the team's.'

I nod, my stomach drops. 'I understand.'

She's shaking her head. 'I'm not so sure you do. I can't put you straight back into the role of deputy senior investigating officer, not right away.'

There's a rock in my stomach, a wedge of lemon in my throat. I swallow — hard. 'I get it.'

'Obviously, I need someone we can rely on to step into the breach, so when the next big case comes in, well, I have asked Amer to take on the role.' I open my mouth; she raises her hand. 'He's earned it, Beth. We both know he picked up your slack during the Brander case.'

The rock in my stomach falls through my guts.

'Even before then, he was on the ball, sharp, on-point.' She tilts her head. '*Trustworthy.*'

The lemon is sour as I force saliva past it. 'I know.' She's right, but it stings. Not only did Amer get promoted while I was suspended, but he's been given the role that should have been mine. Dillon's right — he has earned it. I should feel happy for him, proud, pleased. Instead, I feel jealous and let down.

'What you don't know—' she smiles — 'is that his loyalty extends to you and his career equally.'

My eyes widen. 'Meaning?'

'He won't take on the role unless he has your blessing and you working with him.' She nods. 'That's loyalty, Beth, friendship, partnership. It's what I want in my team. Even if his demands pissed me off initially, I do respect him for making them.'

She rests back in her chair, then picks up her pen and begins rotating it between her fingers. 'There's one more stipulation, and there really is no leeway on this.'

I narrow my eyes. 'And what's that?'

'I need you to speak with a department counsellor.'

I inhale. She holds out a hand, anticipating my interruption. 'No, Beth, it's non-negotiable.'

I've been through therapy repeatedly, but never via work. Letting someone here into my head doesn't sit well with me. I don't want to do it. Looking at Dillon, I know I also don't have a choice. 'Okay.'

'I'll ensure Toby Evans will be expecting your call, soon. Today, even. Is that okay?' she asks.

'Do I have a choice?'

'No. And, what I meant is, is it okay that it's Toby, a man?'

I shrug, like a petulant child. 'Can't say I'm keen to talk to a counsellor at all. Male or female. So, yeah, sure. It's fine.'

She glares at me. 'Don't let me down on this. Sort it.'

'I will.'

'So, are we in agreement, about everything? If so, I want to see you here, ready and eager, first thing Monday morning.'

Looking down at the paperwork Dillon passed me, I flip through to the back pages. If I sign this, I am agreeing to seeing a counsellor, and to taking a position lower than the one I left.

'Yes, ma'am,' I say, as I sign in the two places indicated by small pink post-its. A sense of belonging settles over me like a warm blanket on a winter's night. I'm back.

CHAPTER THREE

The Ordinary Man

He's driven round a few times now, observing, waiting for the right one, at the right time. He's good at being patient when he has to be. He bides his time, anticipating what he will do to her. The *who* is unimportant. He'd been procrastinating. Wasted years. Years when he could have been leaving his mark on the world. Living out his fantasies. And now here he is, anticipating what he's about to do. Sometimes it takes another like-minded soul to set the example, and the example had been well and truly set. Now it is his turn.

If that 'like-minded soul' hadn't been going after kids, he might have felt they were kindred. But he is far superior. He has standards, morals.

A young stunner stumbles into view, swaying beneath the streetlights, almost stumbling into the road a couple of times. She's wearing tight black trousers, a red top that skims her waistline and shiny heeled shoes. Most likely thinks she's a cut above the ones wearing miniskirts and cropped tops. She's wrong. She's carrying a Styrofoam tray, her fingers repeatedly jabbing into it to retrieve a mouthful of fries.

He times it to perfection; she ditches her rubbish in the bin, then as she reaches the kerb, he pulls up alongside her. Staring straight ahead, he makes no move to invite her inside. She grabs the door handle and throws the door wide, then clambers in. He smiles in the rear-view mirror as she reels off her address, before leaning back against the headrest and closing her eyes. His pulse races as he clicks the auto lock and seals her inside.

Her strikingly beautiful blue eyes are closed; he thinks of the word *striking* and smiles to himself.

Putting the car in gear, he pulls away from the kerb. With a rush of excitement, he imagines striking her with the hammer he has sitting on the passenger seat under the old rags. The ones he uses to clean dirt and grime from the steering wheel. He can't abide filth.

She's a blonde, and for once, it's natural. Nothing worse than all these false hair colours. Cheap dyes hiding who people really are, what they are.

As he drives, he drinks her in via the rear-view mirror. Her long, wavy blonde hair glides seductively over her shoulders. She uses her right hand to tuck a few loose strands behind her ear. Her lips part slightly, tempting him further. She wears a slick, nude lip gloss that makes them shine, teasingly. She's young and fresh-faced. The elasticity of her flawless skin is what women a few years beyond her age pay a mint for. She's the picture of naivety.

He visualizes his hands around her throat, the white skin turning red as he squeezes. Her eyes opening and bugging, looking as though they might pop clean out of their sockets. He sees it all so clearly. The images in his mind captivate him, and he gasps. Her eyes spring open. She looks confused, as though she has forgotten where she is, then she rubs at her eyes with the heels of her hands like a sleep-deprived child.

Her head turns, and she peers through the windows. Her confusion intensifies. 'Excuse me? Hello?'

He smirks and lets his silence slither under her skin.

Her blue eyes widen in alarm. Her mouth begins to twitch with fear. 'Excuse me, hey? Where are we? You've gone the wrong way. Hey!'

He stares straight ahead and waits, a thrill bubbling up within him. Sure enough, she starts yanking the door handle. Then, as her panic rises further, she begins to hit the window. He can feel the vibrations of her fear resonating around the car. The shudder of pleasure her torment gives him is close to orgasmic.

Her face appears contorted, her eyes darting around the space as she flings herself from one side of the car to the other, trying both doors. He notes the very moment she realizes the locks have been removed. She lunges forward and begins hammering on the partition between them. 'Please,' she cries, fat useless tears in those sparkly blue eyes of hers, 'I want to go home. Please. I want my mum. Please let me go. Please don't hurt me.'

He sees the hopeful look cross her face as she reaches into her bag and retrieves her mobile. He can't hold it in a moment longer, his low chuckle as her horrified gaze lands on her phone screen. He'd activated the mobile signal scrambler as soon as she'd closed her eyes.

His chuckle transforms into a deep-throated laugh. Their eyes meet in the mirror. He's omnipotent.

Her body is practically convulsing. Mind you, so is his, though for very different reasons. He tightens his hands on the steering wheel, squeezing and twisting. He forces himself to calm his excitement, to subdue his arousal. He's determined to enjoy every moment.

She freezes then, sitting, wide-eyed, tears rolling down her face. Terror has turned her into a mannequin.

21

CHAPTER FOUR

DCI Bethany Fellows

Aunt Margie's pink-and-blue bungalow stands in front of me, her front garden spruced up and full of colour. I turn and glance towards the beach opposite. St Anne's salty sea air fills my lungs for the first time in a while. It's drizzling rain, windy, and grey clouds hang heavily in the sky; the sea is tumultuous today. Even from here, I can see its rage, hear its roar as it crashes against the shore.

The last time I was here was Christmas, a subdued affair, considering what had occurred such a short time before. Just Aunt Margie and me sitting at the table with a roast, more out of habit than anything else. She'd put up a tree, but bypassed the usual fanfare. It had felt wrong even then to be celebrating Christmas when I knew what the victims' families were facing. Their first year without their loved ones.

I see the front door opening. Aunt Margie appears in the gap, and I let out a relaxed sigh as I walk up the path. She has bat ears when it comes to the sound of my car pulling up. Her blonde hair sits atop her head in a frizzy mop. Her wide eyes take me in as I near her.

Emotion wells inside me as I look at my beautiful, kooky aunt. 'Sorry it's taken me a while,' I say, already smelling her familiar scent, Charlie Blue perfume and vanilla candles.

She opens her arms to me, and I rush to her. 'Come here, sugarplum.' She enfolds me, pulling my head into her shoulder, cradling me the way only she does. 'I've got the kettle on.' I feel her mouth spreading into a smile against the side of my head. She lets go, steps back and appraises me. 'Hot chocolate?'

I nod, though my assent isn't needed; whenever I come here in need of comfort, this is our routine. We move to the rhythm that years of practice have established. Walking inside, my body decompresses, my breathing becomes easier, and my heart slows to a steady pace. I'm home. Nowhere else on this earth holds a candle to being here with my aunt.

In some ways, staying away wasn't just to protect Aunt Margie from the fallout of the mess I'd created, it wasn't just for space to heal — it was also a self-exile I deserved. Comfort and homeliness were things now forever denied to the Brander's victims, and they would never have fallen foul of him had it not been for me. I am still attempting to make sense of everything that happened and to stop internalizing the blame, which I know is one of my biggest downfalls. Self-recrimination for the things out of my control is hugely damaging, yet I can't seem to break the habit. Even as a youngster, I held on to the fact I had been unable to identify my mum's killer. I'd been the only witness, the best chance she had at getting justice. That I was only four at the time didn't stop me hating myself for what I saw as my failure. I had finally begun to move forward, beyond that stage, and then it all came back in a storm I couldn't battle through.

I sit at the kitchen table while Aunt Margie busies herself making me a hot chocolate in one of the flamingo mugs. In another, she makes tea. I would offer to do it for her, but I know she needs this, the way I need her. Aunt Margie's role in my life has always been caregiver and saviour, her patience knows no bounds and neither does her love.

Placing the steaming mug in front of me, she sits and holds her own cup, taking a sip before placing it on the table. I lean forward, wrap my hands around my mug and inhale the sweet chocolatey scent. 'I start back on Monday,' I say, still staring down at my drink, avoiding eye contact.

She takes a deep, steadying breath. 'And you're ready?'

I look at her. 'Yes.'

Reaching out, she takes my hand. 'Then there's nothing for me to say, is there?' A minute, reluctant smile traces her lips. 'I never could stop you from doing anything you set your mind to. This is no different. Even if I begged you to think about it, to reconsider, you wouldn't.' She takes my hand in hers and places it on the table before patting the back of it. 'Would you?'

I notice a couple of new lines on her hand and it shocks me. The years and stresses are leaving their mark. Shaking my head, I see a tear fall from her eye, a traitor to her strength. 'I'm sorry.'

She swipes the tear away. 'My worries shouldn't be yours.' She stands quickly and walks to the sink, turning away from me to run the hot tap. She waves a couple of fingers beneath the stream until it's heated enough. Filling the washing-up bowl with water and Fairy Liquid for the scarce items within it. It is a distraction, a way for her to protect me from her pain and panic.

'It's my career, Aunt Margie.' Looking up at the ceiling, I close my eyes momentarily, then stare at her back. 'It's more than that. It's who I am.' Her shoulders are shaking, lightly, almost imperceptibly, but I see it. I don't acknowledge it as she tries her best to hide it from me. She isn't speaking, and I know it's because I would hear the thickness of emotion in her voice. 'How's Zumba going?'

She shrugs, then clears her throat. 'Oh, you know.'

I force a smile. 'I don't. That's why I'm asking.' It's been a while since she joined online Zumba classes in Mauritius. She's been enthused and enchanted by the ladies who see her as something of a star attraction. Usually, her fads don't stand the test of time, but this has been different, I think it's become a bit of a lifeline in many respects.

Turning towards me, her cheeks are damp, and this time, she makes no move to hide the evidence of her tears. 'Zumba is good; it gives me an outlet. But nothing takes this—' she touches her chest — 'pain away. Ever since I found out who killed your mum and why he did it, I can't sleep, I can't eat.'

Only now do I notice just how much weight she's lost; my chest constricts.

'I worry for you constantly,' she says. 'You've needed time; I understand that. But, Beth, I needed you. You haven't been here for almost three months. *Three months*.' The last two words sound strangled.

I feel sick. I had thought I was doing what was best for both of us, but I hadn't been there for the woman who has always been there for me. 'Oh my God, I . . . I am so sorry.'

Standing, I stride to her and pull her into my arms, holding her tightly. She sobs against my chest, huge wracking sobs that shake us both to the core. My tears fall freely; I don't attempt to stop or disguise them. I have let Aunt Margie down. She needed me, and I have been preoccupied with the very people who caused us both this hurt. 'I'm here now, and I promise you, I'm not going anywhere.'

'You can't make that promise, sugarplum, not while he's still out there. Neither of us can make a promise like that. What if he . . .' Her sentence trails off.

Shaking my head against her hair, I breathe her in. 'He won't. I will not let him take anything else from us. They are going to rot in prison.'

'But he's still out there somewhere. He could be anywhere.' She steps out of my hold and looks at me earnestly. 'He could be right outside this bungalow at this very moment. He's free.'

'For now.'

'What are you going to do?'

'My job.'

'Catching him isn't your job, though, is it?'

'I'm a detective, Aunt Margie. Catching killers is exactly what I do. So yes, it's very much my job.'

'They won't let you near the case. And I'm glad. Let someone else find him.'

'I'm not sure anyone else can.'

'What's that supposed to mean?'

'It just means that I am the closest to this. I'm the person he is most likely to come after.' Her face crumples, and I grab her hand. 'Don't worry about me. I know that's easier said than done, but please don't. I'm ready. I'm prepared for whatever he brings, whenever he brings it.'

Her eyes narrow. 'What are you saying?'

'Look, Aunt Margie, I know you're scared; I know how much you love me. I appreciate you and everything you have ever done for me, I do. I adore you; you know that. But I'm a detective. It's my job to deal with the bad guys. This is no different.'

'But it is, Beth. You know it is.'

I brush aside the use of my name, realizing she's getting irritated. 'I don't want you to worry about me. I know it's hard, but please try. Trust me.'

'I do trust you. But I also know you. I didn't miss what you said you know, about being prepared. What did you mean by that?' She tilts my chin up with her finger. 'I *know* you were insinuating something more than it being your job. You were getting at something, tell me what it is, Beth. Now.'

I sigh. I should have known better than to think she would overlook my wording. I should have come with a script in mind, dammit. 'I just meant that I haven't been sitting around crying about what's happened. I did a bit; of course I did. But then I picked myself up and I started getting myself sorted for what is going to happen.'

'I don't know what you're talking about. You're scaring me, sugarplum.' I'm giving her answers, so it's back to 'sugarplum'.

'I don't mean to. I just want you to know that you have no reason to be worried. Not for me. I'm okay.'

'I'm not sure that's true.'

'It is. Honestly, the best thing for me is to get back to work and to some semblance of normality, and to do what I'm best at. The rest will come together as and when. Anyway—' I sit back down at the table — 'our drinks are getting cold, and I fancy an episode of *Wynonna*. You up for some TV time?'

She nods, but I see how unsure she is as she examines me with her eyes. She sits beside me and drinks her tea, but is uncharacteristically quiet as we settle in front of the TV. I want to tell her everything. I hunger to offload, but now isn't the time. She'll only worry more, and that wouldn't be fair. Pulling the blanket over us, I snuggle closer to Aunt Margie, her arm wraps around me and I feel the hardness of her ribs. I have to find a way to be more present and protect her simultaneously. Her age and vulnerabilities are showing more than ever. I won't add to her angst. I only wish I'd kept my counsel entirely. I'd had no choice but to stay away before, for this very reason. Aunt Margie has a way of wheedling the truth out of me. There are certain things better left unsaid. Exactly what I have planned, and how I have planned for it, are things I won't speak of. I can't. Not yet.

CHAPTER FIVE

The Ordinary Man

He reverses the car onto his drive, then sits for a moment while his heart rate settles. He retrieves a tissue from the glove compartment and mops his brow. He's home; it's over.

Friday night has the entire street lit up like fucking Christmas. Everyone's living room lights are ablaze. No one seems to give a shit about their bills or their carbon footprint. He gets out of the car and notices the black bin is still out. It'd been bin day on Wednesday. He'd clean forgotten to take the bloody thing back up the drive. Laurie will whinge her head off if she's noticed. Traipsing over, he huffs as he grabs the handle.

He is repulsed when he feels something sticky. 'Fucking disgusting,' he mutters under his breath, as he wheels it up the drive before placing it by the side gate.

He opens the front door then he kicks his muddy trainers off on the brown welcome mat.

'Daddy, Daddy!' Kira shouts, as she pelts through the lounge door and into the hallway. She flings herself at him and wraps her arms around his legs like a little monkey. 'Mummy said I could wait up for you because it's Friday.'

Their elderly black Labrador, Kickers, trots up behind her, patiently waiting for his master to scratch his head. He obliges, using the opportunity to rid himself of some of the sticky remnants from the bin handle. 'Alreet, Key. Good boy, Kicks.' He addresses his daughter using his pet name for her and she grins up at him. Kickers, happy with the bit of attention he's received, mooches back into the lounge. His sigh is loud as he settles down again.

Kira is the image of him as a kid. Mousey brunette flyaway hair, big brown eyes, and thick eyelashes. She's a cute kid, and of everyone in this godforsaken world, she does own a piece of his heart. He even loves her, in his own way. Perhaps not in the same way most fathers love their children, but he can't help how he was born. He simply isn't built that way. He accepted it a long time ago. Now, he embraces it. His lack of feelings for others offers him a sense of freedom most people will never know.

He tuts as he looks down at the top of Kira's head. At five years old, she should have been in bed hours ago. It's typical of Laurie to let her stay up. He sees right through her; it's obviously a ploy to leave the hassle of putting their daughter to bed up to him. Laurie has never been the most attentive mother. For better or worse, she's his wife, so he puts up with her. She has her uses, after all.

He walks, or rather shuffles, into the lounge with Kira still attached to him, her arms and legs curled around his leg. She refuses to put her feet on the ground and walk. Kickers is flat out on the floor in front of the couch. Laurie uses one foot to half-heartedly stroke his back.

'Come on, Key,' he says. 'Daddy needs his leg back. Stand up.'

She giggles happily to herself. He looks down and notices a bit of blood on his trousers. It must have seeped through from his wounded leg; the bandage was clearly a bag of shit. With a lurch, he realizes some of the blood has transferred onto Kira's pyjamas, leaving an unmistakable red blemish.

Laurie is unmoving, apart from her foot. As always, she's glued to the television. She hadn't even looked up when he walked in. An episode of that crap medical programme she loves so much, *Grey's Anatomy*, is twittering on in the background.

His ankle and hand are really starting to throb now. Having Kira hanging from his leg like some annoying little chimp isn't helping one iota. Shaking his leg, he manages to loosen her grip. As she falls backwards onto the floor, the relief is palpable.

'Hey, love,' he says to Laurie, while simultaneously reaching down to fully detach his daughter. 'Just going to wash my hands; won't be a sec.'

He walks through to the kitchen, then stands at the sink looking through the window at his small but perfectly presented back garden. He removes the dressings, then smothers anti-bacterial soap all over his hands, right up his wrists. It stings his wound like fuck, but after touching that crap on the bin handle, he has to disinfect it. He doesn't want frigging tetanus or sepsis; he ensures both injuries are aptly cleansed. After washing with the thoroughness of a surgeon, he opens the drawer next to the sink with the first aid supplies inside. Finding the bandages, he rewraps his hand and ankle as quickly as possible. Laurie hadn't looked up to notice, and Kira was only interested in his presence, not whether or not he was hurt. They could both be bloody selfish, but on this occasion, he was glad of it.

Kira comes charging into the kitchen, running so fast her legs go from under her. Skidding across the floor, she crashes headfirst into the cupboard and lets out a high-pitched wail.

He bends down and scoops her up. Kira flings her arms around his neck, snuggling her head into his shoulder and sobs violently. Laurie comes rushing into the kitchen, maternal concern plastered across her face. He hadn't missed the fact she'd paused the TV first. It annoys him that her priority was to ensure she wouldn't miss a beat. Laurie stands beside him, rubbing circles against her daughter's back, trying to soothe her.

'What happened? I heard a crash.' She sounds to all intents and purposes like the loving mum.

'She came a cropper against the unit. Came flying in here like a bat outta hell. Probably overtired and not with it—' he narrows his eyes at Laurie — 'it's gone midnight, for Christ's sake. She should be in bed.'

Kira's sobs begin to slow, and she pants, attempting to stop her tears. Her shoulders rise and fall dramatically. He sits her on the sideboard to examine her head. There is already the beginning of an angry red lump forming. Wonderful, he thinks, it will be at least another hour before she can go to bed safely.

He takes a long soak in the shower, then comes downstairs to find Kira waiting patiently with her storybook. She's sitting beside Laurie on the couch. The lump on Kira's head is now egg-shaped and bruising fast. Laurie doesn't look at him, no doubt sulking after his barbed comment.

He sits next to Kira and starts reading a fairy tale.

'You could do that upstairs. I'm trying to watch the telly,' Laurie complains.

He doesn't respond; a pointed look is enough. He carries on reading fairy tale after fairy tale, about princes rescuing princesses from impossible situations. After an hour, her little eyes are sparkling with tiredness. They remind him of her *eyes* as the reality of her situation had hit home. He can still see the tears springing up in them. He smiles as he finishes the last story with a flourish.

CHAPTER SIX

DCI Bethany Fellows

I wake up with a groan. My neck cracks, sending waves of revulsion through me. In my wisdom, I had decided to stay the night at Aunt Margie's. As my old bedroom is now a newly kitted out doll's-house-building area, I have been cramped up on the couch since I nodded off during *Wynonna Earp*. Aunt Margie has wrapped the blanket around me in some sort of stranglehold and I have to fidget and wriggle my way free, further angering the nerves in my neck. Checking my mobile, I see that it's only 6 a.m., and as it's Saturday, Aunt Margie will be having a well-deserved lie-in. I quietly amble into the kitchen and flick the kettle on.

Every time I think about starting back at work on Monday, butterflies begin a rave in my tummy. It's not about the job; that I am ready for. It's not even about being demoted and having Amer leading the team. He's more than earned it. What's spinning around in my overwrought brain are thoughts of facing Millie and what I'm going to say to her. I had managed to miss her while I was at the station, and I've sent her a couple of texts apologizing for being out of touch for so long. The problem is, she hasn't replied to a single one, and I can't stop the panic setting in. I'll have no option but to face her on Monday. Christ, we'll be working alongside each other. She is clearly opting to ignore me, so I am not anticipating a warm welcome back.

A clattering noise reverberates from Aunt Margie's bedroom. I run to her door and am just about to barge in when she appears. 'What's up with you?' she asks, staring at me wide-eyed. 'You look like you've seen a ghost.'

My pulse vibrates in my ears. It takes a moment for my heart rate to settle. 'I heard a bang, what happened?'

She's shaking her head. 'Sugarplum . . . see, this is why I'm so worried about you. Just look at the state of you. And all I did was knock over a few things.'

I look around her into her bedroom and see the items from on top of her chest of drawers lying haphazardly on the floor. I point at the mess. 'How did you manage that?'

'Dancing.' She points to a set of pink headphones on the end of her bed. 'I lost my footing. Anyway, don't divert. So, I knocked a few things over? Who cares. I'll pick them up quick enough. What I am more bothered about is how pale you've gone and your panicked expression.' She swivels her finger in front of my face. 'You don't look like you've slept properly since I last saw you, and we both know that was far too long ago.'

'When did you get headphones?' I again attempt to change the subject.

'I had an early start and didn't want to disturb you. I bought them a while ago; you'd have known if you hadn't been AWOL for so long.'

'An early start? It's Saturday. What kind of early start?'

'This room.' She glances around, looking dismayed.

I raise my eyebrow. 'What about it?'

'The feng shui is all wrong in here. I'm rearranging a few things.'

I smirk. 'The what now?'

'You heard me, you cheeky sod.'

'Since when were you bothered about all that "airy-fairy nonsense"?' I make air quotes as I speak, repeating her own words of the past. Though how Aunt Margie can call any-one or anything *airy-fairy* I don't know. I chuckle, my stress washed away by the sheer Aunt Margie-ness of this situation.

She waves a hand. 'I've been revaluating things, and . . .' She rolls her eyes at me and tuts. 'Everyone is entitled to a change of heart, even your haggard old auntie.'

'You're not *that* old. And you certainly are not haggard.' I stop laughing, but my smile remains. 'Fancy a cuppa?'

'Seeing as you're offering, how can I refuse?'

She saunters behind me through to the kitchen, then sets her iPod on her new bright pink docking station. Thankfully, today's playlist of choice is Motown and soul. Whenever she's prepping for Zumba, it's full of old pop songs and suchlike that make my ears want to close in on themselves.

For some reason, Aunt Margie's computer has a new and inconvenient home on the kitchen counter. I work around it to make myself a coffee and Aunt Margie a tea. 'What's with this being in here?' I tap the mouse and the computer springs to life.

Aunt Margie moves like lightning, reaching past me to hold the power button in, forcing a shut down.

'What the hell was *that* about?'

'Nothing,' she says quickly.

I open my mouth to speak, but my mobile rings, cutting me off. We glance at each other. No welcome call ever came before at least 8 a.m., especially not on a weekend. I dash through to the lounge and grab my phone from the arm of the couch. Dillon's name flashes across the screen.

'Hello?' A sinking sensation lands in my stomach. Is she about to retract her invitation for me to start back on Monday?

'Beth.' She sounds breathless. 'You're familiar with the Shaw's Arms?' Without giving me chance to answer, she adds, 'As in, you know where it is?'

'You mean the one directly off Walton Bridge, near work? If so, then yes, I know where it is.' A new weight lands in my stomach, this time for entirely different reasons. Is this a case?

'That's the one.' Her tone is all-business. 'Behind that, just down by the river near the entrance to the Guild Wheel cycle path. How long until you can get there?'

Looking towards the kitchen, I see Aunt Margie standing in the doorway appearing stricken. 'I, erm. . . ' I turn away from my aunt. 'I'll get there as soon as I can. I stayed at Aunt Margie's last night. So, I'm in St Annes, but I'll get ready and on the road.'

'Okay, good. Thanks, Beth,' she sighs. 'From everything I know, this is definitely one for us.' I can almost hear her brain ticking over. 'For now, we've set the cordon as far as the garage. To be honest, you would be just as well parking at work and walking up. I don't want to risk disturbing any evidence. If this is what I think it is, then whoever did it may have used a vehicle, and if so, they could have parked beside or driven around the Shaw's Arms.'

'I understand. No problem.'

'Thanks, Beth, and, erm, say hello to Margie for me.'

'Of course.'

'Amer is going to meet you there. I've just come off the phone with him.'

It would have been me she'd called first before. It's a tough pill to swallow.

'It was a dog walker who called it in, a man. God bless early morning dog walkers, eh? If not for them . . . I dread to think of a kid coming across something like that. Right, so we will catch up later. Let me know the moment you have anything, any information at all.'

'I will.' I infer the meaning behind her comment. She wouldn't usually feel the need to remind me of something so standard, but I had kept things from her during the last case. She's ensuring I won't do the same thing again.

'Before you go, Beth . . . It sounds like this is a bad one.' There's a beat of silence. 'Are you certain you're ready?'

I swallow and glance sheepishly at Aunt Margie. 'Yes. I'm certain.' I can't keep looking at Aunt Margie's tormented face, so I turn my back to her. 'Any more information?'

She gives me a quick rundown of what she knows so far. It isn't much, but it's enough to get my blood pumping. 'I'll get there as soon as I can.'

'Okay. I'll see you later today. I think we are going to have to bring as many people in as possible. We need to get moving on this. Weekend festivities are cancelled all round.'

I end the call and turn back to face Aunt Margie, but she's vanished into the kitchen. 'Dillon says hello.' I attempt to inject a note of cheeriness into my voice as I walk in to find her sitting at the table, brew in hand.

She looks up at me, dejectedly. 'You're already there, aren't you?'

She knows me too well, because she's right — my mind is whirring with the possibilities of what I am about to be dealing with. Adrenaline is already pumping through my veins. The job is as vital to me as the oxygen I breathe. There will be no placating my aunt, but I have to do this. It's who I am.

I get ready, dressing in the work clothes I keep in my old bedroom, then putting the lanyard around my neck that Dillon returned to me yesterday. Aunt Margie's concern drips from her like sweat from a marathon runner. I want to take it from her, the worry, the angst, but I can't do that. The only way it would be possible would be for me to walk away from my career, and that's not an option. When I'm leaving, her hug lasts longer than usual and her hold is noticeably tighter. I can't lie; I hold her tighter too. 'I love you,' I say as I let go.

She kisses the top of my head. 'I love you too, sugar-plum, more than anything in this world.'

She's standing on the front doorstep, waving, and wearing a small smile as I drive away. I notice her hand swipe across her cheeks a couple of times, and my heart contracts, knowing the smile is forced for my benefit.

It isn't long before I am pulling up at work. I don't go inside the building. Instead, I head straight out onto London Road and take a left before crossing Walton Bridge over the River Ribble. I pull the belt of my leather coat tighter and can't help but roll my eyes as I observe the early morning ghouls, congregating, and gossiping along the bridge. I take a mental picture of each and every one of them as I pass. Peering over the side at the river, I notice that the water appears calm despite the windier-than-usual March weather. It begins to drizzle rain, teardrops landing continuously on the surface of the water. Looking up, I notice a crowd of light-grey clouds, and worry what it could mean for our crime scene. As I pass over the hump of the bridge, I see the blue-and-white ribbon of the outer cordon fluttering in the wind. I can see a few police offers milling around, keeping guard to ensure no one passes the cordon at any point. Across the bridge are a number of figures in white Tyvek suits moving around looking for evidence. This is the world I know; the one that both heals and damages me.

I head straight for the outer cordon just beside the garage, where a young female PC stands holding onto a logbook. I pull my lanyard forward from around my neck and hold it out for her appraisal. She signs me in, noting my rank, the date, time and, of course, my reason for entry. She's professional and on the ball. She directs me to the box containing the forensic wear.

The Shaw's Arms has scaffolding erected, brickwork visible where concrete has been chipped away in huge patches. As I pass by, I note a low brick wall with a small patch of green between that and the old pub. It is full of debris. A possible deposition site for a weapon? There used to be a playground behind it. I glance across — it's still there, but completely desolate. The entrance is littered with bricks and cardboard, and probably all sorts of other rubbish, too. Another place to search. Though I'm doubtful anyone would have struggled beyond the rubbish to get into the playground, it will still have to be checked.

Walking down the side of the pub, I see a white tent opposite a small parking area, which is beside the river. The inner cordon goes from one wooden fence to the next, either side of the entrance to the Guild Wheel cycle route. A short distance beyond, past a small copse of trees is the white forensic tent.

The crime scene tent covering the area aims to preserve evidence, particularly as it's now begun raining. The crime scene investigators, as we must now refer to them — talk about bringing Americanisms here — will move fast to gather all other evidence in the area before it's damaged, moved, contaminated, or even washed away. The tent also protects our victim from the morbid curiosity of onlookers, or worse still, from news helicopters going for an aerial shot. The butterflies of earlier have given way to a sickness reminiscent of a hangover. The responsibility I feel is already weighing heavily, and momentarily I wonder whether I really am ready to be back.

Whoever has done this clearly had no care for the kids that could have happened by. And seeing as the Fishwick Nature Reserve runs adjacent to the Guild Wheel, that was a distinct possibility. The psychological damage it would have inflicted would have been severe, something I know about only too well. I am already seething about the audacity and cruelty of this perp, and I don't have any details yet. Looking back at the bridge, past the onlookers who have gathered, I can't get over how close we are to the station. It's as though whoever did this is taunting us.

Turning back around, I notice Amer within the inner cordon ambling towards me via the common approach path, which has been decided upon as the least likely area to disturb evidence. Like me and everyone else, he is covered head to toe in a white Tyvek suit with the hood up and he's wearing overshoes and gloves. Even looking like he's wearing a questionable onesie and standing at a bit of a distance, I can tell it's him by his walk alone. He balances precariously on the stepping plates, then ducks under the yellow inner cordon to join me.

His huge eyes stare over the face mask. 'Beth.' His voice is slightly muffled by the material. I see a sadness in his eyes and know Dillon was right: this is going to be a bad one. 'Dillon contacted the coroner straight away.' He begins to fill me in, then pauses and starts rubbing at the back of his neck through the papery material. 'This is awkward,' he says.

Normally, his nervous habit would have him fiddling with his belt, but right now the suit makes that impossible. 'I take it Dillon explained about . . .' His eyes flicker away from me uncomfortably. 'I told her that if you're not okay with it, I'll step down. I won't do it.'

I shake my head. 'It's fine, Amer. She told me and I agree with her. You did prove yourself. You've earned this. I am honestly happy to be led by you on this one.' He still appears unsure, so I stare him out. 'I swear it.'

He nods and uses a gloved finger to scratch his head through his hood. 'Good. So long as you really are sure.'

'I am,' I repeat.

'Bloody itchy, these things.' He continues to scratch. 'They make me sweat like an Eskimo in a sauna.' His eyes crinkle at the edges, giving away his smile, but it disappears as quickly as it appeared. 'This poor kid, Beth.'

'Kid?'

'Well, judging by the body shape and clothes, I would guess they're young, but you can never be sure.'

'Male, female?'

'By the length of hair and the clothes, I would hazard a guess at female, but I suppose it could be a lad with long hair. They're face down, filthy and plastered in blood, so until we turn them over . . .'

'Christ,' I say, the lead weight in my stomach unmoving.

I spot Hannah Edwards as she stands up. She's within the inner cordon, past the wooden cycle gate where she'd been crouched behind a tree looking at something.

She stretches her back out and her eyes crinkle with a smile when she spots me. Amer and I duck under the inner cordon and move cautiously across the stepping plates towards her.

She's rocking on the balls of her feet, a movement I would be terrified of making on one of these things. 'Oh my God, Beth, I heard you were coming back. What a sight for sore eyes you are. How're doing, my friend?'

'Hey, Han.' I can't help but smile myself. The sight of her warms me, despite the situation. 'I'm all right. You know how it is. Just glad to be back.' I feel a tad embarrassed, as though my shame at having been suspended is written all over me. 'Bad one?' I say, nodding towards the tent.

Hannah's expression darkens. 'I would say so, yeah. First impression is that the back of the head has been caved in with something. But until we get them out of here, clean the muck off and get a good look, that's about all I have for you.'

'Mind if I take a look?' I ask.

Hannah nods. 'Of course. I think Doctor Sanders is probably about done. Dillon asked him to come by and take a look while the body is in situ.' She's referring to Doctor Damien Sanders, the Home Office Forensic Pathologist.

The tent shifts and a short, skinny figure emerges: Mick Reinhardt clutches a camera in his hands. He's distinguishable among his colleagues. If he replaced Wally in a *Where's Wally?* book, he'd stand out a mile, especially when his long hair is on display. This time, like the rest of us, he is fully suited up, meaning his hood is covering his hair.

Amer and I follow Hannah to the tent. She parts the opening just enough to get through.

Doctor Sanders looks at us as we enter. 'I'm just finishing up. I'll leave the rest in your capable hands, Hannah.'

'Thanks, Doctor Sanders,' she says.

'How many times, Hannah? It's Damien.'

I can practically feel the heat permeating from her. I'm pretty sure she's been harbouring a crush for years. 'Sorry, yes, I forgot . . . again.'

'Mick has taken video footage and photographs. I'll let you do the swabs and tape lifts.'

'No problem.'

He looks to me. 'Good to see you back, Beth.'

'Thanks, Damien.' I look past him to the body. 'I was due to start Monday, but Dillon called.' I nod towards the body that is lying face down, long hair trailing down their back. 'Any idea regarding time of death?'

He nods towards Hannah. 'We got here just before six a.m., and the body was just about in full rigor mortis at that point.'

'Help a layperson out,' I say.

'We could put time since death at approximately six to eight hours. So, you're looking at an approximate time frame of between ten p.m. and midnight.'

'Thanks,' I say.

Anything else for us?' Amer asks.

'There's also the livor mortis.' Damien bends and uses an outstretched gloved finger to indicate purplish skin discolouration. 'It's all accumulated around the front of the body, so I would say this is where they died or were placed very shortly after death.'

Amer nods. 'That's useful, thanks, Damien.'

'Happy to oblige. I've advised Hannah and the team on how best to recover the body. I'll take a closer look once we have them back at the mortuary. I'll schedule the PM as soon as possible.'

I look down at our vic and can see what Amer means about body shape and clothing. They are wearing dark trousers — at least I'm assuming they are; they're covered in mud. Their hair is thick with what looks like blood, and a decent amount of grime. It's reminiscent of matted hair that hasn't been washed for a month. They are wearing some kind of short top, which from what I can see I'm almost confident is red, but I could be wrong. There's what appears to be blood on the ground around the victim, too. Dillon was right; this is bad.

I've been staring for so long, I think I might have slipped into some sort of trance. Hannah waves a hand in front of my face, and when I look up, Damien has gone. Amer gives me a funny look but keeps his counsel.

'I assume a divisional surgeon attended to confirm life extinct?' I say.

Hannah's brow furrows, then she shakes her head almost imperceptibly. 'Of course. The poor old sod who called it in was very shaken, but he could tell they were beyond help.' Hannah looks down at the body, shaking her head. 'Bloody tragic.'

'Right, yeah. I think I've seen enough.' I swivel towards the exit. Amer will have to go out first to allow me to pass. 'You done here too, Amer?'

He looks me up and down. 'Sure,' he says, and steps out of the tent.

'Au revoir,' Hannah mumbles.

'Adios,' I mutter.

Once we pass through the inner cordon, Amer stops and turns to me. 'You okay, Beth? You can tell me if you're not. I won't judge you. First and foremost we're mates; remember that.'

Glancing around I ensure there's no one in ear shot. 'I'm fine, Amer. But first and foremost, you're deputy SIO.' I touch his upper arm. 'Don't let personal feelings cloud your judgement the way I did. I won't be responsible for you not giving it one hundred per cent.'

He steps back and places a hand on his chest. 'I am giving it one hundred per cent. Me caring about you and working this case to the best of my ability are not mutually exclusive.'

I feel my eyebrows hitting my hairline. 'I didn't mean to imply you weren't capable, or that you were messing up in any way. I'm sorry.'

He shrugs. 'It's fine. Look, I think this—' his hand waves between the two of us — 'is just going to take a little time. Like wearing in a pair of new shoes.' His face brightens. 'Before long, we'll be gliding.'

Hearing the click of a camera, I look to my right and see a tech snapping photographs, Mick completing a video diary of the wider scene, and a few more techs leaving an array of numbered yellow markers around the area.

The poor soul: no one deserves to end up like this. Such a cruel and unnatural fate brought about by someone full of rage. After seeing them, I already have a feeling about the case. The kind of person who left them that way could do this again. They're so full of vitriol and bile, it's only a matter of timing and circumstances and they'll explode again. I feel a sense of gratification that my gut instinct has resurfaced and that my first impulse isn't to doubt it. My decision to return to work has been reinforced. This is why I needed to come back so badly, to stop these monsters and lock them away before they can hurt anyone else.

CHAPTER SEVEN

As we head back to the station, I anticipate seeing Millie and the rest of the team. Once I arrive, I gratefully scan my pass and enter the code to get through the security door beside reception.

'Just nipping to the loo,' I say to Amer.

'See you in there. First, I'm going to check where we're at with HOLMES2.'

I dash to the back of the office, passing rows of people sitting at the computer banks. They're inputting data into the HOLMES2 system that will link information and generate leads for us to follow. Once in the ladies, I do a quick recce, pushing doors and checking under them. Then I lean against the bank of sinks and close my eyes, taking deep, steadying breaths. Splashing water onto my face, I tuck some loose strands of hair behind my ears, force a calm look onto my face and leave the ladies.

The Major Incident Room (MIR) has little more than the nameplate on the outside and the desks and laptops arranged inside. The whiteboards are, so far, completely blank. This barren room will soon be the hub of a major murder investigation. It's a different room to the one we used last time, but looks exactly the same. They're all decorated with magnolia-painted walls, grey carpet, white-topped tables, and black chairs. There are noticeboards and framed inspirational quotes dotted around the walls. Four large whiteboards stand on wheels at the front, waiting to be filled with photographs, notes, all the inner workings of an investigation. I stand in the room, allowing the silence to soothe me. I can just about make out the chatter and tapping of keyboards drifting through from the main office. The door is slightly ajar, but as I turn to close it, Dillon pushes from the other side. I almost leap off my feet.

I place my hand over my heart and gasp. 'Jeez, Dil . . . ma'am, you scared me half to death.'

She steps inside, then closes the door. 'Sorry about that, Beth. How was it?' She looks from me to the closed door and back again, as if confirming that we are alone, and I can speak freely.

'It was fine.' I shake my head. 'What I mean is, *I* was fine. I still am.'

Dillon places a hand on my shoulder. 'Good, I'm glad. But if that changes—' she stares into my eyes, almost hypnotically — 'seriously, if that changes *at all*, I want you to come to me. Did you call Toby Evans after we spoke on Friday?'

I avert my eyes towards the empty whiteboards, trying desperately to conjure up any plausible excuse as to why I am yet to make contact with the department counsellor. I can hear every tick of the wall clock and can't throw up a single word of use.

'I'll take your silence as a no, shall I?'

I turn back to face her, pulling my bottom lip into my mouth and chewing.

'Beth, I need you to keep up your end of the bargain. You agreed. You signed. It's part of the deal. You can't avoid it, I'm sorry. Hell, I'm *not* sorry. I don't know why I even said that. You *need* to speak to someone. We both know you do. Please get onto it sooner rather than later. He's expecting your call. You need to get the ball rolling on it ASAP, as agreed.'

I'm unable to think of a counterargument, so nod my acquiescence. I did sign that paperwork; I want and need to be here, and as such I have no choice. 'I'll call him. As soon as we have this room set up and things in motion.'

Dillon eyes me suspiciously, raising one eyebrow.

'I will, I promise.'

'Okay, fine.' She removes her hand from my shoulder. Walking towards the front bank of tables, she perches on the edge of one. 'We have a preliminary ID. I received the call while you were en route back. She had a bankcard in her pocket.'

'She?'

Dillon nods. 'It matches with a MISPER we received about an hour and a half ago. Parents called to say their daughter didn't come home after a night out. Mum went in to check on her and her bed hadn't been slept in. Apparently, it was so out of character they called us right away. A couple of PCs attended swiftly. They were in the area.' She sighs. 'Unfortunately, I guess it's our ballgame now. It's extremely unlikely it isn't the same girl. Pending the official ID, we can't be one hundred per cent certain, but . . .'

A girl, not a woman, *please not a kid*. 'Who is she?'

'Twenty-one-year-old Jasmine Foster, a student nurse. She was reported missing by her parents, Frank and Penny Foster. She'd been on a night out with friends. PC Imelda Roberts and PC David Matthews attended. There was nothing standout, apart from her parents insisting that she has never stayed out before. They contacted the friends she was with, knocked them all up early. They claimed to have no idea where she was, although they did say she was complaining of hunger. The consensus being she left the group early, about ten p.m., and went to get something to eat. The last they saw of her was in the Baluga Bar and Club on Lancaster Road. She posted a couple of tweets while she was out, then nothing.'

'Crikey, they got all that quickly.'

Dillon leans forward and nods. 'PC Imelda Roberts is one to watch, I'm telling you. She's been on my radar for a while. Intuitive, smart as they come and very proactive.'

'Great. They turn up any leads at all?'

She side-eyes me. I suppose I was blunt. 'Jed Armstrong, the ex-boyfriend, came up a couple of times. Amer's arranging for him to be invited in for questioning. Seems they had a contentious relationship, but the parents insist he wouldn't harm her. But then again, that was before we found her body. They still think she's simply missing, poor bastards. They're worried sick. We need to get out there and speak to them. Break the news, before they hear it from somewhere else. If they find out a body has been discovered, they could make the link themselves, and that would be awful. I want you to take Millie with you. She's the people reader, after all. Besides, I want her as family liaison officer.'

'Shouldn't Amer go out with her?'

'He's in interview room one right now. Someone from one of the houses beside the river has come in, reckons he might have seen something.'

'The houses that are opposite the scene, across the river?' Pressing my lips together, I shake my head. 'From there?'

'Binoculars, apparently. Reckons he's a twitcher.'

'So, you want me to inform the family?'

She tilts her head. 'If you think you can handle it, then yes.'

My heart sinks, but I nod. It's not an enviable task at the best of times, but I also have to see Millie, after months of me being MIA from her life. Dillon is right; Millie is the right person to be there with me. I only wish she'd answered my texts yesterday, because this is going to be a baptism of fire. 'Is she in the office yet?'

'Yes, she was with Aaliyah last I saw her. They were checking out HOLMES2 to see what enquiries have been thrown up so far.'

I must have walked right past her; she hadn't come after me. 'Right. I'll go get her then.'

'I'll get DC Giovanelli—' Antonio, she means — 'to start setting up the MIR while you're out and Amer's in the interview. DC Conan Dunn and DC Marsha McLeish are already en route to the Baluga to question the staff and request CCTV.'

'Good.'

I'm at the door when Dillon's words make me freeze. 'Are you sure about this, Beth? Are you really ready for this?'

Without turning, I grit my teeth and answer: 'Yes.' As I walk out of the MIR, I wonder whether I have just told her or myself the biggest lie.

CHAPTER EIGHT

Millie has her back to me as I walk across the office space. She's chatting away to Detective Constable Aaliyah Kimathi. It takes everything I have to keep walking and not run in the opposite direction. My heartbeat speeds up exponentially with her nearness. I wonder momentarily whether I am in the throes of a panic attack. Her hair has grown; her silky, long black locks shine beneath the overhead strip light. I can smell her expensive floral perfume, the fruity shampoo she uses. Something turns over in my chest. I reach out my hand to tap her shoulder and pull it back quickly. Aaliyah notices me and nods knowingly at Millie, who turns and pins me with her gaze.

'Hi.' My mouth is barren, and I can't get enough moisture to form another word.

'You're back,' she says, her voice even. There's no hint of the usual affection, and it gives me a further jolt. The threat of tears stings the backs of my eyes.

Aaliyah steps around Millie. 'Nice to see you back where you belong, Beth. How have you been?'

I divert my eyes to Aaliyah. 'Okay. I've been okay. Thanks.' I look back at Millie. 'Mills, Millie, I . . . erm, can we have a chat? Dillon, she, erm, thinks . . . she wants you to come out to see the family with me. That okay?'

Millie looks towards Dillon's closed office door, then back to me. 'Yeah, sure. I'll just grab my things. Won't be long. Are we driving separately?'

'Yeah, I suppose we should. In case they want you to stay on. You're okay being family liaison officer on this one, I take it?'

'I'm fine doing whatever needs to be done, Beth. It's my job. Excuse me.' She sidesteps me and walks across the office to the staffroom, leaving me stinging from the exchange.

Aaliyah looks awkwardly at me for a moment, while dancing from foot to foot. 'You two will sort it out; don't worry. She's been upset these past few weeks, months even. She's had a lot to deal with.'

So, they've become close. I stepped back, and Aaliyah stepped straight into the space I left behind.

No, I'm not being fair. They're both good people; they're both my friends. Millie needed someone, and I'm glad she had Aaliyah. I shouldn't be jealous.

'Anyway,' Aaliyah says, 'I'm dying for a pee. I'll see you when you get back.' She dashes off, across the office and into the ladies.

I look towards the staffroom and see Millie emerge. She gives a single nod in my direction before heading for the security door. I jog to catch up, but she dashes out of reception and down the concrete steps ahead of me.

She turns at the foot of the stairs and shouts, 'I have the address. I'll meet you there.' I stand frozen as she runs to her car. My legs feel like jelly. I take a few steadying breaths while I regain my composure, then follow her lead and head to my own car.

* * *

I pull up behind Millie, a couple of doors down from the Fosters' home. I get out of my car, then catch up to Millie at the side of hers. 'Millie, can we clear the air before we go in there?'

Millie's upper lip curls. 'You think we have a few hours to spare?'

'Don't be like that, please, Mills.'

'Are you being serious?' She stares at me incredulously, looking me up and down. 'I see you felt up to visiting the gym. But coming to see me, or even taking my calls was, what, a step too far?'

'I, err, I . . .'

'Oh, for God's sake, Beth! I'm a professional and so are you. We don't need to have this conversation now. We are here to give the most horrendous news any parents can ever receive. I really don't think our problems compare right at this moment, do you?' She doesn't wait for a response. 'If I can put them to one side, I'm sure you can too. Come on. Let's get this done. They might spot us out of the window. Let's not prolong their agony.'

'Okay. You're right, I'm sorry.' I tug at the belt of my jacket while attempting to put my thoughts and feelings to the back of my mind.

We walk up to the door of their semi-detached via their front garden and knock. A man who looks to be in his sixties answers. He's ghostly pale. I imagine he must be Jasmine Foster's father, Frank. Stress is etched into his features like engravings on a tree stump. He stares at us in silence. His mouth slowly falls open as something in his eyes dies — they go completely dull.

Journalists refer to what we are doing as the "death knock". I can tell the moment it hits Frank Foster, the most likely reason we are here. It's about four seconds after he opens the door, when silence along with our sombre faces communicate that something terrible has befallen his child, something so awful it has brought two plain-clothed police officers to his door.

I hold out my lanyard and speak in a low but clear voice. 'Mr Foster?'

He nods, slowly, his mouth still wide, no sound falling over his trembling lips.

'I'm Detective Chief Inspector Bethany Fellows and this is Detective Constable Millicent Reid.' From the corner of my eye, I catch Millie holding out her own lanyard. 'May we come in, please?'

'Oh no, no, no, no . . .' Frank Foster finds his voice and cries out as his legs go from under him. Millie and I step forward simultaneously, catching him before he hits the floor.

Over his shoulder, I spot a woman I presume to be Penny Foster. She appears in the doorway at the end of the hall, her hand raised over her mouth, her eyes wide in horror. 'W . . . w . . . what's going on?' Penny whimpers, so afraid of the answer she seems terrified to pose the question.

With our help, Frank Foster has managed to get to his feet, and we are standing in the doorway, trying to ignore the intrigue of neighbours who have appeared behind us in the street.

'Is it Jasmine? Is everything okay? Penny? Frank?' A woman's voice carries from the street. A few other people join in with their questions. Penny nods at me and we step into the porch completely, before closing the front door and shutting the world outside.

'It is, isn't it?' Penny cries. 'It's my baby; it's Jasmine.' She turns, then walks unsteadily back into the lounge and practically collapses onto the couch. 'She's not with you, you haven't found her.' Her voice is monotone, then rises suddenly with panic: 'Or have you? Oh my God.' Her hand covers her mouth, and tears fill her eyes.

Once we are all sitting, Frank and Penny side by side, Millie and I on the armchairs, I begin. 'Would you like Millie to get either of you a drink? Maybe some sweet tea?'

'No. We don't want a bloody drink.' Frank's voice is both gruff and filled with emotion.

Penny Foster looks pleadingly from me to Millie and back again. 'Please tell me this isn't about my daughter; this isn't about Jasmine. I was wrong before, wasn't I? Please God, tell me I was wrong.' Tears are coursing down her cheeks. She knows what I'm going to say. She doesn't want it to be true, but she knows.

Before I can speak, she starts talking again. 'We struggled to conceive. IVF — the lot, it failed twice, then on our third and final try, it happened. Our perfect, wonderful daughter conceived, then born safely. That's why we're older, you see.' She indicates her greying hair. 'I was forty years old when she finally came along. Frank was forty-five. She was so wanted. So, so badly. You see all these people having babies, not looking after them right, then there was us and Jasmine. She was our miracle. Before we had her, Frank's brother suggested we adopt, and who knows — perhaps we would have considered it. But Jasmine was a gift, and she was enough. She has always been enough for us. Please do not sit here, in our home, and tell us she's gone. Don't you do that to us. Don't you come here and destroy our lives. Please, I'm begging you. Please. Just don't. She's all we have. She's everything to us. Our baby. She has a future, a wonderful, glorious future just waiting to be lived.'

She turns to her husband, a thick sob escaping as she curls into his chest. 'Oh, Frank. No, Frank, no, don't let it be our Jasmine. Please, Frank, I can't, I just can't. Don't let them do this to us, Frank, don't let it happen.'

I try to swallow past the hard lump wedged in my throat. My heart is cramping in my chest. I look around at the many photographs on the mantel, sideboard, walls — all beautifully framed. Images of a happy, smiling girl. Jasmine Foster, her face throughout the years only becoming more and more beautiful. Blue dungarees and red wellies as a small child. Dresses and sandals at a party. Arms around both her parents' waists, posing at a petting farm. With friends, marker pen scrawled all over their school shirts. So many happy moments, documented with love.

I clear my throat, then take a breath. I catch a glimpse of Millie via the corner of my eye. 'I'm so very sorry to have to tell you this.' I almost choke on my own words as I watch a bulge rise in Penny Foster's throat, see her noticeably attempt to swallow it down. Frank Foster is staring straight ahead, looking lost. One more breath, and I blow their world apart for good. 'I am afraid we have found a body, and . . .'

'Nooooooooo!' Penny Foster screams. 'No, you, you're wrong, it isn't her, it isn't Jasmine, it's *not* my daughter, she isn't dead, she's twenty-one years old, for Christ's sake, our miracle baby, our baby, ours. She's young. She's healthy. There's no reason for her to . . . She can't be gone. She just can't be. I'm her mother. I would know. A mother would know. Please. Please. Please. Please . . .'

'I'm so, so sorry, but we do believe that it is Jasmine, I'm very sorry.' I can't help but picture her pale, rigid body. I look up once more, towards the large canvass image of her over the couch, *alive* and smiling. My stomach squeezes painfully. 'Jasmine's bank card was recovered.'

Penny's anguished cries increase. Frank pulls her closer but, his pallor has me worrying he might be about to pass out. 'Did Jasmine have a tattoo?'

Frank's eyes widen. 'Why?'

Penny hiccups a few times, attempting to control her tears. 'She has a robin, the bird, her nanna's favourite bird, it's on her thigh. It's symbolic. It's, erm . . .' She loses the rest of her words when she takes in my expression, and Millie's too. I have no doubt she understands the significance.

'The pathologist, Dr Damien Sanders, he is currently undertaking an examination. But I am so truly, sincerely sorry to tell you that the victim does have a robin tattoo on her thigh. At this stage, I would say there's little doubt that it is Jasmine.'

Penny's eyes widen. 'But there is doubt; you're not certain. Not one hundred per cent, and that, that means there's hope, right? There's some hope. There must be loads of girls, women with robin tattoos. I mean it has to be fairly common, right?' Penny is clutching desperately, gripping the edges of the cliff she is hanging from and trying to keep from hurtling to the ground.

Frank coughs, clears his throat. 'Victim? You said victim. Does that mean . . . was Jasmine hit by a car? Did she fall? What happened to our daughter?'

Penny's voice catches on a sob as she says, 'It mightn't be Jasmine, Frank.' She looks up at him. 'Don't let's give up. It might not be her. They're not sure; that's what they said. She's only been gone one night. Remember what they said when we reported it this morning? They said she was probably with a friend or something like that. Maybe she is. Maybe she's okay.'

Frank's stare is unwaveringly on me. 'Victim?' he repeats.

'Yes, I'm afraid it appears that what happened to Jasmine was not an accident. We believe someone may have hurt her. We won't know anything for certain until the post-mortem, but—'

'You're going to cut open my daughter?' Frank splutters. A small amount of vomit splashes over his feet and onto the floor.

Penny is frozen as she watches the ground. Frank's vomiting stops almost immediately, and he turns to face his wife. He reaches out and takes her hands. He has liver spots on the back of his hands, and his skin is thinning with age.

'Pen, darling, look at me . . . look at me.'

She looks up, their eyes meeting, their tears falling.

'It's Jasmine. It's our daughter. We know it is. Denying it won't make it not be her. It's our baby, love. It's our Jasmine.'

Penny Foster sobs. 'Noooo . . . My poor, poor baby. Why? Why would anyone hurt her? She's never done anything to hurt anyone. She's a good girl. Everyone says so; they're always saying she has a heart of gold, and she does, she really does. There's no reason for anyone to do this.'

Millie reaches down to retrieve the satchel she had carried into the house, the one containing the clear evidence bags. Inside the bags are a shoe and a handbag. She lifts the evidence bags out, holding them towards Penny and Frank. 'Do these belong to your daughter?'

The dam completely bursts, both parents sobbing relentlessly, to the point of gasping for air. I give them time, as Millie replaces the items into the black satchel.

'We understand this is very hard, but may we ask you some questions?'

Frank exhales loudly. He holds out his hand, indicating for us to proceed.

'Is there anyone at all you can think of who may have wanted to harm Jasmine?'

'Hard?' Penny Foster cuts in sharply. 'Hard? You call this hard? It's not hard — it's excruciating, it's impossible. You have just told us you think our only daughter is dead, that, that someone has done this on purpose. That's what you're saying, isn't it? They must have, if you're asking about people wanting to hurt her. That it wasn't an accident. Well, no, there is no one, no one in the world that would ever want to harm Jasmine. She's a lovely, kind, intelligent soul. Why would anyone want to hurt someone like that?'

'We don't know anything for certain yet.'

Millie leans forward. 'I am here to help guide you through this, whatever you need. Time and space, support, someone to talk to, to explain things to you. Anything at all.'

'What we *need* is our daughter, home safe. Can you do that? Can you make that happen?' Penny hiccups on a sob.

'I think we've heard enough for now.' Frank interjects. 'I want you to go away and come back when you have something more to tell us. When Penny and I have had time to process, to . . . I just think you ought to leave. Please. Just for — just for a little while.'

Penny stands, then turns to stare at the canvas of Jasmine. Her hand flies to her mouth as her knees buckle.

Frank jumps to his feet and catches her. He wraps his arms tightly around her, pulling her into a cocoon. 'I'm here, I'm here.' Frank holds fast to his wife as she weeps against his shoulder.

I'm pretty sure the only things keeping Frank Foster standing are pure shock and his determination to be the strength Penny needs. Frank's pallor is now almost translucent. Millie and I wait patiently for the right time to speak. We both know instinctively, and from years of experience, that for now this couple need to hold each other up. Like cards leaning into one another, they're each other's support, but the slightest increase in pressure and they'll fall.

I will have to ask my questions; there's not a choice to be made about that. If we are to catch the person responsible for taking their daughter, then time is of the essence. The Golden Hour can be literally an hour. It can be more; it can even stretch to days or weeks. But the more time that passes, the less potent our evidence trail. Everything weakens with time, with age. People, evidence, cases. Not to mention that whoever did this could do it again. I wait Frank and Penny out — unlike the Brander case, I won't leave as soon as they ask me to because of my morality. I will stick it out and hope for the answers that will advance the investigation. We have yet to inform them that one or both will need to make a formal identification.

I feel terrible for the Fosters, I really do, but that's also why I am determined to stay. Millie explains this and remains seated. We listen to the sound of their grief. It's palpable; a relentless contagion that is by now infecting the very bones of this house. A dark sadness washes over us all. And for me, along with that comes a stark determination to catch the person responsible and make them pay.

CHAPTER NINE

The Ordinary Man

It's Saturday morning, and he sits on the couch watching television. His feet are up on the ottoman and the remote control is in his hand. He's unwilling to risk Laurie getting her mitts on it and putting some of her crap on.

He's watching a true crime documentary about Son of Sam. He likes this guy, respects him. He'd had a plan, a desire to kill, and he hadn't let society dictate what was right and wrong. He'd simply gone for it. David Berkowitz was inspirational — the only downside being that the idiot went and got caught. The fool had not only let himself stand out and get noticed by some nosey woman, but he'd then gone on to leave blatant evidence in his own car for the cops to find.

Maybe David Berkowitz wasn't that inspirational after all. Perhaps he was a lesson in what not to do.

Boredom is setting in. The documentary is a little slow-moving for his liking. He looks at the time and gets up from the couch. It's gone 10 a.m.; there might be something on the news, or the internet. He presses back-up on the remote. He'll watch the rest later.

He's been on tenterhooks ever since last night, anticipating her being found. He's scared and excited about it happening. It hasn't yet and he's beginning to get impatient. She's hardly well hidden. Witnessing what comes next will be a thrill. He can't wait for the rumour mills to start churning. All the armchair detectives will be out in force, and he can sit back and read their commentary online. He's eager to hear what people have to say about him. When he's out and about, he'll listen to them making assumptions. He'll revel in the knowledge that they're all clueless. Hell, some of the morons will no doubt talk to him about their suspicions. They'll go on about their dodgy neighbour, or the weirdo from work, whoever they decide is suspect numero uno. Hiding in plain sight will be his disguise, and he's itching for the games to begin.

He's in the bathroom brushing his teeth when he hears Laurie gobbing at Kira to get dressed. They're going out for the afternoon, and he knows exactly where to. He smirks to himself in the mirror. 'Hey, Key, do as your mum says,' he calls.

'Put your friggin' socks on, Key, how many times do I have to repeat meself?' Laurie's screechy voice carries through to him. He winces at the pitch of her tone and at Kira's huffing and puffing in response.

He heads downstairs, humming loudly.

Laurie catches up to him in the kitchen. 'What's got you in such a good mood?'

He kisses her cheek. 'It's the weekend, ain't it? Come on, Laurie. Cheer up; it might never 'appen.'

She snarls. 'I don't get a day off; I am always mum, Monday through Sunday and over again. It never ends.'

He raises his brow. Is she serious? 'Well, today, we're out as a family, so we all get a day off.'

She huffs. 'Yeah, right. I have a picnic to make, then I'll be stuck disciplining madam while you swan about being Mr Fun Guy. It's always the same.'

He sighs. 'I work my arse off for this family. I only get to spend quality time with her on weekends and evenings, so excuse me if I don't feel like screaming my head off at her about pointless shit.'

'Pointless? Fine, you make her get ready; she's still only half-dressed. You deal with her.'

He's steaming. How the hell dare she talk to him like this? He goes to the bottom of the stairs, grabs the end of the banister and yells, 'Get ready now, Kira! I ain't messin', you don't come down here in the next five minutes, I'm coming upstairs. And you won't like what happens if I do.' He storms into the kitchen, his light mood gone.

Laurie is standing in front of the open fridge scowling at its contents. 'We need to do a shop.'

'You happy now? I lost me rag with her. That please you, does it?'

She grabs a half-used block of cheddar and the margarine, then swings the door closed with her hip while glaring at him. 'If it gets her arse ready, yeah, sure. I'm sick of always being the bad guy. You come home and do the stories, the playing, the fun stuff. I do *everything* else.' She drags out the word *everything*, ensuring he gets her point.

She opens the cupboard above her head and takes out the cheese grater. 'Instead of just standing there, you could pack the rest of our picnic.' He shrugs, and Laurie rolls her eyes. 'Oh, for God's sake, a small sausage roll, cheese puffs, a Dairylea dipper thing, yoghurt, and an apple and whatever for us. It's not bloody hard. You should know what your own daughter eats.'

He starts snatching everything and shoving it into a carrier bag. 'It's not like I don't go to work, Laurie. I do my share. I mean, what do you expect, really?'

She's grating the cheese with gusto, and he infers that she's pissed off rather than just rushing. 'Ah, shitting hell.' She pulls her hand back and peers at her wounded finger. Blood drips down the length of it onto the floor. 'I need a new one, I keep telling you. This piece of shit—' she lifts the grater, stands on the pedal of the stainless-steel bin, and launches it in — 'is fuckin' dodgy. I mean, look.' She juts her arm out, finger extended, almost poking him in the eyeball.

'All right, you're bleeding everywhere. Stick a plaster on it. Your finger ain't exactly gonna drop off.'

Kira rushes into the kitchen, everything on but one shoe. 'Ouch, Mummy, did you cut yourself?' Her expression is full of concern, and he wonders how much like him she can really be. Laurie's dramatics mean nothing to him, but it has sparked an idea. One that is fast taking root, and bringing his good mood back.

Laurie gets the first aid kit and runs the cold tap. She holds her finger underneath, the blood draining down the side of the washing-up bowl. 'See,' she whines. 'Kira is more bothered than you. Have you ever grated your own skin off?'

He sneers. 'I ain't that thick.'

'More like you never cook, or do anything in the kitchen, for that matter. We need to get a proper one. Preferably one that doesn't slice me to ribbons.'

'A bad workman and all that, Laurie, but sure, whatever.'

She dries her finger with the dish towel before chucking the towel into the laundry bin, then she puts on the plaster and finishes their sandwiches.

'It's okay, Mummy. I'll kiss it better for you.'

Laurie holds her injured finger out to Kira, who gently kisses the plaster.

'All better,' Kira says. 'Where are we going?' There's a glint of excitement in her eyes.

He smiles down at his daughter. 'The nature reserve for an adventure.'

'Can we go to the park instead, Daddy?'

'No.'

'Pwease . . .'

'Don't whine,' he snaps. 'You like the nature reserve. Besides, we're gonna have a picnic, too.'

She turns to Laurie. 'But I wanted to play on the swings.'

Laurie stares at him. 'What difference does it make if we go to a park instead?'

His blood is boiling. 'Jesus, fine, we'll do both. That suit the pair of you?'

Kira clutches a fist and pulls her arm down at the elbow. 'Yes!' she exclaims.

Every movement and sound she makes after that irritates the hell out of him. She can never be happy with what she's got. Like her mum, it is never enough. He counts to five. He calms himself by focussing on Laurie screeching about how painful cutting herself on the grater was. The rest of the morning, a fizzing feeling of anticipation travels throughout his body.

CHAPTER TEN

DCI Bethany Fellows

I arrive back at work ahead of Millie. Normally, I would want to be with her, but right now the frostiness coming off her in waves is distracting. My focus needs to be on the case.

Amer is walking out of the MIR. I dash over and grab his arm. 'Amer,' I say. 'What happened in the interview with the neighbour?'

He scratches his head, his face pained. 'Nothing much. He has a set of binoculars, which he says he was using last night—' he frowns — 'at gone ten. I mean, he claims to be a twitcher, but who birdwatches from their home at that time, with a set of bog-standard binos?'

'What did he reckon he saw?'

'Said there was a group of teenagers hanging around looking suspicious. To be honest, I got the feeling he has a gripe with some local troublemakers and wants to turn the tables. He had a few names for us. I have Aaliyah and Antonio out at the moment. They're gonna ask a few questions to see if anything comes of it.'

'Do you think they were there? They might be witnesses.'

'Possibly. But to be honest, I'm not certain the old boy isn't just poking the bear. He used the opportunity to tell me all about their antisocial antics, which we have on file anyway. It's the usual revolting racially motivated crime, graffitiing his bin, setting fire to it, posting dog shit through his letterbox. All disgusting, but nothing that would normally escalate to what we're looking at. Besides which, Jasmine Foster was white, and these little creeps seem to like picking on us brown folk.'

I frown. Amer's right. It is disgusting, but like he said, Jasmine Foster's murder doesn't fit. 'I'd have them brought in anyway, cover our bases. If there's something to get out of them, being here might pressure them enough to spill.'

Amer fidgets with his belt. 'Yeah, sure. I'll call Aaliyah and Ant.' He looks down momentarily. 'Good call.'

I touch his arm. 'It's tough being at the top of the pyramid. Decisions are crucial and they fall to you. But I'm here, Amer. Use me.'

He smiles weakly. 'Cheers, Beth.'

Millie walks past us, going straight into the MIR. Amer grimaces. 'Ouch, she not forgiven you yet?'

I shrug. 'Definitely not yet. I'm working on it. Anyway, what about the ex-boyfriend, Jed Armstrong?'

'Rock-solid alibi. He was at his aunt's fortieth. At least a hundred witnesses. He DJ'd. There are photos. The poor lad is cut up. I mean, seriously cut up. He was all tears and snot. I felt bad for him. I think he still loved her.'

'So, we have nothing then.'

He shakes his head. 'Zilch.'

I nod towards the MIR. 'All set up?'

'Yeah, Antonio and a few of the guys had it done by the time I came out of the interviews with Hasim Patel and Jed.'

'Anything from Marsha and Conan?'

'They've questioned most of the staff who were on at the Baluga last night. Nothing out of the ordinary was noted. They have a couple more people to talk to, then they'll be bringing the footage from the CCTV in. The manager couldn't have been more accommodating.'

'That makes a refreshing change.'

'She has a daughter a year younger than our vic. So it hit home. She wants to help.'

'Good. Well, let's just hope there's something of use on the CCTV.'

Dillon's voice calls across the office. 'Beth, you're needed.'

I turn to see her head poking through her doorway.

Amer's eyes widen, and he holds his palms up towards me. 'Whatever that is, it's nothing to do with me.'

Chloe smiles sweetly as I pass her. I wonder whether she knows what this is about. Stepping into the office, I see a man and a woman sitting opposite Dillon, and a third empty chair to the side of them.

Dillon extends her arm. 'Please, sit down.'

They introduce themselves as Detective Superintendent Niall Grant and Detective Chief Inspector Abbie Waring. The introductions aren't entirely necessary. I have seen Abbie around the place, and Niall's reputation proceeds him.

'What's this about?' I ask, looking at them, then Dillon.

Dillon drums her fingers on the table. Niall darts her a look and she stops. 'They have come to talk to you about the ongoing investigation into the twenty-eight brands that were found during the Brander investigation.'

The floor falls away from beneath me. I stare at them. I can't speak.

Dillon snaps me out of my trance. 'They're here about Stanley Baker.'

CHAPTER ELEVEN

The Ordinary Man

Kira is a bundle of energy. She sits up front in the truck fidgeting with her seatbelt, her coat, then she stretches to reach the buttons on the music system.

'You got ants in your pants, Key?'

'No, Daddy,' she says, grinning up at him.

Laurie stares out of the window, ignoring the both of them. He drives towards Avenham Park, his anticipation growing with every mile covered. As they near the bridge, he sees the commotion ahead.

'Wonder what's going on,' Laurie says, suddenly snapping out of her sulk.

His hands tighten around the steering wheel. 'No idea.'

'Mummy, what can you see?' Kira tries to peer above the dash, but her view is obscured. 'Are we going to the nature thing or the park first?'

'I doubt we'll get anywhere near that reserve today.' Laurie can't drag her gaze from the police and people in white. She's staring with hunger at what's happening.

'We could park on Avenham and walk across. It mightn't all be closed,' he says.

Laurie turns, looking at him like he's an idiot. 'Don't be so stupid.'

He has an urge to reach across and punch her in the face.

She rolls her eyes. 'There's people stood on the bridge watching. Look.' She points. 'And there's police tape all over.' She points out the windscreen again. 'Must be something serious. You got credit? Where's your mobile? I left mine at home.'

They turn towards the park, away from the scene — he's desperate to get closer. 'What do you want my phone for?'

'Durgh, to look it up online. You know what Facebook's like; there's bound to be something on there about what's going on.'

'You ain't using my phone to be a nosey—' he glances at Kira — 'parker.'

Laurie glowers at him. 'Like you're not dying to know.'

'Are we going on the swings, then?' Kira is bouncing in her seat; he feels the same level of excitement, but displays nothing.

He parks up in the car park nearest the playground. There's a marked police car parked up along with what he suspects to be a couple of unmarked. They'll be doing the rounds, asking questions. There are already a number of kids on the playground. Their rowdiness is audible as soon as they get out of the truck.

He looks at Laurie. 'Why don't you go on ahead to the café, grab a nice coffee while I tire madam out? Then we'll join you for the picnic.'

She eyes him. 'Why do you want rid of me?'

'Rid of you? You were saying how you do everything and never get a break. Well, I listened.' He smiles, takes her hand and places a five-pound note in her palm. 'So I'm offering you what you asked for.' His grin deepens. 'A break.'

She hesitates, for just a second. 'Okay.' Laurie goes to kiss the top of Kira's head, but Kira jumps up, almost head-butting her in the chin. 'Whoa, careful,' she says, before successfully planting a kiss and walking away.

It's going to be a bit of a walk from here, but he needs to be incognito. He bends in front of Kira, putting his hands on his knees. 'Hey, Key, how about we go on an adventure walk first?'

She swings her arms, her expression sullen. 'But I wanna go on the swings,' she moans. 'You promised, remember.'

'And we will, but first—' he injects as much joy as possible into his voice — 'we're gonna look for . . . mermaids.'

Her eyes widen. 'Really, Daddy?'

'Yes, really. Come on, it's just us now. Let's go on a secret mission,' he holds his finger to his lips. 'We won't tell anyone. Not even Mummy.'

Kira grabs his hand and starts swinging from his arm. 'Yes, Daddy, yes. We're gonna have—' she releases his hand, bends her elbows, and clutches her fists, scrunching up her face with barely contained glee — 'so, so, so much fun, aren't we? And we might even make friends with a real, real mermaid.'

He smiles down at her. 'That we are, our kid; that we are. Come on, then, what are we waiting for?' He laughs. 'Let's start our adventure.'

He skirts around the sports court, avoiding passing the playground, and heads up towards the riverside that runs through Avenham Park. Despite her agreeing to the adventure walk, Kira would still be seduced by the sight of the big slide, the swing set and the helicopter climbing frame. She's holding his hand and he's walking fast; he can't seem to stop himself. He knows he shouldn't appear too eager, but all the same, he can't help it. There's a vibration through his body, like his heart is a tuning fork and it is reverberating outwards against his ribs. Kira pulls free from his hand.

She stops stock-still and proceeds to rub her hand. 'Ouch, Daddy, you hurted me.'

He frowns. 'It's "hurt", Kira. Not "hurted".'

She scowls at him, looking too much like her mum. She's clearly unimpressed by his correction and lack of apology.

'Come on, Key.' He sighs and walks back to her. 'I'm sorry, okay? I didn't mean to hurt your hand. Now, are we gonna carry on walking?'

'I want to go play on the swings.' She places her hands on her hips, looking petulant. 'You promised, and you shouldn't break promises.' She stamps her foot angrily. It's all he can do to keep his arms at his sides and not sideswipe her head.

'Adventure walk first, then swings. That's the deal. No walk, no swings. Got it?' His expression is stern, and he watches her features loosen. She stops rubbing her hand, and as he sets off, she falls into step close behind him.

The last thing he needs is for her to make a fuss and show him up for forcing her to go on this walk. It could raise eyebrows and suspicions. The police presence is not lost on him — far from it. He begins jumping from side to side, laughing playfully. 'Watch you don't step off the edge and fall into the water,' he says.

They are getting closer to London Road. He can see people gathered along the street, gossiping. His heart rate accelerates.

Lifting Kira, he swings her out towards the water. 'Careful, I might throw you in,' he laughs.

Kira lets out a squeal, halfway between scared and thrilled. 'No, Daddy, don't.'

Before long, they are within a stone's throw of the site. The hairs on his arms stand on end. Adrenaline shoots through his veins. He won't go any nearer; he won't draw attention. He is close enough, but far enough away, too.

He looks down at Kira, poking his bottom lip out. 'Oh no,' he says. 'We can't go and see the mermaids today, look.' He points towards the people up ahead, the nosey buggers, and the coppers.

'Mummy told you that already,' she complains. 'Why'd we come, then?' She's smart, but then, she is his kid.

'I forgot. Listen, we still need to keep it a secret, or we won't be able to come back and find the mermaids. So,' he hushes her again, his finger in front of his lip. 'But first, how about a photo?'

He ensures they are at a respectable distance as he quickly encourages Kira to pose. He takes the snap within seconds. No one was looking in their direction. All eyes are on the scene.

He sees the dumb bint bleeding, visualizes himself dragging her over the rugged earth. It's as though he remembers it from outside his own body — hovering above, watching.

'Daddy, Daddy.' Kira snaps him out of his reverie. She's tugging on his sleeve. 'Look, a policeman.'

His nerves fire like a pinball, zigzagging around his body. He follows Kira's line of sight and sees a copper heading in their direction.

'Come on, Key. Let's go on the swings, then we'll go and find Mummy.'

'Yay!' she yells, while jumping up and down.

He grabs her hand, leading her away as quickly as he can without drawing further attention. 'Remember, this is our little secret,' he says, breathlessly.

His heart is thumping with the threat of the copper's hand landing on his shoulder. He'll be asked questions, and he had prepared answers, but they evade him now as panic sets in. After a couple of minutes, he holds his breath and looks over his shoulder, the copper has walked away. His heart rate settles, and he laughs, feeling giddy with euphoria.

'What's funny, Daddy?'

'You are.' He tickles between her neck and shoulder blade, eliciting high-pitched giggles.

'I'll race ya,' he says, jogging towards the playground with Kira in pursuit. The close call has his adrenaline pumping. It is akin to riding a coaster. He's almost eager to go again already.

CHAPTER TWELVE

DCI Bethany Fellows

Dillon's words ring in my ears: 'They're here about Stanley Baker.'

I shift in my seat, feeling the weight of their stares. I suck in my cheeks, coaxing saliva into my suddenly barren mouth. 'What about him?' I croak.

'Do you need a drink, Beth?' Dillon asks, gently. I nod and she lifts the handset. 'Chloe, a glass of water, please, quickly. Thank you.'

There's an uncomfortable silence, then the door creaks open and Chloe walks in carrying a glass.

'It's for Beth,' Dillon advises.

Chloe hands me the glass, and I take hungry gulps. The door opens and closes as she leaves and it's the four of us again.

DS Niall Grant leans forward in his seat, angling closer to me. 'He won't talk. He's refused every opportunity presented to him to give up anything about the brands — who they're from, what they mean. We have twenty-eight brands; that's potentially twenty-eight murder victims. That's twenty-eight families waiting for answers.'

He settles back in his chair, silent again. He's allowing me time to process his words and their meaning before he strikes.

Dillon looks concerned, her expression soft, unlike when she was reading me the riot act just yesterday — it seems a million miles away now. 'Beth, they have come here to ask for your help. I've told them that it's up to you. That I am not going to force your hand on this in any way. The ball is in your court.'

I turn to look at DS Niall Grant. 'What do you want me to do?'

'He wants to see you. He says he'll talk, but only to you.'

'But I'm working a case.' I look to Dillon, searching for rescue. 'It's important, surely DS West explained.'

DCI Abbie Waring pipes up. 'She has, and we agree it takes priority. However, this case is important, too. Especially with Tom still out there. He could kill again. This might be the way we get to him before he has the chance.'

I inhale. 'How would it work?'

DS Niall Grant takes up the lead again. 'If you're in agreement, we will have him brought here or to Preston City Police Station, wherever feels most comfortable for you. We'd like to arrange it as soon as possible. Time is of the essence. So, Beth . . .' He focusses on me, his gaze unwavering. 'Will you talk to your father?'

I swallow the wedge of bile that's risen into my throat and give the only answer I can. 'That monster is not my father. But yes, I will do it.'

* * *

I wake up before my alarm and feel groggy as hell. Sound sleep was a goal I never quite reached last night. Dillon had ordered me out of the building yesterday evening and warned me not to return before my shift. She's worried about my already somewhat fragile state, especially considering the deal I've struck with the twenty-eight-brand team. Before I left, she called me into her office to remind me to make contact with the department counsellor, without delay. It's Sunday and most people will be enjoying a lie-in, time with the family — not the likes of us. Not during a case like this.

Last night, my mind was turning over everything: the case, speaking to a counsellor, making things right with Millie, and worst of all, the notion of coming face to face with Stanley Baker. I had planned to keep looking into the twenty-eight brands. I'd even planned for what might happen if Tom comes after me. I had not planned to be the conduit between Stanley and the truth. It feels like yet another aspect of my life that is out of my control.

I get up and head into the bathroom. Standing in front of the sink, I stare into the mirror. I'm a mess: bed hair, smudged make-up, and a month's worth of luggage under my eyes. A dizzy spell catches me unaware, and I grab the edge of the sink. When I look into the mirror again, I see Jasmine Foster's features blurred with my own. I try to refocus, but the blend of myself and Jasmine turns into a blend of myself and Stanley. Blinking fast, until all I see are black spots, causes me to almost pass out. I grip the sink tighter. Closing my eyes, I wait for a while, and when I dare look into the mirror again, it's just me.

It's not quite 6 a.m., and while I have been told not to go into the office early under any circumstances, Millie will not be under such strict guidelines. I need to speak to her before work, so I grab a shower and dress hurriedly. I can't cope with the atmosphere from yesterday dragging into today. It won't aid the investigation going forward. I can't bear for us to be estranged the way we are.

Millie and I rarely fall out, and whenever we do, it's usually over and done with pretty sharpish. This time it's different, and it's my fault. Cutting her off the way I did has hurt her more than I anticipated. I had thought I was the injured party; my life had been turned on its head by the Brander case. I needed time to acclimatize to my new reality and find a way to move beyond it. Millie had spent her time trying to get through to me, to reconnect, but I'd shut the door in her face — figuratively and literally. First, it was because I needed time alone, then it was because I needed to take measures that I didn't want her to witness. I'd dragged her into too much already. I made the choice to turn my back on my best friend and now I'm paying the price. There were reasons, ones I can't reveal to her right now. However, I do have to make her understand how sorry I am for the hurt I've caused.

At the Fosters', we had been at their disposal, focussed on them and nothing else. We'd stayed for as long as it took to glean all the information possible. Millie had been as brilliant as ever, able to lead them through the questions with as little added trauma as possible. She was the person I would always go to when it came to understanding people and their subtle and not-so-subtle nuances.

We were shaken by the time we left the Fosters'. Being caught in the turmoil of such all-consuming grief was powerful. It ripped you to shreds if you let it. Tore into your heart and laid it bare. Telling a mother and father their only child had been snatched from them by an incomprehensible act of violence put us in their firing line. There was no one but us standing between them and the truth they didn't want to face. There was, as yet, no monster to turn their anger and hatred towards.

We had played the part with them; we had been a team as we ought to be. Professional and together. Then we'd left, and Millie had headed to her car without a word. Seeing her back at the station, I'd tried to talk to her about us, about my poor decisions after the Brander case, even during, but she hadn't wanted to hear it. She was right, of course. Millie often was. During a major investigation was not the time or place to get personal.

She'd been gone for the latter part of the day. Millie had had the task no one envied: being with Frank and Penny Foster during the formal identification of their daughter. I hadn't seen her again, and had wanted to check she was okay. I know how much it shakes her foundations to be at the epicentre of such heartache. It shakes us all.

Selfishly, I also yearned to tell her about DS Niall Grant's request of me. That I would soon be facing Stanley Baker again. I ache to turn to Millie, but I haven't decided yet whether to involve her.

As I'm leaving the house, I notice something poking out from under my doormat. Bending down, I retrieve it. Another bloody postcard, blank again — this time from Marseille, in France. I check the date stamp. It was sent four days ago. It probably arrived yesterday; I must have kicked it under the mat. Damn it. *That bastard*. He's taunting me. Tom. I want to screw it up, tear it up — but I force myself to squirrel it away in the back of the kitchen drawer with the others.

I pull up outside her house and I am relieved to see her car in the drive. I click the handbrake on and get out, feeling like a teenager on a first date. My hands shake as I put my keys into my pocket and walk to the front door. Her curtains flicker and I realize she knows I'm here. My heart races as the door opens. She's standing in her work clothes, her expression stern, unmoved by my gesture. Turning up unannounced has not impressed her; still, she opens the door wide and steps back. I walk inside the house I know as well as my own. I'm a stranger here today, as welcome as a Jehovah's Witness on a recruitment mission.

'What are you doing here, Beth?' she says, while closing the door. She walks past me, goes into the kitchen, then stops at the breakfast bar. I stand across from her as she lifts her coffee mug and takes a slow drink while eyeing me over the top of it.

'I, I erm, I wanted, I need us to talk, to get this thing sorted out before work.'

She puts the mug down and sighs. 'Oh, so now *you* want to talk, you're willing to see me. I see how it is.'

Touché. I deserve that. 'Don't you think it would be better to clear the air? I mean, we need to be professional at . . .'

She glares at me and snarls. 'Don't you dare. I have been professional. I have in no way let this—' she points back and forth between us — 'interfere with how I do my job.' Millie places both hands onto the breakfast bar and leans towards me. 'Please do not come here and try to shift the blame over how things are. You are the one who decided you could do without me. You, Beth. Not me. I didn't choose to go anywhere. I've been right here the whole time.'

I swallow the wedge of guilt in my throat then pull the chair out at the side of the breakfast bar and sit down. 'I'm sorry. I really am.' I deflate, almost sensing the air being expelled from every cell in my body.

'What happened to us, Beth? I don't think I've ever felt so lost from you.' She walks around the breakfast bar and pulls the chair from beside mine, as far away as possible before sitting.

'I guess being suspended was one hit too many. I mean, finding out I am related to the devil knocked me for six, then to top it off, my job, which you know is just about everything to me, was taken. Possibly for good. Yvette lied to me in the worst way. I just, I felt . . . I felt like shit, okay, utter shit. I was ashamed. I couldn't bring myself to face anyone. Especially you and Aunt Margie.'

'None of that was a reflection on you; surely you know that? It should have been us who you did turn to, not us who were the ones you couldn't stand to be around. I felt like I'd done something wrong. Like you were punishing me. For the life of me, I couldn't figure out what I'd done. I tried everything, calling, texting, emailing, writing, showing up. None of it worked. You cut me out like a cancer, Beth. You hurt me. When you were in hospital, I realized . . . I thought, before that, that . . . Oh, never mind. It doesn't matter what I thought. I just don't understand why you stopped seeing me. I don't get it.'

I look into her eyes, feel that familiar juddering of my heart. 'No, Millie, what . . . what did you think? What did you realize?' Something pulls in my chest; I feel as though what she was going to say could change everything.

She stares at me for a few seconds; it feels weighted, intense. My pulse races, but then she looks away. 'Look, it doesn't matter now. But you really hurt me.' She looks back at me, the intensity is gone, instead there is only sadness. 'You really did.'

Shame colours my cheeks, I can feel the heat spreading. 'I'm sorry. It wasn't how you think. I didn't see it that way. I would never have intentionally hurt you. I am sorry, Mills. I really am. You must know what you mean to me . . . don't you?'

She sidelines my question: 'When I came to see you at the hospital, you were okay with me and with Margie. What changed? Why'd it change? I don't get it.'

'I was suspended. Like I said, that was the last straw for me. The one that broke the camel's back, as they say.' I smile.

'Don't be flippant. Please . . . just don't. This is serious in every which way. I was going through something, too. I needed you.'

A burst of anger and indignation bubbles up and bursts. 'What was going on?' I shoot, before catching myself and reining in my annoyance. My problems don't negate hers or anyone else's. 'Sorry,' I add, quickly, trying to douse the newly lit fire.

'I had a miscarriage,' she blurts out, then looks down at her coffee cup like a fortune teller gazing into a crystal ball.

A weight lodges itself in my guts, heavy and unyielding. 'What?' I falter momentarily. 'Oh my God, Millie. I am so, so fucking sorry. I should have been there. You're right, you're one hundred per cent right, I have let you down. I really am so fuckin' sorry . . . You weren't seeing anyone as far as . . .'

'You don't need to be in a relationship to have sex, Beth.'

'Sorry, I didn't mean. I know that sounded . . . shit, I'm just sorry, okay. Truly, honestly, deeply sorry.'

Millie looks up, her eyes are misted with tears, and it rips into my heart. 'You're sorry. I get it. Anyway, Aaliyah has been great. She was a real friend.'

Her words hit me like an arrow straight into the red zone. 'I'm glad you had someone.' I mean it, I am glad. Jealous, too. I have no right to be, and I understand now why the two of them are suddenly so close. Going through something like that together solidifies a friendship. Millie and I have been through our fair share of trauma, shielding each other as best we could. Being there through thick and thin. Now Millie has Aaliyah, too. You can have more than one good friend. And seeing as I wasn't there when Millie needed me, I am grateful Aaliyah was. Even so, it's salt in an already raw wound.

Millie pins me with her eyes. 'I'm being childish. I said that to hurt you. Aaliyah has been great, she has, but she isn't you. I needed *you*, Beth.'

'You have every right to be angry. I let you down. Are you ready to let me be there now? To talk to me?'

'It's dealt with. I don't want to keep going over it. It's too painful.'

'Okay.' I want her to give me a chance to be the friend she deserves. I have to accept her silence, if words will wound her further.

'I had a one-night stand. I know, I know, I don't do that, but I did this time. I was upset about . . .' She looks a little awkward, her cheeks turning pink as she shakes her head. 'Well, that's not important now . . . But once was all it took.'

She's revealing details, even though she said she wouldn't. I'm all ears. 'I found out I was pregnant while you were in hospital. I didn't want to lay it on you at the time. I didn't know how to tell you or what you would say or what you'd think of me. Plus, you already had so much to deal with . . .'

'I would have . . . you should have . . .' The words die on my lips as she side-eyes me, because we both know I might not have been there. I might still have let her down. At least in this way I can pretend. I can convince myself I would have stepped up.

'Anyway, I was shocked, afraid. A baby would have destroyed my career progress. I decided I didn't want it. I wasn't ready. But then, when it came to it, I changed my mind. I got all the way to the doctors, to holding that pill in the palm of my hand . . .' She holds out her hand, staring at its emptiness. 'I was nearly sick at the sight of it. I couldn't do it. I threw it in the bin and didn't look back. I made the choice that I could be a mum and have a career, and if one thing was going to be sacrificed, then it wouldn't be my baby. I didn't even have the chance to get used to the idea. To look through magazines and catalogues, online at baby clothes, prams, cots . . . to get excited. To tell you, to ask you to be there, to help me.

'Then I started cramping, bleeding. And just like that, it was over. I wasn't pregnant anymore.' A tear trickles down her cheek, and she curls her index finger and wipes it away. 'I came to see you. Tried to, anyway. You wouldn't answer. Aaliyah guessed something was wrong. I wasn't myself. I confided in her. She went with me to the doctors to get checked out. She counselled me. She was brilliant. I'm not saying that to hurt you, not this time. I'm saying it how it was.'

'I know. I get it. I'm glad she was there for you. I'm sorry I wasn't. I will never make that mistake again. I promise.'

'Then let's draw a line under it. Under all of it. I miss you, Beth. I really, really miss you. I can't do any of this without you, I don't want to have to.'

'You don't have to. You never will again.' I step down from my seat and rush to her as she does the same. We wrap our arms around each other and settle into the familiarity. It feels like coming home. We both cry out our guilt, our sadness, our relief.

By the time we pull apart, we are composed and ready to face the day. To find whoever killed Jasmine Foster before they kill again. We have found our way back to each other, back to ourselves, and back to the working team that I know is going to crack this case.

I haven't told her about Stanley Baker. I will see him, but I'm going to tell DS Niall Grant to arrange for it to be at Preston City Police Station. I won't put my problems on Millie, not when I wasn't there for her.

CHAPTER THIRTEEN

I arrive at work feeling somewhat refreshed, having sorted things out with Millie. There's still a sourness in the back of my throat, the physical manifestation of my guilt and shame. I should have been there for Millie during what was possibly her darkest time, and I wasn't. I can't turn back the clock. All I can do is be the friend she deserves from now on.

'Beth, can I have a word?' Dillon pops her head out of her office and beckons me.

'Sure.' I turn to Millie, who arrived a moment after me. 'See you in the MIR. Won't be long.'

She nods and walks away. As I step into Dillon's office, my stomach drops when I spot the department counsellor, Toby Evans, his wheelchair turned to face me. His short red hair is slicked back with gel, and his green eyes look knowingly in my direction.

Toby smiles and offers a small wave of his hand. 'Thought I'd be just as well stopping by.'

'Oh, right.' I dare a snide glance at Dillon; she shrugs her shoulders. 'Ambush me more like. And on a Sunday, too. Don't you take days off?'

Toby Evans offers me nothing but a smile. It irritates the heck out of me.

'Take a seat, Beth,' Dillon orders. I do as I'm instructed. 'Toby informs me he is yet to hear from you.'

'I was about to call, actually.' I look at him. 'I didn't think you'd be in today; I was planning on calling you tomorrow morning.'

I look back at Dillon. 'I was busy with a grieving family yesterday. And then DS Grant and DCI Waring came to see me. Not to mention, this is a major investigation, and I . . .'

Dillon raises her palm. 'Enough. We made a deal. You're on the edge of a flaming volcano, and you are skating close to the tip of it right now. I have made it very clear, crystal in fact, that you were not to delay on this. Be careful what you say next. Measure your response.'

I snap my mouth closed like a fish on a line and wait them out.

Toby adjusts in his wheelchair to face me. 'I know counselling doesn't come naturally to you. I know you find it something of a joke, but it isn't. I am a professional like you, and the job I do is important.'

I squirm, lowering myself in my seat. 'I don't think you're a joke.'

He arches a brow. 'I said you thought the process was a joke, not me.'

'I didn't mean to offend you. I just . . . it's my failings okay, not yours. I find it tough to open up to anyone. I also don't think I need it. Counselling, I mean.'

Dillon leans into her desk, closer to me. 'Oh, for God's sake! Whether you think you need it or not, you have signed an agreement, and as such you are required to undertake counselling. Am I clear?' Dillon's curt tone slices through the air.

'I know. I know. I will. When do you want me?' I look at Toby with a forced smile. 'I'll make myself available.'

'Fair enough. Tomorrow, five p.m.?'

'It's the post-mortem tomorrow morning. I might be caught up.'

He smiles. 'I'm sure if you can make it, you will.'

From the corner of my eye, I catch Dillon watching me. 'No problem. All being well, I'll be there.'

Dillon dusts her hands together. 'Excellent. Now we have that out of the way, how about you fill me in on where we're at with the case?' She looks from me to Toby. 'Thanks for stopping by. I really appreciate it.'

'No worries.' He smiles, then manoeuvres to the door and opens it; manners dictate an urge to do it for him, but something tells me he wouldn't welcome my help. He turns to face me again, holding the door open with the back of his chair. 'See you later, then, Beth.'

As the door closes, Dillon starts speaking. 'Amer says the ex-boyfriend's alibi is solid.'

'Yes. He was at a family gathering. Families do lie sometimes, but I really don't think they *all* would. Not to mention, there are photographs. It wasn't him. Jasmine's parents did the formal ID yesterday.'

'I'm aware,' Dillon says.

'Damien is doing the PM tomorrow morning.'

'So, what's your gut telling you at this stage? Stranger attack? Opportunist? Planned? What are you thinking?'

'I'll get back to you on that after the PM, but let's just say I didn't for one second believe it was the kids the neighbour named.'

'They've been ruled out?'

'Yes. The little shits made us jump through a few hoops first, mind. Not one of them would answer questions on the spot. Once they came in — after the hassle of sorting out appropriate adults all round — they talked.'

'Meaning?'

'Meaning they were playing with us. Found the whole thing highly entertaining. Turns out on Friday night they were stopped and searched near Watling Street Road. A concerned member of the public reported a group matching their description graffitiing the local mosque.'

'Was anything found on them?'

I shrug. 'What do you reckon?'

Dillon grunted. 'Of course not.'

'I assume it's been confirmed?'

'Yes. PC Arnie Winters and PC George Vickers carried out the search, then relented to their badgering and drove them home. George said it was to keep them out of further bother for the evening as much as anything else. They dropped all four of them off. They were nowhere near the scene. Turns out they don't even live near the poor old bloke they've been harassing. They go out of their way to wind him up. Sadly, I'm doubtful he's their only victim. The nasty little shites.'

'Who questioned them?'

'DC Vivienne Lee and DC Aaliyah Kimathi.' I smirk. 'They made sure to warn them off bothering Mr Patel. The poor bloke is clearly at the end of his tether if he was willing to come here and attempt to put them in the frame for murder. Maybe he believes they did it, or perhaps he just wants rid of them. Either way, he's scared senseless, by the sound of it.'

Dillon is frowning. 'Kids can be fucking vile, excuse my French.' She shuffles some paperwork, then settles it back down on her desk. 'Anything of interest from the scene?'

'A discarded shoe at one of the scenes, close to where she was found. We think that's where the initial attack took place. There were also fresh tyre marks, so we believe he drove there, perhaps with Jasmine in the car. Casts of the tracks have been taken. They're at the lab waiting to be analysed. Seeing as she'd been in town, we think her having been driven there is the most feasible option. That she was collected, or possibly abducted, and taken to the river. Hannah has surmised, so far, that it appears as though Jasmine was primarily on the ground being dragged. Judging by her footprints, it seems she wasn't on her feet much at all.'

'But she was at some stage? So she wasn't unconscious the entire time?'

I shake my head. 'Unfortunately not.'

'There was also a lot of blood spatter. Some pools had soaked into the ground — there's a lot of mulch, grass, branches. It's going to take Forensics a long time to sift through all the evidence Hannah and the team gathered.'

'Thanks, Beth.' She taps her fingers on the edge of the desk. 'Have you given any more thought to DS Grant's proposition? No one will blame you if you back out.'

'I'm not going to do that.'

Dillon flicks the edge of the paperwork. 'I'm worried about you, Beth; I'm concerned this will be too much.'

'It won't be.'

She settles back in her chair. 'I'm going to level with you,' she says running a hand through her spiky blonde hair. 'I discouraged it from happening. I didn't want them to even bring the idea to you. I fought it, but—' she clenches her fists — 'I lost.'

'I don't know how to respond to that.'

She sighs. 'It's not that I don't believe in your capabilities as a detective; I do. This is something else entirely. We're all fallible. All of us. You're on my team, I care about you. I take my responsibility for your well-being seriously.'

'And you don't think DS Grant and DCI Waring do?'

'I think our priorities differ. I am committed to the Brander case, to finding out who those brands belong to. It's important to each and every one of us. But your mental health and this investigation take precedence for me.'

'Thank you,' I smile, weakly. 'But I'm okay. I want to do this. I thought about it all last night, and—'

'Exactly,' Dillon cuts in, gesturing to me. 'I can tell you haven't slept, and you haven't even spoken to him yet.'

'I never sleep well during a case; you know that. I'll go to my appointment with Toby Evans. I will take all the measures you want. But I have to do this.'

Dillon sighs heavily. 'Like I said yesterday, the ball is in your court entirely.'

'Thank you, ma'am.' I stand and go to find Amer. He will have given the team instructions by now, and will most likely be wondering why I am taking so long with Dillon. I don't want to reveal I am being forced into therapy, and I definitely will not be mentioning Stanley Baker. He's going to think I'm cutting his DSIO balls off by taking on tasks that should be his. This whole situation is untenable.

CHAPTER FOURTEEN

Amer and I stand in the viewing room. I didn't eat this morning and my stomach lets out an audible groan.

Amer turns to me. 'I have a protein bar in my coat pocket.'

I look through the viewing room window at the naked body of Jasmine Foster laid out on the silver examination table, her hands bagged to preserve evidence. I shake my head. 'I'm good, thanks.'

The room occupants are exactly the same as when I was here witnessing the post-mortem of Rose Danes. It jars as I watch Damien Sanders and his assistant Tara Monks carry out the standard tasks. They begin by taking Jasmine's measurements. As crime scene manager, Hannah is in the room and gives me a look of acknowledgement. The exhibits officer, Cath McGraw, is ready to bag, tag and record any evidence. The coroner's officer, James Mascoll-Law is as stern-looking as ever. He is the only member of the team who isn't visibly shaken or moved by the body of a twenty-one-year-old murder victim. Unlike the rest of us, his demeanour appears as though to him it's simply another day at the office.

'How is this happening again, so soon after the Brander case?' Amer says, his eyes remain fixed on the window, following the movement beyond it.

'I don't know,' I admit. 'Do you think it . . . ' I massage the back of my neck, feeling hot and uncomfortable. 'Could they be linked, somehow? Tom is still out there.' I look at him, but he's still watching the others.

He answers without turning. 'I don't know. It's possible. I can't say it hasn't crossed my mind. That it most likely hasn't crossed all our minds. But there's no obvious brand.' He shrugs then looks at me. 'That's their thing, ain't it?'

'Yes, I suppose. But it seems a hell of a coincidence for this to happen so soon. It's not like we're inundated with murders in Preston, especially not ones like this.'

He takes my hand, carefully beneath the view of the window. 'Look, we're going to explore everything. All avenues. If anything leads us to link them, then that's where we'll go.'

'Do you think they're linked?'

He mulls over it momentarily then shakes his head. 'I don't. In some ways, I wish they were, because then it would be one sicko we're searching for, not two. It would mean an end to both investigations, if we catch him. But I just don't think this is him.'

Hearing it said out loud, I realize I agree with Amer. I don't believe Tom did this. Not to mention I received another blank postcard, and it was sent from Marseille a couple of days ago. Theoretically, he could be here. This could be him. But I think I would know; I'd smell the nearness of him.

Amer focusses on what's going on beyond the window. 'Whoever did do this—' he nods towards Jasmine's body — 'we have to find him or her, before they do it to someone else.'

'I know,' I say, it feels like an exhalation rather than a comment.

Damien examines her body for injuries, taking swabs and lifts of any trace evidence, along with measurements of any bruising. The speaker in the viewing room crackles to life. Damien's voice fills the small space. 'A lot of abrasions, consistent with being dragged across rugged terrain. There are cuts on her legs.' He holds up a pair of tweezers, squinting to examine what is clutched between the pincers, before dropping the material into a small evidence bag that Cath holds open for him. 'Small debris, stones embedded in some of them. I've taken swabs of what I believe to be mud and rainwater mixed with blood.'

He continues to move around her body, passing items to Cath that she diligently bags and labels. The speaker crackles once more. 'Significant bruising visible to the chest area. I'll be able to tell you more once we open her up.'

I grimace, imagining what she went through and what her body is about to be further subjected to.

Damien looks at her lower legs, ankles, and feet. He tentatively moves them when needed while dictating a comprehensive list of her injuries. 'Poor girl,' he says. 'Her right ankle is very obviously broken. The fibula bone is protruding.'

My stomach somersaults. It's all I can manage not to dry heave. I press the intercom button to allow my voice to carry via the speaker. 'Any thoughts on how it happened?'

He looks directly at me. 'I haven't completed the exam, of course, but there appears to be a partial footprint.' His eyes darken and he shakes his head, solemnly. 'Like I said, this poor girl.'

Anger surges through me. 'He stamped on her ankle until the bone cut through?' I'm aghast. This was a seriously vicious, unrelenting attack.

'That would be my assumption, at this point.'

It's awful, despicable, but perhaps the footprint, even a partial one, could lead us somewhere.

Damien is now at the head of the silver table. 'She has sustained severe blows to the head. I'll continue with the internal examination.'

I watch James as Damien cuts into the stomach. It's the only time he appears anything other than stoic. The smell in that room will be atrocious. I'm glad to have the thick glass between us.

Damien pokes around with his scalpel and tweezers, gripping something before holding it in front of his face. He scrutinizes it, sniffs it, then rests it on a small kidney-shaped dish. The speaker crackles again. 'I would hazard an educated guess that this is some type of potato product, chips perhaps. It isn't digested, so it had been consumed one to three hours prior to death. There isn't much there, so it was either a light meal, in which case I would estimate consumption being closer to the one-hour mark, or it is the remnants of a big meal, in which case approximately three hours prior. But as there isn't any other undigested content, I would err towards the light meal, one-hour mark.'

I press the intercom. 'We find out what she ate and when, and we can pin down the time of death a little more firmly. Literally follow the crumbs.'

'Exactly.'

Amer glances at me, then presses the intercom himself. 'What about body temp? Won't that clear things up now?'

Damien frowns at us and shakes his head. 'You know better than that detective. I did check the rectal temperature at the scene, of course, but the window would be wide. There is a lot to consider. Using Simpson's Forensic Medicine, I can make some rough calculations. Taking into account the temperature overnight and the body weight of our young lady, I would say that when I attended the scene, the time since death could have been between nine and ten hours—'

Amer hits the intercom again with a frustrated jab, cutting Damien off. I note Damien bristle slightly. 'Could have been? Can't you be a bit more, I don't know, precise?' I want to be able to mute Amer, but he wouldn't thank me for it. I cringe inwardly but remain silent.

Damien's face mask puffs outwards. I realize he has just blown out an exasperated breath, I don't blame him. 'Even then you would have to give or take up to four and a half hours either side. It's really not a reliable method. Rigor mortis had almost entirely set in by the time I attended, so while I would always err on the side of caution,' he emphasizes the word always, 'I would consider prior to midnight on Friday to be a possibility.' This time he puts emphasis on the word possibility. 'I can't really be any clearer than that. I must say, Detective, that this is your area rather than mine.'

Amer gives a quick shake of his head. 'My area?' He smiles. 'I don't do PMs.'

Damien's stance becomes rigid and does not return Amer's smile. 'No, I mean narrowing down the time of death. As I am sure Beth will happily explain, confirmation of the last time a victim was seen alive is a much more reliable and accurate methodology for when it comes to these things. You partner that information with the science. You don't lead with the science.'

'Err, yes, I see what you mean. Sorry I . . . yeah, sorry.' Amer steps back. I know he will be embarrassed, having been put in his place by Damien, so I avoid turning to face him.

He's my mate and colleague, I want to support him. He's wrong on this. He shouldn't be. Surely, he knows the drill by now. He is deputy SIO, but I have to wonder whether he really is ready. Until a few moments ago, I would have said he was. Now, I am not so certain. But I damn well wish Damien hadn't dragged my name into it.

As Damien proceeds with the task at hand, we all fall back into the rhythm of observing his process. I have the utmost respect for everyone in that room. Damien has never steered me wrong. If he could put a time stamp on it, he would. However, he is a scientist and as such he doesn't abide wild guesswork. He also does not like to be pushed for answers he isn't confident or happy to provide.

The rest of the post-mortem yields answers that only heighten my rage and deepen my desire to put cuffs on who-ever was responsible.

'In conclusion,' Damien's by-now-tired voice emanates through the speakers, 'this poor young lady endured a har-rowing, prolonged attack. Her right ankle was stamped on several times; there are partial footprints at differing angles. She was bludgeoned with a blunt, heavy instrument. Wound analysis and measurements would fit with it being some sort of garden-variety hammer. Nothing unusual, irritatingly. She has also sustained serious and what could have potentially been life-threatening chest injuries. Again, blunt force trauma, though as with the ankle, I would say this was due to stamping and kicking. Due to the injuries to her chest, the internal damage was significant. Three broken ribs, a tension pneumothorax.'

'My God,' Amer exclaims.

I press the button to connect the speaker. 'Are you saying the chest injury would have likely killed her regardless of the head injuries?'

Hannah catches my eye and shakes her head mutely. Damien's expression is sombre. 'I'm saying this perpetrator had no intention of giving our girl here a chance. This was overkill, plain and simple.'

Amer and I exchange a look. This isn't the kind of killer who stops at one victim. The sort of fury that exploded within him doesn't extinguish. It burns and sears until another explosion occurs. Maybe even worse than the one before.

CHAPTER FIFTEEN

I arrive at Toby Evans's office promptly at 5 p.m. as arranged, but then I stall outside his door. My hand hovers mid-air as I dare myself to knock. I don't. Instead, I turn and begin walking away. I steel myself once more and swivel back towards his door.

It opens before I get there. Toby appears in the doorway, smiling at me. 'Beth, lovely to see you. Please come in.' This man must have frigging Spidey-sense or something.

I take a seat in the chair at the guest side of his desk. It's tidy to the point of OCD. Everything in its place and perfectly angled. His computer screen glows, casting shadows and light across his face. I glance around the room and note the framed PhD on his wall. He isn't a run-of-the-mill counsellor; he's a qualified psychiatrist. I knew that before I came in here, but the terminology still unnerves me. I'm half expecting the men in white coats to come and cart me off.

'I'm so glad you came,' he says, resting back in his wheelchair. 'I know this must be hard for you. Confronting. I did wonder whether you would turn up.'

I resist the urge to roll my eyes. 'I didn't really get much choice.'

He rests his wrists on the edge of his desk and interlocks his fingers. 'I don't suppose you did. Still, it took courage to come. I commend you.'

I look at his closed office door, sense the room closing inward. 'How long is this for?'

'Today's session, or are you asking how many sessions there will be?'

'Today's.'

'I've nothing on after this, so as long as you need. Or,' he says smiling, 'it can be more of an introductory session.'

I lift a hand and curl a few strands of hair around one finger repeatedly, realize what I'm doing and stop abruptly. I place both hands on my knees, gripping them. My eyes dance, unable to settle. 'Introductory sounds good,' I say.

'You're nervous,' he states.

I bite the inside of my mouth to keep from aiming a retort at him. It's pretty clear I'm nervous; he doesn't need a doctorate to figure that out. 'Yes,' I say instead. I can't help wondering what would entice someone with Toby Evans's qualifications to take on this role. Surely there were better-paying gigs he could have opted for.

'Try to relax. There's really nothing to be afraid of. This—' he encapsulates the room with his arms — 'is a safe space. I want you to try to think of it as such. I only want to help you, Beth.' His tone is gentle, lulling me the way a parent would their child.

'Okay.'

'DS West wanted us to talk through your last case, the one that precipitated your leave from the station.' I nod, and he continues. 'It must have been very hard for you to discover all that you did, during what was the biggest case of your career. I understand your personal connection to the perpetrators must have come as a huge shock. That you worked alongside one of them, Thomas Spencer. You knew him well?'

'As well as you can know someone who is lying through their teeth to you. I thought I knew him. Turns out I didn't. I knew the act he put on. The falsehood he portrayed. I didn't know *him*. My connection to them is genetic, nothing more. It goes no deeper than that.' My defences heighten, and my hackles rise. I am nothing like them, any of them. 'Besides I didn't work *with* Tom. He was never part of my team.'

He interlocks his fingers and nods, completely unruffled by my iciness. 'Stanley Baker, your biological father—'

'My mother's rapist and murderer, you mean,' I cut in. I fold my arms like an angry teen.

'Forgive me, Beth, but I am not here to do battle with you. I don't wish to upset you at all. I do understand that unburdening yourself like this might not come naturally to you. That you are quite obviously uncomfortable with this situation, but I do want to help you. And I will do my very best to do that, if you'll let me try.'

I unfold my arms and blow out my cheeks, sighing deeply. 'Sorry, I know that you mean well. I don't do well talking about myself like this. It makes me feel—'

'Exposed? Vulnerable?'

'Yes, that's right. That's exactly it. And I don't like it; it's as though it weakens me further. Peels back my layers of self-protection. I know I need to do this, that I don't have a choice. I know you want to help. I do understand that. I'm going to try, okay? I will try.'

'You're an intelligent woman, very self-aware. I realize this is going to feel uncomfortable at first, but I'm hoping you'll come to trust me, to trust in the process. This is all confidential, you know, Beth, what you say in here. Unless it will put you or someone else in danger, I won't repeat a word. I can raise the alarm if needed, without going into specifics. This really is a safe space for you to unload. I'm bound by doctor-patient confidentiality. My personal ethics and moral compass aside, I don't believe it would do any good for you to feel as though anything you say will go beyond these walls. Nothing you say will. You can speak freely with me, in here.'

'Thank you. Okay, then.' I fidget in my chair, until I am as comfortable as I think I'm likely to get. 'To be honest, I don't know where to start.'

I ignore the nagging questions I'm dying to pose: *Why are you here? Why not go and work somewhere that pays better? Why not work with people who actually need a psychiatrist?* I'm not here to interrogate him, though that would be easier.

He smiles weakly. 'How about your mum?'

I feel myself blanch; I hadn't expected that.

'You've spent your childhood, adolescence and adulthood not knowing who killed your mum or why. This must have provided some level of closure? Answers to long-ago-posed questions, at least?'

'I suppose so, but at the same time I . . .' I glance at my hands in my lap. 'I feel responsible.' A tear traces my cheek, and humiliation seems to burn beneath it. 'If I'd never been born, she would still be alive.' I swallow hard. My chest tightens with my admission.

'You are a victim too, Beth. You did nothing wrong. No child is responsible for the way they come into the world. You are a detective; you must have come across children born into families in similar situations before?'

'You mean children born as the result of rape?'

'Yes.'

'Yes, I have.'

He pulls a small notepad onto his knee, then picks up a Parker pen and jots something down. 'Would you hold them at all responsible for how they were conceived? For the crime committed against their mother?'

'Of course not.'

'Then why do you hold yourself to account? Why are the rules different for you?'

I shrug. 'I don't know. Maybe because my mother died. Maybe because she died to keep his dirty, disgusting secret. Because I am that secret. It makes me feel sick to think of it. To look in the mirror at the colour of my skin, to finally know where it comes from. Why I am brown, unlike my auntie, unlike my mum. I have always been proud of the colour of my skin. I loved not having to sunbathe, or that when I did, I would just go darker, not red like other kids, other people.

We celebrated my unknown heritage, my aunt and me. Like it was something to be proud of. And it should be, shouldn't it? But it's from him; I know that now. How will I ever be able to see myself the same? How can I be proud of my heritage when it comes from him? My eyes are his. Half my DNA is from him. Growing up, I missed out on having siblings. Turns out I had two brothers and both of them are as twisted as him. I worked alongside Tom for so flaming long, my own brother, and I didn't know. I didn't see it. He must have been laughing at me. Some bloody detective, eh? I met my nieces, looked into their little faces, and they were cute, perfect, but I didn't connect them to myself. I didn't see it — they are my flesh and blood, and I didn't see it. They were living with Tom; they could have been in danger the whole time. He could have snapped at any point, for all I know, and I left them there. With him. I don't know how Aunt Margie can stand to look at me. Because all I see now when I look in the mirror is them. Stanley, Tom, and him, *Simon*.' I'm out of breath, my lungs starved for air — I'm dizzy with the effect.

'You've been through a lot.'

I finally catch my breath. 'You don't say.' I take a moment then level my gaze at him. 'Sorry, I know you're trying to help. I just can't quite wrap my head around all this. I just wish . . .'

'What, Beth? What do you wish?'

'I wish I'd never had to find out any of this. It was easier not to know. Not to have to unlearn hating myself.'

'Hate is a strong word.'

'Yes, it is.'

'You really feel that way? You hate yourself?'

I think about it for a moment, consider how I truly feel. 'I hate the similarities.'

'You mean appearance-wise?'

I nod. 'Yes, and . . . well, Tom was a good detective. I'm a detective. Maybe we are similar, in some respects. And he's still out there somewhere. He will hurt someone again, given the chance.'

'If he does, it won't be your fault. Maybe you do have some similar attributes. But there's a big difference, Beth: you use your powers for good.'

I smile and sense myself rest a little easier. 'Powers? I'm not a superhero.' I laugh, letting the tense sensation between my shoulders ebb away. Damn, Toby Evans is good. How the hell did he coax that motherlode out of me?

'Think of all the people you have helped in the course of your career so far. Calculate how many more people you will help in the future. The case you are working on now. When you catch the person responsible, you will be saving lives. You will be getting justice for his victims, for their families. You do good in this world, Beth. Don't measure yourself by the actions of others.'

'Don't we all do that, to some extent?'

'I suppose we do. But it isn't healthy, because we cannot control what others do. We are only ever responsible for ourselves, for our own actions. For how we respond to the actions of others. You put yourself in danger to meet Simon at that restaurant. You did that because he threatened people you loved. You put yourself in the firing line willingly. That says far more about you as a human being than who your father is.'

'I stood there while Simon was shot and killed. He died right next to me.' I won't go into what I was thinking at the time. That I was willing to let him blow the place to smithereens, with myself and a bunch of strangers as collateral damage.

'How did that make you feel, him dying beside you?'

'Relieved. I thought it was over. Stanley was in custody. I didn't yet know about Tom. I thought that was it; it was done.'

'Have you grieved him, Simon?'

'No. There's nothing to grieve.'

'He was your brother.'

'I didn't know him. He was a murderer. He's everything I despise. He's the monsters I hunt. I hated him.'

'Yet I've noticed you call him Simon, not Sigmund. Simon is the name he chose, isn't it?'

I freeze with my mouth agape; I hadn't realized the significance. I wonder what it means. Whether I am humanizing him too much, caring too much. 'He was bullied because of the name Sigmund, so he began going by Simon. I . . .' I don't know what to say, so I let my words trail to nothing.

'It's okay to feel something. He was your brother. Your emotions are bound to be very mixed.'

'They shouldn't be.' I meet his eyes and see an understanding I wish wasn't there. It's as though he can see into the depths of my soul. 'They aren't. I feel nothing for him.'

'What about Stanley? Do you wonder about him as your father?'

I furrow my brow, and my lip upturns in a snarl. 'Why would I? He isn't my father. He's a despicable human being. He's the reason for all of this. He's nothing to me. I don't have a father. I never have.'

'How do you think you will feel when you sit in a room with him? It's going to happen soon; does it worry you?'

'Of course it does,' I admit. 'But all I really care about is finding out the truth. About the brands. I want to help close the investigation. I want them to catch Tom. I want it over.'

'And do you think you are the right person to meet with him?' He's observing me the way Millie observes a suspect or witness, watching for any nuances.

'I'm the only person. He won't talk to anyone else.'

He doesn't respond.

'I didn't request it. I was asked.'

The silence lingers until he clears his throat. 'What he tells you could potentially lead to more trauma for you, more victims' families to consider, and hopefully, the capture of Tom. Are you prepared for all that?'

'As prepared as anyone could be. I'll do what I have to.'

'Do you think you will feel any guilt? Or perhaps some loyalty to Stanley, to Tom?'

'What?' I exclaim. 'No! Why the hell would I?'

'That's a very strong response, Beth,' he says, in his unnervingly gentle voice. 'Does the mere suggestion of such possibilities upset and anger you?'

'Only because they're preposterous. I want them behind bars. It's where they belong, and if I can help put them there and keep them there, then all the better. I'm good with that. Better than good. I'll be bloody ecstatic about it.' Blood pumps loudly in my ears. I look to the door again, then revert my gaze to Toby Evans.

He clicks the top of his Parker and jots something in his notebook. 'Okay,' he says. 'I think that'll do for today.'

I'm fuming. He's riled me up to send me packing. 'Seriously?'

He cocks his head to the side. 'You'd like longer?' He glances over my head. I turn and see he is checking the wall clock.

'No.'

'Okay, then. Same time next week?'

'I have a case. I'm busy.'

He taps the side of his head. 'As is your mind, Beth. Whatever your emotions — good, bad, or ugly — you need to face them and find a way to deal with them.'

'Is that what that was about? Making me face up to my emotions?'

'Is that what you feel you've done?'

'No, I *feel* like you've pressed my buttons to piss me off.'

He smiles. 'You feel that way because you are afraid to face those emotions. You don't want to be feeling them, but you clearly are. Whatever you say to me, to others or indeed to yourself, you do have complicated feelings towards your father and brothers. It's understandable.'

I stand so quickly the chair rocks. I leave in haste, without pleasantries and without confirming I'll return. I wish to Christ I didn't have to.

CHAPTER SIXTEEN

DCI Bethany Fellows

Work has been hard. Dealing with the worst of humanity always is, and then there's the counselling. It's all been a bit much, not that I would admit that to anyone. Regardless, I am in dire need of a cuddle on the sofa with snacks and a chick flick. I'm exhausted when I arrive at Aunt Margie's. I breathe a sigh of relief as I kill the engine and climb out of the car. I couldn't face going home, looking over my shoulder as I entered my own place. Going through my new routine of checking every corner of the house. Waking in the night, pouring with sweat — having had yet another night terror. Feeling as though Tom is there, watching me, waiting for his opportunity.

My body is bone weary; every nerve ending is shot. My brain feels as though it's on bloody fire. I love it here — no matter where I go in life, this will always be home. Aunt Margie's bungalow in St Annes stands out a mile, mind you; painting a home in bright pinks and blues will do that. She is a kooky, wonderful woman and I couldn't love her more. She's on the doorstep by the time I turn from closing the car door. She's smiling, but I can see the concern etched into the lines of her face. I haven't seen her since I left first thing

Saturday morning when Dillon called. I feel bad that all I've done to ease her worry is send a few texts.

This is my first case after the Brander investigation, and Aunt Margie is well aware I am still dealing with the life-up-ending repercussions of that one. She also knows I have been shutting myself off from the world, and for the first time ever, that included staying away from her, too.

'Come here, sugarplum,' she calls, her arms readily extended. 'Looks to me like you need some TLC, and Lord knows I have missed being able to offer it. Come on, baby.'

Like a needy child, I rush into her embrace. She wraps her skinny arms around me and leads me inside. We sit at the little kitchen table while she boils the kettle and makes herself a cup of tea. For me, as always on a hard day, she heats up milk and passes me a flamingo mug filled with piping hot chocolate. God, I do not half love my crackers aunt. She has always been the constant in my life.

'So, first things first,' she says. 'Have you and Millie managed to sort things out yet?'

Trust my aunt to go there first. She has it in her head that we are destined to be together. Not so long ago, she pointed out that Millie's bi-sexuality and our unique bond are compatible — she didn't so much as hint that we are skirting around each other; rather, she came right out and said it. She pointed out how poorly suited Yvette and I had been. She was right about my farce of a relationship; I'll give her that.

'Actually, yeah, we have. I went to see her before work yesterday morning. We talked. It's, it's erm, all good.' I don't reveal what Millie told me about her miscarriage. It's her business to share, not mine. Aunt Margie is family to Millie and vice versa, but even so, it isn't my place.

She reaches out and places her hand over mine on the table. 'I'm so pleased about that; I really am. It doesn't sit right with me when you two are at loggerheads, and this time it was more . . . what's the word? Ah, well good as any . . . lingering.'

When she can't think of the word she's looking for Aunt Margie will find the nearest to it, sometimes completely altering the meaning of what she's trying to convey. Regardless, I usually get the gist. Though this time, I reckon she's hit the nail on the head — it was *lingering*, and for far too long, too.

'I know. It was all me. I messed up. I should have been a better friend. I'm crap.'

She shakes her head vigorously, her mop of blonde hair flopping around on top of her head. 'You are never that, my love. Look, honey, you went through something none of us can truly understand. It's been hard for me to wrap my head around what happened to my dear sister, never mind discovering the person responsible for her death is your, well, your, erm . . .'

'My mother's rapist. My sperm donor,' I finish for her. I know what she's trying to do, but she doesn't know the full story. She doesn't know that Millie suffered a miscarriage. And, looking at her expression, at the new elements of pain these last few months have drawn into her skin, I realize I have not only been a poor excuse for a friend, but for a daughter and niece, too.

'I'm sorry, Aunt Margie, I really am.' *Sorry* seems to be my word of the moment these days. Tears trail down my face. I can't keep them back, even though I try.

'Oh, sweetheart.' She stands, and steps close to me before pulling me against her middle, cradling my head to her stomach. 'He is nothing to you, nothing. You are my kid. Your mum's kid. Those people are not a part of you.'

She's misunderstood why I am upset. Yes, it burns that they are in my DNA, and I wish more than anything I could change that, but the reason I am crying is not for me or them. It's for this amazing woman who has been there for me my whole life and who I have let down. She doesn't hold it against me; she will never hold me to account for that. The reason being that she will always put me ahead of herself. She might think she's not a born mother, but she's wrong. She is the best mother anyone could ask for, and it astounds me that I have been so unbelievably lucky.

I pull back from her, then look into her eyes. 'I've let you down.'

She places a hand against the side of my face.

'You found out who killed your sister all those years ago, and my only concern was for myself. For how it affected me. I should have been there for you.'

Her eyes moisten as she shakes her head. 'It doesn't work that way. I won't have you punishing yourself because you feel beholden to me. I am the parent; you're the kid.'

I sit further back, forcing her hand to fall from my face. 'No, Aunt Margie, I'm not a kid anymore. I'm a grown woman — a detective, for God's sake. I should have been there with you. We should have been dealing with it together. I fucked up all the way around. You, Mills, work. Everything. Please just let me be sorry. Let me acknowledge my mistakes and make up for them. I need to.'

She moves back to her seat and sits before lifting her mug and taking a slow sip of tea. She replaces the mug and nods gently. 'Okay, okay.' She holds her hands out in surrender. 'You win. I guess, you're a cop and you're programmed to think every bad choice needs to be accounted for and the appropriate punishment sought. So fine, self-recriminate if you must. Go ahead. But I won't jump on board the "I hate Beth train". I won't do it. I refuse.' She grins. 'Now, how about we grab the blankets, choose a film, and have some quality TV time together? Eh?'

I smile, stand, and take my mug through to the lounge. It's why I came here: for Aunt Margie to be the parent I need, and as always, she doesn't let me down. 'I'll grab the blankets; you pick the film.'

I put my flamingo mug on the small side table beside the couch and walk over to the hall cupboard. I grab two folded blankets from inside and go back to the couch. Aunt Margie is knelt beside the pile of DVDs. She turns holding out *Dirty Dancing*, waving it theatrically through the air. It remains our number one go-to movie of all time. I'm pretty sure I could recite the script start to end.

Once we are sitting together and the film is beginning, she asks the question she's obviously been itching to ask. 'Have you heard anything about him?'

I realize right away who she means — Stanley Baker.

'No. I can't be part of the ongoing investigation, so no, I haven't.' It's a bald-faced lie, and I can't look her in the eye while I say it. A shiver flutters through me. I wonder whether she can sense it.

'Okay.' The one-word response tells me she knows I am lying, but isn't going to push me on it. Not yet. The truth is, I'll soon be sitting in an interview room with him listening to him spew his version of reality. I'll do my best to elicit the truth from him. I hate that I am lying to my aunt, but I have to. I won't let her ride this rollercoaster with me. Until there is something solid to disclose, I will leave her be.

There were twenty-eight pieces of seared, branded flesh in the scrapbook Tom Spencer left behind. There was a message at the end that read 'to be continued'. I know instinctively it was left for me, to taunt me and entice me into action. Stanley Baker is the one person other than Tom who can tell me about those brands. He is also the only person privy to the whole truth regarding what happened to my mum. What he did to her. I'm not stupid: I know he will tell lies, horrible or beautiful ones depending on his choice of the moment, but lies all the same. In among those lies there will be the tapestry of the truth.

Aunt Margie and I snuggle together watching *Dirty Dancing*. My thoughts wander to Jasmine Foster, to who her killer might be, the life he might be living right now, what he could be doing. I think about Stanley Baker and what, if anything, he will tell me. I think about the questions I want to ask him. I picture Danielle and the two little girls who are my blood, and wonder how they are. My mind takes a journey of possibilities — where Tom might be, what he might be doing, who he could be hurting. *Dirty Dancing* is playing in front of my eyes, but I don't catch a moment of it. Aunt Margie's hold is the only thing grounding me, keeping me present in the moment. To all intents and purposes, my head is anywhere but here.

CHAPTER SEVENTEEN

The Ordinary Man

He pulls his truck onto Mrs Howe's driveway; since her husband passed it's rarely used. Her daughter uses it occasionally, when she can be bothered to visit her aging mother. He clambers down and lands harshly on the gravel, tutting loudly as his ankle momentarily gives way. He rights himself, then turns and reaches back into the cab to grab his small battery-operated radio. He's hoping there'll be an update on the news, something to get his juices flowing. It's been a few days since she was found, so chances are good there'll be mention of the investigation. She's the biggest news there is right now. *He* is the biggest news there is, he thinks, smiling.

He sets the radio on the low brick wall running the perimeter of the garden and tunes it in, and the music blares. He'll have to put up with the annoying DJ and his musical choices for now. He retrieves his holdall from the truck bed, then heads around to the rose bushes. Grabbing the shears from the bag, he begins pruning them. He takes great pride in his work, everything neat, tidy, and clipped to perfection. There's a certain satisfaction to be had in a job well done and a finished product that he knows would have pleased Mr Howe.

As each song merges into the next, his impatience builds. A hand lands on his shoulder, and he swings around with his arm outstretched. Mrs Howe's granddaughter is holding a mug of tea, some of which jumps ship and splashes onto her forearm, causing her to wince.

'Ouch, sorry,' she says. 'I didn't mean to make you jump. I just brought you a cuppa. Nan asked me to make it for you.'

He looks at the shears in his hand. He'd almost stabbed Mrs Howes' granddaughter in the face. 'Sorry, love. Didn't hear you sneaking up on me.'

He reaches out and takes the mug, smiling at her. He snaps himself out of his trance-like stare. She's captivatingly beautiful, and his breath hitches at the sight of her. The blue dress she's wearing over her black leggings is shaped perfectly around her milky-white breasts. Her neck is long and smooth. A silver chain with a tiny emerald pendant dances at her throat as she moves.

'Thank you. And I'm the one who should be apologizing. Is your arm okay?' He holds out his hand, his fingers extended. She pulls her arm back before he can make contact. He is left with only the idea of what she would feel like.

He notices her eyes flicking back towards the house. He follows her line of sight; Mrs Howe is standing at the kitchen window overlooking the garden. He smiles and waves. Her grey curls don't move an inch as she nods and waves back. She sprays her bonce with so much hairspray she is most likely responsible in part for the gaping hole in the ozone layer.

'Thanks again,' he says, turning back to the young girl. 'You're Eleanor, aren't you? Mrs Howe's granddaughter? She's told me a lot about you.'

'Erm, yeah, but it's Ellie, not Eleanor. Nan's the only one who calls me that. How did you know it was me?'

'I've seen your photograph.' He points towards the house. Mrs Howe has vanished; most likely she will be sitting in the lounge with the television blaring.

'Oh, okay. Fair enough. I'd better go back in. Nan isn't feeling too well today.'

'Really? I'm sorry to hear that. What's wrong with her? Anything I can do to help? I'm more than happy to do some jobs around the house if she'd like. Free of charge, of course. I promised your grandfather I'd always watch out for her, and I meant it.' A strange sensation overcomes him as his chest swells with what he thinks must be pride, or genuine care. He isn't certain which, if either, it is, but there's a fullness in his heart, nonetheless.

Her face softens. 'That's so nice of you. Thank you. But, erm, we're okay. Mum dropped me here earlier. I'm not at college today, so I'm staying all day. We won't leave her alone, don't worry.' She steps back, then stops and smiles. 'But thank you, seriously, it really means a lot. I'll tell Nan what you said. She'll be really touched.' She gestures to the house. 'I'd best get back.' She turns, then spins back around. 'Oh, I almost forgot. Nan's cat, Buster, has gone missing, again. If you see him . . .'

'I'll let you know.'

'Thanks. She loves that thing.'

'I know she does. And Ellie? Thanks again—' he proffers his mug — 'for the tea.'

He watches her walk away. Observes the way her legs push against the material of her dress. Her long brunette hair sashays from side to side as she moves. He can feel a stirring down below and turns away quickly in case she happens to look back, or old Mrs Howe returns to the window. He'd be sacked on the spot, and he can't risk that, or the rumours that might begin circulating as a result.

Flaming Buster. He hates that fucking cat. He's forever finding cat turds buried in the garden. He removes one of his gardening gloves, swipes at his sweaty brow and takes a long, slow drink of tea. Eyeing the Andromeda shrub, he spots Mrs Howe's cat sprawled out beneath it, sheltering from the spring sun. The fucker is happily snoring away, its front left paw clawing at something invisible as it dreams. He goes to his vehicle and places his mug on the truck bed, before walking stealthily back around to the leafy green shrub.

He kneels, then reaches out, stroking the cat's ginger fur, gently rousing it from slumber. It eyes him suspiciously, one eye open, then both of them. It doesn't move, but lets out a low meow, appearing perfectly at ease. *Dumb animal*, he thinks.

He waits for just the right moment, then makes a grab for it, lifting it by a tuft of fur at the back of its neck. 'You've had your old woman worried sick, ya little shit.'

The cat swings its legs, thrashing, baring its teeth, trying its utmost to claw and bite. He holds his ground, keeping his grip, before slowly readjusting his hold into something more reminiscent of a mother cradling her baby. He isn't daft; he knows he won't be thanked for gripping the thing by its scrawny neck.

He walks up to the back door and knocks, plastering on a wide smile while restraining the feral beast as it tries to whip around and bite him. Ellie opens the door, with Mrs Howe close behind.

Mrs Howe's eyes widen as she spots the cat, and she pushes past her granddaughter before reaching for it. 'Oh, thank you, thank you. Dear me, Buster, where have you been? You've had Mummy so worried. Come here, sweetheart.' She takes the cat, cuddling it for all of five seconds before it breaks free and leaps to the ground, running into the house. 'He'll be hungry, Ellie, go make sure he's eating okay. And freshen up his water again; there's a good girl.'

Ellie rolls her eyes and goes back inside. Mrs Howe smiles at him. 'And thank you. Quite the knight in shining armour, aren't you? My Bernard—' she crosses herself — 'God rest his soul, he thought very highly of you, young man.'

Maybe being called a young man or being as good as sainted softens him up, but he once again feels something warm spreading through him. He flushes with the embarrassment of being so easy to please.

He takes in Mrs Howe's pallor and the way she's holding herself. She's off-colour, her skin appears to be hanging a little looser than usual and she's hunched and weary-looking. He nearly offers to help her back inside. He can hear himself saying the words in his head. They don't leave his mouth, but he almost wishes they would.

'Knock if you need anything, won't you?' She slowly closes the door on him, and just like that, she puts him back in his place, the old bitch.

He heads back to his truck and climbs into the cab to finish his brew. Taking his mobile from his jeans pocket, he calls his mum. 'Hi, Mum,' he says, as soon as she answers.

'Oh, hello, sweetheart; lovely to hear from you.'

He smiles, picturing his mum pottering around her little kitchen. 'Just thought I'd give you a buzz, see how you and Dad are doing.'

'Oh, you know, son, same old, same old. You don't need to worry about us. How's Laurie and our gorgeous grand-daughter?' The lilt of her voice lifts on the mention of Kira.

'They're good, Mum. We took Kira to the park on Saturday. We'll pick you up and bring you along next time, if you want?'

'That would be lovely. What park did you go to?'

'Avenham.'

'Oh no, not the one near where they found that poor girl, surely not? You shouldn't go exposing Kira to things of that nature. It isn't right.'

'We were a way off there. Don't worry.'

She sighs. 'Terrible business, that. A young girl should be able to live her life without fear of some sicko . . .' She sighs again. 'It's just so sad. Her poor parents. I can't imagine the pain.'

'Anyway, Mum, I just wanted to check in. I'd better go. I'm at work.'

'Oh, okay, son. Don't work too hard, now.'

He laughs. 'I won't. Love you.'

'Love you too. Bye, honey.'

He hangs up, then gets out of the cab and moves nearer to the radio, stalling, waiting for the news to come on. He passes the time imagining all the things he would like to do to Ellie.

CHAPTER EIGHTEEN

DCI Bethany Fellows

'Beth,' Millie says, cutting me off before I get to the MIR, 'Marsha and Conan wondered if you wanted to have a look at the CCTV from the Baluga.'

I already know they haven't found anything they think is particularly noteworthy, but it wouldn't harm to give the footage the once over myself. 'Sure.'

The room is cramped with all five of us. Amer, Millie and I stand behind Marsha and Conan, who sit before the computer.

Marsha's finger hovers over the mouse. 'Ready?' she asks.

'Yes,' Amer says, and Marsha taps the mouse, setting the screen to play.

We watch for five seconds and then Jasmine Foster comes into view. The image is grainy. I'm unable to make out her features in any discernible way. My chest tightens at the way she moves through the crowd, going in and out of view. She looks like any other young girl on a night out. She's swaying to the music, chatting with her friends, dancing. She's so alive.

'Mind if I sit?' I say to Conan.

He reddens and stands instantly. 'Shit, yeah, sorry.'

'Either of you want to sit?' Marsha asks Amer and Millie, in her strong Scottish accent. They both shake their heads.

'Go back to when she first comes into view,' I say.

Marsha takes the recording back to a couple of seconds prior to Jasmine entering the shot.

I lean close to the screen. 'Can everyone still see?' I ask, conscious that I could be obstructing their line of sight.

'Yes,' Millie and Amer say.

'Good, play it from here, please, Marsha.' I observe everyone around Jasmine, hoping to spot something Marsha and Conan missed. At one point a lad walks up behind her and slides his arms around her waist. She breaks out of his hold, spins around, says something, then laughs and they hug. For a second, I dared to hope for an altercation, something more to go on. I tap the screen. 'Has he been identified?'

Marsha pauses the screen. 'That's Elijah Keane. He's on the same course as Jasmine. We've spoken to him, but he was never a possibility.'

'Because?'

Amer answers, 'He's on the CCTV on and off again for the duration of the evening. He's one of the last to leave the place, just before four a.m.'

'Jesus, do students not sleep at all?'

'Don't you remember what it was like to be young?' Conan says, in his Irish brogue.

I tap him on the back of his head. 'Oi.'

Millie taps him a second later. 'That goes for me, too.'

We continue to watch the CCTV and there's nothing, literally nothing, that we can gather from it. Jasmine Foster was a normal young girl enjoying a night out before evil entered her world. She left at five to ten, just as her friends reported.

'You gathered any other CCTV, anything at all?'

'There are a few possibilities that are being viewed, but so far, she doesn't pop up on them.' Marsha says. 'We checked a couple of cameras from Church Street, which is the most likely direction she would have taken. There's also one from further up Lancaster Road, towards The Guild Theatre, but again, she isn't on it.'

'We're also appealing for witnesses,' Amer cuts in. 'We've received some calls. Nothing helpful so far.'

I look to Amer, waiting for him to say something more. When I realize he isn't going to, I continue: 'Lancaster Road is full of bus stops. If she left before ten, most buses run until at least what, eleven?'

Marsha's eyes light up. 'Bus cameras,' she says.

'Has anyone checked?'

We all look at Amer, who appears to diminish under our gazes. 'I'll get someone out now,' he says.

'What about local takeaways, chip shops?' I say. Despite myself, my irritation levels are rising. Amer's my mate and he's earned his place, but he's missing things. 'She had something in her stomach that contained potato.' I stand up. 'She ate early with her parents on Friday; they eat at five p.m. every day like clockwork. They had spaghetti bolognaise. Damien said she had potato, possibly chips in her stomach, undigested. Her friends said she was hungry and likely went to get something to eat.'

'I'll get Aaliyah and Ant to go door to door round the takeaways, see if anyone remembers her,' Amer offers.

I fight my frustration, remembering how out of my depth I felt when I was DSIO for the first time. 'You never know,' I say, 'maybe we'll hit on something.'

Amer catches me a while later after he's sent Aaliyah and Ant out hunting and gathering. 'Hey, Beth,' he says, grabbing my arm before I can enter the MIR. 'Mind if I have a quick word?'

'Sure.'

We find an empty room. They are few and far between, but we strike gold within a couple of minutes. Once inside, he looks at me, his mouth set, his eyes narrow. 'You have to step back and give me room.'

112

The wind is knocked out of me. 'Excuse me?'

'I said, you have to let me be DSIO. You can't keep cutting across me like you are. It undermines me.'

'Are you being serious?' I yank the belt of my leather jacket tighter.

'Yes. I don't want to piss you off or upset you, but the team are not going to trust me if you don't.'

'Are you referring to earlier with Marsha and Conan?'

'And Millie,' he adds. 'Don't you think I know she goes to you first, that they all do.'

'I'm sorry, Amer, but you're being petty. We're all on the same team. It doesn't matter who they go to, so long as the job gets done.'

'Is that how you would have felt when you were DSIO, if they came to me?'

I hesitate. 'That's not the point.'

'But it is exactly the point. I'm being watched. After what happened with the last case I am under the microscope. We all are.'

'I assume you're insinuating I'm to blame for that?'

He shuffles on the balls of his feet. 'Look, I appreciate you being my second; I'm glad you're back. I am also really bloody grateful that you know your shit, because I know you do. But I am trying to build my career here.'

'And I am trying to stop someone else from dying.'

I turn heel and storm out of the room, before I say something I can't take back.

CHAPTER NINETEEN

It's been a several days, and we haven't made any connections that scream 'killer behind door number whatever'. What we *have* had is confirmation from Yum Yum's takeaway on Lancaster Road that Jasmine went in and ordered a portion of fries at two minutes past ten. If she ate them right away, that would put her time of death at around eleven p.m. to twelve midnight. It has narrowed down our time frame a little, but it's brought us no closer to finding out who killed her. The bloke who served Jasmine has been alibied, along with the other staff who worked that night, and the couple who were there ordering food at the same time. They were known to the owner, so had been easy to track down.

No one at the takeaway noticed anything out of the ordinary. Jasmine was noted as being in good spirits, and gave no indication anything was wrong. There didn't appear to be anyone following her or showing undue interest in her. And if we had any doubts about their ability to read situations and people accurately, we have been able to allay them by viewing Yum Yum's CCTV. They were right; Jasmine appears perfectly at ease, and there is no one unaccounted for who enters the frame at any time.

Unfortunately, the CCTV only covered the inside of the takeaway. The couple who had been ordering food walked via Church Street to get home. They said they walked by Jasmine and waved goodbye. She was heading in the same direction as them, but was ambling along, not rushing like they had been. They hadn't noticed anyone unsavoury hanging around the area — as far as leads go, it's a dead end.

Our lack of progress is frustrating the hell out of us all. Things with Amer and I have remained tense, and I don't like it one bit.

Amer stands at the front of the MIR. Even from here, I can see damp patches beneath the armpits of his light-blue shirt. His fingers are hooked through the belt loopholes on his trousers. His heels rock back and forth.

I walk up to him. 'Amer, we can't carry on like this.'

'I know.'

'I'm sorry if I stepped out of line.' I touch his arm. 'And though I fear doing it again, I am going to say this — you need to take a break. Staring at the boards isn't doing you any good. It will all start blurring into a haze.'

He swipes a hand down his face. 'It already is.'

'Then go in the staffroom, make a cuppa, sit down and have a proper break.'

He peers around the room. Everyone's heads are down, staring at laptops, paperwork — anywhere but at us. I have no doubt some of them are listening. Amer pinches his bottom lip with his thumb and forefinger. 'If only it had been the kids that neighbour offered up.'

'That would have been too easy. This —' I point to an image of Jasmine Foster's brutalized body — 'wasn't down to some kids. And I'm glad it wasn't. Whoever did this is depraved. I wouldn't want to imagine a kid being capable of something so extreme.'

'Kids can be evil; the ones that poor bloke complained about are racist little Nazis, it could have been them.'

'True. But since they were all busy being picked up for graffitiing said racist crap on the gateposts of the mosque on

Watling Street Road, I reckon we can rule them out. Though now I fully understand why Mr Patel has such an issue with them.' I scowl. 'I ever tell you how much I despise racists?'

Amer smirks. 'Once or twice.'

Millie comes into the MIR and makes a beeline for us. 'Amer, Beth,' she says quietly. 'We're all drained, strung out and wrung out — correct?'

We nod. 'Correct,' I say. 'Why are we whispering?'

'This weekend, Sunday to be precise. I want you both at mine, twelve p.m. sharp.'

'Oh, no, Mills, no way,' I protest.

'Come on, Beth, we need this. All of us do.'

'Do you take me for an idiot?'

'Look, I know you hate a fuss; I get that we're in the middle of a case, but we didn't spend any time together over Christmas. We've barely spent any time together at all. You owe me this.'

I squirm at being called out again. 'But you know I hate doing anything for my birthday. Really, Mills, I would rather just ignore it.'

She grabs my arm. 'I won't let you. Not this time. Like I said, we all need it. So make sure Aunt Margie is with you — no excuses. Amer, bring Zarah and the kids. We're going to have some good food, a few drinks and spend time just being normal — we won't put all the focus on you, Beth, I promise. And before you say anything, Mam's cooking, not me — so you're safe.'

I smile, despite myself. 'I didn't say a word.'

She raises a brow. 'You didn't have to.'

'And again, remind me why we're whispering?'

She glances around the room. 'I'm going to invite Aaliyah and Ant as well. Aaliyah's been great recently, and Ant is still struggling with his broken heart, bless him. I'd have the whole team, but there's no way they'd all fit, and I think Mam would have something to say about catering to that many.' She looks at me and raises a brow. 'Plus, I know if I invited everyone, we wouldn't see you for dust, would we?'

'Valid point,' I say. I hate that it'll be my birthday, but I have to admit, it would be great to see everyone.' I haven't seen Millie's parents, Ade and Flora, or Millie's Ouma, Nia, since a month or so before I went AWOL. I usually see them on a regular basis, so I know it's going to be weird at first. I'll be poked and prodded, asked a million questions. That part doesn't sound like my idea of fun, but it's a barrier I need to cross.

'Don't look so scared, Beth,' she mutters. 'They're only mildly annoyed with you. They'll get over it.' She smirks, enjoying my discomfort, then turns her attention to Amer. 'I hope Rayan and Sara won't mind being entertainment fodder for a five-year-old with a motherlode of energy.'

I smile at the mention of Millie's nephew, Luca. His mum, Amara, has raised him alone, aside from the help and interference she's constantly on the receiving end of. It comes in the shapes of her parents, grandmother, me, Millie, and Aunt Margie. All with the best of intentions, of course.

'Is Zane going to be there?' I ask. Millie's younger brother often finds something he'd rather be doing when it comes to family get-togethers.

'He'll be there,' she says. 'Mam's not giving him a choice. She wants "the whole family under one roof for a change."' She imitates her mam's Geordie accent.

Amer's phone buzzes. He grabs it from his pocket and indicates for me to follow as he steps out of the MIR.

'Damien?' he says. 'Seriously? What do you think it means?'

My ears alight at Amer's hopeful and intrigued tone. I am dying to get that mobile from his hands.

'What kind of bud? Right, yes, I see your point. What did he say? Really? Right . . . okay. He have any idea about the meaning? Okay, yes, thanks. I will.'

I can't tell a damn thing from one half of a phone call. I'm rocking on the balls of my feet impatiently.

Amer hangs up and I pounce: 'What?'

'That was Damien Sanders.'

'I gathered that much. Go on; what did he want?'

'He said something was troubling him about Jasmine, something he couldn't quite put his finger on, so he went back and took another look. He reckons he subconsciously took note of a slight bump to her nostril that he initially put down to the violence of the attack.'

'I don't understand . . .' I prod.

'Damien reckons it bothered him enough to investigate further, and sure enough . . .'

I roll my hand in the air, trying to speed him up. 'What? Spit it out, for God's sake.'

Amer widens his eyes and wobbles his head, winding me up, then finally gets to the point. 'There was a flower bud stuffed in her right nostril.'

'A what now?'

'A flower bud. He's consulted a botanist friend, who said it's a white rose.'

'How the hell did it end up in her nostril? I'm guessing she didn't inhale it.'

'It must have been placed there. Damien's botanist pal, Humphrey Drinkwell, said it's almost impossible to narrow down a reason as to why. But it looks like we have another nutter on our hands who likes to leave obscure messages.' Amer appears instantly guilty-looking, and I know it's just occurred to him that he's brought up the Brander case again.

My heart vibrates painfully against my ribcage. 'It's him, it's Tom, isn't it?' Black spots dance before my eyes. I can't catch my breath; it's as though the air in the room is too heavy and thick to inhale. I am forced to take short, sharp gasps.

'Easy, Beth.' Amer has hold of my arm. He leads me to a seat and lowers me into it, then kneels in front of me. 'You're hyperventilating. Come on, breathe with me: one, two, three.'

Millie appears in the periphery of my vision. 'Beth, what's wrong?' She looks from me to Amer. 'What's happening?'

'Damien found the bud of a white rose in Jasmine Foster's nostril, and Beth . . .' Amer looks back to me. 'Come on, Beth, slow your breathing with me. One, two, three.'

After what feels like forever, I am wholly back with them, no longer on the flaming ceiling or desperately attempting to inflate my lungs. I look around and see the commotion has caught the attention of a few people. I feel hot with humiliation. 'I'm okay, I'm fine,' I snap. 'Sorry. I'm okay, though; I am.'

'This doesn't mean it's him,' Amer says. 'There's still no brand.'

'Maybe he's changed tack,' I say, desperately. 'Come on, a white *rose* bud?' I stare from one to the other. 'Rose Danes. It can't be a coincidence. It can't be.'

'I won't lie; we know it's possible, but Rose was Sigmund's victim, not Tom's.' He looks at Millie. 'There's no brand. There would be a brand, don't you think, Millie?'

She's looking at Amer, avoiding eye contact with me. 'I don't know, maybe Beth has a point, but . . .' She appears contemplative, then shakes her head. 'Being devil's advocate, it could be a coincidence, not using the brand, it doesn't seem right to me. No, no, I don't think it's him.'

Millie looks down at me, then grabs both my hands in hers, cradling them. 'Even if it is him, Beth, and that's a big if — we would need to investigate the same as with any case. We have to be open to anything at this stage; you know that. I understand why your mind would go to Tom first. I get it. But you're letting your trauma lead your thinking. I don't need to tell you that a perpetrator who has been using the same methodology, the same calling card for so many years, is unlikely to alter course. Tom coming back here would be suicide. He might as well walk into the prison and tell them to throw away the key. The more I think logically about it, I really don't believe it's him. He's not that stupid or reckless.' She takes a moment. 'But we won't close the door on the possibility. Open minds, always.'

I nod and attempt to convey acceptance of Millie and Amer's logic, but I am not on board. I'm not even riding a train on the same track. My brain is now solely focussed on Tom.

My mobile rings. I look at my phone and see Detective Superintendent Niall Grant's name on the screen. My heart jumps into my throat and wedges itself there — it's choking me so much I can't speak. I hold up a finger to Amer and Millie, ignoring their concerned expressions as I quickly stand up and dash away, out of earshot.

I click to accept the call before it rings off. I was tempted not to, but something tells me it's fate. I could kick myself for thinking it — I don't believe in such things — but Aunt Margie does, and right now, I guess I do, too. I was just thinking about Tom, about the possibility of him being Jasmine Foster's killer and now this.

'Beth?' Niall says. 'Are you there?'

I cough, clearing my throat. 'Yes,' I croak.

'Ah, good.' He sounds hesitant. 'I'm calling because we have a day and time in mind. I've spoken to DS West, and she's cleared you to do it. I just need your okay, and I'll ensure everything runs smoothly.'

My heart beats almost free of my chest. Am I having a panic attack? A heart attack? *Jesus.* 'When?' I ask, sheepishly.

'Friday, three thirty p.m. at Preston City Police Station, as you requested.'

I sense he added in the *as you requested* comment to demonstrate their accommodation of me and my requirements. He's ensuring I won't back out, because I committed. I agreed, and they met the requirements I asked of them, therefore now, I need to reciprocate. I don't want to. Christ, I really don't want to be near that man. He raped my mum. He killed her. He's the monster I've had nightmares about since I was four. There is somewhere I need to go, something I need to do. I've come to rely on the release, on the sense of preparation. It's the only way I know to self-soothe, and by heck do I need that.

'So? Friday?' Niall says.

'Yes.' I hear the weakness in my voice. I take a deep breath. 'I'll be there,' I say with conviction.

CHAPTER TWENTY

I park outside Preston City Police Station. The last time I was in here, I was with Yvette; it was when I learned about her lies. I feel sick. It's the last place I want to be and the last thing I want to be doing. I stayed at Aunt Margie's last night, as I needed the comfort she offers. I didn't tell her about coming here. I can't help feeling it's a betrayal. Keeping this from her is the only way forward right now. I can't begin to explain why I agreed to meet him. I can't tell her or anyone else what I hope to get from it. I can't say how far I am willing to go and how deep I am prepared to delve into the worst time of our lives, and what I am going to do once I have what I'm looking for.

Being a detective is everything to me, but I am willing to risk it. I'm willing to risk my life if it comes to it, so that I can stop Tom, stop the damage that those linked to me through DNA are hell-bent on inflicting on the world. I can't let it go on if there is any way, any way at all, that I can derail them. The words 'to be continued' haunt me. They have since I heard them. Tom is out there somewhere hunting; I feel it in my bones. He may well have already claimed Jasmine Foster as a victim. The only person I have in my orbit who can help me stop him is languishing in prison. Stanley Baker is wasting away in a cell, which is exactly where he belongs. For some reason beyond my understanding, he thinks we have a connection, that him raping my mum and impregnating her with me really does make us father and daughter. The only option I have is to exploit his sick arrogance.

I checked in with Amer before coming here, made sure all avenues are being covered at the station. There was no news, no headway at all. Thankfully, there was also not another body. I am bracing myself for it. I reckon it's a matter of time. The evil that was unleashed on Jasmine Foster will strike again. A human being with that malevolent force heaving inside them cannot contain it. I am not naive anymore. I have seen it, have been so close I could feel it. Like venomous blood coursing through every fibre of their being. Unlike Amer and Millie, I haven't practically discounted Tom, far from it.

DS Niall Grant and DCI Abbie Waring are waiting for me when I walk into the station. Niall holds up a hand in greeting and walks swiftly towards me, with Abbie close on his heels.

'Thank you for coming. We really appreciate this, Beth,' Abbie says.

Niall nods. 'Yes, we do. We understand you might find this difficult. Please know that if you need to, you can back out at any time. You are under no obligation.' He twists his mouth. 'However, it would obviously be beneficial to the investigation if you feel able to see this through.'

I ignore his half-hearted demonstration of duty of care. 'How is this going to work?'

'He is in an interview room; he's cuffed at the moment, and we think for now it would be better to keep it that way. He has expressed a desire to have them removed, but we will see how cooperative he is, first. He has refused legal representation. There's an officer in with him. Abbie and I will sit in the interview with you. Now—' he clears his throat, three short grunts — 'he has asked that it be just the two of you. We've said no. He isn't happy, and to be honest, he might well refuse to talk.' He claps his hands together. 'But we'll give it our best shot. And that's that. Okay, how are you feeling?'

I try to absorb the influx of information, to detangle it and make sense of it. 'I'm fine. Let's get this over with.' I pull the belt of my leather jacket tighter, finding comfort in its embrace.

'Let's,' Abbie says, smiling at me. Clearly this investigation is important to them. They want it solved. But it's not personal for them. They're removed enough to be able to leave here and enjoy the television, a book, a coffee, time with their family. They might have moments of preoccupation — sure, that's likely, rather than possible. But me, I'm going to be locked in this. I'm stepping into my own prison and I'm doing so by choice.

Niall holds the door open as Abbie and I walk through. A police constable stands to the right of the door and there's a table and several chairs inside. Facing us is Stanley Baker. He looks up and beams at me.

Stanley stands up awkwardly, the metallic rattle of his cuffs loud in the quiet room as they impact his freedom of movement. Niall holds a hand up. 'Sit down,' he commands. The police constable moves quickly. He's suddenly at the edge of the table, a looming presence beside Stanley. I see why they chose him for the job. He's huge, broad, tall, intimidating. Though not to Stanley Baker, it would seem; my sperm donor doesn't so much as flinch. His smile is immoveable.

He's put on weight; his grey prison issue joggers are snug around his waist. I remain standing, alongside Abbie. I won't give him the satisfaction of a reaction.

'I said, *sit down*,' Niall repeats, grinding out the last two words.

Stanley ignores him. He has eyes only for me. 'Beth,' he trills, 'my beautiful daughter. How are you?'

'I believe you were instructed to sit down,' I say. 'If you choose to ignore us, I will leave.' I say 'us' purposefully, giving him no doubt which camp I am in.

He hesitates, his expression unsure. I can tell he's in two minds about what to do, whether to heed my warning or to continue his stand-off. It's a power play. His attention remains on me. I note the slight flicker of darkness as he reluctantly gives in and slowly lowers himself back into his chair. There's the slightest hint of a black eye, a small graze beneath it. A certain amount of satisfaction soothes me. I'd love to have been the person to give that to him. The worst kind of scumbags are housed in the same prison as he is: rapists, abusers, murderers. Stanley is right where he belongs.

Niall nods at the police constable. 'Thanks,' he says. 'We're good.'

As the constable leaves, Niall sits in one of the chairs opposite Stanley and indicates for me to take the one beside him, leaving the one off to the right for Abbie.

As soon as I am sat down, Stanley smiles at me again. His cuffs clink against the tabletop as he moves his hands towards me. Niall stiffens beside me. I sense Abbie bristling, too. Stanley stretches his arms closer to me, his hands bent outwards, open as though preparing to clasp mine between them. I snatch my hands out of reach and rest both hands on my legs beneath the table.

'Don't be like that with your old dad.' He pouts, his bottom lip protruding.

'You are not my father,' I snap.

He grunts and shifts in his chair; he spills over the edge of it. They are narrow, plastic and not made for comfort. 'How about a nice cup of tea.' He clasps his hands on the table then, in a deliberately lethargic movement he turns to face Abbie. 'Two sugars and milk, please.' His tone is defiantly mocking. He is making a point. We all know it. I can't control what he says. He is in control of what information he offers up — we can't force his hand.

'Fine.' Abbie stands up, glares at Stanley, then looks to Niall and me. 'I won't be long.'

'It would be lovely if we had a few biccies — I find a nice treat keeps the blood sugars up, the attention span going, and as such, the conversation flowing.' He grins at me. 'Wouldn't you agree, Beth?'

Abbie is at the door, about to leave, Stanley calls to her, 'I adore a custard cream.'

As the door closes behind Abbie, I look at Stanley and smirk. 'I reckon you could do without them, don't you?' I nod towards his thick middle and watch as he frowns.

His smile is back quick smart as he clasps his hands together on the table. Abbie doesn't take long to return, carrying a tray with four cardboard cups and a small packet containing two digestive biscuits. I smirk up at Abbie as she places them in front of Stanley.

'Digestives,' he purrs. 'My second favourite.' He smiles at Abbie, then me, sidelining Niall entirely.

It galls me that he claims digestives are his second favourite. I hope he's lying to save face. They are my second favourite after Bourbons, and I don't want to have anything in common with this monster. Not even what biscuits we choose to dip in our brews.

Abbie places three cups on the table, puts the empty tray on the floor near the door then sits holding her own cup. The liquid is lukewarm and an unappetizing beige colour, but I take a sip, my mouth acrid. There's a certain amount of satisfaction to be had in watching Stanley struggle to open his biscuits and lift his cup. The cuffs create a clumsy impediment, and I can tell it's irritating him.

Being the senior officer and the one leading the twenty-eight-brand investigation, Detective Superintendent Niall Grant takes the lead. I knew this was how matters would proceed; we have put an interview strategy in place. Niall, Abbie, and I are aware of our roles, our intentions and what methodology we are planning on using. Niall advises Stanley of the use of a secure digital network to record the interview, both visually and audibly.

Niall's tone is crisp and clear: 'Present are Detective Superintendent Niall Grant,' he says, then he looks towards Abbie.

'Detective Chief Inspector Abbie Waring,' she says.

Niall looks at me. I glare at Stanley. 'Detective Chief Inspector Bethany Fellows,' I say. We are not the same; we are at opposite ends of the spectrum.

'If you could say your name for the recording, please,' Niall says, looking at Stanley.

He takes a sip of his tea, awkwardly replacing the cup onto the table. 'Stanley Malcolm Baker,' he says, finally.

'The date is the ninth of March 2022, the time is—' Niall shuffles his sleeve up to read from his Apple watch — 'three forty-two p.m. and we are in Interview Room Four of Preston City Police Station. Stanley Baker has declined legal representation at present; however, I will make you aware once again that you are free to change your mind about that at any point. Do you understand?'

'I do,' Stanley says, 'and you're right I did indeed decline legal representation and I have not changed my mind about that, nor will I. However,' he says glancing at me, 'I also stated that I wish to speak with my daughter alone.'

Niall shakes his head. 'Not going to happen. This is the best we can offer.'

I understand from what Niall has explained that they have had to gain special permission to make this happen at all. Stanley is making them jump through hoops, and we all know it. The worst thing is that Stanley knows it, too. We also know that as he is the only person other than Tom who can offer answers about the identity of the twenty-eight-brand victims — he holds the power. With Tom missing, Stanley can dangle the carrot and snatch it away as he pleases. It galls that I am having to kowtow to his whims.

I look into my cup at the unappetizing beige liquid and my stomach turns over. I raise my eyes to Stanley's. 'I want to talk about the brands, where they came from.'

I notice the unmistakable glow of glee on his face. The small twitch at the edge of his lips as he barely suppresses a smile. A sourness rests heavily in the base of my throat. I swallow hard, but it refuses to shift. 'Are they all dead? All twenty-eight of them? Are there more?'

He drums his fingers lightly against the side of his cardboard cup. The metal of his cuffs clinks against the tabletop. 'This is really what you're choosing to talk about now? Not your mother? Not your brothers or me, but this?' He appears incredulous at my chosen topic. But there's nothing about this man or my so-called brothers I want to know. They are a scourge on the earth, as far as I am concerned. I want to rid the world of them. One down, two to go.

I sense Niall and Abbie's judgement. I don't know whether they are even looking at me, but right now, I feel the weight of their stares, their scrutiny. 'Yes. Look, Stanley—' I lean towards him, my chest skimming the top of the table, and Niall tenses — 'you can try to taunt me all you like, it doesn't matter. I am here so that you can tell me the truth. All of it. There's nothing else making me come here, so if you play games, if you don't cooperate, then I have no reason to be here at all. I will happily leave you to rot. I will never come back. You do understand that, don't you?'

He doesn't react, just slowly lifts the cup to his lips, then blows across the liquid and takes a sip. 'Yes, they're all dead.'

I hear Abbie's intake of breath, Niall's sigh. This is the most they've got out of him. He's been tight-lipped, until now. He gave them his word he would reveal the truth if they arranged for me to be here — but none of us trusted him.

'And, no, there are no more. As far as I'm aware.' He puts the cup down and leans his head to one side. 'Now what's next? What question are you going to throw at me now?' He looks pointedly at the clock on the wall to the side of us. 'Time's ticking on. I wouldn't want to end up missing dinner.' He laughs, a hollow sound, devoid of humour.

'Where are the bodies? Have they been found?'

He sits back and rests his hands together over his middle. 'Some, I believe. We always made sure that by the time of discovery they would have degraded enough that the missing skin, the brand, would not be noticed. We preserved them, cared for them. Treasured them.' He raises his chin, his eyes focussed on my own, unwavering. 'The rest of them, their flesh, their bones, it was all disposable.'

The sour lump in my throat rises, almost choking me. 'Who were they? There are years beside each brand. Let's start with the first. 1993 — so, you would have been what, twenty-six, twenty-seven? Was that your first?' My throat tightens, squeezing the lump — I fight the urge to gag. 'After my mum, of course.' I'm gripping the material of my trousers, clenching my fists so hard they begin to shake.

He smiles, actually smiles, his eyes glistening. He's silent momentarily, lost in his memories. 'I won't talk about your mother in the same vein as the others. They aren't the same.' He shakes his head. 'They are worlds apart.'

I want to jump across the table and throttle him; I want to rip his head off. It takes all my willpower to remain outwardly calm. 'I am not here to talk about my mum. You don't deserve to even think about her.'

He raises his cuffed hands stiffly, then clumsily uses two fingers to tap the side of his head. 'I think about her all the time, my dear.' He closes his eyes, and his bottom lip quivers as his inhales jaggedly. 'She's with me whenever I choose for her to be.'

Niall hits the table with his open palm, making me and Abbie start. Stanley languidly opens his eyes. 'Enough!' Niall barks. 'You asked for Beth and she's here, but I will not have you manipulate this situation to torment her. We stick to the brands, as agreed.'

Stanley looks at me and shrugs. 'Is that what you would prefer, my dear?'

I grit my teeth. '1993 . . .'

'Very well. Yes, 1993 — ah.' He angles his head back and stares at the ceiling as though he is searching his memory. 'Yes, I remember her very well.' He looks at me, and licks his lips slowly before smiling broadly. 'A truly beautiful young woman. It was summertime, fourteenth of August, to be precise.'

Abbie makes a note in the flip pad she has on her knee. The interview is being recorded, but she can refer to this information and act on it as soon as she leaves the room. Studying the video and audio will come later. Keeping copies is vital for legal reasons — even more so since he's refusing any legal representation.

'Do you know her identity?'

He frowns. 'She might have been beautiful, and she was, but she was also a whore, excuse my French. I did you a favour.'

'How do you figure that?' I retort.

'I meant the police, not you specifically.'

'Again . . . how do you figure that?'

'You lot don't have the time, the power, the ability to rid the streets of their kind. I do. Or rather, I did.'

I glower at him. 'Her name?'

I know the reality — if she was a sex worker, then the likelihood that she was reported missing at all is slim. And if she was, then it could well have taken some time for anyone to notice and respond to her absence, which would mess with the timeline. Her body may or may not have been recovered, and if it was, it may or may not have been identified. We need him talking. We need more.

Stanley drains the remainder of his tea, grimacing at the now-cold liquid. 'Stephanie. She only gave me her first name. I don't believe she was found. Perhaps she was eventually, but not at the time, and I have never come across mention of her in the news.'

I hear Abbie's pen scratching against the paper. 'How old was she?' I ask. 'Where did you meet her?'

'We didn't exchange measurements, surnames or birth dates,' he chuckles. 'I met her in Liverpool by the Albert Dock. I was there to deliver a talk at an arborist conference. Very fascinating, you know; it takes a great deal of knowledge and skill to be able to cultivate—'

I look pointedly at the clock and drum my fingers on the table. 'I'm not interested in being lectured to about your day job, Stanley.'

'Career, and how about we try "Dad" not "Stanley".'

I sneer. 'I will never refer to you that way. You are not my dad; you never were, and you never will be.'

Stanley turns to Niall. 'I'm feeling a bit weary. I think perhaps we are done here.'

'What did you do with Stephanie's body?' Niall prods.

'I will only repeat myself so many times before I stop speaking entirely,' Stanley warns us. 'I will talk with Beth. I will divulge everything you want to know, but I will not answer your questions DS Grant. I am already compromising by allowing you and the charming DCI Waring to be present. I will not compromise any further.'

I lean towards him. 'What did you do with Stephanie? How did you kill her?'

He holds his cuffed hands up, wrists touching, fingers splayed and palms facing outwards. 'With these.' He grins. 'I strangled her. Then I seared the raven in place before removing the piece of flesh it was on. I got her into the boot of my car and then I drove to the Mersey in Warrington, I remember I went via Wilderspool Causeway.' He snarls with contempt. 'I recall thinking it was a revolting-looking place and that it was perfectly suited to someone like her.'

'Why not just dispose of her in the docks where you killed her?'

'I thought it best to put a little distance between her body and where we met. Where she might be known. It was quieter there, and I wanted her in the tidal water. Clearly it worked out well. She wasn't discovered. I doubt she was missed.'

'Everyone is missed. Everyone matters. She was a human being; she'll have had family. Parents, brothers, sisters, friends, maybe even children. They all will have had someone.' The words spill out of me. I can't stop them. He is sitting here talking about his victims as though they were inconsequential. My blood boils.

'Not everyone has someone, Beth.' He yawns, exaggeratedly. 'Not everyone matters. If Stephanie had mattered so much, I would have read about her in the news after-wards, wouldn't I?' He sits straighter and glares at me. 'Well, wouldn't I?'

Niall clears his throat. 'I think you're right about one thing, Baker; we are done for today.'

'Wait,' I say, quickly. Before coming in here today, I made a request of Niall and Abbie. Now is the time. 'I understand you read the newspaper every day?' I pose it as a question, though I know the answer.

'I do.' Stanley sounds intrigued.

'Jasmine Foster, the twenty-one-year-old woman who was murdered a week ago.'

He is nodding along.

'Was it Tom?'

He holds up his hands, rattling his cuffs again. 'How would I know? I'm currently incommunicado with my son.'

'I think you would know.'

He smiles. 'Was there a brand?'

I shake my head. 'No.'

'Then it wasn't him. Tom stopped killing some time ago. The last one the three of us did together was in 2016. Then, the following year, he made a mistake with that young girl.'

He's referring to Celine Wilson. Tom raped her, and Sigmund attempted to kill her to cover it up. In his haste with-out aforethought, Sigmund left the brand in situ and Celine alive. She's been in a vegetative state ever since.

Stanley's expression darkens. 'Tom cut contact with me and his brother and married the girl's sister. The only joy he brought me after that was my lovely granddaughters. I don't get to see them anymore, of course. Shame, really. But Tom, no, he hasn't been involved nor has he had anything to do with me since 2017.'

'He could be striking out on his own, starting a new ritual.'

Stanley laughs. 'Tom? He never had the imagination. He wouldn't change method. No, I don't for one moment believe he is who you are looking for. But,' he says grinning, 'I am always happy to consult, should you find my advice at all helpful.'

'There is no way I would—'

Niall nudges my leg with his own beneath the table. I clamp my mouth shut, heeding his warning. I won't rise to the bait Stanley is throwing out. Niall details the information relevant to officially conclude the interview recording.

In one fluid motion, I scrape my chair back and stand. I need to get out of here quickly. I don't want to breathe the same air as Stanley Baker for a moment longer than necessary.

'Beth,' he croons, and a shudder travels the length of my spine. 'I'll see you again soon, my darling.'

CHAPTER TWENTY-ONE

The Ordinary Man

He drives through Preston; it's Saturday night and the street-lights bathe the pavements and roads in streams of amber. He relaxes, feeling his taut muscles loosen as he rolls his neck and hears a satisfying crack. Laurie will have his guts for garters when he finally rolls in. This time, he will be truthful; he'll tell her he simply couldn't stand the thought of being cooped up in his sodding house.

He glances in his wing mirror and spots a brown-haired girl stumbling down the street. Her ankles turn one over the other as she tries to navigate the pavement. He licks his lips and slows the car while watching her tugging self-consciously at her skirt. It's so short it is almost riding her arse. There's no one else around. He slows further, then, from around the corner, another girl springs into view. He stops a short distance ahead of them. Lowering his window slightly, he strains to listen in on their exchange.

'Wait! Don't be like this,' the raven-haired girl shouts. She's got a crop top on despite the nip in the air. This one makes no move to tug her skirt to a more respectable length.

She's confident, and to be fair, she has every reason to be. He smiles as he observes them via the rear view.

'Fuck off! Leave me alone,' the brunette barks.

'Fine, then. Suit yourself.' The raven-haired one turns and strides back around the corner out of view.

The brunette swipes at tears with the backs of her hands.

For a moment, he's torn between them, like deciding between Coco Pops and Rice Krispies. He idles the car along the road, feeling antsy. Neither is blonde like Jasmine, but they have other things going in their favour. He can picture the raven hair of the other one held tight in his fist. But then, the brunette is mouthy, and he'd love to shut her up. He drums his fingers against the top of the steering wheel, mulling over his options.

After making his decision, he drives alongside her, pokes his head out of the window and smiles. 'Need a ride?'

She screws up her brow and wrinkles her nose, looking at him like he's a piece of shit. 'No thanks,' she hisses. 'Piss off, ya perv.'

The little bitch. He has the steering wheel in a death grip. 'Charming.' His lips quiver as he struggles to maintain his smile. 'I was gonna say I'd give you a lift home for your bus fare, but you can forget it. Cheeky little madam.' He looks away from her and starts to roll his window up — anticipating her interruption.

'Wait, sorry,' she says. He barely suppresses a smile as he turns to face her and rolls his window back down. She steps closer. 'I've had a crap night, that's all. Sorry. But just my bus fare? Are you sure? I mean—' she steps back again and eyes his car — 'you are a taxi or an Uber or somat, right?' She tilts her head.

'Course. Wouldn't be offering you a lift otherwise, would I?' He grins. 'It's not safe for a pretty young woman like you to be out alone. I have a daughter; I'd hope someone would stop to help her. You know, keep her safe.' He holds his hands up and out. 'But hey, if you'd rather walk home, alone, at night — it's your call. Whatever you think best.'

He observes the moment it registers: he is a dad, he's Mr Safe Bet. He bites the inside of his lip to keep from laughing. He isn't even lying.

Slowly, almost lethargically, she nods. 'Thank you. I mean, if you're sure?'

He quickly looks in the rear view, the wing mirrors and around the car — it's deserted. Getting out, he opens the back door and gestures for her to enter. 'Hop in.' He smiles broadly.

She slides inside. He scrunches his nose at the stench of cheap cider emanating from her pores. 'And, erm, thanks for the lift,' she says, settling in and fumbling to fasten her seat-belt. He eases the door shut, listening to the satisfying click.

Getting in the front, he takes her address while simultaneously activating the locking mechanism. 'I know a short cut; I'll have you home in a jiffy.' He releases the handbrake, observing her via the rear view. 'I noticed you and your mate arguing. She seemed like a bit of a cow, to be honest.'

She sniffs and looks out her window. 'Yeah,' she whines, 'she can be.'

He watches as she bites her lower lip, pulling it inwards on one side. She's perhaps a little younger than he first thought. For a moment, he considers actually driving her home, but then he remembers Jasmine — how he'd felt, the euphoria, and he can't bring himself to do it.

It had happened too fast with Jasmine; this time would be different, better. It amazes him how gullible women are. They almost spoil the fun by making it too easy.

He drives round the roundabout and over the small bridge taking a left onto Lightfoot Lane. It's a long country road, and as such there is zero lighting and complete isolation.

He drives past the turnings for Lightfoot Green Lane and Wychnor. There's a small dead end off to the side of the road. He finds it and pulls over. He smirks into the rear-view mirror, watching the confusion on her face as her eyes lock on his reflection. Her look of confusion transforms into alarm — then, in quick succession, to unadulterated horror.

'Why have we stopped? Are you lost?' Her voice is shaking. She unclips her seatbelt and sits forward. 'What's going on?'

He sits in stony silence, observing her. Seduced by her fear, he licks his lips.

She stares wide-eyed at the back of his head; he watches as she gulps, then as she tries to open the door. He bites down on a chuckle that's trying to escape as he waits for her to realize there's no lock. He knows when it hits her, because her face blanches of colour and she lets out an ear-splitting shriek. She kicks and hits the door, then the partition between them. She grabs her mobile from her bag and taps fruitlessly on the keys.

He counts the seconds until she notices she has no signal and braces himself for her shrill scream that ricochets around the car. She's crying, wailing, desperately clawing at the door. 'Don't you touch me! Don't you touch me! As soon as I get out of this car unless you let me go, I will scream my fucking head off, I swear it. Do you hear me? Are you listening?'

Finally, he twists to face her, half smiling, half sneering. 'And who do you think is gonna hear you?' He laughs.

CHAPTER TWENTY-TWO

DCI Bethany Fellows

I picked Aunt Margie up on the way here. I park on the street, because Millie's driveway is full — Ade and Flora's three-year-old Citroen C4 Cactus is behind Millie's red Peugeot. The neighbours won't be best pleased, but no one wants to complain to a cop about unfortunate parking. I forced Aunt Margie to leave my gift at home. I haven't opened it yet, and I certainly don't want to do so with an audience. Having everyone stare while I tear into a present puts me on edge, the pressure to react too high. I don't do squeals of excitement, or over-the-top shows of gratitude. I do quiet appreciation.

Aunt Margie swivels in her seat to face me. 'Before we go in,' she begins, her voice gentle, 'will you please tell me what's wrong? I didn't hear from you all day yesterday, and since you collected me, you have barely spoken a word. Something's not right, and I want to know what it is.'

I look at Millie's house, and I see movement via her bay window. 'I'm fine, Aunt Margie.' I sense her eyes on me, so meet her gaze. 'Honestly, I'm just exhausted. There really is nothing wrong.' I don't promise. I can't bring myself to do that on the basis of a lie.

Aunt Margie shakes her head. 'If you say so.' Her focus lingers on me, and I know her bullshit detector is going like the clappers. After a couple of beats, she opens her door.

'Anyway, you're one to talk,' I say quickly.

She turns to face me. 'Meaning?'

'I dunno.' I tilt my head and eye her suspiciously. 'You've been different lately.'

'Oh really? And how do you figure that?'

'I'm in the middle of a big case, and you didn't call or text all day yesterday.'

'Neither did you.'

'Exactly. Normally you would have bugged me until I responded.'

She scowls. 'Oh, thanks a lot.'

'You know what I mean. Don't pretend to be offended; we both know I did not offend you.' I laugh.

She smirks. 'Yeah, fair cop, no pun intended.'

'So?'

'So, what?'

'Why didn't you call or text yesterday?'

She sighs. 'Because I'm giving you the space you reckon you want. I mean, you did cut me off for a while there. I don't want that to happen again now, do I?'

'I wouldn't do that again. I won't.'

Before either of us can say anything else, the front door opens, and Millie is standing with her hands on her hips. 'Are you two planning on coming inside?' she calls.

Aunt Margie looks over at her, smiling broadly, then gets out of the car. She opens the back door and retrieves the foil tray of cupcakes before walking up to Millie. I stare after her for a moment, incredulously. She had me, she well and truly bloody had me. She managed to make me feel guilty and back off with my questions. I watch her saunter up to Millie, hug her and waltz inside without a care in the world.

As I near Millie, she looks at me questioningly. 'What's up with you?'

I point into the house. 'Did you see that?' I mouth. 'She's happy as Larry.'

Millie narrows her eyes. 'And why shouldn't she be?'

I blow out a breath. 'Never mind.' I pull Millie into a quick squeeze then walk past her.

'And who the hell is Larry, and why is he always so flaming happy? I'd love to know his secret,' she says to my back. I can hear the smile in her voice, which makes me smile, too.

'Ha ha, Mills. You really wouldn't make a good comedian. You throw out the same jokes way too often.'

We are in the small hallway when Amara's little boy Luca comes hurtling towards us.

'Whoa,' Millie says, making a show of diving out of the way. 'Careful, me laddo.'

He stands beside her, grinning. Millie tickles the tops of his shoulders, making him squirm and break out into fits of high-pitched giggles. I've seen Millie with Luca countless times. She's always great with him, but this time, watching them together feels different — this time, it sucker-punches me. Millie is a natural with kids. I'm sure she's had the whole maternal instinct thing imprinted in her since birth. When she'd decided to keep her baby and then lost it, I can only imagine the pain she must have been in. My heart aches for her.

Luca twists away from Millie, ducks beneath her arm as she pretends to make a grab for him before he vanishes into the lounge, leaving behind echoes of laughter.

Aunt Margie comes from the kitchen. 'I've given Amara the cakes for later,' she says.

Millie smiles. 'There was really no need, but thank you. I'm sure the kids will devour them. If Zane doesn't find them first, that is,' she chuckles. 'For one so skinny, he has hollow legs.'

Then Millie looks at me, her expression now devoid of humour. 'Right, come on; let's go get this over with.'

She knows I'm dreading this. I take a steadying breath and walk into the lounge behind Aunt Margie and Millie.

My anxiety levels are rising at the possibility of the dressing-down I know I am wholly deserving of, but desperately hoping doesn't come.

Luca stands breathlessly beside his Uncle Zane. Amer, Zarah and their gorgeous kids Rayan and Sara stand beside the fireplace. Millie's mum and dad sit beside Millie's seventy-eight-year-old Ouma on the cream couch; they're all looking up at me. The weight of everyone's stares rest on my shoulders, which almost slump in response.

Millie's mum is the first to speak. 'Margie, lovely to see you.' She struggles up from the couch. She takes Aunt Margie's hands, then lightly kisses both her cheeks before stepping back and turning her attention to me. 'It's been a while, Beth,' she tuts, 'what were you thinking of young lady, cutting us off like that?'

'I'm sorry,' I say, feeling like a chastised child. 'I really am.'

Millie pulls three red balloons from the wall, where they had been held in place with tape. I hadn't even noticed them until now. 'Here you go,' she says, handing one each to Rayan, Sara, and Luca. Rayan skews his eyes at the balloon, then Millie, but takes it anyway. She leans down and whispers something to Rayan, who smiles and bats his balloon against Luca's head. Luca giggles and sets off running from the room, the other two kids in pursuit.

Flora looks at me and shakes her head, her lips a strict line. I blush under her scrutiny and judgement, but then she smiles. 'Come here, sweetheart.' She pulls me into her arms and holds on tight. For some reason a lump forms in my throat, and the threat of tears stings the backs of my eyes. She strokes my hair with one hand, then leans back and kisses my forehead. 'Dear girl, don't you ever do that again, okay? My poor Millie was beside herself with worry.'

'I won't, Flora. I didn't intend to upset you all.' I face Millie. 'I'm sorry,' I repeat.

Ade stands and envelopes me in a hug, his thick arms offering instant comfort. He's the closest I've ever come to knowing what having a father would be like. For a second,

Stanley enters my head, which pisses me off — I don't want him in there. I don't want him here with me, now.

Zane's tall, lanky frame hovers to the side of us. He's six foot three with the darkest eyes I have ever seen; they sparkle when he smiles, flashing his perfectly straight white teeth. I am transferred from Ade to Zane like a human pass the parcel, while Ade gives Aunt Margie a bear hug. Amara steps into the room carrying a silver tray adorned with Jamaican dumplings, their fried buttery scent make me salivate. She swiftly hands the tray to Millie, then rushes at me, nudging Zane out of the way to give me one of her renowned cuddles.

Once the hugging has abated, I go to Ouma and give her a kiss on the head. She smells of peppermint, hairspray, and musky perfume. Ouma puts her soft hands either side of my face and stares into my eyes. 'Lovely girl,' she says in her strong Jamaican accent. Her skin looks and feels thinner than the last time I saw her. It terrifies me that she's coming up to eighty. I can't imagine our lives without this beautiful, wizened lady.

Five minutes later, there's a knock at the door and Millie dashes through to the hallway, coming back shortly after with Antonio and Aaliyah. The house feels ready to burst at the seams. Millie has dragged fold-out chairs into the lounge but there still isn't enough room for everyone. For the most part, we stand chatting, moving fluidly, forming one collection of people after another.

Antonio doesn't seem his usual chirpy self, and it occurs to me that Millie was right to ask him along. She's an empath by nature and profession. Noting Ant's broken heart, even months after it was shattered, is typical of her. I was oblivious, the end of a relationship seeming somewhat unnoteworthy in the grand scheme of things.

We've been at Millie's for over an hour when I find him standing by the back door. 'Hey, Ant,' I sidle up to him. 'How are you doing, mate?'

He shrugs. His whole demeanour is dejected and sombre, the way someone would appear at a loved one's funeral. 'Oh, you know, holding up.'

'I'm sorry about your break-up.'

'It was a while ago now; you'd think I'd find these things easier. It's not even like I'd have brought him here, but I feel like something's missing. My life's felt so empty since he left. To be honest, he's all I think about. I'm struggling to move on.'

'Why wouldn't you have brought him? I mean, why didn't you introduce us to him?' I wonder whether his fella was in it the way Ant clearly was. In the past, Ant would have paraded his boyfriend around, puffing his chest out with pride. My heart breaks for him.

He laughs sardonically. 'Didn't want you lot scaring him off. Turns out that should have been the least of my concerns.'

'I'm sorry it didn't work out. You sure there's no going back?'

He twists his lips, then half smiles. 'Nah, it's well and truly dead in the water.'

'Come on, mate,' I pat his shoulder. 'Let's go through.' I indicate the inner sanctum of the house. 'Trust me, I don't wanna be in there when Millie brings the cake through, but you know it's gotta happen.' I laugh. I have absolutely no doubt there will be a delicious chocolate cake adorned with enough candles to risk setting the smoke detector off. I told her not to, but we both knew the inevitability of her ignoring me.

Aaliyah catches me just before we go back into the lounge. 'Can I have a quick word?' she says. Ant smiles, nods, and carries on into the lounge, leaving me to head to the kitchen with Aaliyah.

The oven has warmed the room and I instantly feel too hot. 'What's up?'

I want to get this over with as soon as possible and go back through to the lounge. Not that the body heat in there isn't making it warm as well, and stuffy, but it's still more comfortable than in here. I can't quite put my finger on why Aaliyah is making me bristle. Or is it me that's making her bristle? Perhaps that's the problem.

142

There's a pan on the stove with a wooden spoon in it, the glass lid sitting askew, leaving a small gap for the steam to escape. Aaliyah lifts the lid and begins absentmindedly stirring the food, the spicy smell rising with the steam. 'It's Millie,' she says finally. 'I know she told you.' She looks over my shoulder, then whispers, 'About the miscarriage.'

I nod. 'And?'

'She's struggling still, badly.'

She'd told me she was doing okay now, that she was out the other end, for the most part. How have I missed this? 'Has she said that?'

'She didn't have to. It's obvious.'

I look down, staring at a spot of sauce that's dripped onto the grey tiled flooring. 'I'll talk to her.'

'Good. There's something else,' she says. I look up as she stops stirring and replaces the lid. 'She's been disappearing somewhere, and I'm concerned.'

I do a double take. 'What do you mean, disappearing?'

'I mean, there's been a number of times now that she's been out of contact for an hour or two, and when I ask her about it, she goes off on a random tangent. You know what Millie's like; she can't lie. She starts waffling on about all sorts, trying to cover her tracks, and it ends up so convoluted that you know she's misleading you.'

She doesn't need to tell me this. I know Millie can't lie. I know what she does when she tries. 'It could be anything. Maybe she just doesn't want you to know. Maybe she's dating someone.'

Aaliyah shakes her head. 'No, she'd tell me that, and besides she isn't ready, not after . . .'

'Yeah, I suppose not. I don't know. She hasn't mentioned anything to me, either. I'll talk to her.'

'Thanks, Beth.'

'You don't need to thank me,' I say, my words carrying more than one meaning.

Amara comes through to the kitchen and Aaliyah smiles, then quickly walks past her. I grab a couple of sheets from

143

the kitchen roll, wet it beneath the tap, then bend to wipe the spilled sauce from the floor.

Amara walks over. 'What did I just walk in on?' She raises a brow as I stand to face her.

'Nothing.'

'Yeah right, I coulda cut the tension with a knife. You two got beef or honey?'

I roll my eyes. 'Neither. Don't be ridiculous.'

She nudges me out of the way with her hip, then grabs the oven gloves and opens the oven door. 'Whatever you say. Mmm, would you get a whiff of that. Mam's been cooking up a storm.'

My stomach is screaming for sustenance. I look down as Amara retrieves a roasting tin full of piping hot jerk chicken.

I hear a bit of a commotion coming from the hallway, so pop my head through to see what's going on. I can hardly believe my eyes. Danielle is standing in front of Millie, who spins to face me with a huge grin on her face. Erin and Ava, my gorgeous little nieces, are wearing matching red party dresses and little white cardigans. Erin, whom I know is coming up for five in a couple of months, proudly holds out an atrociously wrapped gift and grins at me. Three-year-old Ava leans into her mum with her thumb in her mouth. With every passing day, she looks more and more like her auntie Celine. It stalls my heartbeat momentarily.

Millie looks down at Erin. 'What have you got there?'

'It's a birthday present for Beth,' she says. Her eyes find mine and my chest swells with love.

'I didn't expect—' I begin, falter, and catch myself. 'Wow, thank you so much, Erin.' I walk to her slowly, fearing scaring her, or making Ava cry. I don't want to ever them to see me as someone to fear. I kneel in front of Erin, and she hands me the present. 'Did you wrap it?' I ask, smiling.

She nods enthusiastically, and points to her sister. 'Ava helped.'

'Thank you so much! Both of you have done such a wonderful job.'

Luca appears in the lounge doorway, unable to resist the intrigue of new guests and children's voices. 'Who are they?' he demands, as only a child would.

Millie tuts and shakes her head. 'They are our guests, Luca. Go on back in the lounge and play with Ray and Sara. They'll be through soon.'

He scrunches up his face. 'Ray won't play with me, and Sara is boring.'

'Don't be unkind, Luca. Go on now.'

Amara walks out of the kitchen, a tray of nicely presented and heavenly smelling jerk chicken in hand. She pauses and faces her son. 'That wasn't nice, Luca. Now then, come on and help me with this. Grab the paper plates from the side.' She nods back towards the kitchen. Luca drops his shoulders, sulking, but then thinks better of it and runs through to the kitchen, narrowly missing slamming into Amara. He returns seconds later with a stack of paper plates that he holds as though they are Wedgwood.

I don't want to overwhelm the girls, so I lead them into the kitchen. Erin sits on a tall stool at the breakfast bar. Danielle goes to sit beside her, but Erin shakes her head vigorously. 'No, Mummy,' she whines, 'that's for Beth. I want her to sit next to me.'

Danielle appears stung, but it quickly passes, and she smiles at Erin. 'Okay,' she says.

Millie quickly scoots a chair closer. 'Here, Danielle, sit on this one.'

'Thanks,' she says. I could be imagining it, but she sounds curt. She sits with Ava perched on her knee. I smile at Ava, but she twists until her face is buried in her mum's jumper.

I make a show of admiring the wrapping paper and shaking the parcel. 'Oooo, what could it be? A car?'

Erin giggles and shakes her head.

I rattle the parcel beside my ear. 'A Barbie doll?'

Erin chuckles. 'No, silly. It's a Boots set. Mummy says all girls like smellies.'

Danielle gives what I think is her first genuine smile, and my heart rate settles; I hadn't even noticed it was elevated. Danielle rolls her eyes dramatically. 'Oh, Erin, you always tell people before they have the chance to see for themselves.'

'I'm sorry, Mummy, I got 'cited.'

I grin as I open it with a flourish. 'I don't mind one bit, and Mummy was right, I *love* it, thank you.' I hold the Sanctuary bath set up to show Millie. My eyes are glistening, I feel the sting of tears. For once they are happy ones, but I can't cry — not here, like this. Crying might unnerve the kids.

Erin gives me permission to cuddle her, and her little arms squeeze tightly. She smells of strawberry shampoo and vanilla ice-cream. I could bottle that scent. I decide not to push Ava, but I stroke my hand down the back of her head, feeling her soft flyaway hair against my skin. After a while, Luca re-emerges and entices both girls with balloons. Ava looks up at Danielle, who smiles and nods. Erin takes her sister's hand and I watch them run from the kitchen into the hall.

Danielle waits until we hear the sound of them playing coming from the lounge. 'Don't read too much into this,' she says.

My heart sinks. 'I won't. Thank you, Danielle, for bringing them. It means,' I place my hand over my heart, 'so much.'

She nods towards Millie, who is standing close to me, protectively. 'You can thank her.'

I look at Millie. Danielle continues, and I face her while feeling Millie's comforting hand on my lower back. 'She fought your corner. She's been on at me for months. I wouldn't,' she shakes her head, 'I couldn't consider it before. But then last week she came to me, and she told me how hard you're working to sort your head out. She told me how much support you have—'

'I am. I do,' I interject quickly.

Danielle shrugs. 'None of that is why I'm here, or why I brought my daughters here.'

'Then why did you?'

'I know, Beth.'

I stare at her mutely, then impel myself to speak. 'You know what?'

'I know you've been visiting Celine. I know that you have been every week. I also know that Mum knows about it, that you made sure you had her consent first—' I sense Millie's eyes on me, feel the tenseness in her hand on my back increasing as Danielle speaks — 'and that you've been paying for Mum's therapy. I know you drive my mum—' she swallows; I'm sure she's battling tears — 'to the therapist and then you sit with Celine. Mum's off most of the meds now, and she doesn't drink. She's doing so much better; she's been able to help with the girls more and more since we moved in. I don't know if I could have managed like we were before. I know I owe you for that, we all do. What happened with Tom,' she spits his name out like venom, 'with his brother — none of that was your fault. I know that. Millie has been telling me how amazing you are, how much the girls would miss out by not having you in their life. She's told me about your relationship with your aunt. They don't have Celine, not really, not the way she is in the home, laid out like a living doll. They could have you, though. Maybe.'

'I'll do whatever you need. I'll take it as slow as you want. I promise I won't push things. I won't hurt them.'

'You'd better not. But seriously, it has to be slow, Beth, I mean it. And no "Auntie Beth" stuff okay, not yet. I'm not ready for that. They aren't either. They've had so much upheaval already.'

'I understand.'

She smiles and places her hand on top of mine. I stare down at our hands on the breakfast bar, surprised. 'Okay,' she says.

Danielle goes through to the lounge to check on the girls. I stand, turn towards Millie, and feeling overcome with emotion, I pull her into my arms. I hold her against me, and I don't want to let go. 'Thank you, thank you,' I say, the thickness of tears in my throat.

'Why didn't you tell me about Celine, and about Diana?' She speaks into my hair, her warm breath tickling my ear.

'I knew how much Danielle and her girls would need Diana. You saw the state she was in — she wouldn't have been capable. I wanted to help. It was the only way I could.'

'And visiting Celine?'

'I had to, Mills; please try to understand. I need to see her, to be there for her after what they did.'

She pulls me closer. 'I do understand.' She takes a breath. 'That's what scares me. You blaming yourself, it won't change anything, you know. Danielle was right — none of what they did was your fault.'

I don't answer. I simply hold her.

We hear Amer clearing his throat and we separate; I feel flushed, as though I have been caught doing something I shouldn't be.

'Beth.' Amer's at the kitchen door, his expression strained, and he's holding his mobile tightly. 'Dillon called. We're needed. A girl has been reported missing. She wants you and Millie to go talk to the family.'

My stomach drops. *Here we go again.*

CHAPTER TWENTY-THREE

Millie and I arrive at the teenager's home. It's a modest terraced, privately owned, by the look of things. There's no garden. A warped wooden door that has seen too many bad winters is to the left of the white PVC front door. It's one of those that has a small pathway behind it, leading to a tiny backyard. Depressing grey stone and concrete. It's little more than a space to store the wheelie bins.

'You okay?' Millie asks, as I park half on, half off the kerb.

'Did you see Danielle's face when we had to leave like that?'

She nods, solemnly. 'It must bring back memories of before, of Tom. It's probably also a challenge, because she is letting more cops into her life and she knows that can mean danger, worry. It's a lot for someone who's been through what she has.'

'What are you saying? Do you think I'm being unfair, wanting the girls in my life?'

She grabs my hand. 'What? No, not at all. She'll get used to it. She'll realize it's very different circumstances. For one, she isn't married to you, and you are not leading a double life or lying to her.'

I can't help thinking of Aaliyah's concerns for Millie. Is she keeping something from me? I am dying to ask her where she's been going, what she's been doing — but now is not the time. 'Thanks, Mills. Okay, let's go.'

I open my door, but pause to read a text that's just come through. 'One sec,' I look at Millie. 'Amer still can't get hold of Antonio.'

'Really?'

'Yeah. Apparently, he vanished while we were in the kitchen with Danielle. Amer reckons he seemed out of sorts, and then he went out the room and didn't come back. What's going on with him? This isn't like him at all.'

Millie sighs. 'I think this last break-up really got to him. He's finding it hard to move past whatever brought their relationship to an end. He seems so lost. I'm really worried for him.'

'Maybe so, but Jasmine Foster needs us all at our best. And Lord knows what we're about to walk into here. We need a solid team.'

Millie looks out of her window. 'It's hard, Beth, if you love someone and they don't love you back the same way. I'm sure he'll call Amer as soon as he sees the missed calls. Like you said, this isn't like him. Cut him some slack.'

'You're right. I'm stressed, that's all. I'm worried about how Danielle reacted before . . .' I almost tell her I'm worried about her, too, but stop myself. 'Anyway, come on — let's speak to these poor sods and pray to God it's not connected to Jasmine Foster.'

I press the doorbell; the loud, rhythmic chime sounds through the house. The door opens a moment later to reveal a stocky man in his thirties or early forties with receding hair. He's wearing a navy-blue work uniform.

'Mr Adam Collins?' He nods. I hold out my lanyard. Millie follows suit. 'Detective Chief Inspector Bethany Fellows and this is Detective Constable Millicent Reid. May we come in?'

He steps back and gestures for us to enter. He's wearing grey socks and his left big toe is peeping through a hole. There is a short beige carpeted hallway leading into a lounge with the same carpeting. A chocolate-coloured corner sofa dominates most of the room. An old-fashioned gas fire is on full blast — it's stifling.

A woman is sitting on the couch, worrying the necklace around her neck. If the outside of the house looked less than homely, the inside makes up for it ten-fold. A yellow waffle-style knitted blanket is folded across the back of the couch. There is an array of cushions with pictures of various woodland animals on them. There's one small dresser positioned at the edge of the couch; it is adorned with bronze animal ornaments. A large ornate stag takes centre stage.

'They're detectives,' Adam says. The weight of our rank sits heavily in the room. 'I'll grab some more chairs.' He walks into the adjoining kitchen and returns a moment later, carrying two chairs. He places them opposite the settee, then sits beside the woman I assume to be his wife.

Millie and I sit. I'm glad they didn't expect us to sit on the couch with them; that would feel too intimate. Right now, we need to be objective. This could all come to nothing. She could have snuck out with friends. Run away. Anything. Lord knows, I hope it's one of those options.

'Mrs Melanie Collins?' I ask, to clarify.

'Yes.' Her voice quivers.

I introduce Millie and myself once more, and note that Melanie swallows again, the movement stiffer and more intentional than before. 'I understand your daughter, Kelly, didn't come home. It was this morning you were expecting her, is that right?'

Melanie nods. Her breath catches, and a short, sharp sob escapes her lips. She clasps her hand across her mouth as though it was a betrayal. Her body acknowledging how serious this is. 'She was meant to be staying with her friend, but then when she didn't come home today, I got worried.'

She looks at Adam and grabs his hand. 'I'm not one of those neurotic-mother types. I didn't panic as soon as the sun came up. But look—' she indicates the lounge window, outside the streetlamps are coming to life — 'I tried her mobile but got nowhere, so I tried to call Fiona. That's her mate. She's ignoring my calls. Her phone's ringing out, then going to voicemail. I called Fiona's parents, and they said she's staying at her sister Chelsea's house. We called Chelsea, and she reckons Fiona's there, but she doesn't know where our Kel is. Fiona refused to talk to us, so I dunno what's gone on there. We assumed Kel would show up eventually but then it got dark again, and we . . . we thought we'd best call you. I mean, it's probably nothing. She'll most likely come walking through that door with her tail between her legs. Her brother is out looking for her. He has been all day.'

'Kelly is sixteen?'

'Yes.'

'How old is your son?'

'Max is three years older than Kelly. He was nineteen last month. He's worried sick. We all are.'

'Do you have any idea where Kelly might have gone? Who she might have gone with?'

'Not a clue. Max has already looked in the obvious places.' Melanie slips a tissue down her sleeve and into her hands. She wipes her eyes, then her nose, before wringing the tissue between her fingers.

'When exactly did you last see or speak to Kelly?'

'When she left to go to Fiona's. What time was it, Adam, do you remember?'

Adam drags his palms down his face. 'I dunno, I guess it was about seven, maybe half past. She shouted that she was off while we were watching *Emmerdale* on catch up. So yeah, that time abouts.'

'We didn't even see her off,' Melanie says. 'I didn't speak to her after that—' she looks at Adam — 'did you?'

He shakes his head. 'No.'

'You said you've tried Kelly's mobile?' Millie asks them.

152

Adam sits forward. 'Yeah. It rings out, then goes to answerphone. Her mum's left message after message. We've all tried it. Me and Max, too. She never lets it run out of battery. We've drummed it into her, the importance of having it, of being able to call us if ever she's in danger . . .' He chokes, as though his throat tightens around the sentiment.

Millie perches on the edge of her seat. 'Is this the first time she hasn't come home?'

Adam's brow furrows. 'Yeah. We don't stand for that sort of thing. I mean she takes the Michael sometimes; all teenagers do. But not like this.' He looks back at his wife. 'Right, love?'

Melanie Collins nods. 'She wouldn't just stay away like this, not for this long, not unless something was really wrong. She's not a troubled kid or anything like that.'

Millie smiles. 'I'm sure she isn't. I can see your kids are well loved. That this is a happy, family home.' Millie looks pointedly around the room, at the wall-mounted photographs of smiling kids throughout the years. She nods towards one of Kelly wearing cream jodhpurs, black wellies, a black riding helmet and standing beside a stunning brown horse.

Melanie follows Millie's eyeline and smiles, pride shining brightly. 'Kelly rides. She loves Delilah with a passion. Those two are bonded. We might not be rolling in it, but our kids are our priority. We do our best to help them realize their dreams, their potential.' She's talking ten to the dozen, trying to convince us they are good parents, already worried she's failed. 'Max used to be into football. He doesn't play much anymore. But he won a lot of trophies when he did.' Her eyes light up. 'He's at university now. First one in the family to go. Kelly is going, too. She already has a plan for her entire future. It's all mapped out. She's really got her head screwed on.' Her face drops, and her bottom lip is trembling. 'That's why we're so worried. This isn't like her. She just isn't rebellious, not at all. She would never worry us like this, not intentionally.'

'Has she got a boyfriend?' Millie is watching both parents intently. She's doing her thing, reading them. Inspecting the curves of their words, the things they don't say. The minute expressions that flicker across their faces so rapidly they would likely be missed by anyone else. It's Millie's speciality, and it is why Dillon will have insisted she be here with me now. Amer is already at the station, looking for any possible links between Jasmine and Kelly.

'Boyfriend?' Adam scoffs, before turning to his wife, doubt settling over him like a mass of grey clouds. 'She doesn't, does she?'

'No. She doesn't have a boyfriend.' Melanie looks at Adam. 'Really, honestly, she doesn't. I'd know.'

She seems convinced, but then I wonder how well she knows her teenaged daughter seeing as she is missing, and she has no clue where she could be. Parents often think they know their kids inside and out. In reality there are parts of their children's lives, hidden depths of their souls, that may as well belong to someone they have never met, and likely never will. As people age, they seem to lose the connection with their youthful selves, the way they lived back then conveniently wiped from their memories. It protects them from facing those aspects of their kids' lives they would rather didn't exist. Ignorance is bliss, until it becomes harmful.

'We will need Fiona's full name and contact information so that we can talk to her ourselves.' I take out my flip pad and pen and hold them poised. 'Do you know her sister's address?'

Melanie shakes her head. 'No. I have her mobile number, though, if that helps?'

'Yes, please,' I say, and jot it down as she reads it off her own phone. 'And her surname?'

'Smithy. She's got a different dad to Fiona. Fiona's surname is Thompson,' Melanie says.

They answer a few more questions, and then we leave the two worried-sick parents behind. I am still hopeful there is no connection to Jasmine. Even so, we have uniforms out scouring the streets, appeals going out on our own social media pages, as well as the Lancashire Evening Post's.

Considering Kelly's age, we are able to move fast and get the appeals online straight away. We will cover all bases and hope we end up with egg on our faces when Kelly Collins turns up sheepish and apologetic for causing her parents such distress.

Once we are outside, Millie stands holding her car door open as she looks back at the closing front door. 'What do you reckon?'

'I don't know. I think Dillon's right to be cautious. Better to throw everything at it and look like we've gone OTT than not to take action, and find out too late that we should have.'

'Agreed.'

I lean close to her, aware there could be flapping ears close by. 'Yeah. I'm hoping there'll be something new from Forensics. I'm gonna get Jed Armstrong brought back in tomorrow. I want to talk to him myself, and I want you in there with me. No offence to Amer, but I want to be sure nothing's been missed.'

'Okay, but I'll tell Amer it was my idea — that I want to talk to Jed.'

I give her a sideways look. 'You've noticed it too, then?'

'Amer being a bit put out by you? Yeah. He's just feeling insecure, that's all. He'll be reet. Even so, I reckon it'll be better if he doesn't think it's your call to bring Jed back in after he alibied him already.'

'Thanks, Mills. And it really isn't that I don't trust Amer's judgement, or that I doubt Jed Armstrong's alibi. A different perspective is always good, that's all,' I say. Then I add, 'I just hope this hasn't put his nose out of joint.'

'Dillon asking us to come here rather than him, you mean?'

'Exactly.'

'I'll try and talk to him. It's all his own hang-ups really. He's a good detective; he needs to trust in that more.'

'Thanks, Mills, and you're right. He is a good detective — a great detective, even.'

'And I get it. You wanting to talk to Jed again, I mean. It is worth seeing if anything was missed, or if he's thought of anything worth mentioning since he was last interviewed. I agree with you.'

I nod, relieved she understands. 'Good.'

On the drive to the station, I can't help thinking about what Millie's been through. How much she must have been hurting when she lost her baby. I won't tell her about talking to Stanley. I can't put that on her. Aaliyah's worries are now my own, and I need to find out what's wrong with Millie. My mind is so preoccupied I only vaguely notice the car behind taking all the turns I do. My breath catches.

Millie turns to face me. 'What is it, Beth?'

I take a sudden left, causing Millie to slide against her door. 'Sorry,' I say. I look in my rear view, the car is gone. 'I thought I . . . never mind.'

Millie twists to look out the back window, appearing worried as she settles back into her seat. I feel heat creeping up my neck and turn the radio on. I switch to a news channel in an attempt to drown out my thoughts and take the tension out of the moment. It's the weather forecast, and the peppy voice of the presenter defuses the tense mood.

We pull up outside the station and my mobile rings. 'Amer,' I answer, seeing his name on the screen.

'I'm coming out to you now,' he says breathlessly. 'I saw you pull up from the balcony.' He sounds panicked.

'What's happened?'

'There's a second missing girl.'

CHAPTER TWENTY-FOUR

The Ordinary Man

He drives to Mrs Howe's house with the radio on full whack. Rock music blasting through the car. The windows are down, and he has his arm outside, his hand pushing against the air. 'Wooo!' he yells. 'Wahoo! Fuckin' yeah!'

The lights ahead change from green to amber, so he puts his foot down and races through. He's pretty certain it's red by the time he crosses the line. He's always so careful, making sure he has no reason to end up in any police system. Not even for a speeding fine. Today, he can't contain himself. Life is for living. As he approaches Mrs Howe's, he slows the car and turns the music low. He dampens down his mood appropriately. Remaining professional at all times during working hours is vital.

He pulls onto the drive and spots Mrs Howe sitting in a deckchair in the front garden. She's overlooking the street; an ideal position for an old lady with nothing better to do than spy on her neighbours. She has a cup of tea in one hand and a women's mag in the other.

'Hello.' She smiles. 'I'm being spoiled today. Young Eleanor is looking after me. Brought me a magazine and everything. She's set me up out here, insists the vitamin D will do me the world of good. She's such a sweet girl; she takes care of me so well.' She's like a peacock fluffing her feathers with pride.

He steps down from the truck, leaving the windows down, and closes the door. 'Glad to hear it.'

'She will no doubt pop the kettle back on once she knows you're here.'

He smiles. 'That'd be lovely, thank you.' He heads for the truck bed and starts unloading the items he will need.

He gets to work, starting in the front garden so he can amuse himself watching Mrs Howe none-too-discreetly spying on the comings and goings of the street. She almost falls out of the chair a couple of times; she's straining her neck that far.

'Do you want another cuppa, Nan?' Eleanor stands in the doorway, her hair pulled back into a high ponytail, a ready smile on her face. His eyes linger over every inch of her, imagining his hands roving her body, his fingers squeezing around her neck. She notices him watching and her smile slips. 'Sorry, I didn't realize you were here. Would you like one too?'

'Thanks, coffee please.' He turns away from her, making a point of busying himself. The flush of being caught staring travels up his neck. Using the shears, he gets to work trimming back the bushes. He'll mow after they've had their drinks; otherwise, bits of grass and debris will end up flavouring them.

There isn't a great deal to do today; he's been so thorough lately that everything is already pretty neat and tidy. Being efficient and hardworking pays off, as far as getting him new clients goes. When it comes to his existing ones, it can be to his detriment in some ways. A lot of his competitors do a half-arsed job so they will be needed sooner and for longer.

He heads round into the back garden and sees that blasted cat sprawled out in the middle of the lawn, basking

158

in the unusually sunny spring weather. He grins as he envisions the mower cutting straight through the little fucker. He feels the sun's warmth beating against his face. Removing his T-shirt, he tucks it into the waistband of his blue jeans. It rests there, flapping against his leg as he walks. He works hard and fast. Sweat is soon trickling down the centre of his back, irritating him. He's attempting to reach the itch when Eleanor comes out the back door carrying his coffee.

He's sure he catches her blushing when she sees he has no shirt on. She walks towards him with the cup extended, as though she's afraid to get too near. 'Here you go. I didn't realize you'd be here, what with it being Sunday and all.'

As he wraps his hand around the mug, his strokes his fingers over hers. Slowly, softly he pulls the cup free from her grasp, his fingertips trailing her skin. 'Thank you.' There's heat between them; he can feel it. An electrical current — he can only imagine what it would feel like to press his body against hers. 'Ah, I sometimes call by over the weekend. You know, to keep on top of things for your nan. Plus, it frees up some time during the week for me.' He smiles.

'Fair enough,' she says, stepping back slightly.

He fixes his eyes on hers, unwavering, intense. She looks away, her body shaking as she turns and scurries back indoors.

A flurry of sensations come alive within him, and he knows he has to have her. Tending the roses, mowing the lawn, tidying the garden, everything he does afterwards is done with an unshakable image in his mind. More than an image, a movie. Life-size and real. Palpable. It's him and her, it's her and him, and it is his best yet.

CHAPTER TWENTY-FIVE

DCI Bethany Fellows

Amer, Millie and I are in my car en route to Fiona Thompson's house. She's Kelly Collins's missing friend. Amer has calmed down on the journey here. We managed to pull him from the brink of a full-on meltdown. This is unlikely to be down to Jasmine Foster's killer. To go from murdering one twenty-one-year-old woman to taking or hurting two sixteen-year-olds doesn't ring true. After having spoken with Kelly's parents, we are looking to maintain continuity and speak to Fiona's family, too. It may well be that we will soon be passing this investigation over to another team. Or, better yet, the girls will turn up safe and well.

I glance at Amer and open my mouth to speak, but he holds his finger in the air and pulls his jacket open, taking his mobile from his inside pocket.

'Damien,' he says. 'Tell me you have news?' Amer's eyes glisten. It's subtle, but it's there. Damien has something.

I look at Millie via the rear-view mirror and see she's craning her neck towards Amer. We're both doing our utmost to discern what Damien could be calling about. I pull over as soon as I can and endure the agonisingly long wait. As soon as Amer hangs up, he smiles.

'What is it?' I ask.

'That was Dr Sanders—'

'Well, yeah,' I say.

Amer skews his eyes at me. 'The swabs he took from inside Jasmine Foster's mouth—' he's almost breathless — 'it was concentrated alcohol, but not the kind you drink. Well, you certainly shouldn't. He's come across it before during PMs in prisons, hospitals. It's isopropyl alcohol.'

I look at him questioningly. Millie is doing the same, as she has now unbuckled her seatbelt and is leaning between the front seats.

'Rubbing alcohol,' he adds. 'Basically, once he broke the components down and identified them, she had hand sanitizer in her mouth.'

'What?' Millie says. 'Why? An attempt to poison her? But . . .' She shakes her head. 'It makes no sense. The brutality of her murder, she'd have died of those injuries long before—'

'That wasn't why,' I say, catching Millie's eye. Realization slowly dawns on her face, and I nod. 'He was trying to destroy evidence, wasn't he?'

Amer looks up and exhales, then adjusts in his seat until he is facing me. 'Damien found a minute piece of skin between her lateral incisor and her canine; he's kicking himself for not spotting it during his initial examination, but it was wedged tightly. He took another look once the swab results came back.'

'Is it enough to get a DNA profile?' I understand Damien will be full of self-recrimination, but right now all that matters is the answer to my question.

'He's hopeful, but it's a small skin sample. He's going to do his best. As soon as he has any results. *Anyway*, he will be in touch.'

During the rest of the journey to the Thompsons' house, we are all on pins. Like me, Millie and Amer are doubting whether these missing girls have any connection with Jasmine Foster. If they are simply off doing what kids do, worrying their parents sick and causing mayhem, then great, but it will be time away from an investigation that needs our full attention. I know Dillon is right, and we have to work on the assumption that there could be a link. We can't say that to the families or anyone else, but we have to be mindful of it. If we ignored the possibility, and were wrong, all hell would break loose. And rightly so.

Once at the house, Amer knocks on the door. Dean Thompson answers. He is not what I expected, which I immediately chastise myself for. He is wearing a smart grey suit and tie, his black hair slicked to one side. He's about five feet two inches, slim and wears wire-rimmed glasses.

'Come in,' he says, after we have shown our identification and introduced ourselves. His accent is southern, posh even. I am taken aback by him.

The house is a small end terraced. It's neatly kept externally and minimalistic on the inside. Given its location, I had jumped to judgement and expected the family to be a bit on the rough side. Nothing wrong with that, of course; I know plenty of rough diamonds. But Dean Thompson is not one of them.

In the long, narrow dining room sit two women. One I know to be Fiona's mum, Jeanette. She's the polar opposite of her husband: she's overweight with long blonde hair, and even while sitting down, I can tell she is a tall woman. Sitting beside her is a younger version of her, who I'm assuming must be the elder daughter, Chelsea. Aside from her narrower frame, she is the image of the older woman beside her.

Amer interlocks his fingers and rests his wrists on the table in front of him. Once the introductions are out of the way, Amer looks at Chelsea and asks. 'Why did you tell the Collinses that Fiona was with you?'

She looks down. 'I feel bad about that.' Her eyes drift to land on her stepdad, then her mum. 'Mum called looking for her first. I assumed Fiona must have lied and said she was staying at mine. I didn't want to drop her in it, so I said she was in the bath. I was mad as hell; I would have given her what for when I clapped eyes on her. I *will* give her what for. But then Kelly's mum called me, and I was stuck in a lie. I thought they must have been up to something together, but then when I saw the Facebook stuff—'

'You mean the missing person posts on Preston Police's page?'

'Yeah, the ones about Kelly Collins. I got worried. I called Mum and admitted that Fiona wasn't with me. That she never had been, and that I honestly don't know where she is.'

Jeanette's eyes widen, staring across at Amer. 'Has something happened to my daughter? You must think so, if you're here.'

'There is no evidence that something has happened to either of them. At the present time, they are simply unaccounted for. We will do everything within our power to find both Fiona and Kelly and bring them home as soon as possible.'

Dean stands up abruptly. 'You're twenty-two years old, Chelsea. It's about time you flaming grew up.'

Her face reddens. 'I'm sorry.'

'Well, this time "sorry" isn't enough. It won't bring your sister home safe.' He walks around the table, so he is standing at the top end of it, putting distance between him and Chelsea.

'I really am sorry. I didn't know this was going to happen. I didn't have anything to do with her lying in the first place. I wasn't in on it.'

Dean angrily shakes his head. 'You should have come clean as soon as your mum called. It's lost time. We could have been looking for her for hours by now.'

Chelsea attempts to take her mum's hand, but she snatches it back. 'No, Chelsea, he's right. If anything's happened to her . . .'

I sit straighter. 'This isn't going to help. Blaming each other never does. You need to be united,' I say. 'Do you have a recent photograph of Fiona?' I divert their focus. We have plenty of images from her Facebook account, but this will give them something practical to do.

'I do,' Chelsea says quickly. Picking her mobile up from the table, she flicks through images, then holds the phone out to me. 'I took it a couple of days ago. It's face-on, but it gets her whole body in, so you can see her height and build, too. It's a good one, isn't it?'

I nod, Millie and Amer glance at the image of the beautiful ebony-haired girl smiling coyly at the camera.

Dean scoffs, 'That's some help, I suppose.'

'Stop it!' Jeanette explodes. 'Enough! She's right—' she points at me — 'this isn't helping, you two being at each other's throats.' Chelsea opens her mouth, I guess about to protest in her own defence, but Jeanette shushes her and continues. 'Blaming each other. You're on about lost hours, Dean.' She glares at him. 'Get out and look, then. Sitting around here complaining about my daughter won't bring Fiona home.'

The atmosphere isn't any less toxic before we leave. There are issues in that household, ones that predate Fiona's disappearance.

I exhale loudly as soon as we are in the car. 'Well, that was tense.'

'It really was,' Millie says from the backseat.

Amer adjusts his seat to allow him more leg room. 'What are we all thinking?'

'That I hope they are off drinking or getting high,' I say. 'It would be preferable to what could have happened, or might *be* happening.'

'But do you think it's linked to Jasmine Foster?' he says.

I shake my head, pop the car into first and pull away. 'I can't imagine our guy taking two girls on. But then again, we don't really know him well enough yet to judge that for certain.'

'So, what *are* you saying?'

'That we need to keep an open mind about everything: these kids, Jasmine's killer, everything. We don't know what he's capable of yet, all we do know is that if Jasmine Foster was his first, then he's got a lot of anger stored up. For him to unleash that amount of rage on her, he either knew her and it was personal, or he's on fire with his need to do harm. If it's the latter, then I have no doubt there will be more.'

I don't voice all my thoughts. To do that, I would need to tell Amer and Millie that I fear Tom could be behind it. If it is him, then he's had years of practice, and he's also a trained detective. He'll know how to evade us, as he's proven to date. If this really is Tom, and he took those kids, then they are already dead.

CHAPTER TWENTY-SIX

By the time I arrive at Aunt Margie's, I am close to collapsing. I haven't called ahead; however, I fully anticipate seeing her on the doorstep, arms spread ready to welcome me in. She has supersonic hearing when it comes to the sound of my car pulling up. I need one of her hugs like a coffee fiend needs Costa.

The evening air is still and close as I step out of my car. The March weather has been uncharacteristically kind to us for the past couple of days, and it's unseasonably warm. I throw my leather jacket onto the passenger seat then lock the doors. I can't help feeling a stab of disappointment that she's not at the door as I'd expected. The house seems to be lacking the usual signs of life. I amble to the front door and try my key. It won't turn.

A slither of panic traces the length of my spine as I bend and peer through the letterbox. I can't see or hear anything. This is not like my aunt at all. I go to the lounge window, cup my hands against the pane and gaze through. I don't understand it. She wouldn't put her key in the back of the door and leave the bungalow. She couldn't — she wouldn't be able to leave it locked from the inside. It makes no sense.

My brow beads with sweat. I kneel in front of the letterbox once more. This time, I shout her name. There's no response. I grab my mobile and try calling hers. I hear her phone ringing from inside, but she doesn't answer. What's the point in having a mobile, for Christ's sake?

'Aunt Margie, it's me. Are you in? Is something wrong? Answer me.' I stand and pound the door, then press the doorbell repeatedly.

Eventually her neighbour, grumpy-old-man Ralph, appears. 'What are you doing? Do you know what time it is?' He pointedly shoves his sleeve up and arches his wrist in my direction. 'It's going on for eight in the evening. What on earth do you think you are doing?'

Aunt Margie has told me more times than I can remember that Ralph is as deaf as a lamppost. It's why she claims her music doesn't bother him. And yet here he is, giving me grief. What was it, the vibrations of my knocking that alerted him? Or the sense of impending doom that's pulsating from my body?

'She isn't answering,' I say, exasperated at his lack of care and the sudden re-emergence of his hearing.

'Well, that's obvious. Have you considered the possibility that she's out? In the bath? Doesn't want to see you? You're disturbing the entire street with this, this carry-on.' His face shakes as he speaks, his jowls wobbling. A wisp of grey hair at the front of his head flaps in the light breeze.

I'm not making that much of a commotion, surely? There would be more people out nosing if I was. He's just in a mood, and now so am I. 'She might be hurt in there. Have *you* considered that?' I say, feeling my face flame with anger, panic, stress.

My panic is escalating, and I'm on the verge of kicking the flaming door in when I hear the keys jangling and there she is, right as rain, standing in the open doorway with an incredulous look on her face.

'Jesus, Beth, what's going on? You'll have him raging about me at his flaming neighbourhood watch meeting again.'

Ralph turns, huffs, and slams the door. I stare at Aunt Margie, disbelievingly. She never locks me out, never. What in the hell is going on with her? 'Why were your keys in the back of the door? Why didn't you answer?' Tears of relief prick the backs of my eyes. I am so close to the edge right now that I can smell the sea beneath the cliff.

'Am I not allowed to have some me time?' She shakes her head. 'What's the matter, Beth? You look shook up.'

'Well, yeah, you nearly gave me a heart attack. I thought you were lying unconscious in there or something.'

'That was your first thought? I locked the front door, and you couldn't get in, so I must be half-dead? Talk about calamitizing.'

'It's "catastrophizing". And I wasn't. I was scared. Scared for you—' I peer around her, looking up the empty hallway. 'So, are you gonna let me in, then?'

She looks behind her, then back to me. 'Well, I—'

'What?' Aunt Margie is always the first to pull me into her arms, to make me a hot chocolate, to tuck me up on the couch. 'Is something wrong?'

The intense worry is back, dread darkening my thoughts. I gently use both my hands to reposition her nearer to the wall, so I can squeeze past. I stalk up the hall, through the empty lounge, then into the kitchen. I don't know if I expect an assailant to be lying in wait, a guy behind the kitchen door clutching a knife or a gun. But I didn't expect what I actually find.

'For God's sake, Beth,' she calls, before following me into the kitchen a moment later. 'Can't I keep anything private?'

'What is this?' I ask, gesturing to her little yellow kitchen table that has been dressed in a posh tablecloth and fancy placemats. It's set with her best plates, polished cutlery, and sparkling wine glasses. There are even candles lit in the centre. And no sign of a flamingo mug or her teapot. What the hell?

'What do you think it is? Don't act dense. It's bad enough that him next door has decided to poke his nose into why I make my every move and complain about it. Now my own child is here doing the same.'

'I'm complaining about nothing.' I look around the room, then walk to the doorway, past Aunt Margie, and peer back into the empty lounge. 'Is someone here?'

'No.' Blushing, she throws her hands up in the air and sits at the table, looking like a child whose classmates have bailed on their party. 'I feel foolish now. What am I even doing?' she tuts. 'Silly old mare.'

She seems to shrink into herself. I feel embarrassed for her, realizing she must have been stood up. And just look at the effort she's made. I want to find this Lothario scumbag and wrap his balls around his throat. She deserves someone who will at least show up; she deserves to be flaming worshipped.

I sit opposite her. 'Oh, Aunt Margie. I'm so, so sorry.'

'For what? Gate-crashing? Showing me up?'

'It's nothing to be ashamed of. You put yourself out there; you will do it again. You deserve someone in your life. Whoever—' I use my arm in a gesture to encompass the table — 'this was for, well, he didn't deserve it.'

'What are you talking about, sugarplum?'

'Well, he obviously hasn't shown up, and—'

There's a crackling noise, followed by a deep, French-sounding male voice. 'Margorie, my darling.'

I almost jump clean out of my skin. My mind instantly recalls the postcard I received from Marseille in France. Surely not? I twist to see a handsome black man with salt-and-pepper hair staring back at me from the computer screen. 'And who is this beautiful lady? Bettany?' He pronounces my name wrong, but I must admit it sounds better with a French inflection.

I narrow my eyes. I don't understand what's going on. I look at Aunt Margie, who suddenly looks less like a birthday girl with no party guests and more like a smitten teenager. 'Aunt Margie?'

'Beth, this is Maurice. Maurice, meet my niece, Bethany.'

She never calls me Bethany, never. I look at her questioningly, waiting for her to explain, but all I get is gooey eyes and an impish grin.

'It is surely my pleasure, Bettany,' he says.

It's much later wherever he is. France is only one hour ahead. He isn't in Marseille. My heart rate settles slightly, but I remain on high alert. He's sitting in a garden. There are a few lantern-style lights hanging from an expensive-looking trellis. There's the flickering of a flame shining against his face, reflecting in his eyes. I can see trees behind him, and I am fairly well convinced he isn't anywhere in France, and certainly not in Britain, either. The trees are a mixture of gorgeous-looking palm trees and ones with stunning flaming red flowers.

'Where are you?' I ask, before realizing how rude I sound. My mind joined dots at the sound of his accent, drawing parallels out of coincidences, and I'm now rushing to rearrange my thoughts. 'And, yes, lovely to meet you too, Maurice.'

He laughs, light-heartedly. 'I am in sunny Mauritius, my dear.'

He must be on a laptop, because his face nears the camera until all I can see is his cheek, then he lifts the laptop. The movement of the screen is reminiscent of the *Blair Witch Project*. He swivels it around so we can observe his surroundings. He is sitting outside the most stunning white-bricked building, with huge glass windows and doors. There's a balcony, and there are spotlights under the rim of the roof. It's gorgeous. As he turns the screen, I see where the flickering firelight is coming from; he is sitting in front a pale-grey circular stone firepit. Logs are burning in the middle of it, the flames dancing in the centre.

'Wow, you have a lovely home,' I say. I mean it, but I still don't grasp what this is. At least he isn't linked to Tom, to those postcards. Anything is better than that.

'I met my Maurice during my Zumba classes.' She grins at him; I have never heard her call a man "my" anything before. 'You remember, the ones I've been attending online? They are such lovely ladies, my Mauritius sisters. And then, along comes Maurice. The only man in the entire class. We hit it off. So, we decided to spend time together without the others.' She's speaking to me, but her eyes are focussed on Maurice and his on hers. 'We've been talking for a while now. He is a lovely, lovely man. You are, Maurice.' She chuckles, girlishly. I've wanted her to meet someone for such a long time, but this feels strange to me. Regardless, she's gushing, happy. 'We cook dinner and eat together. Same meal, sadly not in the same place. Yet.'

The "yet" worries me further. I don't want my aunt to be taken for a ride. I can't exactly vet this guy, when he doesn't even live in the UK. I can't help worrying that it might not be his house. That Maurice could be lying about who he is. And that my dear aunt could be about to become the victim of some sort of love scam.

But I look at her face and decide to put aside my concerns for the time being. 'What time is it there?'

'He's four hours ahead,' Aunt Margie answers. 'We take it in turns to be the night owl or early riser.' She's grinning like she's holding a winning scratch card. I glance at the plates. They're all pristine. I can't smell food. Aunt Margie follows my line of sight. 'We're having a takeaway this evening. Biriyani. It's a traditional Mauritian dish.'

'I'm gonna go and leave you two to it,' I say.

I'm cautiously happy for her. I have reservations, but her happiness is clear. If he's making her feel that way, then who am I to put a spanner in the works. He'd just better be for real. I haven't seen my aunt light up like this since . . . well, I never have. If he is setting her up, I won't be accountable for my actions. I am itching to offload about my case, but there's no way I am bringing Aunt Margie's mood down with talk about missing and murdered girls.

Aunt Margie holds my wrist. 'You can stay for some dinner, Beth. There'll be plenty.'

I stand up. 'No, honestly—' I turn to face Maurice — 'it really was lovely to meet you. Be good to my aunt; she's a wonderful lady. One of a kind.' I can't quite mask the warning tone that slips into my voice, and notice Aunt Margie raise her brow.

'Of course,' he says, obliviously.

I lean down and place a light kiss against Aunt Margie's forehead, inhaling her typical scent of face cream and Charlie Blue perfume. 'Have a nice evening. I love you.'

She grabs my hand, hers gripping tight. 'Are you okay, sweetheart?'

'Yes, yes, I was just stopping by. Honestly, Aunt Margie, I'm fine.' I smile, doing my utmost to keep the truth from my eyes.

I came here tonight for the comfort I always seek during any struggles. But my lovely aunt deserves to be happy. I need to sort my own problems out.

By the time I get home, it's almost pitch-black outside. The streetlamp near my home is flickering again. I'll report it tomorrow, if and when I get the time. Then I give myself a ticking off: I'll *make* the time. Good lighting is paramount to security. I look up and down the street before turning my back on it to put my key in the lock. I hear rushed footsteps and spin. A jogger flies past me, adjusting his earphones. My breathing settles a little, but I look up and down the street again, sensing someone there.

I look up at the camera I had installed on the outside of my house. It's pointing at my front door; I'll check the footage before I settle in for the night. There's a pile of mail on the mat, and I steel myself for another blank postcard from Tom. Relief floods me as I shuffle through the usual bills; there's no postcard. Then again, perhaps he wouldn't send one if he was here, in Preston. If he is the person responsible for Jasmine Foster. In the kitchen, I set the kettle to boil and then do the rounds of my house: opening every door, checking every room, wardrobes included. I lie on my stomach to peer beneath the beds. I leave no possible hiding place unchecked.

Finally, brew in hand, I sit in front of the computer screen and play the footage from the security camera. Once I start yawning, that's it — my eyes are streaming, and one yawn merges into another. I'm exhausted. I move through the footage as quickly as possible, speeding the content up — past the postman, the Amazon delivery woman. I slow it down again as night falls. I sit up straighter; I can just about make out the shadow of someone moving beyond the camera's view. I can see their silhouette on the side of the fence. They are there and gone in a matter of seconds. It was most likely someone innocently passing by, but they piqued my attention. As I rest my hand over my chest, I can feel the hammering of my heart.

CHAPTER TWENTY-SEVEN

It's Monday afternoon, and what we had all hoped would happen hasn't. Neither Kelly Collins nor Fiona Thompson have come home. They have been missing since Saturday evening, and so far, no one has heard from either of them.

Millie and I watch Jed Armstrong leave the station. The interview with him yielded nothing. As far as the investigation into Jasmine Foster goes, he has been eliminated from our enquiries. He's never heard of Kelly or Fiona, and so he had nothing of value to offer either investigation. Mills having the ability to really "see" people, she's convinced me Jed Armstrong is not hiding anything. It was worth a shot. A desperate attempt at clawing something from the depths. The water is deep and vast, and we're fishing for minnows. Millie advised Amer she wanted to speak to Jed herself, to get a read on him. He accepted her explanation without argument. If I had said the very same thing, he would have been irritated.

Millie and I stand together in the staffroom; she's making us both a strong coffee and I am waking my ass up after sitting for the best part of an hour.

Millie heaps a large spoonful of Nescafé into each mug. 'I'm getting a really bad feeling about Kelly and Fiona.' She adds sweetener and hot water, the steam rising in a plume before her face.

'Me too.' I take the mug she proffers. 'It would have been so much easier if Jed Armstrong was guilty, and the girls are hiding at a friend's place.' I sigh.

'The longer they're missing, the more unlikely that is — there are posts being shared all over social media. Someone would have said something by now, surely?'

'You would think, wouldn't you? Kids can be arseholes; this might all be a bit of drama for them. I mean, you used to work with them; you know that.'

The colour drains from her face. I shouldn't have brought that up. Millie's reasons for leaving her career as a therapist for troubled kids is not an easy topic for her. She loved what she did, working at a school dedicated to kids with issues. She was bloody good at it, too. But then there was a kid who she couldn't save, the outcome was disastrous, and I know she still blames herself for it. She probably always will, no matter what anyone says to the contrary.

She takes a drink of her coffee. 'Jed might be a bit of a Jack the Lad, but he's no murderer,' she says, changing the subject. 'What was done to Jasmine was brutal. He wouldn't be capable. Plus, his alibi is solid.'

'And we're saying he didn't pay someone to get it done for him?' I'm grabbing the straws and clutching, even though I know how far off I am.

'No, I don't think so.'

I blow across the liquid and take a sip. 'I know. If only that was the case. I still can't help but think . . .' I let my sentence trail off and blush under Millie's scrutiny.

She shakes her head. 'There's no evidence it's Tom.'

I rub the nape of my neck with one hand and grip the handle of my mug with the other. 'There's also no evidence it isn't.'

Millie puts the milk into the small fridge to her right, then looks at me. 'I know this case is getting to you, Beth. I understand why you're thinking what you are.' Her eyes search my face as if she can see beneath the layers of skin and read words written there. My soul etched onto a scroll. 'Is it getting too much for you? You need to be honest if it is. It would be completely understandable, and—'

I cut her off: 'Please, Mills, don't you start with all that. I'm fine. I wouldn't be here if I wasn't. I came back because I'm ready.'

She cocks her head to one side, arching her brow.

'I am,' I say, with conviction. 'Me considering him as a possible suspect has nothing to do with my state of mind.'

She leans against the counter. 'Have you spoken to Toby Evans yet?'

Blood rushes to my face. It pumps hard and hot in my ears. I haven't told her about having to see the station counsellor. Gossip must be rife. Dillon won't have said anything; she wouldn't be so unprofessional. Our office walls have bloody ears, all right, and a great big fucking gob. I am so annoyed, I realize it might show on my face, and Millie is on the receiving end, unfairly. She cares about me. Of everyone in this building, I can be sure that Millie has my best interests at heart. Then again, her question pretty much insinuates I am barking bloody mad in thinking this could be Tom.

'Yes, I've seen Toby Evans. Like I said, I am ready to be here. Me mentioning Tom, a known murderer who is MIA, is not so far-fetched, surely?'

'I'm not saying it's far-fetched. I'm saying he would have had to change his MO after all these years, and while that's not likely, it is also not impossible. If we follow the evidence and it leads us to him, then good. Two birds, one stone. I'd love to get him off the street, to not have to worry about you every waking moment.' She gasps. 'Sorry, I shouldn't have said that.'

'What, that you worry about me?'

'I know you hate it when any of us worry for you, Beth, but we love you. Jesus, when I saw you with Sigmund — when he had a knife to your throat, I . . .' She swallows, tears glistening in her eyes. 'Losing you would have killed me. I can't bear to think of Tom out there, and knowing he might come after you. I can't breathe when I think of what could happen.'

I reach out and take her hands in my own — they're clammy. I can't maintain eye contact with her; instead, I look down at our hands clasped together. Beads of perspiration tickle my hairline. 'I don't know what to say.' Slowly I raise my eyes to meet hers. My pulse quickens further as a heat rises within me, my chest swelling with the sensation. Our gazes are locked; our breathing quickens.

Millie steps closer, her body only a couple of inches from my own.

My heart is racing. The door opens and the tension is broken. Millie drops my hands and steps back.

Amer stands in the doorway, his face ashen. 'There's a body.'

CHAPTER TWENTY-EIGHT

Amer looks green around the gills at the news. The Brander case took its toll on all of us. We saw the worst of humanity and were faced with the unpalatable truth that we had unwittingly worked alongside such evil and been clueless. We'd allowed the devil into our home and given him the freedom to roam.

'Farmer found the body off Lightfoot Lane. Forensics are on their way. There's a uniform guarding the area; she's cordoned it off. But she said she's as sure as she can be that it's a kid, a teenager. It has to be one of the girls. It must be.'

'Body face down again?' I ask.

Amer nods, his hand massaging the side of his forehead. Amer having young children of his own means cases like this hit harder. A shovel right between the eyes. He'll look at the victim and see his newly nine-year-old daughter Sara, or his twelve-year-old son Rayan. Knowing there is evil out there willing to do harm to the most innocent of us is incomprehensible. 'It's PC Louisa Milligan at the scene.' He shakes his head, his expression solemn. 'She says it's a mess.'

'What do you mean, a mess?'

'She didn't want to interfere with the scene, but she said it was obvious she was beyond help. There was no point having a paramedic trampling the area. They had a divisional surgeon attend — she confirmed life extinct. Louisa says she could see enough, and that . . .' His face is pallid.

'What, Amer?'

'She said she was in a state. The body, I mean. She'd been hurt very, very badly. Maybe worse than Jasmine, by the sounds of it. If it is the same perp, he's upped his game. If this is one of the girls, where's the other one?'

'Jesus, I dread to think.' I sit down next to the table and swallow the same sickness that rises from my guts to my throat, choking me whenever a case gets personal. And I take nothing more personal than a murdered child. 'Shit.'

'Dillon wants us out there ASAP. Then once we know who it is, we need to speak to the parents before they hear it from somewhere else.'

I sigh. 'Fucking hell. I really hoped they'd be okay. That they were runaways, up to no good. Anything but this.'

Millie pours our coffees down the sink and quickly rinses the mugs. I can see her hands shaking, but say nothing. 'We'd best get moving,' she says. 'You want me as FLO?'

'Thanks, Mills,' Amer says.

Millie being the family liaison officer is the best option. Not only can she be there to look out for anyone appearing on the scene who seems suspicious, but she's met the families already. There's a pre-existing relationship of sorts between them. It's a seedling now, but by the time this case is over, it will be an orchard.

I trust Millie more than anyone with the hearts of the families. She'll know when to step in and when to step back. She'll pass on any information pertinent to the case, even if they don't realize they've revealed anything. They will leak it through their tone of voice, their expressions, their behaviours, and she will see it like no one else can.

I don't envy Millie the job she does. We all work these cases, but to get that close to the bereaved, the emotionally wrought and injured, is another level of self-flagellation. Being able to remain sane while submerging herself in the insurmountable grief of families whose loved ones have been ripped away by an act of violence is an ability I will never develop. Each case I work chips away a piece of my armour. With every new case I am less protected, more open to pain, to infection.

I think about the photographs I've seen of the girls, of the love and worry I have seen on their parents' faces. I can't wish one of them alive, because that will mean wishing the other one dead. But we've had no other reports of missing teens. Whichever one it is will be frozen in time, and her parents will no longer have a daughter. We are going to hand-deliver a bomb into their home, into their hearts, then we are going to have to detonate it.

As for the other, where the hell is she? Did he take them both? Why wouldn't they be found together? My stomach clenches, imagining where she could be, what she could be going through.

I grab my leather jacket from the coat stand beside the door. Slipping it on, I pull the belt tightly. I've lost weight; only now is it clear how much.

Amer moves nearer to the door. 'Mills, I'll call as soon as we know who it is,' he says, before walking out into the main office.

We are standing in front of the exit door, next to reception. Amer holds it open. I look back towards the MIR, watching as Millie vanishes inside. There will soon be more photographs and notes filling the whiteboards in there. There's no confirmation yet that it is the same person responsible for murdering Jasmine Foster, but I am certain that it is.

* * *

Amer and I arrive at the scene, a secluded area off Lightfoot Lane. I can't imagine anyone walking in this lonely, dismal place, especially a sixteen-year-old girl who lives nowhere near here. 'Must have been brought here. Driven. Kidnapped, maybe.'

A young female PC stands clutching a folder in her gloved hands. She sees us approach and smiles weakly while nodding her acknowledgement. We sign in with PC Louisa Milligan, then she directs us to the box of forensic wear. We are about to put on the forensic gear when I spot Hannah Edwards approaching. I see other crime scene investigators moving within the cordon, laying yellow markers wherever they find evidence.

Hannah passes beneath the tape of the inner cordon, strips off her forensic wear, then places it in a box to the side of her. Even from this distance, I recognize her by her ample bosom and the distinctive way she walks. Hannah will be coordinating her team, making sure all bases are covered, and with the utmost integrity. Nobody can attend more than one scene for fear of transferring evidence, either material from one scene to another or their own DNA. All staff have their DNA and fingerprints on file for exclusion purposes. The scene where Jasmine Foster's body was discovered has been closed, which is why Hannah is now able to attend here. Hannah is the best at what she does, and I trust her implicitly to get it right and not to miss a thing.

She dashes over, ducks under the outer cordon and heads us off. 'Hey guys,' she says solemnly.

Hannah appears stricken with a ghostly pallor and a sadness in her eyes I seldom see. Hannah is seasoned; she deals with terrible situations all the time. Kids always affect us deeply, but I get the feeling there's more. Something else is turning my friend inside out and leaving her raw.

'Han, what is it?' I look around, doing a quick recce to make sure there's no one within listening distance.

The fields allow for a decent view in all directions. It's secluded but fairly open. Our guy must be familiar enough with the place to be confident he wouldn't be seen. Or at least, to know that the chance was slim. I'm guessing he's a local. He has to know the area. It's the only thing that makes sense.

Hannah's tongue rolls around the inside of her lip, causing it to protrude from one side to the other repeatedly. It's a nervous habit I've started noticing recently. It makes me want to grab her and pull her into a hug.

She moves closer to the two of us. 'I needed to step away,' she whispers. 'I couldn't . . .' Her voice trails off, her hands are shaking, her bottom lip is doing a Mexican wave, demonstrating her extreme distress.

I take her hand and clasp it within both of mine. If Hannah couldn't take it, then I can't imagine what state the kid is in. What this sicko has done to her.

'Han, why did you need to step away? I'm not picking or anything, I completely get it, but you just don't do that.'

She stares down at her hand in mine, avoiding looking me in the eyes. 'How bad?'

Her eyes remain averted. I watch her take a breath, composing herself. She slowly raises her eyes to meet mine, and there is new steeliness there. 'We need to nail this bastard, Beth. He needs to be off the streets *now*. Whatever it takes. I don't give a fuck if some vigilante cuts him to pieces. In fact, I hope they do. He's a monster. Worse than I've ever seen.'

Hannah has a tendency to waffle, and normally I would butt in, cut her short. This time I let her speak, allow her the time and room to purge herself of the darkness clawing its way into her mind.

I wait until I am certain she's done. 'Han, what's been done to her?'

She pulls her hand free from mine, then clenches both fists by her sides. 'He tortured her brutally. He showed that kid not a single, minute ounce of mercy. I can hardly believe I am saying this, but—' she's shaking her head, disbelievingly — 'it looks as though he *grated* her. Fucking grated her, Beth. I mean what the fuck?'

Revulsion ripples through me, and a surge of vomit rises in my throat. 'He did what?'

Amer angles his neck forward, his eyebrows knitted together. 'What the hell do you mean, he *grated* her?'

Hannah shrugs, resigned to the inevitability of revealing what has been done. It can't be changed now; all we can do is react.

Hannah looks pointedly between us. 'I mean, he literally grated her. He left the fucking cheese grater behind, tossed it beside her body. Her back has been savaged by it. I can't imagine the pain, the terror. Her final moments must have been so hellish, dying would probably have been a relief. That poor child. And her parents. How the hell are you going to tell them what's been done to her? How will they ever get past this? I don't think I will, and she's not my kid. But she is a kid. Just a child, and this fucking sadistic prick has killed her in the most torturous way I have ever seen, and I've seen some shit. Sorry, I know I'm going on, I know I am, but I can't believe what I've just seen, or what I'm going to have to continue to see. Never in my career have I wondered whether I can do it, follow a case through, work a scene to completion. This time, I wondered. But coming out here, taking a minute, walking past my colleagues, some of 'em barely out of college, I know I can't pass the buck on this. I hope Damien has a stronger constitution than I do.'

Dr Sanders is on route at Dillon's request. The pathologist doesn't always attend scenes, but sometimes it's necessary. Sometimes a scene needs to be witnessed personally, to be felt, absorbed. If the case is a particularly trying or complicated one, then we might implore the pathologist to attend.

If this is the same perpetrator who murdered Jasmine Foster, then he is just getting started. He's escalating in levels of violence. If we don't unmask the monster, he will retain his power. An unknown entity is so much more fearsome. We need to lift the mask, show his ugliness. Take away his power. Bring him in and lock him up for the rest of his miserable life. This guy won't stop of his own accord. He won't be rehabilitated, or have an epiphany and become Mr Nice Guy. He's the devil, and the only way he'll stop is if he's dead or behind bars. Personally, I don't have a preference.

'Do we have a preliminary ID?' Amer asks.

Hannah nods. 'Yes. It's Kelly Collins.'

'Jesus,' I say. 'Then where the hell is Fiona Thompson?'

CHAPTER TWENTY-NINE

Millie and I arrive at the Collins' terrace at almost exactly the same time. Kelly had identification on her. Both Amer and I have seen enough photos of Kelly to recognize her body. This is the worst aspect of my job. Bringing this kind of news to anyone's door is bad enough, let alone to the parents of a teenager. My heartbeat trembles in the base of my throat.

Together Millie and I walk with leaden steps up to the white PVC front door. I sense Millie's anxiety levels rising in time with my own. I spot Melanie Collins in the window; I recognize the moment her expression transforms from one of hope to one of sheer horror. She turns away from the window and shouts something, I hear the tones but not the words. I have a flashback of arriving at Rose Danes' parents' home with this very same news. A moment later, Adam Collins opens the door. His feet are planted slightly apart, his hand is flat against the wall — it's as though he is physically bracing himself for impact.

I clear my throat. 'Can we come in, please?' I ask, ensuring my tone is gentle. I feel the colour draining from my face.

He steps back, allowing us to enter. There's a teenaged boy standing at the top of the hallway, beside the entrance to the lounge. I gather he must be Kelly's nineteen-year-old brother, Max. He has dark hair swept to the left. His fringe hangs over one eye. He flicks it out of the way, but it moves back instantly. As he walks into the lounge, he repeats the movement, his fringe winning the battle once again. He sits next to his mum on the couch and pulls her into his side. Adam slowly lowers himself onto the corner settee beside his son. This time, he doesn't fetch chairs for me and Millie. We are intruders on this family; they instinctively know we are not bringing them good news.

'What's happened to her?' Melanie's voice quivers. Her fingers dig into the material of Max's jeans.

'I have some very difficult news.' The thudding of my heartbeat in my throat intensifies. There's no way to soften this blow. 'I am so sorry to tell you that we have found Kelly's body.'

I get no further before Melanie's animalistic cry of agony erupts. An almost otherworldly caterwaul of utter heartbreak and torment spills from her lips, slicing through the air. Tears stream down her face. She looks completely stricken — her grief is palpable.

Max folds his body into itself, his hands clutching his ankles, his head hanging low as he wails. Adam stands on shaking legs, virtually staggering until he is in front of his wife, where he slumps to the floor and kneels at her feet. He is sobbing as he pulls her forward and cradles her head against his shoulder. After a while, his cries become a breathy hiccup. His shoulders quiver with the effort to restrain his torment, to be strong for the remaining members of his family. He holds Melanie close, as though he is attempting to absorb her grief.

I walk through to the kitchen and grab a couple of chairs, then carry them through to the lounge in silence. Millie and I sit and wait for the temporary passing of the storm.

Eventually, as though a grey mist is lifting, Adam separates from his wife and turns to look at us. 'What happened to her?' he asks. His expression is desperate. He wants us to tell him she died peacefully. If he can have nothing else, he wants that at least. For him and his family. Some kind of solace, but I am unable to offer it. All I have is the truth, and it is brutal.

'We believe she was murdered.' The best way is to be direct. Dancing around the truth only prolongs the torture. 'I am so very, truly sorry.'

My words hit akin to bullets through their hearts. I see the moment of impact, listen as Melanie's cries escalate into hysteria. She's shivering wildly, her face blanched, her teeth chattering. She's going into shock. The best thing we can do for her is get medical attention; she needs sedating. She'll be no use to us like this.

'Millie.' I look at her, then nod in Melanie's direction. Millie stands and walks into the hallway to make the call.

We need a positive identification from a family member. I can't bring that up now, not with Melanie like this. I'll wait it out. Help will be here swiftly, and then I will ask Adam to do the unthinkable and confirm that the body we have found is his daughter. We already know it is, and this formality seems cruel to me. It's necessary, but how I wish it wasn't. I won't reveal the extent of her suffering, though in time, they will need to be informed. The court case, God willing we will have one, will go through everything in excruciating detail.

Melanie might well accompany Adam to see her daughter one last time, or she might come later, after the official identification. Neither parent will be able to hold her; they won't even be allowed to be in the same room as her. There will be no holding her hand, kissing her head. Not until after the post-mortem, after her body has been officially released by the coroner, and by then, it might be too late. She might well be beyond what is deemed appropriate for in-person visits.

I listen to the sound of the front door opening, hear hushed tones as Millie advises the paramedics. They come through in their green uniforms, eyes heavy with the knowledge of why they are needed.

'Hi, my name is Nick,' the blond man says, as he crouches beside Adam but looks directly at Melanie. 'I am going to give you an injection to help you, okay? This is my colleague, Sue.' He nods up towards the gangly woman standing behind him.

The rest happens rapidly, the injection calming Melanie almost instantly. Her face slackens, her features loosening into a baggy show of grief. Her eyelids are leaden and drooping. Max and Adam ease her into a lying position on the couch. Max dashes upstairs before hurrying back with a quilt, which he wraps around his mother. He kisses the top of her head, as I imagined her doing to Kelly given the chance. Melanie is hiccupping on sobs the entire time.

'Shall we go into the kitchen?' I suggest, as I stand from my chair and lift it without invitation. Millie follows suit and we head through, followed by Adam and Max. The paramedics leave quietly, their moods sombre.

Once we are seated around the small circular table, Max gulps a few desperate breaths before saying, 'I thought I was going to find her. I thought she'd be okay. Was it Fiona? Did they have some sort of fight? Or is she . . .' he falters. 'Is she okay?'

My throat tightens around the heartbeat. 'Fiona is still missing, but no, we do not believe she is responsible.'

'Then where is she?' Max demands.

Millie shakes her head. 'We are doing everything we can to find her.'

Adam bangs his fist onto the table, making it shudder. 'Like you did everything you could to find my child?'

He sucks in breath after breath for a few minutes, Millie and I waiting until he is calm enough to proceed. Rage blazes in his eyes.

Finally, Adam's breathing settles. The waves of anger emanating from him dissipate and he places his hand on top of his son's. Adam looks at me and Millie, his face weary. 'What did they do to her? You said you don't think it was Fiona. Why? Was she . . . did he . . .' He looks at Max. 'Go and sit with your mum, son.'

'No, Dad, I wanna hear this. I need to know too.'

'Not this. You don't need to hear this. Please, son, go in the other room.'

Max shakes his head and pins me with his eyes. 'He wants to know whether she was raped.' He faces his dad. 'Don't you? That's what you were trying to ask, right?'

Adam nods, fearfully.

'We haven't completed her post-mortem yet. I'm sorry I can't give you the answers you want yet.'

Adam glares at me. 'You think I *want* these answers? I want my daughter home. I want her here, now, alive. Laughing, being a cheeky madam, being an arsehole — I don't care, I just want her here.'

'I wish we could give that to you,' Millie says. 'I am so sorry we can't, but what we can do is everything within our power to find the person responsible and put them in prison. We can help by making sure they are punished.'

'So, if you don't know whether she was raped, then what makes you think it isn't Fiona?' Max asks, his eyes narrowed.

He's smart, reading between the lines. Finding meaning in the things we aren't saying.

'We can't disclose any further information right now, but—'

'We've seen the news,' Max interrupts me. 'We ain't stupid. Was it the same person who murdered Jasmine Foster? Is that why you don't think it's Fiona? Has he got her too? Is she next?'

I can't have rumours like that starting; Amer and Aaliyah are with the Thompsons now, explaining what's happening. I can't imagine the fear they will feel, the panic. 'I understand why you are making assumptions and looking for answers, but please don't talk about any of this with anyone. It won't help our investigation, and all that matters right now is finding who did this to your sister and looking for Fiona.'

Max folds his arms on the table and places his head in the centre. 'I get it,' he mumbles.

Adam chokes on a sob. 'Post-mortem.' His eyes are wide, as though it has only just registered. 'You're going to cut my baby up. You're going to destroy her.'

It is always such a difficult concept for a newly bereaved family to comprehend. 'I'm so sorry; we have no choice but to carry out a post-mortem. I assure you it will be done in the most respectful way possible. There are questions only a post-mortem can provide the answers to. We need those answers so we can bring the person responsible to justice.' I am dancing around the truth, that it was a violent death, that she is already destroyed.

'Are you sure it's her? I mean, I know this sounds horrible, but what if you've got them mixed up? What if it's Fiona, and my Kelly is still out there somewhere?' There's a spark of hope in his eyes, the last sparks of an ember.

'We will need an official identification from you, but we are certain. I've seen her myself. I'm so sorry. Millie will accompany you to do the identification. She'll be with you to talk you through it, to support you. Will you want to wait until Melanie is well enough to go with you?'

Max shakes his head vigorously. 'No way. I'll go with him. Mum can't do that — have you seen her? I'll do it.' His shaking hands bely his bravery.

'It's okay, son. I'll be okay. Your mum will need you with her at home. I'll do it on my own.'

Max looks towards the door leading to the lounge, then back to his father. He's torn between two impossible choices. 'No, I won't let you do that.'

Adam sits lower in his seat, the weight on his shoulders unmanageable. 'When?'

'We'll be in touch soon, as soon as possible. But in the meantime, I have this.' I retrieve the evidence bags, one containing Kelly's bank card and the other a necklace with a horse pendant. I hold them in front of Adam. He appears to stare right through them, unable or unwilling to connect with the reality that this is happening.

Then I see it hit him — he can't continue lying to himself. That last spark of hope that was in his eyes dulls to nothing. Snot bubbles from his nostril. His eyes shine with tears that gather and bulge as he attempts to hold them at bay. It's a useless battle, and they soon cascade down his cheeks, running over his trembling lips, down his chin, dripping onto the table. 'She never took that off.'

He stands unsteadily, then walks to the wall. He pulls his arm back and throws a punch so hard his hand vanishes into the plasterwork. Max looks at his dad, then at the pendant. Max collapses from his seat and curls into a ball, keening. His family is broken beyond repair. His sister is dead.

CHAPTER THIRTY

I sit in my car, letting the grief wash over me. Millie has stayed on with the family, offering what comfort and information she can. She will be talking them through the official identification process, attempting to prepare them.

I spot the response to the email I sent Damien earlier and click to open it, holding my breath, then feeling nauseous at his response. He hasn't yet got a DNA profile from the piece of skin he retrieved from Jasmine Foster's teeth, and it's driving me insane. According to him, the sample is so small it increases the timescale and the precariousness of running tests. But if he can get a useable DNA profile, we can run it against Tom's. He's an ex-cop; he's in the system. We'll know for sure then, one way or the other. Frustration makes me want to scream. I clench the steering wheel with one hand and my mobile with the other.

My phone rings. The sound and the vibration make my heart almost leap out of my chest. I'm like this even all these months after the Brander investigation, when I'd received texts and calls from the killer. I had no idea who I was dealing with when that started. This time, I can't shake my suspicions that it's Tom — we just need the DNA test, then I'll know. We all will. Amer's name is flashing on the screen.

'I'm on my way back in. How did it go at your end?' I ask.

I hear him exhale. 'She turned up while we were there.'

I fumble, almost dropping my phone. 'What?' I say, once I've steadied it in my hands.

'Fiona Thompson, she showed up like nothing had bloody happened.'

'You're joking? I mean, it's fantastic that she's okay but . . . where the hell had she been?'

'She'd argued with Kelly apparently, on Saturday night, after that she wandered off and eventually went to her boyfriend's. Her parents didn't know he existed until today. She admitted it when she realized matters with Kelly were serious. The parents went from relieved she was unharmed to furious about the lies and unnecessary worry — then back again. I doubt the rollercoaster is over yet.'

'Yeah, and I'll bet there's a lot more bloody drops on the one the Collinses are riding right now. Jesus. Does she know about Kelly?'

'I told the parents before she came home. I didn't want to give much away, especially not when you were only just telling the family, but I felt it necessary to give them some idea of things. I didn't want them hearing it through the grapevine and thinking it was Fiona.'

'Have you got the boyfriend's details?'

'Yeah, she gave them up without too much prodding. She's coming in tomorrow morning for an interview and to provide a statement about the last time she saw Kelly.'

'We need to look into the boyfriend: how old he is, whether he was with Fiona the whole time. We need to find out if there's any connection at all between him and Jasmine Foster. How old is he?'

'Beth,' he says, 'all that is in hand, don't worry. He's seventeen, only a year older than the girls. No previous run-ins with the police. Not so much as a caution for littering. He's clean as a whistle.'

'That doesn't mean—'

'I know, I know. But he lives with his parents. They were home the entire time.'

'Didn't they see the posts online? They didn't think to contact us and—'

'Beth,' he almost snaps. 'She was hiding in his bedroom. They had no idea she was there. We'll be confirming that, along with everything else. If he left that house, we'll find out. If he had anything to do with what happened to Kelly or Jasmine, we'll find out. I know you're likening this to the Brander case, but you need to stop. We have to keep open minds and clear heads. Okay?'

I clench my mobile and take a breath. 'Okay.'

* * *

Fiona Thompson is waiting in Interview Room Three with appropriate adult Sharon Holten. Fiona's boyfriend Robert Sinclair is being interviewed simultaneously in Interview Room Six. We already have his movements on the night detailed. He is not personally responsible for what happened to Kelly or Jasmine. Another brick wall. I just hope we get some golden nugget from one of these interviews, something that will move the investigation along.

Amer stands by the door, his hand over the handle. 'She's a bag of nerves, though she's doing her best to hide it. She's trying to look tough. Remember, she's just a kid.'

'I know that,' I say, insulted — what does he take me for? 'Okay. Let's do this.'

He opens the door, and sitting at the far side of the table, staring straight at me, is a blast from the past. It smacks me in the face like iced water thrown up from rough seas. She could be Jenny Lambert, a kid I interviewed during the Brander investigation. I don't know whether I am drawing comparisons that aren't there, but I feel it regardless. She's leaning back in her chair, cockiness personified. Her legs are stretched out, her arms crossed defensively across her chest.

Sharon Holten's white permed hair has grown since the last time I saw her. She's as cuddly and as maternal-looking as ever.

Fiona's black hair skims the tops of her shoulders, her brown eyes wide and glaring. She sniffs loudly. 'I didn't know anything bad would happen when I walked off. I didn't know.'

Amer sits down, simultaneously pushing two buttons on the tape recorder. 'I'm Detective Chief Inspector Amer Anwar. Also present is . . .' He looks at me.

'Detective Chief Inspector Bethany Fellows,' I say.

Amer picks it up again. 'We will be recording this interview both audibly and visually. We are interviewing Fiona Thompson. Accompanying Fiona is . . .'

Sharon leans forward, talking into the recorder. 'Sharon Holten, appropriate adult.'

'I'm sorry,' Fiona mutters.

'We understand that, Fiona.' I offer her a small smile. 'We're here to get as much information as possible, to help us understand what happened to Kelly Collins. All you have to do is answer everything as honestly and fully as you can.'

She swipes her long sleeve across her eyes, then under her nose. 'I will, I promise.'

'Good girl. Now, firstly, when was the last time you saw Kelly?'

Tears streak her face. 'We were hanging around town. We fell out because she wanted to go home after she'd already lied and said she was staying at mine. I told them—'

'Who's them?' Amer asks.

'My mum and dad. I told them I was gonna stay at her house, Kelly's. But really we were going to sneak into Rob's — my boyfriend's — house and stay there. I wanted to see him, and if Kelly went home and told the truth, then I wouldn't have been able to, and her parents would have probably grassed on me. I was scared and I was mad, so . . .' She trails off, sobbing.

'What happened, Fiona?' Amer asks.

'I told her she was a wimp, a rubbish friend and that she was just a jealous cow. I was horrible to her. I'm sorry. I want to be able to tell her I'm sorry.'

Sharon Holten sits straighter. 'I think perhaps Fiona would benefit from a comfort break.'

I grit my teeth. 'Do you need a break, Fiona?'

She shakes her head. The relief I feel is palpable, and I sense Amer relaxing a little beside me. 'I want to help,' she says, her voice shaky.

'Thank you,' I respond. 'What happened after you argued?'

'She stormed off. I followed her and said something like "don't be like that" and she told me to eff off and leave her alone. I was really angry, so I said, "fine then" and I walked away. I shouldn't have. I was stressed, because I thought she might go home and tell her parents, and then they'd call mine and it would all kick off. They aren't even that bothered about Rob. I thought they would be, but they aren't. None of this had to happen. This is my fault, isn't it?'

Once again, she reminds me of Jenny Lambert, I shake my head and inch closer to her in my seat. 'It isn't your fault, Fiona. You didn't hurt her, did you?'

'What? No, of course not.'

'Then it isn't your fault. Where were you exactly when you were in town?'

'We were hanging around the Flag Market, drinking and stuff. Rob was coming to meet us after he finished work. He does deliveries on his moped for a takeaway in Fulwood. I just wanted to stay with Rob, and I used Kelly, so I had a way to do it without anyone finding out. She's soft, so I knew if I just lied and said I was at hers, and my mum or dad asked her about it, she'd fold. I needed her to have a reason to lie, too. I thought if she was with me, she'd be scared to get found out — I thought she'd have fun, too. But it was selfish. I'm so fuckin' sorry. Oh my God, I am so, so sorry.'

She crumbles as she lays her head on the table and curls her arms around herself. The force of her cries cause her body to rock, vibrating like the start of an earthquake or the threat of a volcanic eruption. Her distress is powerful enough to filter through everyone in the room, making us burn with sorrow and rage for what has befallen Kelly, Jasmine and everyone who loved them.

Sharon places a hand on Fiona's shoulder and keeps it there. We will get a last known sighting and state of mind from Fiona, but no more. We will be able to check CCTV in the area, and be more precise in our search; with any luck we will strike it lucky. I can't imagine it, though. A killer like this one won't take chances. He will be clued up; he'll have chosen a CCTV dead area. I have little doubt that we will not catch him on camera, not unless he happens to have passed a dashcam or video doorbell. Those eventualities are much more difficult to foresee, and they are also much more difficult to procure.

We are at the start of our investigation, and already we have two bodies. The brutality of the killings and the area both girls were last seen lead me to believe we are hunting one killer. He isn't yet a serial killer, by definition. One more victim and he will be. I will do everything in my power to stop him before he can be given that accolade.

CHAPTER THIRTY-ONE

Dillon ambushes me as I walk into the office on Wednesday morning. Her expression conveys her mood and it's dark. 'Beth, a word. My office. Now.'

I follow behind her, practically having to jog to keep up. Chloe gives me a look of empathy as we pass. My stomach hits the floor.

Dillon storms around her desk. 'Door,' she snaps. I close it quickly, and turn as Dillon slams into her seat, then indicates the one opposite her. 'Sit.'

My nerves are shot. 'What's going on? Have I done something wrong?'

Her eyes are throwing flames at me. 'Have you?' she huffs, and snickers. 'Really, Beth?'

I wrack my brains and only one thing shakes free. I swallow. 'Toby Evans.'

She claps her hands together. 'Give the girl a sticker, for Christ's sake, Beth, it was a condition, a very serious, important condition of your return here. What the hell are you thinking?'

'It's only been one—'

She holds a hand up, silencing me. 'Don't give me "it's only been one missed appointment", blah, blah, blah. One appointment is enough. Toby has been trying to contact you since. He didn't want to flag it right away and get you in trouble. More fool him. I told him, *any* problems, *any* concerns whatsoever . . .' She waves her hand. 'Anyway, the point is this, you either go to your appointment at five p.m. today or you're off the case.'

I open my mouth. 'I mean it, Beth. Off the case, out of this office, potentially, out of the force entirely.'

My eyes widen in alarm. Dillon's expression softens. She seems to come down from hysteria to just mad, which I'll take. 'You have to engage, Beth, you must. Toby had hoped you'd be in touch before his hand was forced. I called him earlier, after . . .'

'After what?'

Her eyes flicker away.

'Dillon, after what?'

'Some concerns have been raised. I am not going to start naming names. I won't have you going all gung-ho, trying to pin the blame on someone else for your situation. You have to talk to Toby, Beth, or I really will pull you from this investigation, and neither of us want that.'

'Who complained about me?'

'That's not important.'

'It is to me. I have to be able to trust my team. Especially after—'

She holds out her hand. 'See, this is exactly why you need to talk to Toby. You are focussing on Tom; on the fact you didn't see what he was. None of us saw it, Beth. Are you going to start doubting us all, doubting yourself? Are you going to suspect all your colleagues? Because that is not tenable to a successful working environment.'

'I don't doubt my colleagues. I don't doubt myself. But if I can't trust everyone implicitly anymore . . . well, can you blame me? Do you trust everyone?'

'Yes, I do. I trust my colleagues. I have to. You do, too. We put our lives in each other's hands every day, so unless someone in particular gives me a reason not to trust them then I will. I must. And so must you.'

'I don't know if I can.'

'Which is precisely why you must see Toby today as planned. I meant what I said, Beth, I don't want to pull you from this investigation, especially not now we have another victim — with relationships formed. The families deserve continuity. They also deserve the very best minds to be working these cases, and you're top of the list. You know you are.'

I can't help a small smile. 'Okay. I won't miss another appointment without good reason.'

'Even then, you can run that reason by me first. I don't care if you have to ring me mid-surgery while having your appendix removed. I want full disclosure at all times, understood?'

'Yes, but, ma'am?'

She waits me out.

I smile. 'I had my appendix out when I was eight.'

She blows out an exasperated breath and shakes her head while pointing at the door. 'Out, now.' She shakes her head, tutting. 'For pity's sake.'

Once I reach the door, her words still me. 'Anything you find, bring it straight to me. And one more thing: DS Niall Grant wants you to see Stanley Baker again. I'm not happy about it, Beth, not one bit. I won't lie, we had a rather heated exchange — but the upshot is, if you are willing to do it, then he still wants to proceed. Apparently, what Baker has given up to you has been the most he's said since his incarceration.'

I nod, without turning around. 'Then I'll do it.'

'Another reason this therapy is vital to you, Beth.'

I leave without another word and with my stomach in knots.

CHAPTER THIRTY-TWO

I arrive at Toby Evans's office at five to five. I don't dare risk pissing Dillon off by being late. I steel myself and knock.

'Come in,' he calls.

I open the door. He's sitting in his wheelchair behind his desk. He smiles. 'Beth. Lovely to see you at last. Do come in.'

Is it just me or do I detect sarcasm?

'Please.' He gestures to the chair opposite him.

'Well, you did call DS West,' I chide. I smile, then attempt to settle into the seat. I readjust myself a couple of times, but give in and remain uncomfortable.

He rests back in his seat and puts his hands behind his head. He looks reminiscent of a cocky teenager, and it rubs me up the wrong way. He's watching me in silence; I know this trick. Allow the silence to linger until the other person feels compelled to talk — to take away the awkwardness. Millie has taught me well. I've used the same method myself countless times. The difference being I used it on suspects and witnesses, not a detective.

'So,' he says eventually. I hold back my smile of accomplishment. 'I'm glad you could make it today. I understand the investigation is very demanding, and that this isn't necessarily convenient for you. It's probably not what you would consider time well spent, either.'

I shrug. 'Yes, it's a very demanding investigation.' I turn and glance at the clock on his wall. It's barely a minute after five. The ticking sounds loud and intrusive, impossible to ignore. His slicked-back red hair isn't as neat as normal. A couple of strands are sticking up.

He runs a hand over his head. I refocus on his face. 'Look,' I say, exhaling slowly, 'you're right, I don't think this is the right way to spend my time. But I'm here. I have no choice; we both know that. So, cards on the table: what is it I need to do? What do you want?'

He sits straight. 'It's not about meeting my needs, Beth; it's about understanding yours and meeting those. It's about you being healthy up here.' He taps the side of his head. 'You coming here isn't for my benefit.'

'Then how do you suppose you can help me? What is it you think I need?'

'What do *you* think you need?'

This time, I take a moment and actually consider his question. The sooner I engage, the sooner this will be over. 'I suppose if I'm being completely honest, my anxiety has been a bit . . .'

He cocks his head slightly. 'What, Beth?'

'Heightened. I feel like I'm constantly on high alert.'

'Okay . . . do you think you need to be? You're a detective. Surely being alert to possible dangers is necessary.'

'Well, yes, of course, but I mean about everything. I jump to conclusions. I struggle to trust people. Even people I know I should trust.'

He grabs a notepad and pen. 'Do you mind if I make a few notes? I will type them up and file them, then destroy this copy afterwards.' He looks at me. 'You have my word.' He didn't offer these assurances last time.

I nod. 'Okay.'

'Thank you. Now, about this lack of trust, are we talking friends, family, colleagues, people you meet within your line of work?'

'All of the above, I guess.' I watch as he jots something down. Frustratingly, the writing is small, slanted and upside down.

He notices me attempting to read his notes and smiles knowingly. I couldn't make out a word anyway. 'DS West tells me you have been finding your current case challenging?'

I frown. 'That's not strictly accurate. All investigations are challenging, especially ones like this one, but that doesn't mean it's any more challenging, if you know what I mean. DS West has had someone in her ear.'

'Hmm, are we back to the trust issue, do you think?'

'No, she told me she has. One of my colleagues has been complaining about me. Why whoever it is didn't just come to me, I don't know. It's what I would have done.'

'Perhaps whoever it is was just worried about your well-being, about the investigation—'

'I'm not harming the investigation.'

'I'm not suggesting you are. But you must see that you're a formidable detective. You were DSIO on the Brander investigation — approaching you could have been an intimidating prospect.'

'So, you're saying whoever it is, is a coward, anyway.'

He shakes his head. 'No, that is not what I'm saying at all. I'm suggesting that perhaps going to DS West seemed like the preferable option.'

I roll my eyes. 'Same thing if you ask me. Regardless, I am not struggling with this investigation any more than anyone else. Okay, so I have suspicions that Tom Spencer could possibly be behind it — I don't think that's such a leap. In fact, I think it's bloody short-sighted not to give the idea serious consideration.'

'What do your colleagues think of the possibility?'

I scratch at the edge of his desk with my fingernail. 'They admit it's possible, but I don't think they reckon it's plausible. This killer hasn't used brands, for one thing. But there are other aspects that do tally . . .'

'Such as?'

'It's an active investigation, Toby. I can't really divulge that.'

'I understand. How about you tell me how you would feel if it was Tom Spencer?'

I stop scratching the table. 'Relieved, if we caught him. These poor kids would be dead either way. It's not like we can bring them back; obviously I would wish them alive and well, if it were possible. But seeing as this is where we are, then if it did turn out to be him and we hauled him in, that would be it. Both cases would be solved, and he would spend the foreseeable rotting in prison where he belongs.'

I almost let slip about the postcards I have been receiving that I am certain are from Tom, even though every last one is blank. Who else would send postcards from around Europe and have nothing to say? It must be him. I haven't received any since the one from Marseille, which is only adding to my suspicions.

'That would be one brother dead and the other in prison, along with your father.'

'I've said this already: they are not my family. Blood does not make a family.'

'Maybe so, but technically they do share your DNA, and that must resonate on some level.'

I think again of the piece of skin Damien is attempting to extract DNA from. I'm itching to check my mobile for any updates. 'Not really, no.'

'What about Thomas Spencer's daughters,' he looks at his computer, reading something. 'He has two? Erin and Ava?'

'Yes.'

'Your face changed when I mentioned their names.'

'Oh?'

'Yes, you.' He smiles broadly. 'Lit up. It was good to see, Beth.'

'I saw them recently. Their mum, Danielle, brought them to see me on my birthday. Millie arranged it.'

'There you go again, glowing.' His eyes glint. 'Is this something that will be continuing? Contact with the children?'

'I hope so, yes. Though we got a call about a missing girl and had to leave, and . . . I saw Danielle's face. She was . . . ' I shrug. 'I dunno, sort of wrong-footed, I guess. I don't know how me being a detective will sit with her, after Tom. I'm worried about getting closer to the girls and then her pulling back. What that would do to me; even worse, what it could do to them. They've already lost their dad — they're too young to understand what he is, that they're better off without him. Having someone else in their life whipped away could compound their feelings of abandonment. I don't want to be the cause of any pain for them.'

'It might take time, but you and Danielle have both taken a huge step forward in your relationship. Take that as a win.'

I smile. 'That's down to Millie.'

'You glow when you mention her, too.'

I blush. 'This anxiety,' I say. 'I feel like I have a heartbeat in my throat, strong, hard, and sometimes it steals my breath. It's starting to remind me of how I used to be, years ago. Back then, I had therapy. It was useful in the end. I remember using coping mechanisms, but I'm struggling to implement them now, for some reason.'

'Okay.' He leans towards me. 'What you are talking about with regards to your anxiety, is the fight-or-flight response. It's the body's reaction, coping mechanism if you will, to extreme stress. Your mind is struggling to process a situation, or your thoughts and feelings. I've noticed while speaking with you that you jump ahead and worry about what hasn't happened yet, and possibly never will.'

'I'm a detective. I anticipate.'

'Maybe so, but in some instances anticipating is not useful, it's detrimental. When you talked about things you're worried about, such as Erin and Ava getting hurt in some future hypothetical scenario.' He's making me feel neurotic. 'I noticed you talked faster, your breathing quickened, your body tensed. Your whole demeanour altered.'

I hate to admit it, but he's right. I still feel slightly breathless. 'What can I do about that?'

'You can utilize a little mindfulness.' He smiles. 'I see by your face you think that's pie-in-the-sky nonsense. You're sceptical, aren't you?'

'Sorry, but yes, I am. It sounds like something my Aunt Margie would recommend. I'm not one for sitting on the floor with my legs crossed, humming, and choking on incense fumes.'

'Then it's a good thing that I'm not suggesting you do that.'

'What are you suggesting?'

'I want you to keep an open mind for a moment.' He smirks. 'I realize that's a tall order, but please try.'

I laugh. 'Okay.'

'Imagine a box. Can you see it?'

I squint. 'Yes.'

'I want you to breathe in through your nose, slow and steady — as though you are breathing as your eyes travel up the side of the box. One. Two. Three. Four. Okay, now exhale through your mouth, slowly, across the top of the box. Good. Now follow the shape of the box, go down the other side. In, one. Two. Three. Four. And across, breathe out. Good. Good. Do that until your breathing evens out, until it slows and feels steadier. Until you sense yourself relaxing.'

I carry on for a couple of minutes, my chest loosening, my lungs filling and feeling lighter somehow. 'Wow, I think that actually worked.'

He smiles. 'Good. Now, whenever you feel yourself getting worked up, if your anxiety is heightened, as you said, if your breathing is fast, do that. Take some time out, find a quiet spot — it can be your car, an empty room, the loos, a quiet corner, if needs be. Just somewhere you can go, where you can concentrate on slowing your breathing.'

I don't mention the impracticalities. 'Okay, thanks.'

'There's another exercise you can do, to bring you back into the moment. To stop this—' he waves his hand upwards — 'escalating thought process. The next time that happens, I want you to feel around yourself, to really concentrate on what you can feel. The chair beneath you, how does it feel? Really focus on it. The floor beneath your feet. You could even remove your shoes and socks, dig your toes into the carpet.'

I cringe. That sounds rank.

'Okay,' he chuckles. 'If that doesn't sound appealing, keep your shoes on.' He runs his hand over his desk. 'How does the desk feel?' He reaches out and grabs a stapler. 'This, how solid it is; as I hold it, the metal bit feels cold, smooth. I want you to find five things you can physically feel, focus — on those at the exclusion of everything else. Utilize your five senses. So, touch, smell, sight, sound, taste. You get the idea?'

I raise an eyebrow. 'And if there's nothing to eat, you want me to go around licking windows or witnesses? It might be frowned upon.'

'Hmm, yes, very funny.' He smiles. 'So, that's your homework. Got it?'

'I'm not an imbecile. Yes, I've got it. So, we done?' I grin.

'No. Not so fast. We still have some time.'

I turn to face the clock, frowning. 'Oh, so we do.'

'I understand you have now had your first visit with your fa . . . Stanley Baker?'

I nod. 'Yes.'

'How did it go?'

'I'm not at liberty to divulge information from an ongoing investigation. You know that.'

'I'm aware. But I didn't mean in that regard. What I meant was, how did you feel about it?'

'As you would imagine. I hated being in a room with him. He makes my skin crawl. He's a revoltingly evil, disgusting excuse for a human being.'

He jots something in his pad. 'There's certainly no love lost there, then?'

I raise my top lip in distaste. 'Would you expect there to be?'

'No, I wouldn't. But if there was . . .'

'There isn't.'

'But there are feelings other than love, Beth. There's intrigue, wonder, loss, grief, sadness, anger, rage. There are a whole host of feelings one can associate with a parent-child relationship. Yes—' he holds his hand up — 'even one when the father has never acted in that capacity and never will.'

'I can relate to the anger and rage. The rest, nah. Maybe add disgust and shame into the mix, though.'

'Shame?'

'In a way.'

'In what way?'

'That we come from the same DNA pool — me, him, Tom and Simon.' I could bite my own tongue off for referring to him as "Simon" again.

'Their actions are not your shame.' He might not have mentioned me calling Sigmund "Simon", but I can infer from his expression that he noted it. His pen furiously scratches across the paper of his notepad. 'Has he kept to his end of the deal? You don't need to go into specifics, but has he opened up to you?'

I'm really not sure I like Toby Evans having any access to this type of information, but then I remember all the comments about my lack of trust. 'Yes.'

'And that is going to negatively impact his situation, I assume?'

'With any luck.'

'Then he must value you, in his own way.'

I couldn't contort my face into one showing more distaste if I tried. 'If you say so.'

'Have you considered asking him more about your mother, about what happened to her? You must be curious.'

'That would afford him power over me. It would offer him some semblance of importance in my life. He is nothing to me, and I want him to never doubt that.'

'Wouldn't it be worth it to get the answers to questions you have been asking your entire life? Would it be worth it to your aunt?'

I pause. 'She hasn't asked that of me.'

'Does she know you're visiting with him?'

'I am not visiting with him. I am questioning him as part of an ongoing investigation. It isn't the same thing. I would never, ever visit that man.'

'But does she know?'

I shake my head.

'Does Millie know?'

Again, I shake my head. 'I haven't told anyone. It's a need-to-know situation.'

'But Millie is important to you.'

'Which is exactly why I haven't told her.'

'Don't you think she would want to support you through this? That your aunt would, too?'

'I haven't been there to support them recently. It wouldn't be fair for me to ask that of them now.'

'I really don't think they would see it that way.'

'They wouldn't, but I would. I do. Moving on . . .'

He glances over my head to the clock. 'Saved by the bell, Beth. Same time next week?'

I stand and stalk to the door.

'Beth?'

I spin to face him. 'What?'

'Remember the techniques I taught you.'

I eke out a smile. 'I will. Oh, and—' I look at the top of his head — 'you might want to add another handful of the gel you love so much.'

He pats his head. 'Ouch, that was harsh. Thanks for the advice . . . and, Beth?'

'What?' I say, through gritted teeth.

'Sometimes your gut instinct is spot on. Even so, trust is important to anyone. It is especially important to an officer on the front line. A lack of trust could put you in just as much danger as trusting too much. Be careful.'

CHAPTER THIRTY-THREE

The Ordinary Man

He holds Kira's hand as they walk into St Georges Mall and head up the escalators. She's squirming and dancing like a whirlwind on the end of his arm. Laurie's dragged her foul mood out with them. He'll have to buy her something, too, if he's going to coax her out of the doldrums of FOMO. God forbid she miss the latest episode of *Loose* frigging *Women*.

'So, Key, fancy a milkshake and a donut? Any kind you want.' He holds her hand high as she leaps into the air at the top of the escalators.

'Yes, Daddy.' She wriggles until her hand is free before darting ahead.

'Key, slow down, you're gonna run into someone.' He winces as she narrowly misses taking out some old dear's walking stick.

'Doesn't exactly look sick, does she? One look at her leaping around like a flaming gazelle and we'll be fined,' Laurie whines.

'For God's sake, I told you if it comes to it, I'll sort it. Just relax will ya, enjoy the day. It's Friday anyway; just think of it as a long weekend.'

Laurie huffs and slows down outside Marks & Spencer. 'Fine.'

He hangs back until Laurie catches up with him, then links her arm. 'Tell ya what, how about we grab a donut, treat Key like I promised, and then we'll have a nosey for something nice for you to wear? A new outfit, coat, whatever you want.'

Her eyes light up and she grins like the Cheshire Cat. 'Thanks, babe.' She cuddles into his side.

He wraps his arm around her and pulls her closer before kissing the top of her head. 'Just wanted to treat my girls today; so sue me,' he says.

'The school or the cops just might.' She can't resist throwing a jibe back at him, but this time, it is said with a lighter touch. There's less of a bitter undertone.

Kira vanishes past the green signs and into Krispy Kreme. He releases his hold on Laurie, and she shuffles into a booth while Kira races up to the counter. He follows and stands beside her as she licks her lips while appraising the variety of iced donuts.

He watches her eyes widen. Her small hands are splayed against the display cabinet. After a moment, she presses one outstretched finger against the glass, the tip bending. 'That one, Daddy, the pink one with spwinkles.'

'What do you say?' He smiles down at his daughter.

'Please.'

'There's a good girl, now off you go. Sit with Mummy, and I'll be there in two ticks.' She skips away and he turns back to the woman behind the counter, who is sporting the dodgiest perm he's ever seen. 'The pink one with white chocolate sprinkles. Two coffees, two glazed and a strawberry milkshake, please.'

There is a radio sitting on the shelf behind the counter. He strains to listen as the news comes on. He can barely make out what is being said. His pulse quickens and his temper shortens. He wants to ask Dodgy-Perm to turn the volume up, but he can't risk creating suspicion, so he keeps quiet. A couple of old-timers appear behind him, chatting away to one another. He is pissed off at first, thinking they will make it impossible to hear the news, when he catches the tail end of their conversation.

'Yeah, they said so on the news. Two bodies now; it gives me the shivers. No matter what they say on the news, it must be the same sicko. It has to be. Whoever did it could be here, now.'

He remains staring ahead, waiting for his order, but he can't help his smile. He's amused that two old ladies could be so on the money. *Could be here now.* He almost laughs.

His order is placed on a tray in front of him. 'Thanks, darlin',' he says, smiling. He pays and turns, grinning at the oldies. 'Here.' He grabs a fiver from his pocket and passes it to them. 'Have a brew on me.'

'Really?' one of them says, while the other is all too quick to snatch the note from his hand.

As he walks away, he hears them chatting about what a nice man he is. The woman behind the counter agrees enthusiastically. Nothing like sharing the love. He smiles as he slides into the seat next to Kira, opposite Laurie.

'Did you just give those old women money?' Laurie narrows her eyes at him.

'Yeah, so?'

'We ain't won the lottery, have we?'

'It was a fiver for a couple of brews, love, not a three-course meal in Gordon Ramsay's restaurant, ya tight git.'

'Yeah, well, it's not like we know them. Why bother?'

'Where's the harm? I'm in a good mood, Laurie. Don't spoil it, will ya?'

'I wasn't trying to. I just don't get what's got into you today. You high or something?'

'Ha bloody ha, can a man not just be in a good mood these days, without it being second-guessed? Anyway, did you hear the news?'

'What news?'

'On the radio just now. The old women were on about it, too.'

211

'What's that?'

He hadn't heard the radio himself, but he's itching to talk about it. The need is churning him up inside. His chest is fizzing with barely contained excitement. 'There's been another body found. They reckon it could be a serial killer.'

'Bullshit.'

'What do you mean bull—' he glances at Kira — 'poo?'

'I've seen enough crime documentaries to know a serial killer has to have at least three victims. So far there's been one, maybe two, if it's the same person. So, no, not a serial killer.'

He clenches his fists beneath the table and grits his teeth. 'Well, get you, Mrs flaming Marple. One more and he's a serial killer.'

'Or she.'

'What?'

'Could be a she. Why are you assumin' it's a bloke, ya sexist pig?'

'It's always a man.'

'Aileen Wuornos, Joanna Dennehy, Rose West, Myra Hindley . . .'

It feels like his stomach acid is searing its way through his skin. 'You spend too much time on your—' he leans across the table — 'fat, lazy lard arse in front of the TV.'

Laurie sits back, her face aflame. Kira scoots up the seat away from him and presses herself into the wall as though she'll be able to leak into it.

'You horrible bastard.' Her voice is steel, but he hears a quiver snaking its way around the syllables. Her hard exterior has developed fault lines. 'How is it you can be so bloody nice to everyone else, but you're hideous to me?'

He smirks, places his hands on the table and leans close to her again. Kira is shaking beside him, so much so that for a moment he thinks the bench is moving. 'Yeah, well, that's because you're a minging pointless waste of space. We all have our crosses to bear, though, eh?'

'Daddy, stop it,' Kira cries.

He looks sideways, catching sight of his little girl, her eyes brimming with tears, the donut abandoned on the table. He slowly edges back in his seat, lifts his cup, and takes a sip of coffee. He lets the anger ebb away, feels himself calming with every second that passes. They've attracted the attention of the old ladies, who are now scowling in his direction. And after he shouted them their brews too, the cheeky old cows. Even so, he has a captive audience, and that is something he could do without.

He places his cup on the table, then lifts Kira's donut and pretends to take a bite. He has it raised to his wide-open mouth, but she doesn't even flinch. Normally she would have screeched and snatched it back before falling around the bench giggling. This time, her eyes remain focussed on her mother, who is doing a stellar job of looking like the wounded party.

He puts the donut down. 'I'm sorry, Laurie, okay? I am. I've just been a bit stressed lately, with work and that. But I shouldn't take it out on you. It's why I wanted some family time. My two girls.' He grins. Nothing like buttering her up and playing the sympathy card. It sickens him to have to do it, but needs must. He watches her edges soften. 'Hey—' he turns to Kira — 'how about I take you both to the shops and get you whatever you want?'

'Anything?' Kira asks coyly.

'Anything.' He leans down and kisses the top of her head. 'Daddy is really sorry, sweetheart.'

'Anything?' Laurie teases, a small smile creeping across her lips, the opportunistic, greedy bitch.

'Anything. Look, some poor family has just had the news their daughter is never coming home.' He looks at his own family. 'It makes you appreciate what you have.'

Laurie watches as Kira chews a mouthful of sticky donut. 'Yes, it does.'

'What are we waiting for?' He grins. 'Eat up.'

Kira lifts her donut and takes a big bite, icing making her lips shine. Her round eyes, that are so like his own, are sparkling once again. He pictures Mrs Howe's granddaughter Ellie — imagines her lips shining, her eyes sparkling. A shudder travels his spine, anticipation building like the very start of a good orgasm. He can't wait to realize his fantasy.

CHAPTER THIRTY-FOUR

DCI Bethany Fellows

Millie is out doing the rounds with the families, updating them, listening. Comforting the Collinses, in light of their completion of the official identification. This is the start of what is going to be the hardest time of their lives. Something they may never recover from.

I am in the MIR, looking over the evidence we have so far. I am about to speak to Fiona Thompson. She might have remembered something over the weekend. Perhaps she'd even knowingly held something back. It's worth a shot. Dillon is attending the PM of Kelly Collins, freeing me and Amer up to continue with the active investigation. The possibility of getting DNA results from the piece of skin Damien retrieved from Jasmine's teeth is permanently at the forefront of my mind.

Fiona is waiting in Interview Room Four with her appropriate adult. I catch Amer's eye and raise my chin. He gives me the thumbs-up. I can't stop myself wondering whether it was him who went to Dillon. He's been getting annoyed with me lately, thinking I'm stepping on his toes. Would he really be so vindictive? I don't want to think so.

'You ready?' Amer asks. I nod, and we step into the room.

'Hi, Fiona, thanks for coming in again.' I sit opposite her, our knees almost touching. Amer sits beside me. Fiona is wearing black jeans and a black hoodie. She has blue eye shadow up to her brows and eyeliner whips up the sides of her eyes.

We record the interview as always, but this time Fiona's appropriate adult is her father, Dean Thompson. He looks worn out and pulled apart by all this.

'So, Fiona,' I begin. 'I thought we could go back over a few things, see if anything new comes to mind.'

'There's nothing new; there isn't. I've tried remembering. I just can't. There isn't anything else to remember. I wish there was. I really, really wish there was.' She is earnest, tears running down her cheeks.

Dean rests his arm around his daughter's shoulders. 'She's told you everything she knows. She feels terrible enough about what's happened without you making things worse. She doesn't know anything more. She's having nightmares—'

'Dad,' she interjects.

He squeezes her shoulder with his hand. 'I'm sorry, honey, but it's true. This is too much for you.'

She shakes her head. 'No, it's not. I want to try; it's just I really don't think there's anything else. I wish I knew something; I want to help. I really do.'

'I know you do. I can see that.' I smile gently. 'How about this — we go back over your argument with Kelly, when you parted ways and we see if we can jog your memory. That sound okay?'

'Really?' Deans says. 'Again? She knows they shouldn't have snuck out, drunk alcohol or separated. She knows all that. Believe me, she has been punished — and I don't mean by her mum and me. I mean, by this whole awful situation.'

Fiona sniffs, hangs her sleeve low over her hand and wipes her nose with it. 'No, Dad, I wanna try.'

He shakes his head. 'Okay, if you really want to.'

'I do.'

'Look at me,' he says. 'One word: "stop". That's all you need to say, and this is over. You hear me, Fiona?'

She nods. 'Yes, Dad. Go on,' she adds, turning to me. 'I'm ready.'

'What were you arguing about?'

She shrugs, her thumbs poke through frayed holes in the ends of her sleeves. 'It was stupid. We'd been drinking, not a lot, but . . . you know, some. Kelly doesn't really drink normally, so she couldn't handle it and I guess she's one of those people who gets all upset when they drink. Sees things differently, you know, like becomes argumentative and that—'

I let her talk. I've learned from Millie and my own experience that it is the best way to get to the truth.

'—she got scared about being caught and about staying at Rob's. She said she'd be a third wheel anyway. She wouldn't have, though. Rob isn't horrible; we wouldn't have made her feel uncomfortable or aught. We would have just been three friends hanging out.' She glances at her dad. 'That's all. All we wanted was to spend some time together. I wanted Rob and Kelly to get on. They're the most important people in my life.' She looks at her dad again. 'Other than family, I mean. Me and Kelly were okay; we were having a laugh until she got all stressed. I said she was being soft, that she should grow up and then maybe she could get a boyfriend too.'

Fiona looks down. 'It was nasty, but she annoyed me. She walked off. I did go after her. I tried to make up, but she told me to "eff off" and to leave her alone. I did. I shouldn't have, and I wish I hadn't, but I did. I left her alone. I feel like this is my fault.'

'It isn't,' Dean says, quickly.

'You couldn't have known what would happen, Fiona,' I say. 'This isn't your fault.'

'Then why does it feel like it is?' Her big brown eyes stare at me, looking for me to absolve her of her guilt. I can't, because she is the one punishing herself. I can't make that stop. I know how hard it is to let yourself off the hook.

'When you walked away, did you see anyone else in the area?'

She closes her eyes as if she can switch on a replay in her mind. 'I can't remember. I was focussed on Kelly. I didn't really pay attention to anything else.'

'You were near the Miller Arcade, weren't you?'

'Yes, we'd been hanging out on the Flag Market. Kelly walked really fast when she went off, so yeah, by the time I caught up to her, she was round the back of the Miller Arcade.'

'By the back of it, do you mean Lancaster Road or Bierly Street?'

She gives me a blank stare for a moment and shrugs. 'Which one's the one with all the bus stops?'

'Lancaster Road.' Where we know Jasmine Foster had been when she was last seen.

'Not that one, then; the other one. Across from the library and just past Heavenly Desserts. You know that snobby place on the corner.'

It can be a quiet little area once the shopping day is over. You might get the odd reveller passing through, but not much other than that. It's a tiny street too, but it does lead onto a much busier one.

'Leading to Church Street and Fishergate?' I confirm. Church Street is the direction Jasmine had been seen walking; this is all slotting sickeningly into place. He's stalking the same area — and we missed him.

'Yes, I guess.'

'You might not have seen anyone walking, but did you notice any cars?' There are a few spaces beside the Miller Arcade, but it's a restricted zone. Disabled parking only. I don't think our guy would risk it unless he has a blue badge, but you never know.

Fiona closes her eyes again, then they spring open. 'Oh my God, how did I not remember before? There was a blue car — it was pulled up on the right, I think. It wasn't in a space or anything, just over to the side. It was a bit up from us. Kind of outside that men's clothes shop, the posh one.' She's referring to Slaters, and I'm damn sure Bierly Street is one-way, leading straight onto Fishergate.

I try to dampen down my eagerness, but lean forward in my seat. 'Do you know the make?'

She shakes her head. 'I don't know anything about cars. It was blue, like a kind of dark blue—' she closes her eyes — 'the front window was down, I think, and . . . and there was someone in it. Someone just sitting there. I forgot. How did I forget?'

'It can happen after a traumatic event. You wouldn't have been focussed on the car at the time; you were concerned with Kelly. Then afterwards, you zoned in on what your brain decided was important and on information you could cope with. It's perfectly normal for things that seemed irrelevant or insignificant at the time to come back later. This is good, Fiona. This is really, really good.'

Dean looks shocked. 'Well done, Fiona.' Tears spring to his eyes. 'You're doing brilliantly.'

'You are,' Amer agrees.

I nod and smile. 'Yes, you are.'

Fiona returns my smile. 'I might be able to draw the car. I'm dead good at art, like *dead* good.' She stops fidgeting, and her eyes regain some of their lost sheen. She has found a way to help her friend, to redeem herself. 'I might even be able to draw a bit of him sitting in it. The man. He had dark hair. I didn't really see anything else, but that might help right?'

'Yes, Fiona, it could help us a lot. Thank you.'

We wrap up the interview. Once outside, Amer and I take Fiona round to the main office and find her a workstation. We give her everything she'll need and get her settled. Dean sticks to his daughter like glue. Any parent would be the same. I can only hope that what she draws will advance the investigation. For all we know, the car being there was a coincidence, but something tells me it wasn't.

Once Amer and I are alone, I turn to him. 'If we have a description of a vehicle, we can circulate it. Rule it in or out.

We'll also have something to look out for on CCTV, ANPRs and whatnot. If it's our guy and he went down Fishergate, there bloody well should be some cameras around. Have we got any footage from that area?'

'We have some from outside a couple of bars, but they are focussed on foot traffic at the entrance. They don't cover the road at all.'

'Shit! Has anyone come forward with dashcam footage?'

'Not yet.'

'Get someone out to that restaurant on the corner, Turtle Bay. You never know.'

He looks at me sideways. 'I'll sort it.'

'Sorry,' I say, quickly. 'I forgot.'

'It's okay. Don't worry about it, like I said we'll find our way eventually.' He shrugs. 'This is taking a bit of getting used to, isn't it?'

My earlier suspicions of him die away. I nod. Then a thought occurs to me. 'Wait a minute, Church Street, Fishergate . . . they're bus routes, too, aren't they?'

'Yeah, there are a few bus stops along the street. It's one-way now, too. Which means if this is our guy, then like you said, it's one-way, which means his only option was to head towards Fishergate shopping centre.'

'Oh shit, yeah. We need a computer.'

We go into the MIR, grab a laptop, then settle down together. It feels like I'm a kid waiting for Christmas morning while being terrified of Santa Claus. There's a mixture of excitement and trepidation as I log in and pull up Google maps. I grab the little yellow man in the corner and drop him onto the page, right where I need him. The street view springs to life in front of us. I click the arrow and head out of Bierly Street onto the cross section between Church Street and Fishergate. Amer's right — he could only have taken a right out of Bierly Street. There are bus stops visible, but before long it becomes a bus-only route. His only choices were to take Cheapside towards the markets or Glover Street towards Avenham. If it's him, then my bet is he avoided

Cheapside: restricted access means cameras. Glover Street would have been the safer bet.

'Bus cameras, Amer.' I stop myself from issuing instructions. 'I'll get onto Preston Bus Station, Stagecoach, all of them. Let's see what they've got.' I point to the tiny bit of road where he may have shared space with a bus. 'It's a small window, but it is there. We might strike lucky this time. It's worth a try.'

He grins. 'We just might. I'm going to go and see how our resident artist is getting on.' He's heading for the door when his mobile rings. He retrieves his mobile from his pocket and turns to look at me. 'It's Damien.'

CHAPTER THIRTY-FIVE

The Ordinary Man

He knows he's spending far too much time at Mrs Howe's lately, that it might get questioned, but he can't stay away. Ellie is on his mind constantly. He needs to see her, or at least to have the chance of seeing her — that alone gives him a thrill. Besides, if anyone asks, he'll just claim he is being more attentive due to Mrs Howe's current ill health. He promised Bernard he'd look out for her after all.

He arrives at her house around lunchtime, minus any arrangement. He is planning on putting in an hour or so free of charge. Any excuse to get away from Laurie, and with any luck Ellie will be around again. Thinking of her and what he longs to do to her is the only thing getting him through the mundane drudge of his life. Jasmine Foster was his first, so she was always going to be imperfect, but special. Now it turns out Kelly Collins had been anything but right.

The news had come on the radio again while they'd been shopping. He was excited at first, watching as people reacted. Most just carried on browsing, including Laurie. But some froze, listened intently, their faces contorting as they took in what had happened in their home city. He'd stood holding

222

umpteen bags filled with Laurie and Kira's spoils, leaning against the wall casually listening to the news report. What should have been a memorable moment was ruined when they gave Kelly Collins's age. She was sixteen. His mood instantly became morose, and Laurie reverted to sulking. It was all he could manage not to whack her round her hideous head. How could this have happened to him?

Now he can't get Kelly Collins out of his mind, and he's infuriated. He's spent his entire weekend mulling it over. He may as well have been set up by her, by her family. She should never have been out at night, dressed the way she was. He couldn't have known how old she was; she didn't tell him. She didn't behave like a kid. He'd been tricked into becoming a child killer — he knew that's what they'd call him now. It made him feel sick. He never would have touched her if he'd known.

He takes a deep breath, then knocks at Mrs Howe's back door and waits. If he can just see Ellie, he will feel better. Being around her will make everything else fade away. He's getting wound up as he knocks and knocks and gains no response. Being poorly, Mrs Howe should be here, and with any luck she'll be being babysat by her granddaughter again. Surely the world isn't so flaming against him that this would be a waste of time? He needs one thing to go right, just one fucking thing. He cups his hands together and places them against the windowpane to guard his eyes from the sun as he peers inside.

He spots Mrs Howe's outstretched legs lying on the floor. Her top half is in the lounge, so he can't make out whether she is conscious or not. He's tempted to get back in his truck and leave, but then he imagines how he'd feel if this was his mum. He pounds the window and watches, but she doesn't so much as flinch.

He goes to his truck and grabs the first heavy thing he finds, his hammer, then he takes a roll of duct tape and a ground sheet from the truck bed. He dashes back to the kitchen and quickly lays the ground sheet on the floor in front of the window. He unwinds the tape, sticking it all over one side of the window.

'I'm coming, Mrs Howe, hold on. You're gonna be okay.'

Using the metal tip of his hammer, he taps hard against the corner and edges of the window. The glass begins to splinter and shatter, cracking upwards, but it only goes through one layer of the double glazing. He has to remove the rest by hand. Luckily, he's wearing thick gardening gloves, or he might have injured himself. He uses a rag to clear the edges until it is safe enough.

Mrs Howe still hasn't moved, and he wonders whether he's already too late. He angles himself sideways and lifts one leg over the sill. 'Shit!' he exclaims, as a shard of glass slices through his jeans and cuts his leg. 'Fucking hell.' He looks down at the blood seeping through a rip in his jeans. He must have missed a bit of the glass. Great.

He lowers himself onto the floor and goes to Mrs Howe. If the silly old sod hadn't gone and collapsed, he wouldn't be down a pair of jeans or hurt. Kneeling opens his wound further, and it stings to high heaven. He checks her pulse but can't find it. He holds his palm over her open mouth and feels the warmth of her breath.

'Well, you're alive,' he says. 'You're going to be fine, Mrs Howe. I'm here now. I'm going to help you.'

He kind of wishes he hadn't flaming bothered. He looks around, his eyes scanning the room — he left his mobile in the truck. He spots the landline, dials 999 and requests an ambulance. The operator asks him a series of ridiculous but supposedly mandatory questions. What a way to spend his day. He's still answering the operator's dumbass questions when he hears sirens.

The sudden silencing of the sirens is followed by a pounding at Mrs Howe's front door. He's relieved to find her keys sitting on a meter cupboard beside the door. He snatches them up and rattles them from side to side until he spots the one that he reckons it must be.

He inserts it, and thankfully, the door opens. 'She's through here.'

The two paramedics follow him to Mrs Howe and set to work right away. They feel for her pulse, then get her hooked up to equipment to check her heart and oxygen.

'How long has she been like this?' one of them asks.

'I don't know. I just got here. I'm her gardener. I looked through the window when there was no answer and saw her lying on the floor. So, I broke in and called you guys.'

'Well, you've certainly improved your karma for the day. Good job, mate. You just made yourself her hero,' he says, smiling. 'We're gonna take her in now. Do you know how to get in contact with her next of kin?'

He smiles back at the paramedic, keeping the laugh that bubbles up his throat firmly locked down. 'She's going to be all right, then?'

'I hope so. We'll do everything we can for her. They'll know more at the hospital, once she's conscious. Looks like she had a fall. I think she may have been lying here for some time, poor lass. You might well have saved her life.'

'She's been unwell. She shouldn't have been left on her own. Her daughter or grandchildren should have been here.'

The paramedic stands and extends his hand. 'I know how you feel, mate. It's good you got here when you did. Families, eh? Still, if you know how to get hold of them?'

He clasps the paramedic's hand, a thought occurring to him. 'Listen, I'll stay here and look for an address book. I'm sure there'll be one somewhere. Most people her age have them. I'll do my best to contact them. I'll secure the window, too.'

'You're a diamond, mate. They'll most likely have her next of kin on file; try not to worry. We're going to get her to hospital now. You've done a good thing today, sir.'

They get Mrs Howe onto a stretcher and into the back of the ambulance. It doesn't move for a few minutes, and he's tempted to knock on the ambulance and ask what the hold-up is. A couple of nosey-ass neighbours watch from their windows. Finally, it drives off, and the neighbours bog off, too.

He goes back inside and immediately starts ransacking the place, searching every cupboard and drawer. He's certain there will be an address book somewhere. He's about to give up when he comes across a mobile phone. It's an old brick of a thing with no lock or anything. He opens the phone book and scans the list until he finds Eleanor. He ignores all the others and clicks *Call*. His groin comes to life at the sound of her voice.

'Nan?'

'Hello, Ellie, it's your nan's gardener. I'm afraid she's had an accident. I had to break in to get to her. She's been taken to hospital. She needs you, Ellie.' He uses the name she prefers, as though they are more than acquaintances. It feels good rolling around on his tongue.

'Oh my God, what happened? Is she okay?' Her voice is thick with emotion, and he can hear the threat of tears.

'Is your mum with you?'

'No, I'm on my own.' *Brilliant*, he thinks. 'Mum's out of town today. Shit, shit, shit. I'll call a taxi. I have to go; I need to get to Nan. I need to call Mum, oh God.'

'Calm down, Ellie. It's going to be okay. Where are you? I'll come and get you; I'll take you to her. I have your mum's number here, too; I'll call her for you. You just wait for me, okay. It is all going to be fine, just tell me where you are, and I'll set off.'

There's a hesitation — he can almost hear her thoughts as she wonders whether she should accept his offer. He adds, 'I'll be able to get you there quick, take you to your nan.'

'Okay, thanks.' She tells him the street she's on, and he directs her to a quiet spot where she can wait in peace.

'I'll be right with you, Ellie.' He breathes her name, his groin stirring as he does so. 'You just wait for me, okay? I'm going to look after you.'

'Thank you.' She's crying tears of panic and relief as she hangs up.

He runs around to his truck and speeds off.

CHAPTER THIRTY-SIX

DCI Bethany Fellows

'Beth, did you hear what I said?' Amer is standing close, too close. I fear he will notice my fast breathing, feel the heat radiating off me. Despite his nearness, his voice sounds far away.

I step back. 'Yes. I heard you.' My own voice sounds echoey.

'The results of the DNA. It isn't Tom.'

I feel sick. 'I heard you.'

'The DNA wasn't a match to him. It's a good thing. It means he isn't doing this to get to you.'

I want to throw up. 'Yes.'

'Beth.' He reaches out, but I twist away. 'Are you okay?'

'Yes.'

'The flower bud, though, another one — it's definitely one killer.'

'I know.'

'I'd put money on it being the same flower. It must mean something.'

'Yeah.'

'Beth?'

'I need to . . . I need a minute.'

I dash across the office to the bathroom, go inside and check all the cubicles, hitting the doors until they swing open. I'm alone. I go to the sinks and lean against the unit. Running the water, I splash my face. Freezing, cold, wet. I grip the edge of the sink, smooth, firm. I press my feet into the ground, solid, steady. I feel the iciness of the stainless-steel tap beneath my fingers. I run my hand along the edge of the wooden unit. I go through the list of things I can see, things I can smell, hear, taste. I can taste vomit; it's rising in my throat. I picture the box Toby talked about, and breathe up its side, across the top, down, across, up.

The door opens and Aaliyah walks In. I spin to face her.

She comes to me quickly, her arms out. 'Beth.' She grabs me, pulls me close and holds on. 'Amer asked me to come and check on you. What's going on? Should I get Dillon?'

I wrench myself free. 'No. I'm fine.'

'Beth, you're not fine. You are very obviously not fine. What about Millie? I could call her.'

I shake my head, vigorously. 'Don't. I don't want this getting back to her or Dillon, you hear me?'

'There's no shame in needing support.'

'I will be fine. It's just a shock.'

'Finding out this killer isn't Tom is a shock?'

'Yes. Come on; you must have thought it could be?'

'Yes, I did think it was a possibility. But it not being him isn't a shock to me.'

'I needed to get my head around it, that's all. I have. It's done. I'm over it. I just wish there'd been a match to someone in the system.'

'We all do.'

I stare at her. 'Was it you?'

She looks confused. 'Was what me?'

'Did you go to Dillon about me?'

Her eyes narrow. 'No, Beth, I didn't. Why would you think that?'

228

I shake my head. 'Never mind. Look, I need to get back to work, and so do you.'

Aaliyah looks about as convinced by my claims of being okay as an atheist being told God is sitting on their shoulder. All I can hope is that she really isn't the spy I need to worry about, that she won't go running straight to Dillon. Now I am more fuelled by anger at the mystery viper in my nest. My upset at the knowledge that my team will not be actively hunting Tom has abated somewhat. I give myself a talking to and walk through the office with my head held high.

* * *

When I go into the MIR, there are four officers in situ. I spot Antonio and walk up to him. He's completely focussed on his laptop, so when I tap his shoulder he almost leaps out of his chair.

'Shit, sorry, Ant. You got a minute?'

'Yeah, course, boss. What's up?'

I notice a couple of the others' ears prick as they attempt to listen in on our conversation. 'Has Amer spoken to you about the camera situation with regards to Kelly Collins? I want the bus cameras checked, every last one that travelled via Fishergate on the night she was killed. Just as we did after Jasmine Foster's murder. You never know, this time it might pay off, especially now we have a description of the car.'

'On it.' His blond fringe flops low on one side. He's a handsome bloke, but seemingly perpetually unlucky in love. It's been so obvious to see since Millie told me about his break-up. He is subdued, his shoulders permanently slumped under the weight of his sadness. This last bloke really did do a number on him. 'I'll go as soon as I've done this, if that's okay. It'll take me, like, five minutes, that all right?'

I step around to see the screen of his laptop and lean over his shoulder to get a better look. 'What are you doing?'

He looks from the screen to me and back. His expression tells me he isn't best pleased I'm poking my nose in, along with a dose of *oh shit, you caught me.* 'It's nothing.' He leans the screen low, cutting off my view.

'It is work-related, isn't it? Specifically, *this* case?' I'll be shocked if it isn't, and also rightly cheesed off.

'Well, yeah, kind of.' He's nervous. I can feel it coming off him in waves.

This better not be something to do with his ex. Cyber stalking? 'Tell me, Antonio; I mean it. I'm talking as your superior now. What are you doing?'

He puckers his lips and blows, then lifts the screen up again. 'I was reviewing some security footage, that's all.'

I frown. 'Why in here and not one of the booths?' I'm referring to the specific rooms we have set up to look through CCTV and the like. 'And—' I lean down again and squint at the screen — 'where is that? It looks like . . . that's outside Millie's house. Why the hell do you have footage of Millie's home? What is this?'

I straighten up and swivel his chair towards me. I drag another chair from the table behind and sit facing him, then I look at the two nosey parkers who are gawping in our direction. 'You two, get back to work. This isn't a water cooler moment.'

They turn away, sharpish.

'So?' I let my question hang in the air. If he wasn't gay, I would think he was stalking her.

He's akin to a deer in the headlights. 'I'm not meant to tell you.'

'What is that supposed to mean? Why are you watching Millie's home? I'm not messing, Antonio.' I use his full name again, making sure he realizes I mean business, and lean towards him and whisper. 'Tell me, what the *hell* you are doing?'

I lace my words with threat. I will not blindly trust anyone again, not even Antonio Giovanelli, and certainly not when there is a clear reason not to.

He sighs. 'Millie asked me to,' he admits, his voice echoing his betrayal. 'She's gonna kill me. She didn't want you to know.'

'To know what?' My mind is racing with a million and one scenarios, none of them good. 'Tell me, Ant, I mean it. It must be important if you're doing it on our time. What the fuck is going on?'

'Okay, okay — someone's been following her. Hanging around her house. At least she thinks so. She—' he does air quotes — '*sensed* it. She seems certain, though, and call it copper's or woman's instinct but, look . . .' He moves the bar along the bottom of the stilled video until it reads 21.00 and there, on the screen, is a hooded figure. A man, by the looks of it, lurking near her house. 'He's there for over thirty minutes — just watching. It's creepy.'

'Why didn't she report it? She could have called the police out while he was there, had him caught red-handed. Found out who the fuck this is.'

Acid is bubbling through my veins. Someone is messing with my best friend, and it is very far from okay. I can't understand why she didn't come to me. Why Ant? Possibly for the same reason I haven't told her about the postcards, about talking to Stanley Baker, or about the sense I've had that I am being watched. Shit, maybe someone *is* watching me. Maybe it's the same person who is watching Millie. Does this have something to do with her going off radar every so often, as Aaliyah said?

'She didn't know when he was there. She had the feeling she was being followed, so she installed cameras at home and had a dashcam fitted to her car. She wanted to make sure she wasn't, you know—' he twirls his fingers in small circles either side of his head — '*nuts*. Turns out she wasn't. Isn't.'

'Does she know? Have you told her about this?' I prod the screen. 'Why didn't she view it herself?'

'She's been freaking out, didn't want to drive herself crazy watching hours of footage, getting obsessive. She wasn't gonna bother. She thought she was being paranoid and didn't want to make a big deal out of it. She said she was gonna ditch the footage without even reviewing it, get rid of the cameras. I offered to go through the lot, just to be safe.

She's been good to me lately, since my break-up. I owed her. And I'm glad I did it, too, because this—' he points at the hooded figure again — 'is not in her head.'

My heart is racing. 'Why didn't she want me to know? Who else knows?'

He looks guilty. 'Just me and Aaliyah. Millie wasn't cutting you out. She didn't want to pile the pressure on, especially when she thought she might be wrong. She was protecting you.'

I nod, but I can't understand why Aaliyah didn't tell me. She told me how worried she is about Millie, that she's been disappearing for hours and not being contactable. Why didn't she tell me about this as well? It might well be connected.

'Fine. Leave this with me.' I shut the laptop without turning it off, then pick it up and tuck it under my arm. 'You get to the bus station. You should be working on the case. We don't have time to waste doing . . . personal things. Not even for Millie. Not on work time, okay?'

'Sorry, boss. I get it.' He stands, grabs his coat from the back of his chair, then walks out.

I don't give a flying fuck what Millie will say. I intend to find out who the hell is stalking her — possibly us — and why. My money is firmly on Tom. He might not be our killer this time, but that doesn't mean he isn't coming for me and those I love. I take the laptop and ensconce myself in an empty side room where I hope I won't be interrupted. There is no way I am risking Millie. Not for anything or anyone.

CHAPTER THIRTY-SEVEN

I locate the time on the recording that Ant pointed out, 21.00, and there he is — a man, standing in the shadows, watching Millie's house. Chills run up and down my spine as I observe him. I study every moment of the thirty-two minutes he remains there, but not once does he show his face. Surely, he isn't aware of the camera, or is he? If he is, then why the hell go there in the first place? Why stand in its view? A weight lodges in my stomach as I consider what kind of person would knowingly do this. Even so, he is so bloody careful. It's as though he is deliberately scaring her, while remaining an unknown entity. We fear what we can't identify much more than what we can. But I know who it is. I've always known he would come back. It was only ever a matter of time. But why Millie?

He is in the shadow of a tree that hangs over the fence from Millie's neighbour's front garden. He stays on the pavement beneath its overhang. His hood is pulled up to further hide his face. He is wearing dark clothing, nothing with any obvious labels. In my mind, as I watch this man encroaching on Millie's life, I see Tom Spencer. What if he isn't just encroaching on her life, what if he is threatening it? My entire body reacts to the panic, it drives itself through my veins, through my internal organs. It pulses through my skin and bones. I am alive with fear, because this is Millie — she's at risk.

My mobile buzzes in my pocket. I retrieve it and see Dillon's name on the screen. Clicking to answer, my gaze wanders back to the hooded figure on the laptop screen. 'Ma'am?'

'Where the hell are you, Beth?'

I force my eyes away from the screen. 'I'm in the building, I'll be with you in two ticks. Sorry, ma'am, I—'

'I don't care about your sorrys, you can't just vanish — even within the building, not during a case like this. You have to be all-in and available. I need to know where you are. Your team needs to know. This isn't good, Beth; it's not good at all. I don't know how many times we can have conversations like this.'

I swallow past the hard lump that's rising in my throat. 'I just needed a minute.' It's all I can think of to say, and I'm kicking myself the instant those damned words leave my lips. My heart pounds as I await Dillon's response. I can hear her breathing down the line and know she's deciding my fate on this investigation.

'Come to my office. Now, please.'

She hangs up before I can respond. We both know I don't have a choice. I close the laptop, then place it under my arm. I'll stash it in the staffroom on my way to see Dillon. I don't want to invite questions, not until I speak with Millie.

Dillon's voice rings in my ears, the order to come to her office. I attempt to decipher her meaning from her tone. She's pissed, that much is a given, but is she pissed enough to remove me from the case? My heart tramples my ribcage as I head through the main office. I can sense the weight of a dozen or so sets of eyes, my colleagues watching me walk towards the gallows. My face heats as I avoid their glares. After a moment, I dare a glance and they are all focussed on their computer screens or notepads — not one of them is paying me heed. It's my own paranoia coming to the fore, making my cheeks burn and my legs quake.

I open the staffroom door and head straight for my bag. It contains little other than some money and the banana I grabbed this morning on my way out of the house. I'd sensed eyes on me then, too, I'd pushed it aside. Always be aware of my surroundings, be alert, ready to react — stay vigilant. I knew what I should be doing, but I was sick of feeling crazy, so I'd ignored my gut and I'd ignored my training. Idiot. I won't make the same mistake again. Not now.

I place the laptop beneath my bag and hope everyone has the good sense to let it be. You could leave your life savings lying around the office and no one would touch it. A packet of biscuits, however, is considered fair game. A laptop, well, I'm confident it will still be here after I speak to Dillon. I quickly tap out a text to Millie, checking in. I attempt to make it as casual as possible. There's no reason for me to be breathing down her neck investigation-wise. If there was something to report, then she would.

Dillon's assistant nods in my direction. 'She said to just go in.' She smiles, like this is anything to smile about. For a millisecond, I wonder if she's mocking me, if she knows exactly why I am here. I feel like the new kid at school, seeing my potential downfall in the faces of every classmate.

By now, the blood is pumping around my body at a million miles per hour. I stand with my hand clasped around Dillon's door handle. I don't have to turn around to know that Chloe is watching me. I open the door and walk inside. Dillon looks up as I enter, her face puce with pent-up annoyance. It rushes from her eyes to my guts — at least, that's how it feels.

'Sit,' she orders. Her voice is barren of her usual friendliness.

I do as I'm told. 'Ma'am, I—' This is most definitely a time to refer to her as "ma'am" rather than "Dillon".

She holds up her hand, and my mouth clamps shut. 'I am seriously beginning to worry that I allowed you back prematurely. It's my fault; I wanted to believe you when you claimed to be ready.'

'Ma'am, please let me exp—'

Once again, she raises her hand. 'There's no need. I accept some of the responsibility here, I do. Having said that, this case deserves to be headed by the best people — who are also *at* their best. Do you understand?'

I take a breath, waiting to see if I am actually allowed to speak this time. But even as I begin, I half expect her to stop me. 'Yes, I understand. I'm sorry you feel I am letting you down, letting the team down. That I am not equipped to handle this investigation. But you're wrong.' I look into her eyes and see the spark of a fire. She's on the verge of losing it. 'I was taking a little time to think some things through . . . about the case. I have a theory.'

The spark In her eyes shines brighter, but this time with intrigue, with hunger. 'Go on.' She sits forward, her wrists resting on the table, her hands clasped together.

I move closer in my seat, my confidence rising. I can only hope I am not about to make a huge mistake — one I can't come back from.

'Okay, so I have been thinking about the kind of person we are looking for.' Dillon's attention is unwavering. 'It's looking more and more likely that he took both his victims from Preston town centre. To me, that shows arrogance, that he would use the same hunting ground twice, and with a non-existent cooling-off period. Not to mention, he killed and disposed of Jasmine in a ridiculously brazen way, and in close proximity to our offices.

'This guy is forensically aware. He does his homework; I reckon he knew it would be us specifically, here at these offices, who would be investigating him. He was proving his superiority to us. We are dirt to him. This is a game, and he holds all the cards — at least in his mind. He's a narcissist. The world revolves around him, his needs, his desires. He is all-important.

'I reckon the only explanation as to how these girls vanished from the town centre and ended up in the places they did is because he drove them there. The overkill he uses, the way he tortures his victims indicates he is a sadist. A psycho-pathic narcissistic sexual sadist, to be precise. He may not have raped them, but that does not mean he doesn't gain sexual gratification by inflicting pain, watching them suffer.

'He perceives himself to be intellectually above us. We are all inferior to this guy or so he believes. He made a mis-take with Jasmine, gave her the opportunity to fight back, and she did. She bit him. God bless her. He then washed her mouth out with antibac, thinking that would get rid of evidence. I'm pretty sure he thinks he's covered all his bases. But he failed, because our wonderful Dr Sanders managed to find a tiny piece of our perp's flesh between Jasmine's teeth, and what's even better is, he extracted a DNA profile from it.

'Now, as you'll be aware, there was no match on our systems.' Damien Sanders will have informed Dillon of this. It isn't news to her; however, my take on it might be. 'Which means he is not only forensically aware, but has ensured he hasn't ended up on our database. Right about now, our guy is patting himself on the back for a job well done.'

'Your point?' Dillon's hands are no longer poised on the desk, and she isn't sitting forward in her seat. I am los-ing her. 'I know all this, Beth. Yes, you have insight, and of course that's useful, but this—' she throws out her hands — 'is hardly hold-the-front-page stuff, is it?'

'I know, I know. However, I don't think someone like this, someone who is so careful, so *considered*, and thorough about everything would risk a stop and snatch. He got two smart young girls on two separate occasions to get into his car, without anyone batting an eye. He did so in Preston city centre, a place where you run the very real risk of some-one happening by and witnessing any kind of altercation. Some opportunists might take the risk, but not our guy. He wouldn't do anything he hadn't already risk assessed to the nth degree. On top of that, he has to be aware of the killing areas, to know he wouldn't be disturbed once he got them there. However, he wouldn't take the chance of being easily recognized.'

'What are you saying, Beth? Spit it out, would you?' She points to my chair. 'That isn't a soapbox you're sitting on.'

'I'm saying that he knows Preston, but doesn't worry too much about being recognized, so he isn't *from* Preston, but he spends time here. He lives near, works near, perhaps even within Preston itself. He drives a car young women and girls would feel comfortable getting into. So, taxi driver maybe? I think it's a good punt. We have Fiona Thompson sketching a car we believe could be his. She witnessed it on the street idling by with a lone male occupant shortly before Kelly vanished. She's already given a description, and Ant is at the bus station now, checking their cameras. The street connects with Church Street and Fishergate, which is a fairly active bus route. I think we have a shot here.'

'Do you really think someone as careful as this asshole would use his own taxi to lure his victims?'

I halt before responding and give it some consideration. This is how we work best, batting our thinking around from one to the other. Our ideas form a tumbleweed that we bash between us. As it rolls from place to place it releases its seedlings, which grow into new ideas, until eventually we hit on the one that changes everything.

'You have a point; he wouldn't take that kind of risk.' I clench my jaw. 'Damn it.'

'I think maybe you were on the right track, though; he is too smart to use his own mode of business to take them. It could be linked back to him in the blink of an eye. But what's to stop him impersonating a taxi or Uber or something? I mean, come on there's so many different types of these things knocking about nowadays. You'd be hard pushed to know whose vehicle you're getting into unless you ordered it yourself, which it's unlikely either of our girls did. Unless they both used someone else's phone to do it.'

'So, he hangs around and waits? He's like a chameleon camouflaging himself within his surroundings until they literally walk into his path. If the car Fiona Thompson saw was him, then we might get a jump on him. He thinks he is so fucking clever; he thought washing Jasmine's mouth out with antibac would get rid of his DNA. It's tempting to put that out there. He'd hate knowing he failed. That she might be the one to nail him. There might not be a match in the system, but once we have him, she'll confirm it.'

'We can't risk angering him; he'll come out fighting. I have no intention of pushing him to kill again,' Dillon says, vehemently.

'I realize that. I wouldn't really put it out there. If he doesn't live in Preston, but works here or visits, then where do you think he lives? How far away?' I'm thinking up options, places this monster might choose to live.

'Somewhere within driving distance. If he works here, he must be within an hour's drive. If he visits, it could be longer. Maybe he has an elderly relative living here, a parent, perhaps?'

'But that would mean he likely grew up here. Preston isn't somewhere you come to retire, it's where you stay if you've always lived here. If he has family here, then he would be recognizable.'

'He would be if he worked here, too.'

'That's true, but less so.'

'Not if he works for a big company. Think of all the colleagues, customers and suchlike who would see him, know him, potentially recognize him.'

She's right. I shut my eyes momentarily and let my brain map out these options. 'So, what are we thinking here? Maybe he works for a small company or is self-employed. And the work he does is only partially in the Preston area. It would allow him authentic access, but without him becoming too *seen*, if you know what I mean. He would be somewhat invisible, non-consequential to the people who pass by him. Part of the furniture, so to speak. Is that what we're saying?'

'Yes, I think we're on the right track.'

The cogs are turning in my head. I can sense it all beginning to take shape, to come together. 'And what kind of job allows you that kind of freedom and limits your exposure to the general public?'

'I don't know; some kind of healthcare professional. Carer, perhaps?'

'Most carers and healthcare are vetted.' I shake my head. 'I don't think he would find that a worthy risk. Plus, they can become notable, important to the people they care for.'

'What other possibilities are there?' she says.

'Electrician, plumber . . . that kind of thing?'

'Yes, maybe. He wouldn't want to be called out in an emergency. He could end up becoming too familiar in the area, and most people in Preston would use someone more local. But what about if he was a tree surgeon, gardener, car valet?'

'Jesus Christ, that's it! Why the hell didn't I realize it sooner — the significance? The flower buds he puts up their noses. Gardener, landscaper — that's what he does. That's who he is.'

'Oh my God,' she says. 'And those kinds of businesses are very much within the control of the owner.'

Our theory is germinating, firmly taking root in my brain. 'He would be able to pick and choose who he worked for. He could opt for people who live on the outskirts of Preston. He could even choose the infirm, who aren't likely to get about and see him elsewhere. He could do most of his work outside of Preston, but have a few choice clients here. That bastard is a bloody landscaper or something, he is.'

Dillon nods enthusiastically. 'I reckon this could really be something, Beth . . .'

'We need the description of that car; we need to hope to Christ it's his. You okay if I go and check in with Fiona and Amer? She might have done the drawing and gone by now.' I wait, watching as Dillon considers her options. I was brought in here for a dressing-down, potentially to be taken off the case.

'Okay. Let me know as soon as you have anything, and I mean *anything*.'

CHAPTER THIRTY-EIGHT

I barely slept last night; I was on edge about Millie — wondering whether the person stalking her was there, watching her home. I wanted to go to her, but knew she wouldn't thank me for it. I don't yet know how to broach the subject; she has chosen not to tell me for some reason. Me forcing the information out of Ant and then taking it upon myself to view her security camera footage — well, maybe I have overstepped. Even so, the only thing that truly matters is keeping Millie safe.

I text her to see what her plan of action is today; she responds almost instantly, telling me she is going back to the Fosters. They were struggling to take everything in yesterday, and she promised to go back and relay where we are with the investigation. I'm unbelievably relieved to hear from Mills and know she's okay, but if I had my way, I would insist she come into the office. I want my eyes on her at all times. It's impractical — hell, it's impossible — but it doesn't stop me wishing that weren't the case.

It wasn't so long ago she was under threat during the Brander investigation, and it was all I could do not to go insane with worry. I can't believe we are being thrust into a similar situation again. Last time, I kept the threat to myself;

this time, Millie is doing the same. But I know she is in danger; I can't just ignore that. I won't. I will have to talk to her today. The bags under my eyes are clear evidence that I can't go on like this. I get ready and go into work.

Time passes quickly. I am relieved when I receive a text from Millie, telling me she's on her way into the station. I didn't bother with breakfast and my stomach is crying out for sustenance. I remember the banana I didn't get round to eating yesterday and grab it from my bag. It's a bit battered and bruised, but it'll do the job. I have it peeled and poised, about to take a bite, when my mobile rings. Antonio's name on the screen. 'Yes?'

'I have shit loads of bus CCTV for us to trawl through. They've gathered it all together now. I went in first thing this morning to collect it. Turns out there's a tonne of buses travel via Fishergate between seven and nine of an evening.'

'I suppose that's good; it gives us a solid chance of coming across him.'

'If it is him.'

I sigh. 'Yes, *if* it's him. You on your way back in?'

'Yeah. I just thought I'd give you a heads up that we'll need a few people looking through it; it's going to be time consuming. And . . .'

'And what?'

'I wondered whether you've spoken to Millie yet. I want to know whether I should come in wearing a flak jacket. She's gonna be gunning for me for spilling the beans.'

'I haven't said anything yet, no. She's on her way in.' I look up at the clock. 'Actually, she's taking a while. What's the traffic like?'

'Oh, you know. It's Preston, so shit.'

'Okay, see you soon, Ant.'

I toss my banana in the bin, my appetite suddenly eluding me. I spend the next hour or so searching Facebook advertisements, LinkedIn, Trustpilot, every site I can think of where gardeners and landscapers might advertise or be rated. I look for any images with cars in them and try to narrow down our search to any gardener who works in Preston, particularly ones who don't live here.

Not all information is readily available on one site alone. I use various sites and posts to collate enough information to make decisions on order of importance. The idea is to gather a list of possible people of interest, then to gather further intel. Interview them; do whatever it takes to rule them in or out. It's a process of elimination. The problem is that there are far more landscapers, gardeners, tree surgeons, etc, than I could have imagined. It's taking forever. The team has been divided accordingly, and I am not alone in my frustrations. I hear exasperated sighs every few minutes — the pile of information we have printed between us is in danger of toppling.

Millie's still not back, and I'm getting increasingly worried. My concern for Millie is distracting me from the investigation, but I do feel as if we are getting more of a picture of our perp. I'm impatient to get a name, but we are so much closer than we were. I believe our theory that he is a gardener or landscaper is solid. If we are right, then our suspect pool is much more manageable than it was a couple of days ago.

I know what he is, a psychopathic narcissistic sexual sadist, but *who* he is, now that's what's important. But to get to one, we have to traverse the other. Part of that is understanding why he chooses the victims he does. Both have been young; they looked similar, too. Though Jasmine was blonde and Kelly a brunette.

Had he known Kelly was a teenager? She was dressed and made up to appear older. The idea that he might not have intended to go after a child nags at me. How would that make him feel? Would he care? He's a psychopath, after all, so maybe he wouldn't. But what if he *does* care? What if he is out there now, angry, upset? What emotions would he feel? And what would he do about them? Might it make him stop? Or might it drive him to kill again, sooner?

The door clicks open, and I turn and see Millie. My chest swells, my breathing calms. 'Thank God,' I say, then catch myself. 'We're making headway.'

Her face is ghostly pale. 'That's great. How so?'

My chest constricts as though a python is wrapped around me, tightening its hold. 'What's happened, Millie?'

'Nothing. Tell me about the headway.'

I walk to her. 'I will, but first will you just come with me? Please.'

I'm stressing as I lead her into the bathroom. There's clearly something wrong. Is it her stalker? Maybe she is finally going to confide in me. Millie checks the cubicles. One is occupied. We wait in silence until Chloe Adams comes out, washes her hands and leaves.

'What's happened, Millie? What's wrong?'

Her eyes are teary. She shakes her head, her mouth opening and closing mutely. 'I, I erm . . .'

'Look at the state of you! What's wrong? Please, Mills, talk to me. You can tell me anything, you know that.' I want her trust again. I need it. I step closer and hold my hand to her cheek. 'What's going on?'

She turns her face into my hand, I feel the quiver of her lips against my palm; a shiver travels my spine, a heat fills my chest. Our eyes lock, and I can't look away; the sensation that moves though me is impossibly intense. Lately, there have been moments like this between us and I don't know what they mean. I don't know how to react. I'm afraid of making the wrong move. Aunt Margie's comment about how Millie and I should be together has been in the back of my mind since the day she said it. I can't lie to myself anymore: I have always loved her, deeply, madly. But I couldn't admit it to myself; I could never say the words out loud. I am terrified of her rejection, of losing her entirely. My chest is heaving with a rush of wildly alive emotions.

'Beth,' she whispers.

My heart is beating so hard I can feel its rhythm and heat in my ears. Adrenaline surges through me. It's like how you feel as you chug to the top of a huge rollercoaster. As you tilt over the precipice and begin to fall. She leans closer. I feel the softness of her lips against mine, the heat of her

244

breath as her lips part. She gives herself to me. My body is on fire as my hand reaches around and slides through her hair. Our mouths move together as though it's how it was always meant to be. My heart is thundering, but so is hers — I can feel it against my chest. Our kiss becomes more urgent, more breathless. I can't believe this is happening. What if she regrets it, what if it ruins everything? But I'm powerless to stop. I can't and I have no desire to. I sigh her name into her mouth.

The door begins to open, and we jump apart, our chests heaving, her expression one of utter shock, mine no doubt the same.

'Beth?' Antonio calls. He doesn't come in, thank goodness. 'You in here?'

My eyes are on Millie as I catch my breath and call, 'Coming!'

For some reason, I feel we shouldn't leave together, as though if we do everyone in the office will know exactly what just happened. I'm not even sure I know. Millie seems to think the same, because she doesn't acknowledge Ant or make a move to leave. As I walk alongside her to pass by, I let my hand trail hers. A shudder so powerful it almost floors me is propelled up my spine. What the hell have we just started?

CHAPTER THIRTY-NINE

Ant takes me to the MIR, where Detective Constable Marsha McLeish is sitting beside Amer with a grin on her face. 'Me father is like a car encyclopaedia. Mum always said they were his first love,' she grins, winks, and says, 'he pulled it out the bag, and Fiona, too.

I struggle to take my mind from Millie, from what just happened. 'Oh yeah?'

Ant and I drag a couple of chairs to the opposite side of their table and sit. Amer places the sketch Fiona completed in front of us. It's impressive.

Marsha taps it. 'Fiona described the car she saw to my father. Along with that, the drawing and her looking at some colour swatches, she came up trumps — my father didn't want to plant the image of a specific car in her mind until he was as sure as he could be. But he managed to get enough detail to narrow it down to make and model, even the year.'

I grin. 'How in the hell did he do that?'

'Well, I know my cars, but my father, he's a frigging car encyclopaedia. Once he sussed it was a Volkswagen Passat, he had Fiona pin down the colour to midnight blue. They were made in 2014. So, this guy's car is either bloody old and he's had it years, or he bought it preowned. But it's also a typical option for a taxi in the UK. I reckon he either *is* a taxi, Uber or whatever driver, or . . .'

I see where she's going with this, and as Dillon and I already deduced, it makes complete and utter sense. 'He bought a car that would fit the mould. One that could be assumed to be a taxi?'

'Exactly what I was thinking.'

Amer nods. 'That makes three of us.'

I shake my head, smiling. 'I'm going to have to watch out for you, Marsha. You're gonna be on my tail all the way up the promotion ladder—' I wink, I'll support her advancement any way I can. She's got the gift of deduction some coppers struggle with. Clearly, hers is ingrained. 'What's your father's drink of choice?'

'Whisky.'

'I'll shout him a bottle. Hell, if we catch this fucker using what he's given us, I'll shout him a crate.' My mood couldn't lift any higher right now. We are closing in on this bastard; I can feel it.

Marsha smirks. 'Trust me, he'll be your pal for life for a glass, never mind the bottle. He's a Scotsman, after all. The way to his heart and all that.'

'Well, he may well have helped crack this case open, and you too, Marsha, well done. Thanks, honestly, I mean that. I've been mulling over the theory that our guy is a taxi driver, or faking it. How else would he get two intelligent young women to climb into his car without them kicking up a fuss? And no one who plans the way he does would risk that. So . . .'

Amer looks at me. 'That makes sense. I see where you're going with that. He's too clever, or thinks he is, to use his own business in the course of his crimes. So, yeah, faking it would fit better.' He nods enthusiastically. 'You're on the money, Beth.' He turns to Marsha. 'You are a bloody star, Marsha.'

She blushes under his praise. 'Glad to be able to help.'

I can feel us gaining on him. I only pray we get to him before he kills again. I dread to think how much further he might escalate in terms of brutality.

Amer and I send out a request for the team to congregate in the MIR as soon as possible. We take DC Marsha McLeish to update Dillon with what she's uncovered. This certainly feels like a pivotal moment in the investigation. When we go back to the MIR to deliver the update to the team, Millie is there, and my heart practically leaps out of my mouth.

Tummies are rumbling and morale is dipping. The team needs a boost; they need to know we are closing in. Dillon stands at the front with the whiteboards behind her. They contain photographs of Jasmine and Kelly, crime scene snaps, and a litany of information. Amer and I stand beside her. Millie looks at me, then quickly diverts her line of sight to Dillon. I wish I knew what she was thinking.

'Thank you all for being here,' Dillon begins, everyone sits erect and face forward. 'Earlier, Marsha took Fiona Thompson's sketch of the possible suspect vehicle, along with Fiona herself, to see Marsha's father. He is, as Marsha put it, a "car encyclopaedia" and he was able to make an educated deduction that the car is likely a Volkswagen Passat in midnight blue, made in 2014.'

There are a couple of gasps and an excitable *yes!* or two.

She turns and sticks an image of a matching car, along with Fiona's drawing featuring a side view of the driver, to the board. 'We have CCTV footage available to be viewed in the hope of spotting the vehicle. So far, as you know, we have nothing. However, thanks to Marsha's father, we now have much more information to go on. It also occurred to us that the street where Fiona last saw Kelly, the street where she spotted the car, joins up to Church Street and Fishergate. There are plenty of bus routes that pass through that area.'

I notice the eager nods, the dawning realization.

'Antonio went to Preston Bus Station and collected all bus CCTV and dashcam footage from that evening between seven and nine p.m. There's a lot to get through, so we have put together a list of names, and I want you working as a team. I want you to go through every inch of that footage until you find what we need. Ant will divvy out the material and you can use the booths to go through it, two to a room. We need eagle eyes on this. Right then, I will touch base again later. In the meantime, if anyone gets anything, I want to know about it, got that?'

There's a murmur of assent, and satisfied with this, Dillon leaves.

Ant moves to the door as Amer reels off the names on the list; each of them move in turn to join Ant. They leave the room and Amer hands out the rest of the roles. If I wasn't so preoccupied with Millie and what just happened between us, I might be inclined to feel slightly defunct. HOLMES2 has thrown up a few enquiries, a couple of reinterviews. Every role is vital, and needs to be handled with care and diligence.

If we can identify the owner of the car, then we can check his DNA against the profile Damien lifted from the skin in Jasmine's teeth. I steel myself to talk to Millie, but before I get the chance, the door bursts open.

Dillon comes in looking flushed with her fists clenched at her sides. 'I can't flaming believe this,' she spits. 'I've just got off the phone—' my heart sinks, as I anticipate what's coming — 'there's been a report of a missing eighteen-year-old girl. She failed to return home yesterday and hasn't answered her phone or been active on social media. It's completely out of character. Her grandmother is in hospital, and the girl's mother insists her daughter would be there in a heartbeat if she knew. This is not the kind of girl to up and disappear like this, not according to the mother. I had a quick look at the girl's Instagram, at her photo. And that's what is worrying me the most.' Beads of perspiration form on Dillon's forehead. 'Young, innocent-looking, doe-eyed, slender, attractive. She's exactly what this guy goes for. Now, it's not a given that it's him. Maybe it won't be; I hope to Christ it isn't. But, Beth, Amer, I need you to go speak to the mother. Now.'

CHAPTER FORTY

Amer and I dash through the main office and out via reception. As we reach the car park, I turn to him. 'You okay to drive?'

His gob falls open. 'Seriously?' He moves towards me and places his hand on my forehead. 'You sickening for something?'

I knock his arm away. 'Very funny. I just haven't eaten. I'm a bit light-headed.'

He side-eyes me. 'That's not good, Beth. You need to eat.'

'I will. Later.'

On the way, I call through to one of the officers who took the initial missing person's report. I gather all the information available from him as fast as possible.

As soon as I hang up, Amer speaks. 'What we got?'

'Eleanor Grice, eighteen-year-old college student. Her mother Karen reported her missing yesterday after she failed to answer the phone or come home.'

'Eleanor had a class in the afternoon, two thirty p.m. She didn't show. Apparently, she's studious, but she does have an active social life, so her mum thought she might be with friends. That's since been ruled out. There's no response from her mobile phone—'

'Is her mobile off?' Amer interjects.

'It would appear so, yes.'

'When was she last seen?'

'Monday morning, yesterday, by her mum and brother. She saw her nan later that same morning, then she left to go to college, but she never arrived. Her nan had some sort of fall or collapse after Eleanor had gone. She's in the hospital.'

Amer shoots me a look. 'They sure it was accidental?'

I shrug. 'We'll speak with her, just in case.'

'Father?'

'Parents are divorced. I think that's it. That's what we have so far. She last updated her Instagram just after two p.m. with a selfie and a comment saying she was running late for college. Then it stopped, no updates to any of her social media pages since.'

Amer shakes his head. 'I don't know. I'm not convinced. This isn't his usual MO. Maybe she's with friends, nicked off college, then gone on a night out. Battery dead. Scared to go home after breaking the rules. Maybe she even gave granny a shove — you never know. Shit happens.'

'I agree. There are a few possibilities. I hope it's that she's holed up with mates. But none of her friends admit to seeing her. Could be lying, covering for her. Though when you consider the seriousness of being asked by the police, I'm not sure that holds water. Not for a bit of rule-breaking. Not at their age. No one living in Preston is unaware of what's going on right now. I reckon they'd fess up. Besides, from what the officer said, the mum was adamant she wouldn't stay out like this. But you're right — he has never taken a girl during daylight hours before. That we know of.'

'And you think he'd change tack now?'

'He might. I had been wondering how he would react if he hadn't realized Kelly Collins was sixteen. I get the feeling killing a kid might damage his ego, his warped sense of right and wrong. I did consider that he might do something drastic in response. I don't know; maybe this is it?'

* * *

251

When we arrive at Karen Howe's house her youngest, Spencer, answers. He reminds me a little of Max Collins, and I pray I'm not looking at another young lad who's destined to become an only child.

'Spencer, is it?' I ask, he nods. I pull my lanyard forward from around my neck and hold it out to him. 'I'm Detective Chief Inspector Bethany Fellows, and this is my colleague, Detective Chief Inspector Amer Anwar.'

Amer holds his lanyard out. Spencer looks at them both briefly. 'Mum's through here.' He turns and walks into the house. We step inside, close the door, and follow him.

Once in the lounge, I see a frazzled-looking woman in her mid-forties. 'Has there been any news?' she asks.

I shake my head. 'I'm afraid not. We're here to gather some more information.'

I hear a noise coming from the next room, and look over as a man with shoulder-length blond hair and baby-blue eyes steps through from the kitchen.

'Lionel Grice,' he says, his voice silk.

He holds out his hand as he nears Amer. They shake hands, before he holds his hand out to me. His clasp is firm, confident. He looks to be in his late forties, maybe early fifties, judging by the laughter lines at the sides of his eyes. Yet he appears youthful, even the way he dresses in light-blue casual canvas trousers, sandy-coloured loafers without socks and a Guns N' Roses T-shirt.

There is an abundance of places to sit in this stylish lounge. A two-seater sofa that is already occupied by Karen, two armchairs, a red loveseat, and a wicker chair beside the bay window. It's a huge, airy space.

'Please do sit,' Lionel says. I see Karen arch her brow. They're divorced, yet he is treating us as though we are guests in his own home, not hers.

I sit in one armchair, Amer in the other. Spencer settles beside his mother. Lionel remains standing. 'Anyone want a drink?' he asks.

'No, thank you,' I say. 'Please, Mr Grice, I think it would be better if you sit while we talk. It could take a while.'

He looks from Karen to me, to Spencer, and finally opts to sit in the wicker chair. His leg is bouncing up and down, and I realize he isn't being arrogant or insensitive; he's worried sick. He's the father of a missing girl, and like the rest of the world, he's seen the news. He's very much aware that there's a predator stalking these streets. He'll no doubt have seen the images of the previous victims, seen the similarities between them and Ellie. And now, here we are, two plain-clothed detectives. It doesn't take Einstein to make the deduction.

'Amer is going to take notes while we talk, if that's okay?'

'Of course,' Karen says.

Amer nods, smiles, then takes a small flip pad from his jacket pocket. It has a padded black cover. He reaches into his shirt pocket and retrieves his silver Parker pen. He rests the open notepad on his knee and holds the pen poised.

'First of all, I want to get a good picture of Ellie, of the person she is,' I say. They nod their understanding, eager to help in any way they can. 'She's eighteen years old?' More nods. 'Has she ever spent the night away from home without making contact before?'

'Never,' Karen says quickly.

'Ellie was due to attend college yesterday?'

'Yes, in the afternoon. She only has one class on a Monday, and it wasn't until two thirty. I saw her in the morning before work, but she went to my mum's, so Mum was the last person we know of who saw her. We've been kind of tag-teaming her care recently, since she's been more unwell.'

'Can you remember what she was wearing when you last saw her?'

Karen's eyes go up and to the right as she searches her memory. 'Light-blue leggings and a long top; it's navy blue with yellow flowers and comes down to just over her knees. She had on her cream canvas shoes.'

'Okay, thank you. Does she ever turn her phone off for this long?'

'No. Especially not since my mum took ill. She's scared to death something's going to happen to her nan. There's not a chance she would have turned it off or let the battery run out. If she knew Mum was in hospital, she'd be there night and day, she loves her so much.'

'Your mum suffered a collapse?'

'Yes. We were extremely lucky the gardener showed up when he did. He's been so good recently, spending extra time at Mum's.'

CHAPTER FORTY-ONE

The Ordinary Man

He arrives home hoping Laurie will be out, and he can clean himself up in peace. No such luck: the lazy cow is ensconced in front of the television as always. He kicks his boots off by the front door; they're muck-encrusted. He's going to have to give them an epic clean or throw them out.

Laurie pauses *Grey's Anatomy* and calls through. 'What the fuck are you doing home?'

'Had a messy job this morning, I need to clean myself up before I go back out. I have a new client booked in this afternoon — can't turn up looking like Stig of the Dump.'

'Why not? You're a gardener, not a flaming Silver Service waiter.' She laughs at her own joke before turning the television back onto play.

He's just glad she didn't bother her arse coming through. The leg wound he received playing the good Samaritan has opened again and blood is seeping through his jeans. He could explain that away easily enough; she practically sainted him when he told her what he'd done. It's the busted lip and scratches all over his fucking face and hands that he's going to struggle to account for. Laurie is full of suspicion at the best of times. She's forever accusing him of getting his leg over with one client or another. If she could see his customers for herself, it would allay every one of those fears.

He goes into the bathroom, lifts Kira's naked doll out of the bathtub by its straggly hair and dumps it on the floor. He turns on the hot tap, then holds his finger under the stream until it's piping hot before putting the plug in. He looks around the edge of the bath at the ridiculous number of products and adds a good glug of blue Radox bubble bath along with some bath salts.

He strips naked and piles his clothes beside the toilet, ready to take downstairs. He'll be in and out the bath, have his gear in the washer and be on his way before Laurie's shit programme finishes. Once he's added enough cold water so as not to scald himself, he settles down into the bath. He slides in until he is lying with his head against the slope at the back and his feet propped either side of the taps.

His leg stings like a bitch as the soap gets into his wound. Yesterday when he picked her up, he had genuinely considered driving Ellie to the hospital. She'd been so grateful to him and worried about her nan that he'd felt momentarily off-kilter. But then his excitement had taken over, and he'd ended up breaking all his own rules. He went through a red at least once. He might even have been caught on a speed camera, but there was this all-consuming energy at his core as he thought about her, and it overtook him. He'd wanted to see her at Mrs Howe's. What he hadn't expected was everything that followed.

He'd made the call to her, then everything had happened on some sort of autopilot. His brain had been fizzing on the drive to her. Vivid images of her. The way she moves. The way her hair sashays across her shoulders when she walks. The smooth milkiness of her skin. He didn't plan what happened. Everything that followed unfolded naturally. She'd sat in his truck, thanking him over and over for saving her nan, for going to get her. All she cared about was getting to the hospital.

On the phone, he'd promised her that he would call her mum to inform her of Mrs Howe's situation. He'd told Ellie to sit tight and wait for him. There was a risk. A very real risk that she'd have ignored him and called them herself before he arrived to pick her up. It was one of the first things he dropped into conversation on the way to the hospital. If she had spoken to them, to anyone, then maybe things would have turned out differently.

It must have been fate. She was delivered to him; this time she really was. Kelly Collins had been a mistake. But that wasn't really his fault. He'd thought the universe was paying up after things went a bit wrong with Jasmine Foster. He'd genuinely believed that Kelly was a gift wrapped for him. He'd been arrogant to think that. And so, when Ellie sat beside him, sniffling, crying to herself. Distracted. He had turned down a quiet street, taken a quick look around, then elbowed her in the head, hard enough to knock her out.

She'd slumped low in the seat, and he'd pushed her further, until she was squished into the footwell out of sight. He drove like a wild man after that, as the last thing he wanted was for her to come to and start kicking off. He'd already taken too many risks. Ever since he first laid eyes on her, his desire had been impossible to ignore.

He lowers himself beneath the water, almost enjoying the sting of his lip and face as the soapy water gets into his cuts. He'll claim another gardening accident. Laurie won't be interested enough to push him on it. Him being injured is fine. Him shagging someone else, not so much. He blows bubbles and lies with his eyes wide open, watching as they rise above him. As he sits up and breaks the surface, he notices Laurie in the doorway. She's standing in silence, just watching him. It's then he realizes that thoughts of Ellie have had consequences, and his groin aches with his arousal. Laurie stares at him for a little longer, glances at his mud- and blood-encrusted clothes, then leaves the room.

CHAPTER FORTY-TWO

DCI Bethany Fellows

We are on our way to the hospital to speak to Elsie Howe. Karen Howe didn't know the gardener's name. So many people pay little to no attention to those in service trades. Unfortunately, Karen Howe is one of those people. We called the hospital, spoke directly to Elsie. She refused to give her gardener's information, claiming he has been a godsend since her husband died. She refuses to be part of a witch-hunt. Even with her granddaughter missing, she won't be swayed. I'm seriously wondering whether the knock she received to her head when she collapsed has altered her thinking. Surely granddaughter trumps gardener? It will be harder to remain tight-lipped if we are there in person. If I remind her what could potentially be at stake if she's wrong about him. We have to tread carefully. But we need this information. Our best bet will be to judge the situation as we go, to decide on the fly what tactic could yield results.

We arrive at Royal Preston Hospital and ditch the car in the space reserved for emergency vehicles. We race into the hospital, past the shop, the café and coffee stand with its snaking queue. The waiting area in the centre of the ground floor is heaving. There's a line of people clutching numbered tickets for the blood clinic. We have to practically elbow our way through. We run down the corridor and, ignoring the lifts with the crowd of people gathered, we go through the doors to the stairs. We pass doctors, nurses, visitors. The place is manic. We dash straight for Elsie's ward. She's in a bay with a few other elderly ladies and one young girl. The place stinks of bleach, stale urine, and that weird and distinctive smell you get when plates of hot food have those awful plastic coverings over them.

Elsie is fully dressed sitting up in a tall-back patient chair with a brown table on wheels in front of her. There's a plastic jug of water, a half-filled see-through cup and two stained blue-and-white mugs.

Amer stands in front of her. 'Mrs Howe, I'm Detective Chief Inspector Amer Anwar and this is Detective Chief Inspector Bethany Fellows.'

We show her our ID. As she moves her head, I get a strong whiff of hairspray and musky perfume.

'I've already told you on the phone. I won't be giving his information. I'm a woman of my word.'

I grab a plastic chair from a pile at the top of the ward, place it close to Mrs Howe and sit. My patience is wearing thin, but I can't let her see that. I smile, speaking softly, 'What do you mean, you're a woman of your word? Has someone asked you not to give us his information?'

She averts her eyes to the ceiling, like a child in the process of a telling off. 'I don't understand why it matters to you so much anyway. He has nothing to do with what's happened to Eleanor.'

'How can you be so sure?'

She looks back at me, confident, assured. 'Because he's a good man. He is. My late husband, Bernard thought very highly of him. He comes to check on me. Does extra jobs. He saved me from lying on that floor any longer. My own family didn't find me; he did. Someone like that wouldn't do anything to a young girl. He wouldn't. You're wasting your time when you should be out looking for my granddaughter.'

'We just want to rule him out. If you give us his information, we can have a quick chat with him and clear everything up. What harm would that do?'

She shakes her head. 'No.'

'Why not, Mrs Howe? Come on, I don't believe you would withhold his information for no reason. This is an investigation; not giving relevant information when asked is a criminal offence. You could get into trouble.' I'll try anything to coax it out of her. I can't fathom why she won't just give us his name.

'Do what you will. I don't trust the police. You set people up. Innocent people rot in jail, and rapists, paedophiles, murderers—' she punctuates the last three words for emphasis — 'get away with it. Why don't you do some proper police work and go find my granddaughter?'

I try another tack. 'Mrs Howe, would you be willing to let us take a look around your house? There could be something that could help us find Eleanor.' I'm careful to refer to her granddaughter by her given name, as Mrs Howe does. 'I understand from your daughter that you and Eleanor are very close? That she's been spending a lot of time with you?'

She smiles. 'Yes, she's a lovely girl.' Her expression changes, and her eyes fill with tears. 'I'm so worried about her. Please, you have to stop this, this nonsense with D . . . you have to look for her properly.'

She almost slipped up. So, the only thing I have so far is his first initial. *Helpful.* 'I promise you that's what we are doing. So, your house?'

'Well, yes, I suppose that would be okay.' She looks to the drawer set beside her. 'Could you grab my handbag, please? It's in the bottom cupboard, I think. I'm sure Karen brought it in for me.'

'Of course.' I get up, then bend to open the door. There's a black handbag and a small toiletry bag. I pass Mrs Howe the handbag, and she digs around until she finds a set of keys.

She holds them out to me. 'I'll need these back.'

'As soon as we've used them. Can I get you to sign a form just saying you are allowing us access to your home?'

260

She leaves the handbag on the table in front of her and gives me a small nod. 'I suppose that would be all right.'

I take the form I brought with me from my pocket, unfold it, then move her handbag to one side and pass her a pen. I point to the signature line. 'Just there, thank you.' I touch her handbag. 'Would you like me to put this away for you?'

'Yes. Thank you.'

As I'm putting the handbag back into the cupboard, I watch her out of the corner of my eye, and breathe a sigh of relief when she signs. 'Thank you,' I say. I put the form and keys into my pocket, then sit down again. 'Mrs Howe, I know there must be a good reason you aren't giving me your gardener's information. I promise you that if he's done something else, if there's some reason you feel you need to protect him — whatever that reason is, it doesn't matter to us. The only thing we're interested in is finding Eleanor and bringing her home safely. If he can't help us with that, then we will move on. I'm sure you're right, and he's not in any way responsible, but we do have to rule him out. Until that happens, he will remain a person of interest. That won't do him any favours, nor will it help Eleanor. We need to be focussing on her, not chasing dead ends. If we could just rule him out . . . all we need is his name. His information. Please, Mrs Howe, for Eleanor.'

She looks thoughtful for a while; I can imagine her mind working at breakneck speed. It's clear she loves her grand-daughter. She must believe wholeheartedly that I am wrong, and there is a possibility that I am — but surely Eleanor is far more important to her than any loyalty she feels towards this man?

'Just his name; his contact number. Whatever you have. Then I will talk to him, informally.' I add, 'And then we can concentrate on Eleanor.'

She's wavering. She drums her fingers lightly on the table. I wait, not wanting to add more pressure, wanting her to make the right choice.

'Okay,' she says, finally. 'I'll tell you what you need to know. For Eleanor. I still don't believe he did anything. I would have handed him to you on a plate straight away if I thought for one millisecond he might have hurt her. But I will give you what you're asking for. I just hope I'm doing the right thing and he won't get into any trouble. He's a good man.'

As sure as she is that he's good, I am becoming more and more convinced that he's bad. Evil. As she gives me his name and his mobile number, and explains why she was so reluctant to hand them over, my heart drums ferociously.

CHAPTER FORTY-THREE

It's getting late in the day; everything is taking too long. We leave the ward and try David Taylor's mobile number repeatedly, but get nothing. There's not even an option to leave a voicemail. It's switched off. I call Dillon and explain what we've found out.

Next, I call Ant. He picks up on the first ring. 'Beth, I was literally just about to call you. We've reviewed all the CCTV footage now. Aaliyah spotted a car that looks like it could be the one Fiona saw. It made an appearance on the camera of a number 3 Penwortham Stagecoach. It's the only vehicle any of the cameras caught during our time frame that looks remotely possible.'

He doesn't sound enthusiastic; rather, like he is about to hand me a bag of dog crap. 'Please tell me they got a number plate?'

'They did. And they've run it. It's registered to a female driver though, so I don't think it's our perp. All that for nothing.'

'Shit.'

'I know. It's a Lauren Taylor. Another dead end. I'm beginning to lose the will. Please tell me you've had more luck?'

My mind is whirring because this asshole is covering all his bases. 'Fuck, it's him.'

'What?'

'How old is Lauren Taylor?'

'Erm, one mo' . . . she's thirty years old.' He quickly adds, 'Driving licence has her as "Mrs".'

As fast as I can, I run through everything Amer and I have discovered.

'Get scene of crime out to Mrs Howe's right away. He injured himself, there's blood. Have them run it against the sample we got from Jasmine Foster. I need that car tracked,' I say, breathlessly. 'I need to know where it is right now. Get Dillon and the team up to speed. Amer and I are going to go to his home address.'

'Right, shit. Right, yeah.'

After I hang up, I turn to Amer. 'This is it. David Taylor, you bastard, we're coming for you.'

Amer's driving like a man possessed. 'I just hope we're not too late for Ellie.'

'You and me both. If he uses that car to hunt, then of course someone like him would register it under another name. So, he's married then? Urgh.'

Everything happens so rapidly I barely have the time to breathe. It's like that feeling when you are rushing and everything falls from your hands — your shoelace is undone, your coat is in the wash. The world seems to speed up while you slow down. Panic rises inside you like a tide up the wall of a cliff, crashing against it again and again.

No one is home at David Taylor's address. The neighbours either side describe a lovely little family. He's the father of a five-year-old child. Kira. The husband of Lauren Taylor, known as Laurie. He's a self-employed landscape gardener who has clients dotted around Ormskirk, Preston, Southport, even St Annes. My skin crawls at the thought that he could have ended up in the orbit of a loved one. Aunt Margie, Millie, Amer. It's all down to chance and bad luck.

Two houses up, I knock. Amer is doing the same at the other side. An aging woman opens the door to me. She cranes her neck to watch as a marked police car pulls into the street. 'What's going on?' she asks, her eyes lighting up.

'We are looking for the occupants of number six, in particular a Mr David Taylor. Have you seen him today?'

'Yeah, actually,' her voice goes up an octave, 'came home about an hour ago. He doesn't usually, not during the day, so it stood out. He was filthy, from what I could see. Went in, then about forty or so minutes later, he left again.'

'Did he leave in a vehicle? His truck is outside the house. So, car?'

She nods. 'Yeah, he drove the car. There was something a bit weird, though . . .'

'What?' I prod, impatiently.

'Almost as soon as he left, another car pulled up. I saw the wife run out, get in the car and then they sped off after him. Looked to me like they were trying to follow him. Why you asking anyway? He done something? Hey, he isn't that murderer, is he?' She looks excited by the prospect. 'Imagine that, a couple o' doors up from me.'

'Did you see which way he turned out of the street?'

She shakes her head, disappointed. 'No, sorry. Can't see from my window. Wrong angle.'

Amer and I call the station to mobilize and disperse the team along with a number of police constables. They are sent to any place we think we might locate David Taylor. We have put an alert out for the car. We are simultaneously monitoring his house, any workplaces we know of, even his daughter's school. She's in after-school club, but we have social services on alert, ready to step in. We will have a couple of officers remaining at each location in the hope he shows his face.

David Taylor is a chameleon in every way. Psychopaths imitate, and he's done a fine job of it. To the point that he had Mrs Howe believing he was in witness protection after giving evidence about a corrupt police officer. He opened up

265

to her late husband, who had shared the information with his wife. None of it was true; it was a fairy tale. David Taylor is a fantasist.

Elsie Howe believes David to be a good, kind man. She also saw the similarities between him and the late husband she adored. Bernard Howe had a fear of the police, believing us to be untrustworthy. He passed that distrust onto his wife. She wanted to protect David, but when it came to it, her granddaughter mattered much more. She thought we would rule David out and focus on Ellie. The reality might just finish her off.

I am praying there is still blood present at Mrs Howe's from where we now know he injured himself. With any luck, we will be able to get a useable DNA profile to run against the one Damien Sanders recovered. After that, once we have David Taylor in custody, we will compel him to give a DNA sample. All three come back as a match, and there'll be little to no wriggle room.

My mobile rings. I snatch it up, not even looking at the caller ID. 'Hello?'

'Beth, it's DS Niall Grant.' My stomach drops. 'Stanley Baker is demanding to speak to you. He says it's urgent.'

'I can't. We're closing in on our suspect. It isn't possible.'

'I don't mean to alarm you, but he's making claims that you could be in danger and that he can help. He's doing his usual — won't disclose to anyone else. I don't know what to say, Beth, but if what he's saying is true, then it might be best you find a way to come to HMP Manchester. Under the circumstances, we don't have time to arrange for him to be brought to you. I can meet you there? It's down to you.'

266

CHAPTER FORTY-FOUR

The Ordinary Man

He's always fancied himself as a bit adventurous. Urban exploration appeals to him — time alone in a place long forgotten. He's been into the grounds of Whittingham Asylum in Goosnargh, St Joseph's Orphanage in Preston. He's also been inside the Miley Tunnel, which is how he knew it would be the perfect place to take her. He wasn't one of those saddos who felt the need to record themselves and post it to YouTube. He kept his little excursions to himself. And he always went alone. Until last night. That was a first. He still isn't sure what possessed him to do it. The risk was high. He would usually balk at the idea of taking that kind of gamble, but everything about Ellie was different. She was special, so his time with her had to reflect that. He needed to make it last.

It had proven tricky getting her down here. The hill was steep, and she'd been a dead weight over his shoulder. He'd carried her in a fireman's lift. He had waited until dark to take her there. She'd been easy to subdue once he'd knocked her unconscious in the truck. As luck would have it, a client who lived rurally, in an isolated little cottage, was on holiday.

She'd asked him to keep on top of the garden while she visited her sister in Australia. She'd even given him a spare key, so that he could use the facilities and make himself a brew. She was handy to know, that's for sure. Because once he had Ellie, he'd needed somewhere to hold her. She was still out of it when he carried her into the house and while he tied her to a kitchen chair.

He'd rooted through the cupboards for the old girl's sleeping tablets. She was always extremely talkative while he worked. She'd told him all about her trouble sleeping and the pills she took when she really needed to. He'd crushed up a good dose of Zopiclone. He recalls shoving it into Ellie's mouth, swilling it down with a glass of water. She woke up, coughing and spluttering. He held his palm over her mouth, forcing her to swallow the remainder of the water and crushed tablets. Her eyes appeared to swim in her head, before frantically searching the room as she tried to make sense of where she was and what was happening to her.

His groin was pulsating as he stared into her eyes, watching the realization take hold. He wanted to do it right there and then. He resisted. Fought his almost overpowering urges. She tried screaming, but it made no difference; there was no one to hear. He gagged her anyway; the noise had threatened to drive him nuts. She began to drift towards sleep. Her eyes flickering as she'd battled to stay awake until the medication finally won out. Then he waited for darkness to fall. He hadn't been prepared. Ellie had practically been sucked into his orbit, and he'd made the best of it.

Getting her from the house to the Miley Tunnel had not been ideal. She'd practically been comatose, so she hadn't fought back, but it had also meant it was like lugging a dead cow.

He had considered doing it at the cottage. Sense won out. He'd taken enough chances as it was. He'd slung her over his shoulder and carried her down the steep hill towards the tunnel entrance. It was all so much more difficult than the last time he'd been there. The bramble scratched the fuck out of him, and he slipped and nose-dived. She walloped her head in the process and came to. She started thrashing and kicking out. Luckily, the Zopiclone had weakened her, along with not eating or drinking. To look at her, it was obvious she was groggy as hell. He dragged her into the tunnel and thanked his lucky stars that he'd had a torch in his truck.

The tunnel was pitch-black, with weeds crawling up the cracked stone walls. He'd gone deeper into the tunnel, walking alongside the disused, rusty railway line. That place had long since been left to rot. The smell of decay was potent. There was litter everywhere, thrown down the hill and blown inside the tunnel by the wind.

He tied her to the track and made sure she had a good, solid dose of Zopiclone down her neck. Then he left her there. A stress headache plagued him throughout the night; he barely slept. He was worried someone would go in the tunnel exploring and find her, or that she'd free herself. He'd gone back earlier, to check on her and to dose her up again.

He wanted to make this one last. It had to be different, better. Especially after Kelly Collins.

His heart ribbits in his chest as he half walks, half slides down the hill. It rained last night, and the ground is sodden. His bag falls and rolls ahead of him. He's plastered in filth again by the time he reaches the bottom and retrieves his bag, it's soaked through, for fuck's sake. He needn't have bloody bothered with his bath, but his aching muscles feel somewhat soothed. He's as certain as he can be that won't be disturbed; he made sure to do a recce of the area and ensure no one is around before coming down here.

His footfalls echo as he walks into the darkness of the tunnel. Even in the afternoon no light reaches this place. It's expansive. He shines his torch ahead and can't see to anywhere near the end. It feels like it goes on forever. He nears her and sees she's not moving. He panics, worrying she's already dead. Then what? He needs his time with her to be long and exceptional. He's been kamikaze with this one. He knows she could potentially be his downfall. Laurie was weird with him after she saw him in the bath — scratched and bleeding, aroused. She'd stared at him, at his erection, then at his clothes on the floor, but she'd said nothing. He'd put his stuff in the wash and called goodbye, and still she'd been silent.

He's brought his kit this time. He crouches down and unties her, slowly, feeling her skin against his as he does so. His body reacts to every touch. She's freezing, but she's alive. He places his hand in front of her mouth to be certain, and her warm breath caresses him, sending a heat to his groin. He undoes the last bind, the one that ties her ankles to the rail track. Then he reaches down and pulls, rolling her onto her back, to face him. As he turns her, her eyes ping open, wide, alert — staring straight at him.

He jumps back and almost falls; he puts his hand on the ground to steady himself. In one fluid motion, she's on her feet, swivelling her body with her leg in the air — he has no time to react before her foot connects with his nose. There's an explosion of pain and he sees a burst of bright lights. He blinks them away, shocked. He tries to get to his feet, but her foot comes back round before he can. She kicks him in the temple, and he goes down, falling onto his back, which feels like it cracks against the track.

'You sick bastard!' she screams. Her words reverberate through the cavernous space. She bends in front of him as he starts to lift his head. She pulls her elbow back and arcs it so that her hand is up above his face then brings the side of her hand down into the centre of his head.

He attempts to get up again, but this time she lands a punch to his temple. He's dizzy and struggles to stand. He keeps trying, but each time he stumbles and falls. She rains down kicks and punches in such quick succession he can't catch his breath. He's ravaged by pain.

'You bitch!' he yells, spluttering blood. He manages to get onto all fours and is about to stand when she slams her elbow into the middle of his back. 'Ah, fuck!' He falls back down, face flat into the ground.

He turns his head and sees she's running the wrong way trying to get out, the dumb bint. His torch has been smashed and the light it is emitting has weakened. He stretches towards his bag, reaches inside, and feels around for his nail gun. He struggles to his feet, smiles with bloodied teeth, and shouts, 'Oi, bitch!'

She turns. He's holding the nail gun poised as a weapon. She sees it and no doubt assumes he's too far away. What she doesn't know is that he's modernized it for this exact purpose. To make a bit of distance workable. She spins away from him. His finger twitches on the trigger.

CHAPTER FORTY-FIVE

DCI Bethany Fellows

Whatever Stanley has to say will have to wait. We've finally had a hit on an ANPR. David Taylor passed a camera on the motorway heading into Preston. Better still, we have received a phone call from the driver of the car Laurie Taylor was in. It belongs to a friend; she'd been asked to pick her up and follow Taylor, whom Laurie believed was cheating. Now she is parked in Deepdale, scared to death because the last time she spoke to Laurie was on her mobile, and she'd been about to follow David Taylor into the Miley Tunnel. There's no chance Laurie Taylor's mobile will have a signal down there.

We arrive in force and climb down the steep hill that is teeming with bramble and nettles. It comes through the radios that his car has been located in the area. A moment later, we enter the murky tunnel. Laurie's friend is with a couple of officers waiting for news. We use torches to light our way, but there is still only so far that we can see. The place is echoing our collective footsteps, announcing our arrival.

'David Taylor, this is the police!' I shout into the shadows. I can't see anything, but I hear something. It's a strange amalgamation of a muffled resounding noise. It bounces off the damp, graffitied walls. 'Hello?' I call.

I move ahead of the others, turning to hold my hand up as a signal for them to wait on me. I have my baton extended, my hand shaking, and I hope no one else has noticed. I move deeper into the tunnel, following the rust-encrusted track. The muffled noise becomes louder. Someone is crying. My torch catches a movement, making me start. I peer down the beam and see three people. One of them is standing, another sitting on the floor and the last figure is slumped across the tracks.

I turn and flash my torch twice to alert my team to come forward. My view of them becomes clearer the nearer I get. Ellie Grice is standing, battered and bleeding, but alive. She's quivering from head to toe. On the floor, is Laurie cradling the head of David Taylor. He looks as though a train really has travelled through here and smacked right into him.

We check his pulse, then encourage Laurie to release him to us. She lets his head fall with a thwack against the track. As she does, his head turns away from me slightly and I can see that along with all the blood, the back of his head has been caved in.

An officer steps forward and begins CPR, but I already know it will be fruitless; we all do. There are so many questions that will remain unanswered now. We will likely never know why he did what he did, why he stuffed the buds of white roses inside their nasal cavities. He has taken the truths of his perversions to the grave. Not that his reasons matter. He is irrelevant. Jasmine, Kelly and Ellie are who matter.

Laurie stands, then brushes down her clothes. 'It was him, wasn't it? The man who has been murdering women, kids.'

I nod. 'We think so, yes.'

She turns and looks down at him. 'I always just thought he was a bully.' She eyes the officer whose efforts are slowing down with the knowledge that it's a waste of time. 'Don't bother. At least now we're all free of him.'

'Are you okay?' I ask Ellie.

'I'm cold.' Her teeth chatter violently. 'He had me tied up in here all night.' She looks around and shudders. 'There are rats and all sorts. I hate rats.'

'What happened to his head?' I ask.

Laurie opens her mouth to speak, but Ellie beats her to it. 'She saved me. He was going to shoot me with that thing.' She nods down at what I think is a nail gun. 'If she hadn't arrived when she did, I'd probably be dead.'

'I used his hammer,' Laurie says, her voice flat.

Ellie is wan. Her whole body is shaking; she's clearly in shock, and she needs to be checked over at the hospital. We lead her and Laurie outside. Laurie had tasked another friend with collecting Kira from after-school club. The police had stopped her, instead keeping Kira back with her teacher and the headmistress. That poor child is going to be faced with a very cruel reality.

'Is Kira okay?' Laurie asks, as we reach the police cars and waiting ambulances.

'Yes, don't worry. She's being looked after by Mrs Wrathall.'

'Good.' She smiles. 'Kira likes her. She's her favourite teacher.' Her smile vanishes. 'How am I going to tell her about all this? He's her dad; people might think she's like him. How is she going to grow up with this hanging over her?'

I shrug. 'I don't know.' I can't answer those questions. The answers she's looking for might always elude her; they might elude us all. Years of therapy and professional insight may never uncover the truth of what David Taylor was. Of what made him what he was. 'It's just DNA,' I offer. 'One day, you'll find a way to make her understand that.'

Two paramedics have helped Ellie onto a stretcher. She's in the back of an ambulance about to be driven to hospital. 'Just one sec,' I say to the paramedic who'd been about to close the rear door. I jump in and walk to the stretcher, and take her hand. 'I'll come and see you at the hospital. We'll need a statement, but for now just rest. It's over. We'll let your family know where you are. They've been so worried,'

'Was he lying about my nan? She wasn't hurt really, was she?'

'Actually, she was. She collapsed at home. She's recovering now. She's going to be okay.'

She appears puzzled. 'So did he save her, then?'

I nod. 'He broke in and called an ambulance, yes.'

She's confused as hell by his contradictions, as am I. 'So, he saved my nan, and then he called me and lured me to him. He picked me up. Knocked me out and did all this . . .'

The paramedic pokes his head in. 'We need to get going.'

'Sorry, yeah.' I look at Ellie, at this brave young woman. 'What happened in there?'

'That,' she says, 'is a very long story. But let's just say my brother might have a brown belt, but I have a black belt. I knew my parents and Nan wouldn't approve. I've been taking lessons for years on the sly.'

I grin. 'Well, those lessons paid dividends.'

She smiles. 'They did, didn't they?'

'We really do have to go,' the paramedic says, exasperatedly.

CHAPTER FORTY-SIX

There'll be a tonne of paperwork, interviews, information to put together — but we all know we got the right man. The DNA comparisons coming back will seal the deal. He's bang to rights, and dead as a dodo. There will be celebratory drinks for the team this evening, but I won't be partaking. As scared as I am about talking to Millie and figuring things out, I am dying to see her, but right now, I have something else I have to do.

No one but DS Niall Grant and Dillon know I'm here. I'm just hoping Millie doesn't think I'm avoiding her. I am booked into HMP Manchester and led through to an interview room.

There is so much more to find out about the twenty-eight brands. There's more to learn so we can try and locate Tom. I hate that Stanley has successfully summoned me here. DS Niall Grant walks into the tiny concrete room with me. There's a chill in the air. Stanley Baker sits at the far side of a small table. There are metal loops on top of it, which his hands are cuffed to.

He smiles when he sees me, and I'm tempted to turn away and join my team for drinks. I almost smile at the thought of seeing Millie. I grimace as I focus on Stanley.

'I'm glad you came,' he says. 'I was expecting to see you much sooner to be honest. I've been waiting on tenterhooks for our next meeting.'

I sit down next to Niall. 'If this is some ploy just to get me here like this, tell me now.'

He holds his palms outwards, his fingers splayed. 'No ploy,' he says, softly. 'I swear.'

'What is it you have to say? I'm all ears.'

'We have so much to talk about. The last time we were together we discussed Stephanie, my only one for 1993.' He smiles at me, then looks at Niall. 'You found her yet? Her identity, perhaps?' He cocks his head sideways.

Niall bristles. 'No. Nothing you gave us resulted in an identification. We have some Jane Does we are looking at. But currently no means to contact her family, no way to let them know what happened to their loved one. No closure.' There's disgust in his tone. It's subtle — he's attempting to disguise it, but it's there.

Stanley purses his lips. 'Pity. I'm sure you'll get there eventually. Maybe you should have my daughter leading the investigation.' He beams at me, and my stomach turns over. 'She'd have it sewn up in a jiffy. Then again, perhaps that would be a conflict of interest? No?'

'Are you ready to give us another name? More information?' Niall says.

Stanley grins, interlocking his fingers. 'All in good time. I gave you my word I would talk if you got my daughter here. And as far as I can see, I kept up my end of the bargain. Only it's been some time since I last saw her, and I was getting concerned. Isn't this investigation important enough to you, DS Grant?'

'Yes. It is my top priority. I want to bring these women home to their families. I want you and your son to pay for what you've done. I can be here anytime, for as long as you like, if you'll talk.'

Stanley shakes his head. 'And I have told *you* that I will only give that information to my daughter.' His pitch rises in irritation. 'No one else,' he barks.

I clench my teeth every time he refers to me as his daughter.

'Well, she's here now,' Niall says, not reacting to Stanley's anger.

Stanley looks at me and smiles again. 'Yes, I can see that. But now isn't the time to talk about the brands. I needed you here for something else, Beth, something far more important. Pertinent to your safety.' He interlocks his fingers again, and fixes his gaze on me. 'Am I to understand you still believe Tom had some involvement in what Simon did?'

'To Celine, Rose and Jenny?'

'What happened to Celine, yes. He was involved, but after that he cut ties with his brother and me. I did not see him again, and neither did Simon. I believe you received text messages with photographs during your investigation into — well, into your brother. As I understand it, Simon,' Stanley seems to preen with pride, 'had a mobile delivered to you at work, and subsequently you received photographs to the phone. One of which was an image of you, taken at work?'

I look sharply at Niall. He gives a quick, subtle shake of his head. 'How do you know about that?' I stare at Stanley.

He's unflinching. 'Does it matter?'

'Yes.'

'I think the important thing here is that it happened at all, and that for some reason, you seem to believe Tom was responsible for taking it.'

I nod. Where the hell is he going with this? 'He was. Simon couldn't have been there. So, Tom had to be involved in some capacity.'

Stanley is shaking his head. 'Noooo,' he croons, still shaking his head. 'That was not Tom. I can assure you of that; it was not your brother.'

I sideline his reference to Tom as my brother. 'Then who the hell was it? It was taken while I was at work. There's no way it could have been anyone else.'

'You really believe that?' he chuckles. 'Then perhaps you aren't quite as smart as I thought you were.'

'Okay, then, you want me to believe you — give me a name. Convince me you're not trying to mess with my head. That you aren't loving these little games of yours. I see where Sigmund got his perverse pleasure in playing them.'

He frowns. '*Simon* was his own man. What he did to you, to those girls, had nothing to do with me.'

'Rubbish. You created him. You started all this.'

He shrugs. 'We haven't even got that far in our discussions yet. We will, but we're not there yet.' His eyes flare with indignation. 'So don't presume to know anything about my relationship with my sons.' He rests back in his seat and smiles. 'I promise you, Beth, you are going to get to know me much better over the course of things. I have decided to help you with this, I didn't have to. I was under no direct obligation, and I wasn't intending to involve myself. I was,' his smile deepens, 'waiting to see how it played out.'

He shrugs, and the cuffs clang against the metal loop. 'However, I had a change of heart. It's been a while since I last saw you,' he smirks. 'What can I say, I became concerned. So, here we are. I suggest you listen and take heed for your own benefit, and perhaps for those you love, too. I am not a foolish man, I do realize I don't fall into that category, but over time—' he holds his hands outwards, the cuffs thankfully keeping them from coming anywhere near me — 'I'm sure the distance between us will become less.'

My body stiffens. I despise him. I am never going to feel anything but deep-rooted hatred for him. I clench my shaking fists beneath the table, desperately fighting the urge to lunge at him.

Niall leans forward. 'A name now, or we walk. For all I know, everything you've given us so far is a lie. Stephanie could be another game, a creation of yours. Is she one of the twenty-eight? Are you playing us? Getting off on leading us round the houses?'

Stanley's attention remains fixed on me. 'That's not why we are here today. Aren't you listening?'

'Is she real, was she?' I ask.

279

'Yes. I will only ever tell you the truth. I want you to learn to trust me. Where would the sense be in me ruining that trust with a lie?'

A cynical, sarcasm-laced laugh sputters out of me; there's no holding it back.

Stanley narrows his eyes and upturns his lip. 'Really? This is not how I envisioned this going.'

'What the hell did you think would happen?'

'I don't know . . . a little gratitude, perhaps? I am trying to protect you.'

Niall slams his hand onto the table. 'Then give us a goddamn name! I've had about enough of this farce. Come on, DCI Fellows.' He stands. I am about to follow suit when Stanley speaks.

'I don't have a name. I do, however, know without a shred of doubt that Simon was a very resourceful man. He could be quite charming, too, when the mood struck him.'

'What are you banging on about?' I demand.

'Oh, would you look at the time. Best get on; I'll be seeing you soon, sweetheart. We have a lot to talk about.' He smiles widely, then his face straightens, and he leans forward. 'Be careful who you trust, Beth. Watch your back.'

CHAPTER FORTY-SEVEN

By the time I get home from Manchester, I am dead on my feet. Despite not trusting Stanley Baker as far as a flea could throw him, I am unnerved by what he said. What if it wasn't Tom who took that photograph? Who else could it be? It would mean someone else with access to my place of work was helping Sigmund. A civilian member of the force? Another cop? There's no way.

I follow my new routine and check the house. I even do a quick bleary-eyed run through of the footage from my camera. Finally, I settle into bed and fall into a fitful sleep. I didn't get to see Millie because of that scumbag. I wish I'd ignored his demand. I can't stop worrying for her safety and panicking that she's regretting our kiss. One nightmare after another have me shooting awake and pouring with sweat.

That's why, in my half-asleep state, I wonder if I heard the footfall at all. Another dream? I sit up and grab my phone from my nightstand; it's 2.30 a.m. Something feels off to me — Stanley might well have been attempting to play me, but I've sensed someone following me for weeks now. Millie's definitely had some weirdo stalking her; I've seen the evidence. Before today with Stanley, I had been attempting to pull myself together, to move on from all this angst and suspicion. I was tired of always being on high alert. Being constantly primed for an attack is draining. It was taking over my life. It started to feel as though by living that way, I was letting them win.

I've done everything within my power to make my home safe. Everything possible to keep my home a green zone. It's familiar, enclosed, as safe as I can make it. It is an environment entirely of my own creation. It's the only place, other than work, where I've been somewhat able to revert to human rather than vigilant meerkat. I haven't been able to take the same precautions at Aunt Margie's or Millie's; they would have been marching me to the nearest psych ward if I'd tried. But here, I am in control. I am.

I pat my pillow until it's how I want it, then lie back down. I refuse to let Stanley win. I won't let him put more fear into me. I won't let Tom either, for that matter. I haven't received any of his dreaded blank postcards for a while. With any luck, he's been flattened by a truck. Maybe he's done a failed parachute jump and landed in a giant meat grinder. You never know; occasionally good things happen. Every window and door is locked. No one but Millie and Aunt Margie have a spare key. The only way in would be to break a window or kick a door in. I wouldn't have slept through that.

Rolling onto my side, I start to fall asleep. Then I see it, a shadow in the gap beneath my bedroom door. It hovers, then moves away. I am immediately thrust into the red zone. My home is not safe. It's been infiltrated, despite everything.

I swing my legs over the side of the bed, trying to be quiet. But as I make contact with the floor, the footsteps are loud and undeniable as they rush downstairs. I race to the door, swing it open — but whoever was there has already cleared the stairs. I chase after them and trip over the edge of my hallway rug. I swear at another lapse in judgement — I should have taped it down, at the very least. But I right myself, grab the banister, and launch myself down the stairs.

My heart thunders against my ribcage. My breath escapes in rapid bursts. Once downstairs, I round the corner into my hallway. The front door claps gently against the frame, not quite sitting in place. The cold night air invades my home. Sprinting forward, I shove the door wide and stare frantically up and down the dimly lit path.

There's no one there.

No car screeches past.

There's nothing.

But I know they were there.

I doubt myself momentarily, uncertain that I didn't sleepwalk again and leave the door open myself. That everything leading up to now wasn't yet another night terror. But something solid and immoveable in my gut tells me I am not safe. This time, I choose to trust my instincts.

The camera outside my home is set up to point at the front of the house. I glance up and let out a frustrated shriek when I see it's swivelled out of place.

I can't call this in. My position as deputy chief inspector is already precarious. There's no way I am risking them saying I'm not emotionally or psychologically ready to be back at work.

At least if he's here, stalking me, he isn't with Millie.

I step back inside and am about to close the door behind me when I hear a noise that sounds like it came from the darkness of the hallway. My heart is racing as I stare into the gloom. Then the sound is behind me, moving fast. I have no time to react as something hits me hard in the back. The force takes my legs from under me as I plunge forwards. The side of my head glances off the wall. I hit the floor with a crunch and the wind is knocked out of me. I see something moving in the shadows, and the intruder steps forward to stand directly in front of me.

Looking up, our eyes meet. 'Oh my God,' I say, shocked at the sight of the knife in his hand. 'I trusted you.'

He kicks the front door with the heel of his foot. A heaviness lurches inside my chest, my stomach drops, and blood rushes to my head — it feels hot and full. I can't believe what I'm seeing. I need to snap out of it, now. I don't have time to make sense of this. His eyes are wide, and they're fixed on me.

On the floor, I am hugely disadvantaged; add the knife into the mix, and I am easy prey. But this is my home, and I am prepared for this. *Don't push him to react. Keep calm, confident. Defuse.*

'Antonio, what's going on? Did you see who pushed me?' I offer him an out. Attempt to convince him that it's not too late to back out of whatever he came here to do.

I ready myself, one hand on the ground behind me, leg bent with my foot on the floor, the other leg ready to kick out. His stare is piercing; there's no reluctance. He's not going to back down.

There is aggression and hate on his face; he wears it like a mask. He's no longer the man I thought I knew. He's an aggressor, and he's in my home with a weapon. He means me harm. I have a right to defend myself. I just never imagined it would be against him.

Raising one hand up and out, protecting my head, I thrust my foot hard into his shin. He moves back, wincing. I kick again and again with as much force as I can muster until there is enough space between us.

In one fluid movement, I plant both hands firmly on the floor. Using the balance of my foot on the ground, I slide the other beneath my leg and around onto the ground to put further space between us as I stand. As natural as taking a breath, I move into an active stance. Elbows bent, arms upwards protecting my chest, fists clenched in front of my face.

'Stop this!' I shout. 'I am under attack. Antonio Giovanelli is in my home armed with a knife. Call the police.' I shout the same words repeatedly.

There's a flicker of doubt in his eyes. He's panicked, caught unaware — he didn't expect this. I continue with my tirade as loudly as possible; it's my call to arms. It has dual purpose: raise the alarm and interrupt his cognitive function by attacking his senses.

His face shakes with rage, his jaw clenched. 'I loved him. He was everything to me, *everything*, and you stole our last months. I promised him this. I swore I'd finish you, and I will.' He rushes at me with the knife.

I have seconds to accept I am about to be cut; I will be cut. I minimize his access with my guard. As the knife comes at me, I strike out at his forearm using both hands, palms out. I break his speed, striking him repeatedly, watching the pain register, slowing him down further. I don't perceive the pain of the multiple cuts to my arms.

Without breaking stride, I drive my open palm into his face. A short, sharp hit upwards against his nose — I hear it crack. The knife clatters to the floor as I feel the warmth of his blood. I kick the knife away, aiming it behind me. He's in front of the door. I can't escape. My voice is getting hoarse, but not once do I let up shouting. I jab my hand into his face again. This time, I grab at his eyes, pull upwards on his nostrils. His arm shoots out, and I step back fast, raise my arms trapping his between them. Somehow, he breaks free, pivots and is behind me with his fist in my hair. Using a clenched fist, I rap it against his hand, then grip hard, placing direct pressure on his fist until he releases me. It's a second, but it's enough. I swing my head back, feeling the crunch as it connects with his nose.

'Fuck!' he yelps.

When I hear him say that, it makes me realize I've stopped shouting. I twist around until I am behind him this time. I angle one arm around his neck, the crook of my elbow beneath his chin. I pull him against me, securing him in place. I use my other hand to claw at his eyes and nostrils. I rub my hand over his face. I continuously scream in his ear, overloading his senses. I'm tiring, but he is too. I can feel his resistance waning as I overload his brain function.

It happens just as it was supposed to. He slumps to the ground. I follow him down and press my knee onto the side of his head. I know I should escape while I can, but last time I did that, Tom ran, and he's still out there. This time will be different. Antonio bucks, struggling against me. I fiercely grind my knee against his head, pressing it harshly against the floor. His breathing is desperate, he stills and gasps for air. I don't let up. Sirens are wailing, louder, nearer. He gives one last-ditch attempt at dislodging my position, but I hold tight. Then they are there. The door is unlocked, and they flood into my home. It's mayhem. The flashing lights from the emergency vehicles reflect all around me. Uniformed officers crowd the doorway.

'It's over, DCI Fellows. You can let go now. We have it from here.'

I feel a hand on my shoulder, and I let myself fall back, away from Antonio and onto the ground. I shuffle until my back is against the wall. My breathing is rapid, my chest heaving. 'He attacked me with that knife,' I wheeze, nodding in the direction of the weapon.

There are voices filling my head, but I can't make out a word. I barely notice him being led away in cuffs. He's speaking, protesting but I can't make it out. My ears are ringing. Suddenly my entire body is in the throes of agony. Pain like I've never felt tears at my muscles, my skin. My arms hurt like hell; blood is running down them, dripping onto my floor. I put my head between my knees, trying to block everything out.

'Beth? Beth?' The familiar voice yanks me into the present. I look up to see Dillon knelt in front of me, her face ashen. 'Jesus, what the hell happened?'

There are tears running down my face. I am only now aware of them. 'I trusted him,' I whimper. 'Why? How could he?'

'Niall Grant contacted me, told me what Stanley Baker said to you. I am guessing that piece of shit—' she snarls towards the door, where Antonio was taken out — 'was the traitorous little worm?'

'I reckon so,' I say.

Dillon looks me up and down. 'We need to get you looked at by a doctor. You're a mess. And so's he.' She almost smiles. 'Jesus, what the hell went on here? What did you do to him?'

'We have Iain McKinstry to thank for that.'

'Who?'

'I've been attending Rapid Action-Initiated Defence classes.' Dillon looks confused, and I shake my head. 'A place in Ormskirk. I wanted to be prepared, ready in case. I thought Tom might . . . he's a trained cop; I knew I couldn't use our own training against him effectively. I've been training with this ex-special forces bloke.'

Dillon's face darkens. 'Well, whatever it was, whatever you did, it worked. You're alive.'

'Wait,' I say. Something in the periphery of my mind tells me Dillon personally being here this quickly is wrong. Uniforms, yes, but why Dillon? 'How did you get here so fast? Why are you here?'

Dillon averts her eyes. She's holding something in her hand. It's an evidence bag. She looks back at me, shaking her head. 'I don't know how to tell you this, Beth.'

I nod at the evidence bag, my stomach tightening. 'What's in there?' I already know; I can see it well enough. But I don't know what it means. Why Dillon has it. Where the hell she got it from.

'It was found at Millie's house. I'm sorry, Beth.' She's shaking her head, tears in her eyes.

'What? What the hell do you mean, you're sorry? What's going on?'

'Millie is gone.' As she speaks, she holds the postcard closer to me, so I can see the image on the front — it's the Cenotaph. The one in Preston city centre. He's here. *Millie.*

'Gone?' I choke, almost throwing up.

'Missing. A neighbour called it in. There'd been some noises; they didn't think anything of it at first, but her husband went to check the perimeter and found Millie's front door wide open.'

'What are you saying?'

'There was blood, Beth, a lot of blood. Millie wasn't there. The house was in a state. There had obviously been some sort of altercation. There's something else,' she says.

'What else could there possibly be?' Tears are thick in my voice.

'DS Niall Grant didn't just call to inform me of what Stanley Baker had said. He had something else to tell me. As it happens, I would have been going to see Millie myself.'

'I don't understand.'

'Millie had been to see Stanley Baker.' She shakes her head. 'I've no idea for what purpose. She received a visiting order to her home address, and she used it. It was not an official visit, by any stretch.'

'I really do not understand this . . .' Realization dawns on me. He'd known about the mobile phone, the photographs. Why would she do that?

'And then there's this.' She holds up the evidence bag. 'It was recovered at the scene. It's a postcard.'

I struggle to swallow past the lump in my throat.

'The message on it is for you.'

This one isn't blank? 'Let me see it.' I hold out my hand.

'You can't remove it. But . . .' She passes the evidence bag to me. 'Here.'

As I read it, my head spins, and my lungs feel strangulated. This can't be happening.

Hello Beth,
You didn't think you'd seen the last of me, did you? You ruined my life. Now, I am going to return the favour. See you soon.

THE END

ACKNOWLEDGEMENTS

I would like to thank everyone at my agency, Northbank Talent Management. I would especially like to thank Elizabeth Counsell, who is a wonderful support and a champion of my work. I would also like to thank everyone at Joffe Books for believing in my Detective Beth Fellows series and giving Beth a home. I would particularly like to thank Darja from Dee Dee Book Covers for her brilliant cover, as well as Claire Coombes, Tania Charles and Jodi Compton who worked on the book. The sharp eye and insight of an editor is invaluable to any book. *The Ordinary Man* would not be the polished, completed product you have just read without them.

A massive thank you must go to the professionals who have helped by answering my many questions. They include retired senior detective, Graham Bartlett. Working crime scene investigator, Kate Bendelow. Forensic scientist, Brian Price. All of whom are also authors and the loveliest people. Any mistakes are my own. You can't put the entirety of a police investigation into a novel, if you did it would be many pages of detectives completing paperwork. What we as authors must do is create a buyable investigation that a reader can believe and invest in and that keeps the story interesting. I hope I have achieved that.

I would like to thank Iain McKinstry of McKinstry Family Karate in Ormskirk. Iain introduced me to RAID — Rapid Action Initiated Defence — which focuses on modern self-defence and conflict management. Broken down the elements of RAID teaches you to deter, detect, defuse, defend and desensitize. I also referred to the RAID book written by Tremaine Kent and given to me by Iain. If you wish to learn any self-defence techniques do check them out. After the events in *The Raven's Mark*, Beth needed to arm herself with a method of protecting herself that would not be routine knowledge for police officers. To do this I visited Iain at the centre in Ormskirk and learned a great deal. Thank you for being so generous and enthusiastic. It is due to your guidance that Beth was able to pull on the resources she does. I hope you like the mention Beth gives you in the book. To the reader — any mistakes regarding the RAID technique or indeed anything else are my own.

I would wish to thank everyone who has supported me before and since the publication of *The Raven's Mark*, the first in the Detective Beth Fellows series. So, thanks must go to authors such as Diane Chamberlain, Dorothy Koomson, Lisa, Jewell, Nadine Matheson, Harriet Tyce, Mari Hannah, Trevor Wood, Amy McCulloch, Sarah Bonner, Philippa East, A. A. Chaudhuri, Liz Mistry, Amy McClellan and Lesley McEvoy. If I have missed anyone from this list, please know I am immensely grateful even if I do have a goldfish memory.

I want to extend my thanks to the organisers of the festivals and events I have had the honour of taking part in. Lizzie Curle and David Headley at the Capital Crime Writing Festival. Selina Brown, Sarah Bennett and Linda Odongo of the Black British Book Festival. Bob McDevitt at Bloody Scotland. Craig Robertson and Alexandra Sokoloff at Bute Noir. The staff and volunteers involved at all these festivals help to make them what they are. So, thank you. I would like to thank the staff and volunteers at Bute Museum who hosted my panel at Bute Noir and kindly gave us a fascinating tour of the museum. Do pay them a visit. Vaseem Khan and Marc Dunleavy at Harrogate's Peculiar Crime Writing Festival. Jacky Collins at Newcastle Noir. Donna Morfett of The Darkside of Brighton. I was sorry not to be able to attend Iceland Noir in 2023, but I plan on being there this year. Susanne Green at Durham Library. Rob Parker at Manchester Crime Central. Those who interview and champion us, such as my lovely friends Samantha Brownley and Ayo Onatade. The fantastic podcasters, interviewers and reviewers, such as but not limited to the Book Lover's Companion and the UK Crime Book Club. And there are so many more supportive people, I would be hard pushed to include them all — but I am thankful for each of you. I am also extremely grateful to the crime writing community for being such an incredible group of people and becoming my tribe. Much love to you all.

A huge thank you to photographer extraordinaire, Donna-Lisa Healy. I was honoured to have my portrait featured in the *Telling it Like it Is* exhibition at the Glasgow Women's Library. Donna-Lisa met me in Alnwick where she photographed me in the Accidental Bookshop and Barter's Books. She then came to my home the following day. Donna-Lisa managed the near impossible feat of taking photographs of me that I liked. I attended the opening of the exhibition and took part in the Story Cafe, which on that occasion was led by Jacky Collins, aka Dr Noir. It was a wonderful experience. Thank you to everyone involved for being so welcoming.

A special thank you to Helen Stanton the owner of Forum Books in Corbridge, the Accidental Bookshop in Alnwick and the Bound in Whitley Bay. Helen is always supportive and delivers a personal and passionate approach to book selling in all three of her stores. Do check them out if you are in town, or via their website.

Libraries and book clubs are the life blood of books and writers. Their passion helps to keep us going. Berwick Library is a place I truly love and one that has shown me great kindness and support. So, thank you once again to them for hosting my very first launch. In particular, Katy Wedderburn, Diane Wright and Gerard Young. I loved taking part in an interview with the charity book club, Pumping Marvellous. One reason being that they were wonderful hosts, but another is the importance of the work they do. My dad had a quadruple heart bypass some years ago, so when this charity reached out there was no question as to whether I would agree to the interview. It was my honour to take part. I would like to thank the book club at Durham Waterstones run by Fiona Sharp and the Belford book club, that is local to me. Book clubs are places of warmth and friendship. Keep doing the great work you all do.

To the people of Preston, Lancashire — thank you to those of you who showed up to my event at Waterstones. You were a fantastic audience and I hope to see you again. I truly hope you enjoy reading these books set in your home city as much as I have enjoyed writing them. And to the people of Northumberland, thank you so much for welcoming me to this beautiful part of the England.

2023 has been a difficult year for me health wise. As such it has reminded me that I would not be here if it hadn't been for the support, I received in 2015 when I needed life-saving treatment. Back then I was almost entirely bed bound, I was in excruciating pain every day, if I went anywhere, it was in a wheelchair. I spent more time in hospital than I did at home. I was in intensive care/treatment more often than I care to remember. I had given up, but when urged to 'try anything' by my wife, Amy Newport, and my mum, Dawn Newport, I did. We found out about stem cell replacement therapy in Santa Monica, USA. It had a price tag we would never have been able to afford, so I did something that went against every instinct I had — I fundraised. I did not expect to reach our target, I thought I was simply pacifying Amy and my family by trying. But after only two months we had reached target. Doing so restored my faith in humanity. I could scarcely fathom the kindness shown to me. I will never forget it. I will always fight for the life that they gave back to me. This book would certainly not be here without you all. Thank you from the bottom of my heart.

Thank you to my parents, Paul and Dawn Newport, who have been supportive and attended various writing events. It was fantastic to know that they got to witness this stage of my life. Thank you as well to my sister, Kerry Newport, and cousin, Cherie Ali, who remain hugely supportive. Thank you to all my family and friends.

Thanks to Ellie Sedgewick. I stole your maiden name! I hope you like the character of Eleanor Grice.

A special thanks must go to the two who make my homelife just that 'home' — my wife, Amy Newport, who reads everything I write and is honest and always, always encouraging. And our Labrador son, Laddy, who is always ready to lend a paw.

Here's to a happy, healthy (as possible) and prosperous 2024 for all of us. Much love.

THE JOFFE BOOKS STORY

We began in 2014 when Jasper agreed to publish his mum's much-rejected romance novel and it became a bestseller.

Since then we've grown into the largest independent publisher in the UK. We're extremely proud to publish some of the very best writers in the world, including Joy Ellis, Faith Martin, Caro Ramsay, Helen Forrester, Simon Brett and Robert Goddard. Everyone at Joffe Books loves reading and we never forget that it all begins with the magic of an author telling a story.

We are proud to publish talented first-time authors, as well as established writers whose books we love introducing to a new generation of readers.

We won Trade Publisher of the Year at the Independent Publishing Awards in 2023. We have been shortlisted for Independent Publisher of the Year at the British Book Awards for the last four years, and were shortlisted for the Diversity and Inclusivity Award at the 2022 Independent Publishing Awards. In 2023 we were shortlisted for Publisher of the Year at the RNA Industry Awards.

We built this company with your help, and we love to hear from you, so please email us about absolutely anything bookish at feedback@joffebooks.com

If you want to receive free books every Friday and hear about all our new releases, join our mailing list: www.joffebooks.com/contact

And when you tell your friends about us, just remember: it's pronounced Joffe as in coffee or toffee!

ALSO BY CHRISTIE J. NEWPORT

THE PRESTON MURDERS SERIES
Book 1: THE RAVEN'S MARK
Book 2: THE ORDINARY MAN